Prospero's
Children

Prospero's Children

♦

Jan Siegel

DEL
REY

THE BALLANTINE PUBLISHING GROUP
NEW YORK

A Del Rey® Book
Published by The Ballantine Publishing Group

Copyright © 1999 by Jan Siegel

All rights reserved under International and Pan-American Copyright Conventions. Published in the United States by The Ballantine Publishing Group, a division of Random House, Inc., New York, and distributed in Canada by Random House of Canada Limited, Toronto. Originally published in Great Britain by Voyager, an imprint of HarperCollins, in 1999.

Del Rey is a registered trademark and the Del Rey colophon is a trademark of Random House, Inc.

www.randomhouse.com/delrey/

Library of Congress Card Number: 00-190160

Text design by Ann Gold

Manufactured in the United States of America

First American Edition: May 2000

10 9 8 7 6 5 4 3 2 1

Acknowledgments

I would like to thank my long-suffering family and friends for all the support they have given me during the writing of this book, in particular my father, my sister, and my brother-in-law, Jenny and Julian Bell, Jane and Robin Lee, Judith Burns, Ruth McNichol, Clare Hallams, and Dominique Mameczko, and for professional help and advice above and beyond the call of duty Dr. Brian Hinton, John Walsh, Victor Olliver, and most of all my agent, Antony Harwood, who believed in me and backed me against all the odds.

When dawn was gray you went to catch the tide
leaving me waking in an empty bed
for I was loved and loved but never wed
and left alone to hope and pray and fear:
God speed you back to me, my bonny dear.

The storm came screaming from the ocean's heart
shredding the clouds, whipping the waves to foam;
a broken spar was all the sea sent home
when darkling night gave way to morning drear.
No last farewell for thee, my bonny dear.

I went to church but not in bridal white
and sang the hymns, although you did not come,
and laid pale garlands on a vacant tomb
and said a prayer for no one else to hear:
God keep your soul somewhere, my bonny dear.

Where once I kissed your cheek the fishes feed
and mermaid-children steal your finger-bones
to play at dice, and on your bed of stones
the whale-songs echo through your hollow ear:
Sleep well forever there, my bonny dear.

Prologue

The Mermaid

℧he mermaid rose out of deep water into the stormheart. Being a creature with no soul, she was without fear of the elements which had engendered her. She rode the giant waves like a child on a switchback, sucked laughing into terrible black chasms of water, then hurled skyward toward the plunging clouds, riding the sea-crests with her hair lashing in the wind. Lightning illumined her for an instant, an efreet of the ocean, face a-scream with glee, slanting bones and elongated eyes sloping back from the pointed nose and tapering chin. It was a misshapen imitation of a human visage, formed perhaps by some pagan Creator who had caught only the briefest glimpse of Man. Her storm-tossed body was almost androgynous, flat-breasted, fish-pale, the ectopic nether limb glistening steel-silver with scales, each jagged fin shot with the needle-glint of poisonous spines. Above her, thunderhead clouds were piled into toppling cliffs of airborne water; the wind came roaring from the throat of the sky. More lightning-flashes, almost incessant now, picked her out in every motion of her wild play, leaping, diving, tumbling, amidst the heaving mountains and rocking valleys of the ocean. She could not remember another such storm, never in all her uncounted years on

Earth. Always alone, alienated both from Man and beast, a careless elemental for whom the waters were mother and lover, lifeblood and home.

She saw the barque ahead of her through a cleft between rearing waves, broken and desperate, clinging precariously to the skirts of the tempest. Drums rolled from the chasing clouds; storm-fires flashlit the ragged sail streaming like torn skin from a skeletal wreck of mast and spar. She was a small boat, sturdily built; the last remnants of her crew had secured themselves to tilting deck and sides with frayed rigging. Spume-capped ridges lifted her skyward, spun her round, then sent her plummeting nose-first into liquid ravines; but she was in her element even as the mermaid, and each time she would right herself and battle onward.

Strong arms gripped the useless wheel, not to steer but for an anchor against the greedy undertow that would have sucked the sailor from the deck. Lightning gleamed on a sea-glossed interplay of muscle in forearm and shoulder. The mermaid saw him as she drew astern, her hand on the gunwale, cold fingers touching the boat's skin with the chill of the uttermost deep, weed-green hair crackling with secret electricity. He glanced round, some instinct warning him of the deadly gaze on his back. She saw the brine-blackened locks webbing his face, the narrowing of eyes both dark and bright. He saw he knew not what: a mirage of fear, a phantom of the storm, gone too swiftly for his mind to compass it, leaving only the impression of a wild white face and unhuman eyes depthless as glass. Yet moments later when his ears picked up the sound, a single distinctive note within the howling chorus of wave and tempest, he knew what it must be. He knew it in the marrow that froze in his bones and the hairs that stirred on his nape: a recognition beyond memory. It was a high thin keening— a call without words—a piercing thread of sound that sang even in the waves' roaring. It swelled with the wind, until the fragile timbers of the boat shook with it, and he could imagine it penetrating even to the still deep places far below. One of the other sailors shouted a question but he shook his head and turned away. Still grasping the ruptured helm, he whispered to the boat a lover's encouragement—his greatheart, his brave one, his dear-ling, his dear—though he knew it was all in vain. Behind him the siren-call had done its work: the hunt was up.

Orca and octopus, giant eel and electric serpent, countless sharks—sharks tiger-striped and leopard-spotted, ghost-pale and shadow-black—all gathered in their wake. In the coral-groves be-neath, nameless creatures waited with glittering antennae and sharpened pincers, knowing it would not be long now. A mottled flank heaved out of the waves to starboard, many times the length of the boat. Crawling tentacles twined the boom, thick as a man's arm: the water became opaque with a writhing flood of ink. And in the midst of the chase rode the mermaid, mounted on the back of an enormous shark—she whom the beasts of the sea had often hunted, never caught, now summoning them to her need with the feckless arrogance that was her most human characteristic. At the helm, the young man heard his companions' cry of warning, but he did not look back again. The storm had ripped the shirt from his chest; salt clogged his lashes and stung his lips. The wind pricked his eyes into tears that evaporated on his cheek. Some-thing which hung on a chain about his neck glinted against his breast with its own light, but the flicker of power was lost in the raging of the elements, helpless as a firefly in a hurricane.

The end came suddenly. A glassy cavern yawned behind the boat, rushing forward to swallow it; the sweep of a monstrous tail cracked the hull. The crew were borne away between tooth and tentacle, into the gullet of the sea. The young man found himself clutching a wheel without helm or vessel, seesawing between peaks of water, holding on, not in hope or fear, but because sur-vival is Man's first and last instinct. Then he saw the face again, rising from the surge less than a yard away, its flat eyes aglow, its

hair uncoiling like a nest of snakes in the wind. The pale lips were
parted as if to suck his last breath. The fantasies of imminent
death seized his mind, and the alien face became one more familiar, and the din of thunder was blotted out by the sea-surge in his
head. He murmured something—a word, a name—and the mermaid, hearing, though she understood neither language nor affection, knew it was the name of his mortal love, whose spectre had
driven her from his sight. Then she wound her arms around him,
and drew him down and down into the deep.

In a murky grotto a few fathoms below she hid him, weight-
ing his ragged clothes with rocks to keep him from drifting away.
The tiny nibblers of the reef did not touch him for they were
afraid of her: she would pull off their claws in hunger or caprice
and suck the jelly from their transparent shells, or tear slender
bodies apart with wanton fingers. Even the giant crayfish and
monster crabs were wary of her, for she was a cunning huntress,
thrusting a sliver of rock into the chink under horned carapace or
between linked plates and using the makeshift tool to wrench
them asunder. Too quick and too clever for the larger predators,
she roamed her domain in fear of nothing, having not yet learned
the fear of Man which would soon infect all living creatures—
Man her cousin and her kinsman, a killer more ruthless than the
shark, deadlier than the kraken. She gazed on the sailor's still face
with a strange yearning, a tugging at her heart, or where her heart
should have been, touching his cheek with her cold caresses,
closing his eyes with shells, binding his hair with weed. Then she
would grow irritated or bored with her dead plaything and swim
away, forgetting him for an hour or a week, only to return and gaze
on him again.

He was beyond the reach of the sun but the thing on his
breast still gleamed erratically, sending glancing rays through the
moving currents. Sometimes it seemed to grow hot, as if emitting

pulses of fretful power: the water around it would hiss and shrink, forming bubbles full of steam which floated upward in broken trails. When the mermaid tried to remove it her fingers prickled as if with pins and needles; once her whole hand grew numb. She left it alone, and as time passed it became dark and dull, and the face of the sailor was eaten away by creatures too microscopic to torment, and the sea washed his bones, leaving them moon-white among the hidden colors of the coral, and an anemone blossomed in one empty socket, and angelfish kissed his hollow cheek. Yet still she came back, once a month or once a year, as a miser returns to his hoard, and her gloating dwindled and her games, and she gazed long and long on the mystery of his death. She had never before been so close to a being which resembled herself, having no memory of parents, brother or sister, if indeed she had ever possessed any, born of the wind's breath and the sea's tears. Ever alone, for the first time in the aching shallows of her spirit she knew that she was lonely, and the seeds of her ultimate destruction were sown.

The Earth turned, season melted into season, the timeless morning of the world drew on to noon. The years were numbered, events arranged into history; the age of magic gave way to reason and science, knowledge and prejudice, religion and heresy. Men attempted to limn the continents with maps and web the seas with charts. A fisherman from a coastal village, more daring than his compeers, was casting his nets in unfamiliar waters when he hauled in a clotted mass that looked like weed. He bent over the side of the boat and plunged his hands in it to free it from the net, and it felt lithe as silk and curiously alive, writhing between his fingers. He pulled hard, sensing an alien weight below, and the weed parted beneath his hands even as the head emerged from the water. A terrible head with the blanched clammy complexion of the drowned, bloodless mouth agape, glaring eyes above slanting bones. But the head lived. The eyes flashed like the glint of light on broken glass and an eldritch wail came from between the pallid lips, rising in pitch and slowly strengthening, vibrating from the long throat as from a living flute. The fisherman knew that call from race memory or traveler's tale, and he dragged the head close to the ship's side and laid the naked blade of his gutting knife against her neck, ordering silence in a tone that transcended the barriers of language. Her mouth shut tight and he called to his sons to help him heave her on board, staring in wonder as the water ran from the unnatural tail squirming against the bonds of the net. One of the boys received a handful of spines in the struggle, and in the night he sickened and lay in the cabin burning with fever, but the fisherman would not throw the mermaid back. He poured water over her to keep her moist and fed her raw fish from their catch, drawing near to press his knife into her flesh even while her live hair coiled about his ankles.

Whether this was the same mermaid or another no legend tells: certainly this one understood something of mortal speech, or learned understanding in the extremity of her need. She was alone as always, divided by a few flimsy planks from the sea that was her element, prisoner of her enemy, her only real predator, her kin. Perhaps she had sought that capture, driven by centuries of isolation or a fatal curiosity; but here was no storm-tossed seafarer, his hard beauty softened by the phantom of love, here was only a weather-weary peasant, toughened by the long slow battle for survival, and in his face the blending of fear and anger, and a deadly greed.

After two days in a babbling delirium the boy died, and in the morning the fisherman went to his captive with a raw heart and new-sharpened knife, grasping her green hair and dragging her head back for the death-blow. Her angled eyes stared into his, impenetrable as the eyes of an animal, and he could not tell if there was terror behind them, or intelligence, or deceit. And then for the first time in memory or legend she spoke, and her voice throbbed harshly from unused vocal cords; but there was an echo in it of the wind, and an echo of the sea. "Don't," she said. "Don't kill." She could not say *please* because the word was beyond her understanding.

"My son is dead," said the fisherman. "A death for a death. You should have found your voice the sooner. It is too late now to beg."

"Your son was careless. He died easy. If not now, then later. Is no loss."

"I loved him," said the fisherman, and his hand tightened on her twisting hair and the knife gleamed before her.

"You have other sons. What is love?"

The fisherman knew few words for the gentler emotions. "He sprang from my loins," he responded at last. "Flesh of my flesh, bone of my bone. You could offer me the treasures of a dozen shipwrecks, the pearls from a hundred oysters, but it would not buy your life. That is love." The blade sank into her flesh until a thin trickle ran down her white skin, and he saw with something close to desire that her blood was as red as his.

"I have not found love," said the mermaid, and her voice was as thin as the wind hissing through a chink in a wall of ice. "There is none in the deep sea. But I have treasure. I have a great treasure."

The knife was withdrawn an inch or two; the fisherman's tone changed very slightly. "What treasure?"

"From a ship," said the mermaid. "A ship that sank long ago. The treasure lies in the coral. Even the bones are coral now."

"What kind of treasure?" the fisherman reiterated, and there was no mistaking the eager glint in his eye. "Gold?"

"It glittered," said the mermaid. "In the dark beyond the sun it gleamed like the storm-fire. It is my treasure, my secret."

"I will trade you this treasure," said the fisherman, "for your life. My son is gone and neither love nor gold can bring him back. But I will take your treasure as blood money, the price of my revenge."

At that his two remaining sons cried out against him, for their brother had been very dear to them, and they found the mermaid both alien and unchancy, too wayward to trust, too perilous to spare. No oath would bind her to her bargain: principle and mercy alike were outside her comprehension. "Release her," they said, "and she will swim fast and far, and we will have neither vengeance nor payment. We want blood for our brother."

"Gold is better than blood," said the fisherman, and they were silenced. Then he cut a single tress from the mermaid's hair and knotted it, though it seemed to resist him, the separate strands seeking to slip away between his fingers. "I will let you go," he told her, "and for three days I will keep this lock of hair in a jar of water. But if in that time you do not return—if you try to cheat me—if you do not bring me the treasure, then I will pin the lock to the mast and let it dry in the wind, and if you never come at all then when I am back on shore I will lay it out in the noonday heat until it shrivels away, and even in the ocean's depths you too will shrivel, burned by a sun you cannot see. Do you understand?"

"I understand," said the mermaid.

"Go then."

He snapped the rope that held her and she pulled herself over the side, diving like a flying fish in an arc of silver, lost in an instant beneath hurrying waves. "You will not see her again," said the boys.

But the fisherman clasped the lock of hair and smiled a smile without humor, confident and grim.

"I will see her," he said.

On the afternoon of the third day the mermaid returned. The fisherman had lingered in the area against the wishes of his sons, although the body of the youngest was starting to putrefy and the sweet smell of death had begun to permeate the whole boat. By day they fished, but the nets which had been replete now came up empty: only a sprat or two twitched on the brine-washed deck among a few knots of weed, and some strange creatures which resembled living fungi and leaked a noxious ooze at the pressure of a finger. The wind had dropped; the sails hung limp as the drapes on a tomb; thin tides of cloud had seeped across the sky, blearing the face of the sun. Late that day the last rays, issuing from beneath the cloudline, filled the narrow space between sky and sea with a concentrated brilliance. The clouds were burned bronze, the air turned to gold, glancing fires sparked from every wave. The mermaid rose from a pool of dazzle, dark against the brightness, her long hair netting the sea-fire. She swam warily to the side of the boat, staying out of reach of both the fisherman and his knife. Her hands were hidden under the gilded water; her face was as expressionless as that of an animal.

"Where is it?" he demanded. "Where is my treasure?"

"I have it," she said. "Where is my hair?"

One of his sons brought him the jar; he lifted the contents out and held them up for her to see. The single tress still twitched and twisted like the newly severed tail of a live serpent.

"My treasure?" he repeated.

Her hand emerged from the water; she stretched out her arm. The fisherman closed hungry fingers on a hard irregular shape, lumpy with tiny polyps, slimy with tendrils of weed. The touch of the mermaid's skin was colder than the coldest fish. In the same instant one of his sons, bitter beyond any gold-lust at his brother's death, started forward to seize her, knife at the ready. But she was too sudden and too slippery for him: she had broken free even before he tightened his grasp, before his father's shout, before the knife had done its work. She was gone in a swirl of fractured sunlight, leaving only a wisp of blood—too little blood—uncurling beneath the bright reflections. The fisherman still clasped her violated hair. In the silence that followed he looked down at the object in his other hand, the small, jagged thing, coral-studded, begreened with weed: the treasure. It took him a minute or two to realize what it was. A key.

The fisherman was seized with a fury far greater than the anger he had known for the loss of his son, the pent-up fury of his toil-filled, empty-bellied, mean-hearted life, the fury of a dream shattered, of greed cheated, of hope extinguished forever. It distorted his mouth and dragged his features this way and that, it mounted in him like a tidal wave, it howled through him like a storm. His sons shrank from it; the very boards of the ship seemed to quiver in fear. Yet after the first terrible curse he grew quiet again; poverty had taught him the hardest lessons in self-control. "A key!" he said. "A *key*. And no doubt the lock that it should fit is fathoms deep, in a treasure chest accessible only to the crabs. God damn the lying nixie! May she writhe in a waterless hell for all eternity!" So saying, he went to hurl away his useless prize. Then, with an abrupt change of mind, he thrust it into a deep pocket and descended into the cabin, the fury set like stone in his face. When he returned he was carrying a tinderbox. He struck a light and held the tress of hair above it. The strands parted, billowing, fanning away as though trying to escape the lethal fire. Then he lowered the hair onto the flame and slowly, smiling, he watched it burn.

Deep below the surface the mermaid felt herself scorched with a sudden, impossible pain. Heat flared on her cold skin, bubbling it into blisters, searing into her flesh. Her bright tail blotched and blackened, molting poisonous spines that charred even as they fell. Water surrounded her, yet she burned. Her body arched and buckled, struggling to be free of the agony that invaded it. The last clear note of her clouding mind was one of utter incomprehension. Then the sea fizzed around her as her very substance withered, melted, and was dispersed, minute grains swept away on the many currents of ocean, feeding the unseen creatures who are the seeds of all life.

Part One

The Key

◆

⋅ I ⋅

S he had been standing in front of the picture for several minutes before she began to notice it. The other paintings in the gallery were purely abstract but as she stared at this one, waiting for her father, passing the time, shapes began to emerge from the field of nondescript color, vague as shadows on smoke: disconnected fragments of stair, random archways, openings into nowhere, ghostly glimpses of an unfinished labyrinth. Here and there a detail was highlighted, a splinter of sky beyond a broken vault, a segment of window with branching latticework, eye blinks of clarity which seemed to flicker into being even as her gaze skimmed over them. The artist drew her attention to and fro with a skill that was almost disquieting, letting her roam the boundaries of image, then pulling her gradually toward the focus, where an irregular patch of vividly contrasting color was set like a gaudy postage stamp at the very center of the picture. Initially the truncated rectangle, perhaps three inches high, appeared so crowded with microscopic detail that it resembled a vast and complex mosaic, miniaturized until all coherence was lost. But as she studied it, either because her vision became acclimatized or by some contrivance of the artist, the tiny shapes seemed to shift, like a kaleidoscope falling into place, and she found herself looking through a doorway or casement out over a city. Wide streets lined with columns and colonnades, clustered roofs hiding secret alleys, glistening domes, steeples, spires, palaces and terraces, temple-walls and tavern-walls, courtyards, backyards, fountains, gardens. Everything was bathed in the gold of a falling sun, enriching paint-work and stonework, touching the gilding on the domes with pure fire. She did not know what city it was yet it looked both ancient and timeless, a Rome that lived on free of traffic and tourism, a new-built Jerusalem unscarred by warring factions, the seat, maybe, of a higher civilization, older than history, fresh as the world in which it flourished, whose ruins had since crumbled to dust and whose wisdom had long been forgotten. She was not a fanciful girl, or so she told herself, yet her dormant fancy was stirred: she was pierced by a nostalgia for a place she had never seen, for the fairy-tale realms she had always rejected.

"Do you like it?" inquired a voice behind her. "You seem to be rather absorbed."

She turned abruptly. The gallery was carpeted and the owner—she was sure he must be the owner—had approached so quietly she had not heard him. "I don't know," she said. "I haven't decided. It's very interesting."

"So you don't believe in impulsive judgments." The voice was as smooth as pouring cream with a faint intonation of mockery, but whether lofty or merely teasing it was impossible to tell. There was little humor visible in his expression. Glossy pale gray hair framed his face like a steel halo; his café-crème complexion was unlined, creating an effect of careful preservation rather than enduring youth; his eyes were almond-shaped and flecked with glints of yellow light. He was delicately suave, discreetly elegant, gracefully tall. She disliked him immediately, on impulse. "It's an etching," he went on. "Did you know?"

"No, I didn't." Of course she didn't. "I thought etchings had to be in black and white."

"The technique is very complex." Once again, that trace of superiority. "Bellkush has always favored the most difficult approach. The effect, I think, is almost unearthly—those diaphanous layers of subtle color. Almost unearthly. Appropriate, perhaps, to the subject matter."

"What is it called?" she asked, rather as if the question had been wrung out of her.

"*Lost City.*" There was a pause while she felt herself drawn back to the contemplation of that crowded portal. "Are you here to buy?"

"I'm waiting for my father." She dragged her eyes away from the picture. He must know who she was: he had seen them arrive.

"Ah . . . yes. Robin Capel's daughter. And your name is?"

"Fernanda."

"How pretty. Also unusual." Her name might have been a piece of bric-a-brac which had attracted his wandering attention.

"I had a Spanish grandfather," she explained, lapsing into her routine excuse. It was untrue, but she had always felt such an exotic appellation needed more justification than her mother's erratic taste. She did not approve of foreign names without foreign blood to back them up.

"Fern!" Her father, his discussions concluded, came toward them, wearing his habitual expression of slightly anxious goodwill. The young woman who worked at the gallery followed in his wake. "So you've met Javier. Er—terrific. Terrific. What were you chatting about?"

"The pictures." The man answered for her.

"I'm afraid you must have found my daughter's taste a bit— well, conservative. She's a very down-to-earth young lady, you know. Likes sitters in portraits to have all their features in the right place, trees to be the proper shade of green—that sort of thing. Only abstract painter I've ever known her to admire is Mondrian. She says he'd make nice kitchen wallpaper."

"That would be a very expensive kitchen," said the man called Javier. Robin and the woman both laughed.

"Daddy, don't make me sound so boring," Fern said, wanting to leave.

"Just a joke, darling. Oh—I'd like you to meet Alison Redmond. We're definitely going to collaborate on the witchcraft book. She'll organize several of the artists here to do the illustrations. It should be a big success. Alison, my daughter Fernanda."

They exchanged a polite handshake. Close up, the woman was not so young: her face was long and pointed with an incongruously full mouth adorning its thin structure and pale narrow eyes between heavily mascaraed lashes. Her off-blond hair was waist-length and worn loose. Had Fern not been too prosaic for such comparisons she would have thought her father's future collaborator resembled a witch herself.

"Terrific," murmured Ms. Redmond. Possibly Fern imagined the same elusive mockery in her voice that she had detected in Javier's smooth accents. For a moment, seeing her father standing between them, she was visited with the illusion that he was somehow trapped, hemmed in by two predatory figures, the man with his superior height and superior smile, the woman with her warmth of manner and coldness of eye. The impression of danger, though fleeting, disturbed her because it seemed out of all proportion to the actual threat. In the six years since her mother died Fern had monitored her father's love-life with the skill of an international statesman, dismissing a succession of unsuitable candidates out-of-hand. The menace here was surely similar, the standard hazard of marauding huntress and hapless prey; she had dealt with it a hundred times, and she had never before experienced any doubts or premonitions. But then, Fern did not believe in premonitions.

Robin shook more hands in farewell, while she resisted an irrational urge to drag him away.

That was the beginning, she decided long afterward. The meeting at the gallery, the sense of menace, the picture. The incident seemed trivial enough at the time but it left her feeling vaguely perturbed, as if the outlying penumbra of some far-flung shadow had brushed the borderline of her bright safe world, or she had caught a few isolated notes of an eerie music which would soon come booming from every corner of the universe, obliterating all other sound. The events of that extraordinary and terrifying summer became perhaps easier to assimilate because she was in some sort prepared: from the moment of that initial encounter an unfamiliar atmosphere began to seep into her life, unsettling her, unbalancing her cultivated equilibrium, making her vulnerable, unsure, receptive to change. She was sixteen years old, well-behaved, intelligent, motivated, a product of the Eighties in which she lived, viewing the world with a practical realism engendered by the early death of her mother and the responsibilities which had devolved on her as a result of it. Her father's easygoing manner had acquired its undercurrent of anxiety from that time, left alone with a small daughter and smaller son, but it was Fern who had gradually taken charge of the household, trading au pair for housekeeper, seeing the bills were paid, bossing her surviving parent, attempting to boss her younger brother. She had coasted through puberty and adolescence without rebellion or trauma, avoiding hard drugs, excessive alcohol, and underage sex. Her future was carefully planned, with no room for surprises. University; a suitable career; at some point, a prudent marriage. She thought of herself as grown-up but behind the sedate façade she was still a child, shutting out the unknown with illusions of security and control. That summer the illusions would be dissipated and the unknown would invade her existence, transforming the self-possessed girl into someone desperate, frightened, uncertain, alone—the raw material of an adult.

The day after their visit to the Holt Gallery they collected her brother from school and drove out of London to see the house. That was the next thing. The house. On the death of a distant relative Robin had inherited a property in a remote part of Yorkshire, and before putting it on the market his accountant had suggested he might like to take a look at it. "Good idea," Robin had responded. "Could do with a break. Nice for the kids. They're a real pair of townies: need a taste of the country. Never know, might decide to keep it, do it up a bit, that sort of thing. Use it for weekends and holidays. Good idea." Perceiving too late the pitfalls ahead, his accountant's heart sank visibly. Robin Capel had a flair for turning potential assets into costly liabilities. Fortunately, Fernanda could be counted on to veto the additional expense. Robin ran a small but lucrative publishing company producing coffee-table books of the type bought by the illiterate as a substitute for reading, but although he was an excellent editor with a genuine enthusiasm for the banal, financial management was beyond him.

"We never take a holiday in England, Daddy," Fern pointed out en route north. "We generally rent a villa in Tuscany in the summer and go skiing in France or Switzerland in winter. You can't ski in Yorkshire and they don't make very good Chianti. It just isn't sensible to keep a place we'll hardly ever use."

"You're obsessed with being sensible," said William from the back seat. "Women go through life with a shopping list, and when someone gives them anything that isn't on it—even if it's something really precious—they simply throw it out of the basket."

"Who said that?" Fern asked sharply.

"Mr. Calder. History."

His sister shook her head. "You're slipping, Will," she said. "Last time you made a nasty remark about women you attributed it to the English master. You can't expect me to believe all your teachers are male chauvinists."

"Why not?" he retorted, unabashed. At twelve, he was as tall as his sister and slight and supple as a whip. His face had that quality of luminous clarity, common to elves and angels, which the unwary so often mistake for innocence. He changed the subject without apology or embarrassment.

"If Great-Uncle Edward barely knew you," he asked Robin, "why did he leave you his house?"

"No one else to leave it to," Robin surmised. "He wasn't really my great-uncle. Or yours. My grandfather's cousin. Might make him my great-cousin, I suppose. Maybe a couple of greats."

"One will do," said Fern.

"He must have been awfully old," Will mused.

"Youngest of his family," Robin explained. "Lots of sisters. Story goes, he ran away to sea when he was a boy—merchant navy—and didn't come back till they'd all died. Part of the Capel legend. Don't know if that's what really happened. None of the sisters married—unless some of them were widowed—anyway, there were no children. Ned Capel didn't marry either. Overdosed on women at an early age, I expect. The sisters all lived in that house until they sort of faded away and then he came home and vegetated there too. Must have been about ninety when he died. The sisters were fairly ancient as well. Remember visiting once with my grandparents: I think I was about Will's age. There were three or four of them left by then: Esme and Deirdre and Irene— don't recall any other names. Esme—no, Eithne—they called her the baby. Seventy-five at least. Very small with a wrinkled little face all eyes, like a marmoset in flowered chiffon. 'I made the seedcake myself,' she told me. Frightful stuff. Tasted of sand."

"What's seedcake?" asked Will, intrigued.

"Told you," said Robin. "Sand."

They arrived in Yorkshire around ten that evening. Fern, normally a faultless map-reader, was in an edgy mood after losing them twice. Although it was May the weather was cold and a thin drizzle misted the windscreen whenever Robin tried switching off the wipers. The lights of a straggling village glittered through the rain as they crossed the Yarrow and climbed uphill; few lights and far between, lurking behind deep-set windows and close-drawn curtains, not unwelcoming but distant, keeping themselves to themselves. Following directions conveyed by Ned Capel's solicitors they left the village and continued on into the dark, turning off at last up a steep drive which proved to be more like a cart-track, their rough passage shaking the Audi until its Vorsprung seemed about to come unsprung. The drive widened and leveled out in front of the house and Robin stopped the car. Little of the façade was visible through the rain-swept gloom except for the tall windows, many of them arched, black in the gray wall. The former housekeeper, a local woman, had been informed of their advent but there were no lights showing, no indications that they were expected. The house might have stood unoccupied for years. It looked dour, unfriendly, desolate as the surrounding countryside, hugging itself around the hollow darkness of its dusty rooms. Fern produced a flashlight and the roving beam picked out the entrance, tag-ends of creeper casting wavering fingers of shadow across the front door. In the blurred lozenge of light this was seen to be of unvarnished oak, splintered and weather-bleached, and as solid as the door to a dungeon. A modern Yale lock had been added, but the key turned reluctantly and the door creaked open under duress, scraping over bare boards. The hall inside was chilly and almost pitch-black. Fern took a long time finding the lightswitch: the skittering beam glanced over the lower treads of a winding stair and flicked in and out of curious niches and past angled doorways, blinking back abruptly from the depths of a stained mirror. Low-wattage illumination did little to improve matters, showing the details of cobwebs trailing from ceiling and lamp-shade and patches of discoloration on walls which might originally have been painted white.

Will gazed about him without enthusiasm. "Fern's right," he said. "What's the point of a house we won't use? I think we should sell."

"I must say," Robin averred, "it looks a bit off-putting. Could move on, I suppose. Find a B & B. Come back in the morning."

"No." Fern's tone did not admit of argument. "We're here and we're going to stay. You were both so set on coming: well, I don't intend to run away just because there isn't a red carpet. Mrs. Wicklow was asked to leave us tea and milk and so on. Let's find the kitchen."

She deposited the flashlight on a table and opened the door to her left, flicking an adjacent switch. A yellow glow sprang into being, no mellow radiance but a tired, sickly, off-color light, as if the bulbs which provided it were continuously on the verge of expiring. It illumined a long drawing room with a few pieces of cumbersome furniture, the velvet upholstery rubbed raw by past occupants, a carpet mottled with age and dirt, and a wide empty fireplace bringing to her the dreary moan of the wind in the chimney. A grandfather clock ticked loudly, but there were no other sounds. At the far end of the room was an alcove, and peering out of it was the Face. For an instant, for all her resolute nerves, Fern stifled a gasp that was almost a cry. It was the face of a malevolent Buddha, not pensive and serene but gloating, somehow sly, the broad lips half parted in an unholy smile, the eyelids creased at some inscrutable jest, stubby horns protruding above a low brow. One of the lightbulbs flickered and she had the illusion that the idol had winked at her. It's a statue, she told herself. Only a statue. Inadvertently, she spoke aloud.

Will and Robin had been investigating other doors but her brother heard her and came back to the hall. "What's the matter?" he said. "Did you call?"

"It was the statue," she said. "It gave me a shock."

Will pushed past her to take a closer look. "It's hideous," he said gleefully. "I'll bet Great-Cousin Ned brought it back from his travels. Sailors always pick up stuff in foreign parts, don't they? This place could be full of strange things. Some of them might be valuable."

"Pirates' treasure, I suppose?" said Fern, reassured by his ebullience. "Doubloons, and pieces of eight."

"I thought a doubloon was something you wore." Will had stopped a couple of feet in front of the idol, and suddenly he turned away. "Actually, I don't think I do like it very much. I wonder what it's laughing at?"

"I don't really want to know," said Fern.

Robin found the kitchen, at the back of the house. It was stone-flagged, cold but clean, with the barren air of a kitchen where nothing had been cooked in a long while. A jar of coffee, packets of sugar and tea, and a plate of sandwiches in plastic wrap stood on the table, looking like the isolated relics of an alien visitation. There was milk in the fridge. They had snacked at a pub on the way, but Will and Robin tucked into the sandwiches, one eagerly, the other absentmindedly. Fern searched for a teapot to make tea.

"It's a depressing sort of house, isn't it?" Robin commented between mouthfuls.

"That's Yorkshire for you," said his daughter.

The building was on three storeys, with eight bedrooms but only one bathroom and an extra loo downstairs. "The Victorians," Robin explained. "Grubby lot. Didn't reckon too much to bathrooms." The cistern slurped and gurgled at the slightest provocation; hot water was not forthcoming. They went to bed unwashed,

like the Victorians. Mrs. Wicklow had made up the beds in three
of the second-floor rooms; Robin chose the front room, Fern and
Will slept at the back of the house. Fern lay awake for some time,
listening to the unfamiliar sounds of a country night. The rain was
silent and there was no traffic, although once she heard the grating roar of an untuned engine on the road below, possibly a motorbike. A strange mewing cry must, she assumed, have been
some nocturnal creature, maybe a bird: it was only the unfamil-
iarity of it which disturbed her. She slept fitfully, falling between
uneasy dreams, not sure if the snuffling she could hear, along the
wall beneath her window, was real or simply another phantom
from the shadows of sleep.

In the morning she woke around nine and got up to look at
her surroundings in daylight. There was a small garden at the
back of the house but the flower-beds were scantily planted and
the grass grew in tufts on what might have been intended for a
lawn; only weeds and a few hardy shrubs thrived there. Beyond,
the bare hillside, treeless and gray with dew, climbed up toward
the moors and the sky. Occasional rocks broke the skin of turf,
moss-padded, the outthrust bones of Earth; a bridle path skirted
the garden and ascended the slope, a shadowy line against the
contouring of the land. Above it Fern noticed something which
might have been a solitary boulder or stump, curiously shaped,
looking almost like an old man sitting hunched up, cloaked and
hooded against the weather. It was not actually raining but a layer
of pale cloud covered the sky and the air felt damp. A budding inclination to explore the path died when Fern realized she had
come without suitable boots.

Downstairs, she found her brother in the kitchen, bemoaning a
lack of cereal, while the water boiled away from the old-fashioned
iron kettle which Robin had left on the hob.

"Dad's gone to the village shop," Will reported. "I asked him
to get me some Frosties. He said he'd bring orange juice too."

"Is there a village shop?" Fern inquired, transferring the kettle to an unheated surface.

"Probably."

Robin returned about three quarters of an hour later with squash instead of juice and no Frosties. "Only cornflakes," he explained, "and porridge oats. Didn't think you'd like those. Sorry about the juice. Said they'd run out."

"No Frosties!" Will bewailed.

"You took a long time," said Fern.

"Met the vicar. Nice chap. Name of Dinsdale—Gus Dinsdale. Invited us to tea. Thought we might like to visit Edward Capel's grave, pay our respects, I suppose. He's buried here: local churchyard. Anyway, I said fine. Nothing else to do."

"A visit to a grave and tea with the vicar," said Will. "Lovely weekend we're having."

They spent the rest of the morning going through the house. Fern found a long-handled broom for the cobwebs and an antiquated vacuum cleaner which made a noise like a small tornado and seemed bent on sucking up the carpets. In the drawing room, she moved the idol to a place where it would not catch her eye every time she opened the door. It was much heavier than she had anticipated and the stone felt rough and chill; she shivered when she set it down. On the second floor, Robin became absorbed in the paintings and estimated that a couple of murky landscapes and the portrait of a little girl with Shirley Temple ringlets clutching a puppy might possibly be worth something. Will, disappointed to find that the vaulted gloom of the cellar contained nothing more promising than a wine-rack with several bottles of superior burgundy, was cheered by the discovery of an attic running the length of the house, colonized by spiders and littered with bric-a-brac, including an iron-bound chest which might have come straight from a pirates' hoard. His enthusiasm was enhanced rather than mitigated when the chest proved to be locked, with no immediate sign of a key.

"Looking for it will give you something useless to occupy your time," said Fern, who had stubbed her toe on a lurking footstool and was determined to find nothing intriguing in an overcrowded attic. She was too old for treasure hunts.

"I say," said Robin from behind her. "Quite a place. Might find all kinds of stuff here—family heirlooms, missing works of art . . . That chair looks like a Chippendale. Pity it's broken. Not much light, is there? We need Fern's flashlight."

They came down finally at lunchtime when Mrs. Wicklow arrived carrying a covered dish. Her greeting was abrupt and her face only slightly less stony than that of the idol but the dish emanated an agreeable aroma of steak-and-kidney and Fern concluded that her attitude was not actively grudging, it was simply that she was resistant to change and unused to the incursion of strangers. "Solicitors told me t' Captain was your great-uncle," she said to Robin over their meal.

"Well, not exactly . . ."

"We decided he was our great-cousin," Will said, "with an extra great for Fern and me."

"You must miss him," Fern offered.

"He was a good man," Mrs. Wicklow conceded, "but tired. He was old and he didn't like it. He couldn't go walking the way he used to. Folks say long life is a thing to wish for, but I'm not so sure. It can't be pleasant to outlive your friends. T' Captain, he wasn't t' same since his dog died."

"Was he really a captain?" Will asked.

"He was that. Been all over the world, he had. I don't know as how he ever really took to it, being what he called a landsman all the time. Of course, we're near the coast here. He'd go down to look at t' sea often and often, and come back sad about the eyes.

Can't say I trust it myself, t' sea: it can seem so blue and gentle, but t' water's always cold and tricksy underneath."

"He must have collected a lot of things on his travels," Will said opportunely. "I don't suppose you know where I could find the key to that big chest in the attic?"

"Could be anywhere." Mrs. Wicklow achieved a shrug. "House is full of stuff. Most of it's rubbish, if you ask me; he wasn't one for throwing things away. T' key'll be tucked in a drawer in t' study or bedroom if you're that set on it."

"Which was the Captain's room?" Will pursued.

"One Mr. Capel has now," Mrs. Wicklow said. She had done some investigative bed-making before serving the pie.

"Er—make it Robin," their father interjected. "Mr. Capel . . . bit formal."

"Mr. Robin, then."

"Might not all be rubbish, you know," Mr. Robin remarked, discarding any further attempt at informality. "There are some good pictures, although I expect those came to him through the family."

"I don't mind pictures," said Mrs. Wicklow. "It's that heathen idol in the drawing room I don't like. Evil-looking object, I told t' Captain to his face. Unchristian. He said it amused him. There's different kinds of God, he used to say, all over t' world. That's not a kind I'd want in my prayers, I told him, nor any respectable person."

"I don't care for it much either," said Fern.

"And then there's that woman," Mrs. Wicklow continued, obscurely. "Carved out of a whole tree, according to t' Captain, painted up as bright as life, and showing her all just like in t' Sunday papers. She came from a shipwreck, he said, back in t' old days when ships had a real lady up front for t' sailors to warm to, only she doesn't look much like a lady to me. T' prow, that's what they call it. He kept it in t' barn next door, and a big piece of t' ship with it."

"We haven't looked in the barn yet," said Will, glancing compellingly at his father, his interest in sea chests temporarily in abeyance.

"We ought to go and see," Robin affirmed. "A ship's figurehead— sounds pretty exciting." His eyes were as bright as his son's.

Fern stayed in the kitchen, although her offer to help with the washing up was firmly rejected.

"Funny thing, what your brother was asking," Mrs. Wicklow resumed. "There was a young woman over from Guisborough, not long before t' Captain died. Something to do with antiques. They're all crooks, so I hear. Wanting him to sell stuff, she was. He sent her about her business. Anyway, I was doing t' drawing room when they came downstairs, and I heard them talking. She was asking about keys."

Later that afternoon they paid a brief visit to the churchyard, where Ned Capel lay in the lee of a dry stone wall, with the turf plumped up like a pillow over his grave. It was a quiet place hollowed into the hillside, with the petals of a hawthorn drifting across the ground like a spring snowfall. "Home is the sailor, home from the sea," Fern quoted, and for an instant she felt, irrationally, that she too had come home—home to the grimness of Dale House and the wild country waiting in the wings. "Is it supposed to be haunted?" she asked the vicar, over tea.

"Extraordinary question," said Robin. "Didn't think you believed in ghosts."

"I don't. It's just—when we arrived, the house appeared, not exactly menacing, but reserved, sort of sullen, unwilling—or afraid—to let us in. I almost fancied . . ." She checked herself, remembering her vaunted distrust of fancies.

"I've never been too sure about hauntings," said the Reverend Dinsdale. He was younger than Fern had expected, probably under forty, with a friendly bony face and a long neck in which a mobile Adam's apple fluctuated expressively. "I can't really imagine a human spirit is going to mope around the same old place for centuries just because it was murdered there, or something equally nasty. All the more reason to move on, I would have thought. On the other hand, some houses have a definite personality. I've often wondered if it's the buildings themselves which remember—and maybe sometimes the memory can be strong enough to reproduce an old image, a sound, even a smell, so that human senses can detect it. Perhaps there's a kind of house-spirit which lives in such places, a degenerate form of something that was once akin to mankind, craving the company of the living even while it resents them, reminded of what it might have been."

"A sort of *genius loci*," Will supplied knowledgeably. He was in a beatific mood after the vicar's wife had donated a packet of Frosties from her larder.

"That's it. Pure speculation, of course. Mind you, it's fairly well grounded in folk mythology. In the past, every house in Yorkshire had its own hobgoblin. The occupants would put out a saucer of milk or a choice morsel of food to keep it sweet, and in return it would look after the house, see off danger and disease, that kind of thing. Much more efficient than a burglar alarm."

"Maybe we should get Fern to put out some milk for ours," Robin suggested slyly.

"Don't be silly, Daddy," his daughter retorted.

"I don't know about ghosts," Will said, "but I heard a weird sniffing noise last night, going along the wall under my window. It was awfully loud." Fern glanced at him with suddenly widening eyes.

"Could be a badger," the vicar said. "They always sound as if they have a cold in the head. What you want to do is go out in the morning and check for tracks. I've got a book in my study with some good illustrations: I'll show you what to look for."

By the time they returned to Ned Capel's house the daylight was failing. The cloud-cover had begun to break up and chinks of fire appeared in the far west above a muffled sunset, while eastward great lakes of pale green had opened up, with a star or two winking in their depths. The motorcyclist Fern had heard the previous night roared past them on the narrow road, a little too close for comfort, his exhaust rattling and a black visor hiding his face. Their temporary home loomed up ahead of them, its unyielding frontage looking no longer threatening but merely solid, sternly dependable, as safe as a castle wall which would keep them from the night. Fern went straight up to her room and gazed out toward the sunset: twilight dimmed the rugged hillside but she could still distinguish the paler thread of the path and the stump or boulder that resembled a seated man on the bank above, maintaining its timeless vigil over the house. Something like a bird swooped past, its wing-beat too swift for the eye to follow, its flight-path erratic. Then there was another, and another. They made a faint high-pitched chittering unlike any birdsong. Bats! Fern thought with a sudden shiver, part fear, part pleasure. She had never seen a bat outside the nature programs on television and although she was not really frightened of them they seemed to her alien and fantastical, messengers symbolizing her transition into another world. The teeming man-made metropolis where she had grown up shrank in her mind until it was merely a blob of meaningless ferment, and beyond it she glimpsed a boundless universe, with pockmarked moons sinking behind drifting hills, and blue voids opening in between, and dusty nebulae floating like clouds across the backdrop of space, and at the last a starry sea whose glittering waves hissed forever on the silver beaches at the margin of being. For a moment she was spellbound, panic-stricken; and then the endless vistas vanished from her head and there was only the hill-side climbing to the barren moor and the zigzagging of the bats. The sunset had faded from behind the cloud-wrack and in the softened light details were briefly clearer: Fern squinted at the view, striving after uncertainty, knowing that what she saw was against logic, against sense. The solitary boulder had gone. The path was empty, the slope bare; in an eye blink, the duration of a mirage, the hunched up rock or stump had disappeared. Fern flinched away from the window with a lurching heart and made herself walk slowly from the room.

Tea had been heavy on scones and cake and accordingly the three of them ate a cursory supper and spent the rest of the eve-ning trying to elucidate the rule-book for a box of mah-jongg tiles unearthed in the attic.

"Good thing, no telly," said Robin a little doubtfully. "Makes you create your own amusements. Stretches the mind."

"We'll have to get a TV here," said Will. "Also a music center."

"No point," Fern said. "We're going to sell. Will, you're cheat-ing. There's no such thing as a King Kong."

"I'm not cheating," Will retorted. "I'm creating my own amusements."

It was well after eleven by the time they went up to bed, worn out by the intricacies of the game. Fern tumbled into a bemused sleep where ivory tiles tap-danced along the table and an elaborate Oriental character uncurled into a bat-winged creature which skit-tered around the room, bumping into walls and lamp-shades. "It's a dragon," said a voice in her ear. "Don't look into its eyes"—but it was too late, she was already falling into the hypnotic orbs as if into a crimson abyss, clouded with shifting vapors of thought, and a single iris dilated in front of her, black as the Pit. Then she crossed into a dreamland so crowded with incident and adventure that she woke exhausted, snatching in vain at the fraying threads of recollection. She had a feeling her dream had possessed some overwhelming significance, but it was gone in a few seconds and there were only the raindrops beating on the windowpanes like the tapping of mah-jongg tiles. She slept and woke again, this time into silence. And then below her window came the snuffling noise, bronchial and somehow eager, as if the animal outside was desperately seeking ingress through the steadfast wall. A badger, thought Fern. I'd like to see a badger—but a huge reluctance came over her, pressing her into the bed like a dead weight, forcing her back into the inertia of sleep, and when she woke again it was morning.

The hot water had come on eventually but there was no shower attachment so Fern had a quick bath. When she finally nerved herself to look out at the view, the boulder—she had decided to think of it as a boulder since the area was virtually devoid of trees—was back in place as if it had never been gone; she could almost convince herself its absence the previous evening had been a trick of the twilight. Will was grubbing around in the flower-bed below, presumably hunting for badger-tracks as instructed by Gus Dinsdale. In the kitchen, Robin was trying to make toast without the assistance of a toaster. Several charred slices on the table bore mute witness to his failure. Fern packed him off to the bathroom and took over; Will came in from the garden, unashamedly earth-stained, in time to appropriate the first round.

"Any luck?" she asked.

"What?"

"Badger-tracking."

Will set down his slice of toast unfinished, a frown puckering his forehead. "No. I can't understand it. I heard it last night, that same sniffing, really loud, just where the flower-bed is. It had rained earlier, and Gus said damp soil is perfect for holding prints, but there isn't a mark. Yet I know I heard it. I was sort of half asleep at the time, and I thought about getting up and taking a look, but somehow I didn't want to, or I was just too tired. I wish I had now. Maybe I dreamed it."

"If you did," said Fern, "then I did too. Both nights."

"Perhaps the house is haunted," Will said after a pause.

"Do you believe in ghosts?" Fern asked.

"Well, Mr. Burrows—Physics—he says Science has proved so many impossible things that it would be a great mistake to rule out the supernatural just because we haven't sussed it out yet. He got us all talking about it one afternoon: he said he'd had an experience which he couldn't explain, and Rebecca Hollis told us about her grandmother's house, and this room which is always cold, and something she'd seen there. She isn't the fanciful type, either, and she doesn't boast; she wouldn't even have talked about it if her best friend hadn't nudged her into it." Absentmindedly, he took another bite of toast and reached for the Frosties. "I rather like that idea Gus had, about the house-spirit," he concluded with his mouth full.

"But the sniffing is outside the house," Fern said thoughtfully, "and it wants to get in."

For a minute Will stopped eating and stared at her. She contemplated telling him about the boulder but decided against it; he was only twelve, and the light had been poor, she might have been mistaken. "I'm imagining things," she said, suddenly impatient with her own credulity. "It's the Yorkshire landscape. Overexposure to nature is bad for city-dwellers. We need to get back to the bright lights of reality."

"The lights are man-made," Will pointed out. "Electricity and neon. Only the stars are real."

And then: "What's that awful smell?"

"Damn," said Fern. "Now I've burned the toast."

They drove back to London after lunch at the local pub, where surly rustics eyed them sidelong and thick Yorkshire accents made the language barrier almost insurmountable. "Interesting house," Robin said in the car. "Must go through all that stuff sometime. Quite a collection. Didn't see the figurehead, did you, Fern? You ought to have a look. She's pretty impressive. Next time we're there—"

"We really have to sell, Daddy," Fern interrupted resolutely. "We don't need the house and we're not likely to use it very much. It'll be far too expensive to maintain just as a storehouse for marine antiquities."

"Of course. Of course." Robin's agreement was too quick and too hearty. "Just a thought. We'll go back in the summer, sort out, tidy up, sell later. No hurry. Market's still picking up. Best to wait a bit. Invest some time and effort in the place: makes good business sense. James'll approve. He's all for investment." James was his accountant.

Fern's grip tightened on the AA Road Atlas.

"We've got to go back," Will insisted. "The house-spirit will be waiting for us."

Fern was not entirely sure he was joking.

✦ II ✦

The summer holidays had arrived before they found time to return to Yarrowdale. Robin was seeing a fair amount of Alison Redmond, apparently in the course of literary collaboration; but Fern did not perceive any reason for undue anxiety. Although they dined out together almost every week he never brought her home, and in his daughter's experience serious intentions always involved getting on terms with the children. On her own terrain, she could demolish all invaders: her sweet, aloof smile quelled both patronage and gush, camaraderie wilted in the face of her perfect manners, domestic aspirants blanched at her competent management and delectable cuisine. As a child, she had used a cultivated artlessness to undermine overconfidence; when she grew older, she honed her conversational skills at the dinner table until she knew to a nicety how to wrong-foot her opponents and expose, as if by accident, pretension, bossiness, self-importance—even when such defects were not really there. Will, an indifferent ally, usually left her a clear field. Robin was the charming, helpless type of man who invariably attracted forceful women wanting to mold him to suit their own inclinations, an ambition that would only work as long as he was unaware of it.

24

Once these plans had been revealed, resistance would set in, and Fern, who had been molding him for years, knew she had won another unobtrusive skirmish. She wanted her father to marry again eventually, but only to someone who would make him comfortable, whose authority would be gentle, who would refrain from pushing him down roads he did not wish to travel. She had almost decided in favor of Abigail Markham, a thirtysomething Sloane currently employed by Robin's publicity department in a low-key capacity, who combined a certain serenity of outlook with a pleasant scattiness over dress and social engagements. But Robin's penchant for her company seemed to have abated under Alison's influence. Fern, keeping a routine eye on him, trusted the friendship would not outlast the germination of the book.

Attending a party at the gallery with her father, she noticed Alison greeting him with an extra inch of smile and a sideways glitter of her pale eyes. She wore several clinging, drooping, fluttering garments of some vague shade between beige and taupe which echoed the dark fairness of her hair, and her overfull mouth was painted a deep red so that it blossomed like a rampant peony against the whiteness of her skin. There was a bizarre fascination in her sidelong gaze, the point-edged smile that never came close to laughter, the sinuous fingers that punctuated her every gesture, the rippling motion of the material that wrapped her body, as fluid and as neutral as water. And her strange, dull, endless hair, veined with hues of shadow, enfolding her like a cloak: Fern wondered what treatment had made it grow so long—too long, surely, for European locks—and what had leached the colors of life from its waving masses. It might almost have provided her with a mantle of invisibility, effective by dusk and dark, hiding her from wary eyes as she stole abroad on some unspecified but nefarious business. Nonsense, Fern scolded herself. What is the matter with me? I'm seeing too many ghosts lately. This is the West End, this is an art gallery, this is a room full of people drinking cheap champagne and chattering about the decline of the image. There are no spectres here. In passing, she glanced at one of the champagne bottles. Long after, she knew that should have warned her, evidence rather than intuition: the champagne was not cheap. She had been attending and sometimes assisting at such parties since she was fourteen and she knew quite well that no normal person wastes good drink on a crowd.

"And what do you think of the pictures tonight, Fernanda?" The voice at her side caught her unawares. For the second time.

"It's a bit difficult to study them properly with so many people around," she said after a moment, mentally putting herself on guard. She had not noticed the pictures yet.

"Of course," Javier Holt responded smoothly. "The problem with a private view is that it isn't private and nobody gets to view anything." His face looked like a mask, she thought, a perfect mask of some seamless metal with topaz eyes and hair of spun steel. The focus of her apprehension shifted. At least Alison Redmond was a living hazard, whereas Javier Holt appeared dead, suavely, immaculately dead, and the spark that animated him might have come from elsewhere, controlled by a pressing of buttons, a turning of wheels.

"You seemed very intent nonetheless," he went on. "If not the pictures, what were you studying?"

"People," said Fern coolly. "You have an interesting selection here."

He smiled automatically. "Anyone in particular?" He obviously knew who had claimed her attention.

"Alison," said Fern with a pose of candor, a hint of defiance.

"Naturally. Your father seems very taken with her. She is a most unusual woman."

"She moves like water," Fern said, "like a twisting stream, all bright deceptive reflections, hidden currents, dangerous little eddies. She might be very shallow, she might be very deep. She's much too unusual for my father."

"I am sure she knows that," Javier responded with that faint mockery in his tone.

Fern was not entirely reassured.

It was something of a relief to be leaving for Yorkshire. Fern's two closest friends were going on holiday early and although she would miss London it was hot enough for the country to have its attractions. Robin might spend part of the week in the metropolis on business but long weekends at Dale House, rifling among the hotch-potch of Ned Capel's collection, would provide both distance and distraction from urban perils. He evidently anticipated the visit with a brand of schoolboy pleasure which even exceeded Will's. Fern found it more difficult to analyze her own emotions when she saw Yarrowdale again: there was no obvious surge of gladness, rather a feeling of acknowledgment, a falling-into-place of her life's pattern, as if she had returned to somewhere she was meant to be after a careless and unscheduled absence. The grim façade of the house seemed to relax a little; recognition peered out of the empty windows. She went up to her room and, with a doubt bordering on fear, scanned the hillside for that strange-shaped boulder. It was there in its place, a silent Watcher, maintaining surveillance through all weathers, unmoving as the rock it resembled. But it *is* a rock, Fern reminded herself, afraid to find she was no longer afraid; it was never gone; I imagined that.

She slept undisturbed by birdcall or badger and in the morning, encouraged by a lightening breeze and a brightening sun, they walked the half mile or so to the coast. Yarrowdale was not one of *the* Dales, being situated on the edge of the moors between Scarborough and Whitby, where a series of steep valleys wind down to a rocky shore buffeted by the storms from the North Sea. That day, however, the sea was blue and tranquil, the waves tumbling gently onto the beach and melting into great fans of foam, while a coaxing wind seemed to take the fire out of the noonday heat. The Capels strolled along the wide sweep of beach and smelled the sea-smell and removed their shoes to paddle at the waves' edge— "The water's freezing," said Fern, and "Got to be careful swimming," Robin added. "Mrs. Wicklow's right: currents are chancy round here." There were few people, no litter. Scavenging gulls skimmed the shoreline in vain: their lonely cries sounded harsh as screams and desolate as the ocean's heart. Yet to Fern they seemed to be a summons to an unknown world, a growing-up unlike anything she had planned, where her mind and her experience would be broadened beyond the bounds of imagination.

On Monday Robin set off for London with a car full of paintings which would undoubtedly prove to be worth a fraction of his optimistic valuations, something that would in no way damage his hopes for the rest of Great-Cousin Ned's jumble. Mrs. Wicklow had agreed to assist with cooking and housekeeping and Gus Dinsdale's wife had promised to drive Fern to Whitby for essential shopping. Will had started on cleaning the ship's figurehead. As Mrs. Wicklow had said, there was a sizeable section of ship attached. "See," Will told his sister, "she's got a name. When I've got the rest of those barnacles off we should be able to read it. I wonder how old she is?"

"This is really a job for a professional," Fern remarked.

"We haven't *got* a professional. Anyway, I'm being careful." He proceeded to notch a kitchen knife against a particularly stubborn crustacean. "She's been on the seabed a while. She must have survived much rougher handling than anything she's getting from me."

"I'll give you a hand," said Fern, abandoning her careful indifference to succumb to the lure of a mystery.

After about an hour of rather awkward chipping the name emerged, semi-obliterated but legible. Fern had known what it would be all along, with the strange prescience which comes from that region of the brain they say is never used, a zone of thought still unconscious and untabulated. *Seawitch*, ran the lettering. The carving did not resemble Alison, for all its flowing hair and parted lips: the improbable bosom was outthrust, the belly a sleek curve, the face as knowing as Dodona. Nonetheless, Fern was unsurprised. Her awareness was touched with an elusive familiarity, but whether from the future or the past she could not tell.

"She's *wonderful*," said Will. "Those tits look like nuclear warheads."

"You're much too young to notice such things," his sister said loftily.

"You're just jealous," said Will.

That evening Mrs. Wicklow left around five. Fern made omelettes and they ate in the kitchen listening to Will's ghetto-blaster pumping out the latest from the Pet Shop Boys. Even when Robin was with them, they never sat in the drawing room: it was always a degree colder than the rest of the house and the stone idol squatted there wrapped in its secret gloating like a diminutive Moloch. Fern did her best to keep the door closed, hindered by Mrs. Wicklow's penchant for opening both doors and windows at every opportunity, in order, so she said, to let in air. "There's air in here already," Will had pointed out, "otherwise we wouldn't be breathing." But Mrs. Wicklow believed air had to be specially admitted.

The sky had clouded over and by the time they went to bed the night outside had grown very dark. "We ought to have candles," said Will, "guttering in the draft, making huge spidery shadows on the wall."

"Don't talk about spiders," said Fern.

Slightly to her surprise, she fell asleep immediately, untroubled by nightmares.

She woke abruptly in the small hours to find herself sitting up in bed, intensely alert, her nerve endings on stalks. The curtains were half drawn but the space between was merely a paler shade of black, barely discernible against the velvet dark of the room. There was no wind and the absolute quiet, without even a distant rumor of traffic, was something to which she had not yet become accustomed. The silence had a quality of tension about it, as if the night itself were holding its breath, waiting for a board to creak, a pin to drop, the warning screech of a bird. Fern's pulse beat so hard that her whole body seemed to shake with it. And then came the snuffling, just as she had expected, horribly familiar and so loud it might have been directly below her windowsill. The rasping, stertorous breath of some creature that left never a print, an incorporeal hunter who had no existence except to scent its prey. The reluctance that held her back she recognized as fear, a fear that was not only inside her but all around her, a dread that was part of the room itself: she had to thrust it aside like a physical barrier. The floor made no sound beneath her tread; the window, thanks to Mrs. Wicklow, was already ajar. She leaned out into the night.

There was something at the foot of the wall, something that was darker than the surrounding darkness, a clot of shadow whose actual shape was impossible to make out. Not a badger: the white bands on its mask would have been visible at that range. Besides, although she had no idea how large a badger was supposed to be she was sure this must be larger, larger than a fox, larger than a sheepdog. It moved to and fro, to and fro, as if worrying at the wall; then suddenly it stopped, and the sniffing was accompanied by a furious scrabbling, the unmistakable sound of paws burrowing frenziedly in the soil, as though seeking to unearth the very foundations of the house. Afterward, Fern knew she must have made some slight noise to betray her presence. The thing below her froze, and lifted its head. She saw neither form nor feature, only the eyes, slanting ovoids filled with a glow that mirrored nothing around them, a livid flame that came only from within. The terror that rushed over her was beyond all reason, a wild, mindless force not pushing her back but pulling her down, down toward the ground and the waiting eyes. With a vast effort of will she wrenched herself free—and then she was back in her room, latching the window with unsteady fingers, and the silence outside was unbroken, and a board creaked in welcome as she stumbled across to her bed. She thought of going to her brother's room to see if he was awake and what he had heard, but a great tiredness overwhelmed her and she decided it could wait till morning. Now she needed to sleep . . . and sleep . . . and by daylight the horror would be a matter for nightmare and the flower-bed would be pocked with the tracks of some mongrel stray.

But it rained before dawn, and any prints there might have been were washed away.

Fern went to the window as soon as she got up, and there was Will searching the ground, still in his pajamas and slippers: the latter would be soaked through. "Come in and get dressed," she called. And: "Have you found anything?"

"No. The rain was too heavy." His upturned face was curiously solemn despite a lavish smudge of dirt. "You heard it too?"

"Yes. Come on in."

He disappeared through the back door and Fern's gaze lifted automatically to the path straddling the hillside. In the gray morning light there could be no mistaking what she saw. The Watcher had gone.

"It wasn't a badger," said Fern over breakfast. "There were no markings. It was big, and dark: that's all I could see." She didn't want to mention the reasonless terror that had tried to drag her from the window. Fern disliked both terror and unreason.

"A dog?" Will suggested.

"Maybe."

"A wolf?"

"There aren't any wolves left in Britain."

"It could have escaped from a zoo," Will theorized, "only . . ."

"Why would it want to get into the house? An escaped wolf would be out on the moors killing sheep—supposing it *was* a wolf, which I doubt. Anyway, I don't think there *are* any zoos near here."

There was a short pause filled with the crunching of cereal. "When you have eliminated the impossible," Will pronounced eventually, "whatever remains, no matter how improbable, must be the truth. Sherlock Holmes. Conan Doyle was a great believer in the supernatural. And that's what we're left with. There's something strange going on, something to do with this house. I thought so all along. So did you really, only you're so grown-up and boring that you won't let yourself believe in anything anymore. Remind me not to grow up if that's how it takes you. Did you know that they've conducted experiments in telekinesis in the laboratory? Did you know that there are alternative universes round every corner? Did you know—"

"Shut up," said Fern. "I'm not boring, just skeptical. That's healthy." And: "Did *you* know . . . did you know there's a boulder on the hill behind the garden that's shaped like a seated man, and sometimes it's there, and sometimes it isn't? It's been there all weekend—always in the same place—and this morning it was gone. How's that for a did-you-know?"

"Perhaps it *is* a man," Will said uncertainly, baffled by the introduction of a new element in the situation. "Perhaps it's a tramp."

"It's a rock," said Fern. "There's nothing wrong with my eyesight. It sits there for days, in all kinds of weather, like a rock is supposed to. I think it's watching us."

"Rocks don't watch," Will pointed out.

"This one does."

"It all centers on the house," Will reiterated. "It could be something to do with the stuff Great-Cousin Ned picked up on his travels. Maybe there's a magic talisman hidden in the attic, or an amulet, or the green eye of the little yellow god, or—what about that chest? It must be in there—whatever it is."

"Too obvious."

"Well, we ought to look. The key should be around somewhere."

An arrested expression appeared on Fern's face. "I don't know if it's relevant," she said slowly, "but Mrs. Wicklow said there was a woman here asking about keys, before Great-Cousin Ned died. She was in the antiques business."

"She must have known about the chest."

"How?"

They spent the morning rooting among the jumble in the attic, finding neither talisman nor key but an assortment of items which Will at least considered promising, including an evil-looking curved knife, a devil-mask which was probably African, a hookah happily empty of opium, and an antiquated map of the Indian subcontinent with elephants, tigers, maharajahs, and palaces drawn in where appropriate. Also a great deal of dust and several spiders, the largest and leggiest of which sent Fern into retreat, claiming it was time she checked out the study. Unfortunately, the most interesting feature of Ned Capel's sanctum was a mahogany writing desk the top of which proved to be locked and, like the chest, keyless. "Damn," said Fern, who had been brought up to moderate her language. "I bet all the keys are in one place. The question is where." Her sweatshirt, she noticed, had acquired several dust-smears as a result of her foraging, and she went to her room to change it. She had no intention of returning to the attic that day.

A routine glance out of the window showed her a sky of gunmetal gray and rain blowing in waves across the bleak landscape.

Her gaze shifted—then switched back again. Seconds later she was running down the stairs, kicking off her sandals at the bottom with uncharacteristic carelessness. In the hall, she plunged her feet into an old pair of galoshes, snatched Robin's Barbour from the peg, and crammed on her head a shapeless waterproof hat which had formerly belonged to Ned Capel. Then she ran out of the back door and through the garden to the gate. The latch was stiff from infrequent use and the wood had swollen in the wet: it took a hard thrust of her shoulder to open it. The oversized boots slopped around her feet as she scrambled up the path. The wind swept across the hillside unhindered. And then she was standing in front of him with the water dripping off her hat-brim and her unfastened jacket letting the rain soak through her sweatshirt. He no longer resembled a boulder, though there was something rock-like about his absolute stillness and the patience it implied. He wore a loose, bulky garment with a pointed hood overhanging his face: the material was heavy and laminated with long weathering, its brindled hues at once earth-colored and stone-colored, moss-patched and grass-grimed. Under the hood she saw a countenance as battered as the coat, with sparse flesh on strong bones and wind-worn, sun-leathered skin gathered into wrinkles about the mouth and eyes, some of them for laughter, some for thought, many for grimness and sorrow. But it was the eyes themselves which held her: they were green and gold and brown like a woodland spring and they sparkled brighter than the rain, so bright that they seemed to pierce the walls of her mind and see into her very soul. And after the first shocked recoil her soul opened in response, and her life changed forever. It was as if the personality she had made for herself, matter-of-fact, positive, conscientiously hidebound, began to peel away like a chrysalis and a different Fernanda, wet-winged and shy, poked a tentative antenna into the unfamiliar air. In that moment she realized that she did not know herself, she never had, and all her certainties had been merely the pretense of a child afraid of maturity; but ignorance did not frighten her now, for *he* knew who she was, and what she was, and in that knowing she could be at ease. She said "Hello," and he said "Hello," and their greeting dissolved the walls of her little world, and let in the unimaginable from Outside.

"You took your time," the Watcher went on. He studied her thoughtfully, seeing a girl with a raindrop on her nose—a very young girl—small for her age, her face heart-shaped, her features delineated with the precision and clarity of a pen-and-ink drawing. The wind slipped under her hat-brim, tugging it back from her forehead, showing hair that was leaf-brown and close-cut, the would-be fringe dividing obstinately into a widow's peak above her brow. Her eyes were wide and wide-set, their gray veined with celadon, and even in that instant of her mind's opening he glimpsed depths that were incalculable, an intelligence that would always be wary. He had made her trust him, an elementary maneuver, but she would not hesitate to return to doubt if—and when—he let her down.

"You looked like a rock," she said accusingly.

"It's useful," he replied. "Nobody wonders what you're up to, if you're a rock. No questions, no trouble. There's nothing as unremarkable as a rock."

"It isn't possible," said Fern, but the conviction was gone from her voice. "I *saw* the rock."

"Appearances can deceive," the Watcher said. "You see many things which are not there. A mirage, a reflection, a star that died thousands of years ago. You should trust your instinct, not your eyes. You knew me long before today."

Fern did not attempt to answer that. "You've been spying on us."

"Observing," he corrected gently. "Fortunately, I am still an observant man, whatever else I may have lost. I seem to have spent centuries just watching."

She was not entirely sure he was exaggerating. "That's how I thought of you," she said. "The Watcher."

"It's appropriate," he said. "I have grown very tired of it, over the years. There are too many things that need watching, and far too few of us to keep watch. Have you found it yet?"

"Found what?"

"What you are looking for."

"I don't know what I'm looking for," Fern pointed out.

"A profound philosophical statement. Not many people do, and if they did, it would be far worse. To find what you seek would be an anticlimax, to fail, a tragedy. But I am talking concepts, which is beside the point. Here, there is clearly something specific to be found. There has been a certain amount of attention focused on this house for some time: callers who were not what they seemed, prowlers by night, some human, some less so. Which reminds me, next time you hear noises in the dark, curb your curiosity. It would be safer."

"You saw it," Fern said. "That creature last night. What was it?"

"Something which should not have been there. Whoever sent it made a thoroughly unsuitable choice of instrument. Don't worry too much: even if it finds an opening, it can't come in, not without being invited. The ancient law still stands. Ignore it and it will go away."

"Are you sure?"

"No. It would be rash to be too sure. But this thing was ill-chosen for our hunt: the sender may well have selected it simply to show that he—or she—has the power to summon such beings." He rubbed his finger along the crooked bridge of his nose in a gesture of reflection. "His next move should be more practical. I hope."

"*Whose* next move?" Fern demanded.

"I don't know. I know very little right now. There are so many possibilities. It could be someone working alone, seeking self-aggrandizement, personal power—alas, we all want those. It could be an agent or emissary. It depends what we're looking for. There are certain indications." His eyes seemed to dim and then brighten again, their light fluctuating with the vagaries of memory. "Something was lost, long, long ago, before the beginnings of history: few remain who would recognize it, fewer still who would know the secret of its use. When it was recovered the recipient thought it an object of no value, the symbol of a cheat; his family kept it as they would keep a grudge, passing it on with legend and moral attached, until a young bride traded it to a tinker for a knot of ribbons. He stole a kiss as well, which was not part of the bargain; they said she looked coldly on her husband ever after. The tinker took his purchase to a collector of such things, sensing its mystery if not its power, a backstreet alchemist one-eighth sorcerer, seven-eighths charlatan. They studied it, he and his apprentice, scanning the smoke for visions and peering into crystal balls, learning the sort of things that you learn from staring at smoke and Venetian glassware. The alchemist also dealt in love potions and poisons—not very successfully: his potions were over-optimistic and his poisons half-hearted. Unfortunately, a dissatisfied client among the warring nobility decided to take his revenge: the alchemist was beaten senseless, his lodgings ransacked, his possessions commandeered. The object was lost again, and never found." He paused, sighed, as indifferent to rain and wind as the rock he had chosen to imitate. Fern was reminded of a venerable hippy, beyond the reach of marijuana or hallucinogen, looking back with cold eyes on the psychedelic phantoms he once pursued. She was damp and chilled; but she did not move. "We searched for it," he went on, "long after, when we learned its importance, but it was too late. The feuding families of that time had hidden their treasures so efficiently that even their descendants could not find them. They left clues, and ciphers, but the clues were mislaid and the ciphers indecipherable.

The trail had vanished. And then, about twenty years ago, a famous chalice was sold at auction—one that had gone missing
during the relevant period. Apparently it had been retrieved in the
last great war when a bomb demolished the wall concealing a secret vault. I could not trace the minor items which might have
been found with it, but I imagine a traveler collecting flotsam
could well have bought one of them for a few pounds from a market stall. It seems a likely theory."

"Great-Cousin Ned," Fern said. "And then? How did you find
him?"

"He was found: I don't know how. A chance meeting, a
spell—it doesn't matter. The interest of others drew *me*. This
thing could be here—may be here—if it is, you must get to it
first."

"*I* must?"

He ignored the interruption. "In the wrong hands, it could be
put to the wrong use. What would happen I'm not sure—and I
don't want to find out. I've been watching the investigations very
carefully: they—whoever they are—know hardly more than we
do. So far. You have to stay ahead of them. You have to find it."

"*What is it?*"

The answer came slowly, softly, as if the Watcher feared to be
overheard, there on the empty hillside without even a bird in
sight. "A key," he said. "Didn't you guess? It's a key."

"Of course," said Fern. "We've been looking for the keys to open
the writing desk and the chest in the attic, when all the time . . . it
was the keys themselves which mattered."

"Just one key. It'll be smaller than the others, made of stone or
something that looks like stone. You'll know it when you see it.
Hide it from everyone."

"And then . . . I give it to you." The doubt crept back, darken-
ing her mind. "And then what? What will *you* do with it?"

For the first time he smiled, an unexpectedly impish smile

which dug punctuation marks in his cheeks and buckled the lines round his eyes. "That's the question, isn't it?" he said. "I've been at this search for decades—centuries—and when I find it, *if* I find it, I won't even know what to do. It could prove the ultimate jest—if we get the chance to laugh."

"Who are you?" she asked, suddenly aware that she was very wet, and cold, and Mrs. Wicklow was calling her in to lunch, and she was standing on a barren slope talking to a rock.

"Who am I?" The mischief faded; what was left of his smile grew ghostly. "That is a short question with a long answer, and we haven't the leisure now. Who do you think I am?"

Fern shrugged, striving to sound flippant. "A Watcher—a wizard—a trickster—a tramp."

"Mainly just a tramp. You can call me Ragginbone, if you need a name. They called me that a long while back, when all this—" he indicated his dilapidated garb "—was merely a disguise. Now, it's my only self. And how should I call you?"

"Fernanda," she said. "Fern will do. I thought you would know that already." There was a shade of disappointment in her tone.

"I read your mind, not your birth certificate," he retorted. "You'd better go now, Fernanda. Your lunch is waiting, and you should change into dry clothes. I'll be here tomorrow. Or the next day. Remember: find the key. You must . . . find the key . . ."

The wind snatched at her hat and as she turned to recapture it the rain seemed to swirl around her, blurring the landscape, and when she looked back up the path there was only a rock—she could see it was a rock—shaped like a seated man with his hood pulled forward over his face. She ran on down the hill toward the house.

For the time being, Fern said nothing to Will about her encounter with Ragginbone. It was not that she expected disbelief: on the contrary, Will was only too prone to believe in the improbable or even the impossible, while dismissing probabilities as too dull to merit his faith. But Fern needed a while to assimilate her own reactions and come to terms with what she had learned. In any case Will, she told herself, was still very young, obviously imprudent, easily carried away by overenthusiasm; oblivious to real danger, he would see this shadowy world into which they had strayed as merely an adventurous game. And she was sure there *was* danger, lying in wait, a little way ahead of her: she could sense it even as the hunter senses the tiger in the thicket.

Will had struck up an unlikely friendship with the vicar and over the next few days, when not rummaging in the attic, he accompanied Gus on leisurely rambles up on the moors, identifying wildlife and listening to local folklore. Fern declined to go with them, beginning a methodical search for keys, turning out drawers and emptying cupboards to no avail. "He'll have put them in a safe place," opined Mrs. Wicklow. Fern, who had done that herself on occasion, was not encouraged. She wanted another talk with Ragginbone but the hillside was bare again, leaving her oddly bereft, and it was small consolation that no snuffling disturbed her slumber. The most disquieting incident was when the black-visored motorcyclist passed her and Will on the road one evening, cutting in so close that they had to leap for the verge. But this, surely, could only be an act of mindless bravado, a young tough out to terrify and impress; it could have no connection with the mystery of Dale House.

On Friday morning, Robin telephoned. There was a lot of background noise and although Fern could hear him he didn't seem to be able to hear her very clearly. He said he was at the airport, about to emplane for New York: an urgent business trip, Alison Redmond had given him some contacts, an American historian working on witch-trials, all very exciting. He might be gone some time. "But, Daddy—!" Anyway, she wasn't to worry. He'd arranged everything. Alison would come and stay with them, take care of things, help fix up the house: she had a real flair for interior design. He knew Fern would get on with her. (Robin always knew Fern would get on with his various girlfriends.) Over the phone she heard the tuneless tinkle that precedes an announcement over the tannoy. "Must go, darling. I'm awfully late—" and then the line went dead and Fern was left clutching a silent receiver, a pale anger tightening her face. Gradually, it drained away, to be replaced by bewilderment. Accustomed as she was to her father's erratic behavior, this level of impetuosity appeared extreme. "I detect Ms. Redmond's Machiavellian hand behind the whole business," she declared over lunch, putting Will and Mrs. Wicklow in the picture. "What I don't understand, is what she's after."

"Happen she's looking for a husband," said Mrs. Wicklow sapiently. Her dourness had long been revealed as purely external and she had evidently ranged herself on the side of the young Capels.

"Well, naturally," said Fern. "That was what I assumed from the start. I've never had any problems dealing with that kind of thing."

"Cunning little lass, isn't she?" Mrs. Wicklow almost grinned.

"But," Fern persisted, "if it's Daddy she wants, why send him to America? It's almost as if—" She stopped, closing her mouth on the unspoken words. *It's almost as if she were interested in this house.* It was not cold in the kitchen but Fern felt a sudden chill.

"What's she like?" Will asked. "I haven't met her, have I?"

Fern shook her head. "She's clever," she said. "I think. I don't really know. She has a lean and hungry look, like Cassius in *Julius Caesar*. But . . . there's something there you can't catch hold of, something fluid. She can look all bright and glittering and slippery, like water, and yet you always feel there's a hardness underneath. I can't explain it very well. See for yourself."

"Is she pretty?"

"Sometimes," Fern admitted dubiously. "She can exude a kind of shimmering fascination one moment, and the next she's just a thin ugly woman with a big mouth. It's not looks: it's all in her manner."

"Those are t' ones you have to watch out for," said Mrs. Wicklow.

"You'll take care of it," said Will. "You always do."

In the afternoon Fern, annoyed with herself for not having thought of it earlier, rang the solicitors to inquire if they had the rest of Mr. Capel's keys. Her brainwave, however, failed to bring results; a man with an elderly voice suggested that she search in drawers, cupboards, and so on. "I already have," said Fern.

"He'll have put them in a safe place, then," said the solicitor comfortably.

"I've been afraid of that," said Fern.

She tried vainly to stop herself looking out of the window every few minutes; Ragginbone's continued absence might be irrelevant, but it provided an extra irritant. At tea, Will startled her by remarking: "That rock's gone again."

"Which rock?" The question was a reflex.

"The one that looks like a man. It's been gone for several days now."

"You're imagining things," said Fern. "Forget it." She was still reluctant to talk about the Watcher.

Will studied his sister with limpid detachment. "This woman who's coming here," he said, "do you suppose she could be part of it?"

"How could she?" said Fern, without pretending to misunderstand.

"I don't know," said Will, "but I can see you thinking."

Alison Redmond arrived later that day, driving a Range Rover loaded with paintings, samples of carpet and furnishing fabrics, several cardboard boxes taped shut, and three or four items of Gucci luggage. She was wearing her point-edged smile and a passing flicker of sunshine found a few strands of color in her dim hair. She greeted the Capels with a diffidence designed to undermine hostility, apologized to Mrs. Wicklow for any possible inconvenience, and demanded instantly to be taken over the house, praising its atmosphere and period discomforts. She did not say "I do so hope we're all going to be friends," nor scatter kisses in their vicinity: her gestures were airy, tenuous, almost filmy, her fingertips would flutter along an arm, her hair brush against a neighboring body, and Fern knew it was paranoia that made her fancy these feather-touches contaminated her. Alison managed to adore everything without quite crossing the line into effusion, drawing Will out on his attic researches so skillfully that his sister grew anxious, throwing her arm around him with unaccustomed affection and digging her nails into his shoulder to silence him. The only thing that checked Alison's flow, just for a moment, was the main drawing room. She hesitated on the threshold, glancing round as though something were missing, her smile blurring; and then she seemed to regain her self-command, and the charm was back in play. Afterward, pondering that temporary glitch in her manner, an explanation occurred to Fern, but she discarded it as too far-fetched. Alison had never been in that room before. She could not possibly be disconcerted because the idol had been moved.

"I'll help you bring your things in," Will offered, clearly reserving judgment.

Alison, just grateful enough and not too grateful, passed him a valise and a book of carpet patterns and began hefting the boxes herself. "Most of the pictures can stay in the car," she said. "One of our artists lives in York: I picked up a load of stuff on my way here to take back on Monday. There are just a couple of mine I'd like to have in my room; I never go anywhere without my own pictures." The sweep of her smile deprecated affectation. "Some people won't travel without a particular cushion, or a bag, or an item of jewelry. With me I'm afraid it's paintings. It's disastrous on planes: it makes my baggage so heavy."

Fern went to assist her, largely out of curiosity. The paintings in question were propped up against the bumper, shrouded in a protective cloth. Alison vanished indoors and Fern lifted the material to steal a glance at the topmost canvas. She had been expecting an abstract but this work was representational, though it struck her as strangely distorted, not for effect but because of some clumsiness on the part of the artist. It showed a horse's head peering over a stable door, a conventional enough subject, but there were bars impeding it and an odd discoloration creeping in from the borders of the image like mold. The horse's mane was unnaturally long and tangled and its forehead seemed somehow misshapen, as though its creator had made no real effort for verisimilitude, yet its eyes were intensely alive, heartbreakingly real, dark wild eyes gazing out at Fern with a mixture of pleading and defiance. Being in London most of the time Fern had had few opportunities to ride, but she loved horses and still dreamed of having the chance to learn. She found herself reaching out to touch the canvas, her hand going instinctively to the lock on the stable door; the paint felt rough and hard, like metal, like rust. "Leave it!" The voice behind her was Alison's, almost unrecognizable in its abrupt alteration.

Fern jumped. Her hand dropped; the cloth slipped back into place. "I beg your pardon," she said with exquisite politeness. "I wasn't aware the pictures were private."

For a second, she thought Alison was discomfited; then both curtness and awkwardness melted away and a thin veil of warmth slid over her face, leaving it as before. "The paintings are old," she explained, "and very fragile. If you touch the paint you could damage them. I'm keeping them for restoration work: my own personal project. As a matter of fact, I think that whole scene has been applied on top of something else. The layers have to be re-moved very carefully. As you saw, I've only just started." The area that looks like mold, Fern thought, only half satisfied. "A lot of stolen masterpieces get painted over to make them easier to hide or transport. I keep hoping I'm going to come across something special."

She carried the pictures upstairs herself. They had installed her, by common consensus, on the top floor—"Out of the way," said Will—in a room that felt chill and gloomy from long vacancy. Alison, however, professed herself delighted with the crooked ceiling, the balding velvet of cushion and curtain, the smoky mir-ror above the mantel. "I trust you won't think me obsessive," she said, "but if I might just have the key? I have this thing about pri-vacy. My own space is vital to me—I can't help it, it's just how I am. I grew up sharing with three sisters: I expect that's how it started."

"I'm sorry," said Fern blandly. "We only have the house keys. Great-Cousin Ned seems to have put all the others in a safe place."

"We've looked everywhere," Will added. "At least, Fern has."

Watching Alison, Fern was convinced there was another flicker in her expression, a momentary freezing-over. "I'd be obliged," she said, "if you didn't come into my room when I'm not here. I'm sure you understand."

Do I? thought Fern.

She and Will went back downstairs, leaving Alison to unpack.

"She's very nice," said Will, "if you like niceness. It's hard to tell how sincere she is. She seems to be working at it—but if she's keen on Dad she would, wouldn't she?"

"The niceness is all on the surface," declared Fern. "All sparkle, no substance. It's called charm."

"Like tinsel," said Will, "on a shoddy Christmas tree. I don't think I trust her. I haven't quite made up my mind."

"I have," said his sister. "You don't."

In the hall, Mrs. Wicklow was putting on her coat. "I'll be off now," she said. "There's a pie in t' oven. I daresay Madam won't eat it, she's too skinny to eat pie: probably lives off brown rice and that muesli. Still, I know you two appreciate my cooking."

"We do," Will concurred warmly.

"Queer thing about her," she added, glancing up in the direction of Alison's room. "Odd fancies you do get sometimes."

"What fancy?" asked Fern.

"Miss Redmond comes from London: that's what you said?"

Fern nodded. "She works in an art gallery in the West End."

"There was a young woman over from Guisborough, three . . . four months before t' Captain died. Happen I mentioned it. Something to do with antiques. I didn't get a good look at her, of course, and she didn't have all that hair—I think she had a kind of bob, just about shoulder-length—but I could swear it was t' same woman. Heard her, I did, chattering away to t' Captain, sweet as sugar. She didn't notice me, mind: she's t' sort who sees them as interest her and doesn't bother to look at t' rest of us. I'd have bet five pounds it was your Miss Redmond." She gave a brisk shake, as if throwing off a cobweb. "Must be my fancy. Still, you take care. Third house from end of t' village if you need me."

"Thanks," said Fern, smiling, making light of the matter. But the smile vanished with Mrs. Wicklow and she went to check on the pie with a somber face.

Dinner was a polite meal. Alison kept the conversation going by discussing her ideas for the house. "I think we could do something really exciting with that barn," she said, having duly admired the *Seawitch* and her current residence. "Your father's very keen to have my advice. He'll be calling from the States in a day or two: I'm going to ask him if I can make a start. I have a friend in the building trade who specializes in these sort of commissions. I thought I'd get him up here to give us an estimate. Of course, we must take care of that wonderful boat. It should be all right outside for the time being, if we cover it in tarpaulins. After all, it *is* supposed to be summer, even if it hasn't reached Yorkshire yet."

"We like the Yorkshire summer," Will said. "It's bracing."

Fern sucked in her cheeks to suppress a smile. Will had never been noted for appreciating a bracing climate. "We only need to tidy the place up before putting it on the market," she pointed out. "Daddy doesn't want to spend any money on it."

"It would be a good investment," Alison insisted. "Convert the barn and you can sell two properties instead of one. I'll discuss it with Robin when he calls."

The inference was unmistakable: Fern was a child, it was none of her business, financial matters were beyond the zone of her responsibility. The hairs bristled on her nape; her small face set in lines that might have been etched in steel. But for the moment there was little she could do: final authority rested officially with her father, and while he was in America it would be difficult for her to counteract Alison's influence. She had a suspicion the telephone would not lend itself to an assertion of filial control. She was conscious of a frustration that bordered on panic, but she fought it down.

"Delicious pie," Alison said, pushing the pastry to the side of her plate.

They went to bed early. Inevitably, Fern lay sleepless for an hour or more before drifting into an uneasy doze. Suppressed anxieties surfaced as garbled dreams: she was at a private view in New York trying to reach her father who was on the far side of the room, but a huge crowd of people impeded her, and her father saw her, and waved and smiled as if there was nothing wrong at all. He was talking to a woman who had to be Alison Redmond, but when she turned round it was a stranger, and Alison was right next to Fern, wearing a dress that rippled like water, and her hair rippled as she moved, so you could not tell where the hair ended and the dress began. "Come," she said, laying a long-fingered hand on Fern's shoulder, and there was Javier Holt, standing beside the etching of the *Lost City*, and the door was open, and the streets unraveled below her, and the drums were beating in the temple, and she knew she must not cross the threshold, but she couldn't remember why. She awoke from a jumble of color and incident more vivid than life, but recollection faded even as she tried to hold on to it, and there was only her heart's pounding and a disproportionate sense of loss. The night-noises that were growing familiar came to her ears: the endless sough of the wind; sudden and startling, the screech of a bird. She was floating back toward sleep when the snuffling began.

Despite the fear that seemed to invade the very air around her she felt a flicker of indignation. She cultivated it, gritting her teeth, smothering cowardice, not forgetting but rejecting Ragginbone's advice. This was her place, her home, if only temporarily, and no intruder, canine or feline, mongrel or monster, had the right to terrorize her here. She had not formed any specific plan for driving it off but she was determined at least to see it, to face it down, to prove to herself once and for all that it was merely a stray dog, half savage maybe but solid, flesh and blood and smell, and no bodiless hunter from a dimension of shadows. She sat up, picking up the flashlight which she now kept beside her bed. She thought she had closed the window but it had to be open: the snuffling sounded so loud and near. And then she froze. The noise wasn't coming from under her window. It was outside her door.

She sat absolutely still, all resolution forgotten. It can't come in, Ragginbone had said, but it *was* in. In the house, in the passage; she could hear it scraping at the floorboards, rucking the worn drugget. Her thought stopped, her limbs seemed to petrify, but she could not control the violence of her pulse: it must be audible even through the barrier of the walls. The door was not locked: something which had no hand to grasp rattled at the knob. For a few seconds, Fern ceased to breathe.

It moved on. She heard the gentle pad-pad of stealthy paws, receding down the corridor, the guttural hiss of hoarse panting. When the sounds had died away she sat for what seemed like hours, waiting and listening. The thudding of her pulse did not abate. Gradually, the tension in the air around her appeared to diminish: the house settled into a nervous quietude. Fern got out of bed so cautiously the duvet barely rustled, feeling her way to the door without switching on the flashlight. It took an effort of courage that made her sweat to turn the handle and peer into the passageway. Her vision was well-adjusted to the darkness and for an instant she thought she saw something, not a black animal shape with glowing orbs but something much smaller, furtive, skulking in a corner by the end window, shrinking into invisibility even as she caught its eye. Her heart leaped into her mouth—but whatever it was, it had gone. The corridor was empty. She could sense its emptiness. She groped her way along the wall to Will's room and entered without knocking.

"*Who is it?*" He was awake.

"Me. Shush." She closed the door carefully, switched on the flashlight. "I don't want to make too much light. Move your legs: I'll sit on the bed."

"Did you hear it?"

"Yes."

"It was *inside*. How could it be inside? Did we leave a door open?"

"It doesn't matter," Fern said. They were talking in whispers and the flashlight was on the table; little light reached their faces. She found she was holding his hand for mutual reassurance, something he would never have allowed if he could see it. "It can't come in unless invited. That's the ancient law."

"What law? How do you know?"

"Never mind. I just do."

"Laws can be broken." Will sounded skeptical.

"Maybe." Ragginbone, after all, had not been sure. "Maybe not." She glanced upward toward Alison's room; Will saw the whites of her eyes gleam, followed her gaze.

"You think *she*—?"

"It's too much of a coincidence. The day she arrives, *it* comes inside. She invited it in. She must have done."

"What are we going to do?"

"There's more," she persisted, adhering to her train of thought. "There was something in the corridor when I came out of my room—something else, I mean. It was quite small and it vanished very quickly but there was definitely something there."

"It's too much," Will said. "Alison Redmond and the Sniffer and the *Seawitch* and the chest and the rock that isn't there and the missing treasure . . . and now this. Whatever it was. It's too much. I can't cope. Do you think . . . do you think we should try to tell Dad?" She knew from the note in his voice even more than his words that he was struggling not to betray the level of his terror. Despite her own fears, she was comforted to feel herself the stronger. If she could only be strong enough.

"Pointless," she said. "For one thing, there's a limit to what you can say over the phone. For another, what *would* we tell him? That we heard some unknown creature sniffing inside the house and we can't find the keys to the treasure chest and we think his girlfriend could be a witch? He'd probably assume we were both on drugs—or raving. And even if he *did* come home, there's nothing he can do. Alison's a lot smarter than he is. We'll have to handle it ourselves."

Will's soft gasp might have been sudden laughter. "You've dealt with all Daddy's girlfriends to date," he said.

"This might be a bit more difficult," Fern admitted.

There was a short pause. She reached for the flashlight but did not move from the bed. "I think you ought to stay here for the rest of tonight," Will said with an air of selfless chivalry which deceived neither of them. "We'll be safer together."

"Okay," she said. "Move over."

The bed was large but they curled up, back to back, each warmed by the other's nearness, falling swiftly and unexpectedly into sleep.

· III ·

Fern got up early the following morning and returned to her own room. Instinct warned her that it would be preferable if Alison did not suspect they were on their guard. However, although it was barely seven she was no longer sleepy, and she dressed and went out into the garden, her footsteps leading her inevitably toward the back gate and the path up the hill. The sun had not yet risen far above the eastern horizon and the shadow of the house lay long and black across the grass, but the slope beyond glittered with dew. There was no sign of the Watcher; he seemed to have been gone so long she had almost ceased to believe in their meeting. As she climbed higher emptiness stretched in every direction. A few sheep grazed across the valley; cloud-shadows mottled the upland moors; a lone bird soared, its whistling call like the music of some unearthly piper, summoning errant spirits back to their hollow hills before the gates closed on the mortal day. The Day—the Day to Man! thought Fern, remembering her Kipling. The wind that touched her cheek felt totally clean and free, a wind that knew neither bonds nor boundaries, which might have blown straight from some virgin height, over grass and gorse, rock and river, to be breathed only by her. The skyline above was unbroken, except where she saw the twin tufts of a wild plant poking upward like the cocked ears of a couched animal. Below, the valley opened out, a river-delved cleft in the rolling plateau, still cupping the last shades of retreating darkness, winding down toward the coast and the distant blue glimmer of the sea.

She was nearly at the brow of the hill when the animal rose up in front of her. One moment there was only turf and that tell-tale glimpse of ear-tufts, and then the grass shivered into fur and the creature was on its feet, pink tongue lolling between ragged teeth, amber eyes fixed unblinking on her face. It was a dog: it must be a dog. It had a pointed vulpine muzzle with a ruff around its neck not quite long enough for a mane and a lean body built for running. Its coat was matted and dew-draggled, white-streaked, gray-flecked, shaded with brown, stippled with black. It might have been part sheepdog, part Alsatian, part vixen, part wolf. But Fern reminded herself that there had been no wolves in Britain since the Middle Ages. She knew immediately that it was female, though she could not have said how. Its unwavering stare was filled with latent meaning.

Hesitantly, half afraid for herself, half nervous of inducing fear, Fern held out her hand. The animal sniffed, then licked. The wicked incisors were less than an inch from her fingers, yet she felt curiously at ease. "Did *he* send you here?" she asked softly. "Do you come from Ragginbone? Are you a Watcher too?" And then, as an afterthought: "Are you on guard?"

The yellow eyes returned her questioning gaze with a steady intensity.

"It was inside the house last night," Fern went on, progressing from the preliminary introduction to a tentative pat, then to stroking the thick ruff. The fur was damped into rats' tails as if the dog—she was definitely a dog—had been outside a long time. "I don't know what kind of creature it is: it moves like a hound, only it's too big for any species of hound I know. Ragginbone recognized it. He said it couldn't come in without being invited, but it did, and I think . . . I think Alison must have let it in. She arrived yesterday, and that's the first time it's been inside the house."

The dog accepted Fern's caresses with a quiver of uncertainty, a dignified restraint. Fern received the impression—she could not say how—that she was, not alarmed, but slightly unnerved, an aloof outcast unaccustomed to such demonstrations. This is ridiculous, Fern told herself. First I talk to a rock, now it's a dog. "I don't suppose you really understand," she said aloud. "There's probably a natural explanation for everything that's happened. My imagination's running away with me. Only why now? That's what's so confusing. I'm too old for fairy tales and anyhow, when I was a child I never let my fantasy take over. After my mother died, when I saw my father cry and I knew she was really gone, I was afraid all the time. I used to lie in bed at night seeing a demon in every shadow. I told myself over and over: there's nothing there. There are no demons, no dragons, no witches, no elves, no Santa Claus. There are no vampires in Transylvania, no kingdoms in wardrobes, no lands behind the sun. A shadow is only a shadow. I made myself grow up, and put away childish things. I thought the adult world was a prosaic sort of place where everything was clear-cut, everything was tangible; but it isn't. It isn't. I don't know who I am any more. I'm not sure about anyone. Who are *you*? Are you a dog? Are you a wolf?" The yellow stare held her; a rough tongue rasped her palm.

"Cancel that question," said Fern. "There are no wolves in England now. I have to go. Take care." A strange thing to say to a dog, but then, Fern reflected uncomfortably, the entire one-sided conversation was strange. She hurried down the path almost as if she were running away.

At the gate, she glanced round to find the dog at her heels. "You can't come in," she said, wondering why the words disturbed her, tapping at something in the back of her mind. Her companion, undeterred, slipped through the gate behind her before she could close it. Reaching the back door, Fern turned with more determination. "I'm sorry," she began, but the dog stood a little way off, making no attempt to cross the threshold. Fern noted that she did not bark, or wag her tail, or do any of the things that dogs normally do. She simply stood there, waiting. "Would you like some water?" Fern said, relenting. And: "Come on then." The animal slid past her in a movement too swift to follow, lying down beside the kitchen stove with her chin on her paws. And in the same instant something clicked in Fern's head and she knew what she had done. For good or evil, she had invited the outcast in.

Later, when Fern had had her morning bath, she found the kitchen unoccupied and the back door ajar. The latch was old-fashioned, the kind that an intelligent animal might be able to lift with its nose. On the outside, however, there was an iron ring which required the grip of a hand. Fern, in a deviation from her usual policy, resolved to see that the door was left slightly open at all times.

It was a difficult day. Fern did not feel she could continue her search for the key with Alison in the vicinity, so she and Will escaped to the vicarage, where Maggie Dinsdale made them sandwiches and Gus drove them up onto the moors for a picnic. Back at Dale House, they found Alison in the barn with a measuring tape. She and Gus shook hands and exchanged pleasantries, thus disappointing Will, who confided in an aside to his sister that if she *had* been a witch she would surely not have been so friendly with a vicar. "Don't be idiotic," Fern responded. "Next you'll expect her to wear a pointed hat."

Supper was happily brief: Alison retired straight afterward claiming she wanted to work on her picture. Will, going up to her room later with the excuse of an offer of coffee, reported that she had brought her own television. "That settles it," he concluded. "I don't like her. Why can't she share it with us? That isn't just self-ishness, it's . . . it's *sadism*. We *must* have a TV. Speak to Daddy about it."

"Mm."

"Do you know, when I opened the door she switched it off, as if she couldn't bear me to see it even for a couple of minutes? I think she's got a video too. I wish we had a video."

"Maybe she was watching something she considered unsuit-able for little boys," Fern suggested unkindly.

They fell back on mah-jongg and a plate of Mrs. Wicklow's biscuits, becoming so engrossed that it was almost midnight when Fern glanced at the clock. "Are you going to sleep in my room again?" Will asked, not looking at his sister, his voice care-fully devoid of any wistfulness.

"I don't *think* it's necessary," Fern said. "Put something against your door, though—something heavy. You can bang on the wall if you really need me. I feel it's important to . . . well, act nonchalant. As if we haven't noticed anything out of the ordinary. Then either she'll think we're unobservant, which means she'll be underestimating us, or she'll be as baffled as we are. She's behav-ing as if there's nothing going on; so can we."

"Do you suppose Mrs. Wicklow was right," Will said abruptly, "when she said she'd seen Alison before?"

"Yes," said Fern. "Yes, I do."

"Can you put a short wig over long hair?"

"I think so. Actresses do it sometimes. I'm sure they do."

"This ought to be very exciting," Will remarked. "I just wish I wasn't scared. Are you scared?"

"Shitless," said Fern coolly, going over to the back door. The vulgarism was unusual for her and Will grinned.

"What are you doing?"

"Leaving the door open."

"*What?* If that creature comes—"

"Our prowling visitor," she pointed out, "can already get in: we know that. I want to be sure—" She hesitated, changed her tack. "I'm like Mrs. Wicklow. I want to let in the air."

"Bullshit."

"And don't use that kind of language."

"But you said—"

"I'm sixteen," said Fern haughtily. "I'm allowed."

They went upstairs still squabbling, falling silent, by mutual consent, at the foot of the second flight. Fern mounted a few steps, but there was no sound from Alison's room. The low wattage lighting favored by Great-Cousin Ned did not reach far, and the upper landing was swathed in shadow. She could see Alison's door but it was firmly closed and she hoped the sense of oppression which seemed to emanate from it was the result of pure fancy and overstrained nerves. She stole quietly back to her brother and the two of them went to their respective beds.

For all his apprehension, Will fell asleep quickly; but Fern sat up, reading by flashlight so no betraying gleam could be seen under the door, her senses on alert, half fearful, half in a sort of desperate expectancy. More than an hour passed while she tried in vain to concentrate on the story, unable to restrain herself from regular glances at her traveling clock: the luminous hands seemed to snail around the dial, spinning out the minutes, dragging her down into slumber. A brief shower battered on the window, until a rush of wind swept it away. When the snuffling finally started, she had almost given up. Her body jerked upright on a reflex, snatching her cheek from the pillow; her breath was caught in her throat; her eyes dilated, though there was nothing to be seen. She switched off the flashlight and retrieved the book, which was slipping floorward. In the corridor outside she heard the sniffing moving closer, hesitating at Will's door, progressing on to hers. There was the familiar ragged panting, the not-quite-noiseless

footfalls, the sudden scrabble of claws on wood. And then silence. A new silence, invading the passageway, tangible as a presence. The snuffling and the clawing had ceased, the panting
changed into a low snarl, a soft, dark noise on the edge of hearing,
rising slowly to a growl, a sound neither feline nor canine but
somewhere in between. Fern thought she had never in her life
heard anything so totally evil. Then came a sudden rush, the skid-
ding of paws on bare board, the swish of bunching drugget, a
clamor of snapping, worrying, grumbling, an ugly yowl. Heavy
bodies seemed to be struggling and writhing; a crash told of an
overturned table, a shattered vase. Yet throughout Fern was convinced it was the intruder who made most of the noise: the chal-
lenger was mute, with no voice to cry defiance or pain. She heard
a scurrying as of something bent on escape: one set of paws fled
toward the stairs, chasing or being chased, and then quiet super-
vened. Out in the garden there was a howl of baffled rage, maybe
of fear; but it died away, and only the wind returned, droning
among the chimneys, and under the eaves. Fern had grown used
to the wind; they had become friends. She lay down, smiling
faintly, heedless of the damage she envisaged outside her door. A
name came into her mind, clear and certain as a call: *Lougarry.*

   She fell asleep.

At breakfast, Alison was irritable. "Nightmares," she said. "I
thought I could hear voices crying, shrieks, moans. I expect it was
the wind." Will looked innocent, Fern bland. She had risen early
to dispose of the broken vase; it was one Robin had said might be
valuable; but then, his daughter reflected, he always said that. A
rapid confabulation had revealed that Will, too, had witnessed
the fight in the night.

   "I slept well," Fern asseverated sweetly.

   Will merely smiled, and attacked his Frosties.

A little to their surprise, Alison chose to go for a walk later, declining company even before they had had an opportunity not to offer it. Afterward the back door, unlatched, swung open; the dog was waiting outside. "Come in," Fern said. "You don't have to wait for permission. You're always welcome." She came in, hobbling on three legs: there was blood on the fourth, dried into brownish crystals, and more blood clogging the thick fur of her ruff. She lay down at Fern's feet and fixed her with that steady unhuman gaze.

"That's a wolf," said Will. "I know it is. Where did you find it?"

"She found me. Get some antiseptic; I've seen a bottle of Dettol somewhere. She's hurt."

"It was her," Will said, "last night—wasn't it?"

"Fetch the Dettol."

The animal was docile while Fern cleaned her wounds and applied cream from a tube of Savlon, crusted from long disuse, which was all they could find. The tears in her shoulder were deep and ugly but her expression appeared indifferent, beyond suffering. "Lougarry," Fern murmured. The tired muzzle lifted; the ears pricked.

"*Thank* you," said Will.

Robin phoned that evening: Alison spoke to him at length and hovered when Fern took over, making confidences impossible. "Of course we're selling," he reiterated a little too forcefully. "Leave it to Alison. Bright girl. Knows what she's doing. Gave me the name of a useful chap over here—professor of witchcraft—they have professorships for everything in America. What's that, darling? Can't hear you."

The line shouldn't be this bad, thought Fern, giving up. We live in an age of satellite technology. Supposing it isn't the phone . . .

Alison left on Monday, promising to return by the end of the week. "She may be involved in this business," Will said, "but I don't believe she's the real enemy. She's not . . . she's not *frightening* enough."

"What do you want?" asked Fern. "The Devil in person? Yesterday you complained you were scared; today you're complaining you're not scared enough. That isn't logical."

"I'm still scared," Will explained, "but not of Alison. She's all slippery charm: you think you've caught her out—you think you can pin her down—but her personality just slithers away from you as if it were greased. Mrs. Wicklow says she saw her before, but she isn't absolutely sure. She must have come here after something, but she hasn't tried to search the house. We think she's controlling that creature that sniffs in the night, but we don't *know*. We can't prove anything."

"I thought you believed in the impossible," said Fern. "Now you want proof." She was anointing Lougarry's injuries as she spoke: once Alison had gone, the dog had come into the kitchen and lain down in the place beside the stove which she had taken for her own.

"Not exactly. I want to know what we're up against." Will cupped his chin in his hand, gazing dreamily into the middle distance. "What's really going on? Sometimes I feel we're tangled in a dark web of supernatural forces, but if you try to snatch at a single strand it frays into a shadow and then there's nothing there. What the hell are we all looking for, anyway?"

"Actually," Fern began, finally resolved to tell him about the key—but Mrs. Wicklow came in, cutting her short, and the impulse to confide passed.

Inevitably, the housekeeper objected to Lougarry. "Great-Cousin Ned had a dog," Fern reminded her. "You told us so."

"That's not a dog," said Mrs. Wicklow. "Looks more like a wolf. It's probably savage, anyway. If it's been killing sheep there'll be real trouble, police and that. I'd better go call someone to fetch it away."

"*Have* any sheep been killed?" Fern challenged, unobtrusively crossing her fingers. She had a feeling that taking mutton on the hoof would be well within Lougarry's scope.

Mrs. Wicklow conceded grudgingly that they hadn't. "Been fighting, though, by the look of it," she said. "Those cuts look nasty. You want to take it to t' vet: he'll see to it. I daresay t' rever-end would give you a lift."

Lougarry's lip lifted in a soundless snarl.

"I don't think she'd like that," Fern said.

"What'll you do about feeding it? Haven't thought about that, have you? You can't just give it Madam Slimline's leftovers."

A picture of rabbits came into Fern's head—rabbits scattering in a panic, scuts flashing white. "We'll fix up something," she said evasively. "Anyhow, she doesn't belong to us. She comes round sometimes: that's all."

"Scrounging," said Mrs. Wicklow, hunching a disapproving shoulder.

A knock on the back door heralded the arrival of Gus Dins-dale, further complicating the argument. "If she's a stray," he said, "you ought to hand her over to the authorities."

"She's *not* a stray," Fern snapped, feeling beleaguered. "She belongs to this old man: I don't know his name but I've seen him round here quite a lot. I think he's a kind of tramp." Will glanced quickly at her, his eyebrows flicking into a frown.

"I know the one you mean," Gus said unexpectedly. "Interest-ing type. Seems to be out in all weathers and there are more lines on his face than a street map, but I've seen him striding over the moor at a pace that puts most hikers to shame. We've exchanged a few words now and then; he's intelligent and cultured, certainly not a drunk. I would guess he's one of those who choose a life on the road—they feel hemmed in by the walls of civilization, trapped in the kind of surroundings we would call home. A free spirit. I never realized he had a dog. I must say, this creature appears to be an appropriate companion. She looks more than half wild. A free spirit herself, no doubt."

"It's wild all right," said Mrs. Wicklow, still refusing to allow the visitor the dignity of gender. "If Fern touches t' cuts it'll bite her for sure."

("Who's the old man?" Will inquired, for his sister's private ear; but she shook her head.)

"The dog seems to trust her," Gus was saying, evidently won over by his own image of the free-spirited wanderer and his maverick pet. "Animals can very often sense when they've found a friend. After all, you've heard the story of Androcles and the lion, haven't you?"

"No, I haven't," Mrs. Wicklow retorted, scoring points where she could.

But Gus had turned back to Fern. "Does she have a name?" he asked.

"Lougarry," said Fern. She didn't say how she knew.

"Odd," the vicar mused. "I wonder . . . it sounds almost as if it might come from the French. Lougarry . . . *loup garou.*"

"*Loup garou,*" Will repeated, struggling with his accent. "What does that mean?"

"Werewolf," said Gus.

It was after lunch and Lougarry had departed on affairs of her own before the Capels were left to themselves. "It's time we had a serious discussion," said Will. "There are too many things you're not telling me. The old man, for instance. And Lougarry. Do you think she really *is* a werewolf?"

"Maybe," said Fern. "She's on our side: that's all that matters. We're rather short of allies."

"And the old man?"

"He watches. I told you. He has a tendency to look like a rock. I thought I might have imagined him, but Gus has seen him too, so he must be real. Perhaps it was the rock I imagined."

"Gus is a vicar," Will remarked captiously. "He's supposed to see things. Angels, you know, and visitations."

"Don't be ridiculous," said Fern. "He's C of E."

There was a pause; then she got to her feet. "Come on," she said. "We'd better get on with it."

"Get on with what?" asked Will, but he knew.

They went upstairs to Alison's room. The landing was gray and dim, surrounded by closed doors; no sunlight penetrated the narrow window in the north wall. Will took hold of the handle and tried to turn it, but it would not move. It seemed to be not so much jammed as fixed, petrified into stasis: it didn't even rattle. He pulled his hand away, complaining of pins and needles. "It can't be locked," said Fern. "There's no key." She seized the knob herself, but her grip squeaked on brass; Will kicked and shoved at panels that did not stir. When she drew back she could see the pins and needles, angry pinpoints of red flickering and fading on her palm. "This won't do," she said. "This is *our house*. We have a right to enter any room we please. She can ask us to stay out if she likes, but she can't force us. I don't know what she's done, but we're going to get in."

"The window?" Will suggested.

From a neighboring room they leaned out to check, but Alison's window also appeared shut. "We might be able to open it," Will said, "if she hasn't done anything fancy to it like she has to the door." He didn't mention the word *magic* but they both knew the omission was not born of modern skepticism. "This window's on a latch; hers probably is too. You could lift it from the outside with something thin enough to slip through the crack. I've seen it done on TV with a credit card."

"I don't have a credit card," said Fern. "We'll try a knife. But first, we're going to need a ladder."

Knowing Mrs. Wicklow's antipathy to Alison, Fern did not hesitate to enlist her aid. The housekeeper had reservations, not about the propriety of their actions, but about the risks of illicit entry via a window more than twenty feet off the ground. Ladders, she claimed, were notoriously chancy, especially under inexpert control. However, suspicion of the alien finally persuaded her. "I don't know what she's done to t' door," she said. "Fair made my hand sting. It must be some kind of electricity."

Introduced to a small-time builder in the village, Fern and Will were able to borrow a ladder long enough for their needs on the following Wednesday afternoon. As instigator of the plan Will climbed up first, armed with the slimmest of the kitchen knives; his sister waited at the bottom, holding the ladder to steady it. Rather to her surprise, the methods of television drama did not let them down.

"Done it," Will called out, and she saw him disappearing over the windowsill. She wriggled the two prongs deeper into the flower-bed and ascended a little nervously after him.

The room was transformed. The balding velvet of cushion and curtain now appeared thick and soft, the dingy carpet glowed with the tracery of long-lost designs. Shelves formerly empty were stacked with books and cassettes, a portable music center, a pair of candles in iron holders, a pot-plant which resembled a cactus, its spines glistening, its single flower gaping like a small red mouth with the tongue-shaped stamen lurking inside. Fern glanced at the books: they seemed mainly concerned with art and antiquities, though there were a couple in a language, and a script, which she could not understand. Several new pictures adorned the walls, one of which looked vaguely familiar: it took her a few moments to recognize the etching she had once seen at the gallery. The imprisoned horse was not on show but in the far corner stood an easel shrouded in a piece of stained cloth. There was a different cover on the bed, all emerald and peacock-blue, embroidered with twining feathers and iridescent eyes: it was very beautiful but somehow it repelled her. She could imagine it stitched in pain by women with blistered fingers and vision weakened from peering at their labor. She caught its reflection in the spotless mirror, turned away; and then her gaze was drawn back to the glass. The image showed her a bedroom within a bedroom, the alien invasion of Alison's possessions, the books, the paintings, the plant. But the sumptuous curtains were threadbare as before, the carpet dim with age, murky with ingrained dirt. "Will . . ." Fern whispered, suddenly pale, struggling with the evidence of her senses.

But her brother was concentrating on the television. He had wheeled the unit away from its place against the wall and was toying with the remote control, obtaining nothing but crackle and snow. He had not noticed the mirror, and Fern found that she shrank from drawing his attention to it, more than half afraid he would not see what she saw. She forced herself to look elsewhere, her glance alighting on a box at the bedside, a rectangle of some dark wood, its somber hue veined as if with faint gold, the lid inlaid with ominous characters in red enamel. When she touched it a scent came to her, as if carried on a nonexistent breeze in a room with barely a draft: the smell of a northern forest, of sap rising, leaves opening, roots drinking, as if the wood still lived, dreaming of the days when it was a tree among trees. She felt round the rim of the lid, encountered the metal clasp which closed it, and bit back the beginnings of a scream. The stab of pain was like a burn, though her hand was unmarked. "What is it?" Will inquired, distracted from the television screen.

"I'm not sure," said Fern. "It felt like the door handle, only worse. I need gloves."

The gloves were in a drawer under the bedside table. Fern noted with disapproval that they were made from the skin of a reptile, snake or lizard; the mottled patterns appeared to alter in a changing light, as if, like the wood, some elusive memory of life lingered in the dead scales, shifting colors like a chameleon. She pulled on the right-hand one: it had looked overlarge but the fingers seemed to shrink onto hers, skin melding with skin, until it no longer resembled a glove and she knew a sudden terror that it would never come off. Her arm would terminate for all time in a claw. "Can you open it now?" Will demanded. She pressed the clasp without ill effect; the lid lifted of its own accord. Inside, the box was divided into sections. There were tiny jars and bottles with labels too minute to decipher; a squat book, leatherbound and handwritten, its pages sere with age; strangest of all, an unmarked video cassette, the tape invisible in its opaque casing. "Let's try it," said Will, his expression bright with a mixture of curiosity and daring; but he could not pick it up. Fern took it in her gloved hand and inserted it in the machine, then they sat on the peacock bed-cover to watch. Will pressed PLAY. There was a click, and the screen disappeared. The square outline of the TV set framed a hole, bottomless as the Pit, a window into nothing. A solitary star, infinitely remote, no bigger than a grain of dust, winked and died in its depths. "They do it with computers," Will said. He did not sound convinced.

The image came rushing up toward them from the point where the star had died, spinning to a halt, shuddering into coherence. This was no two-dimensional film but a spyhole on reality, a street with exhaust fumes and erratic sunshine, an old man getting into an old car. He tugged a bunch of keys out of his pocket, glanced at it in irritation, and put it back, subsequently producing a much smaller bunch which evidently included the key to the ignition. It came to Fern that this must be Great-Cousin Ned, and on that first keyring was the one key they sought. But the image was gone; another crowded on its heels, and another, a quickfire succession of instant and incident, frag-

ments of history tumbling over each other, hurtling back further
and further into the past. A market stall with a tray of trinkets
where sifting fingers brushed over an object she could not see; a
coved cellar piled with cases on which the dust lay undisturbed; a
uniformed figure picking up something from a blood-smeared
floor; two men staring into a flame, their faces lit from below, one
chubby and eager, the other very young but already shrewd, his
forelock limp with sweat, premature lines in his thin cheek. For a
second, his eyes lifted, and they were brown and golden and
green as a sunlit wood. Then the chimera was lost, overwhelmed
in a chaos of other faces: a gypsy, a woman with languorous eyes,
a man with a bitter mouth. A waveless sea trailed at the stern of a
seedy fishing boat, the sails hanging immobile in the torpid air.
The setting sun spilled from beneath the cloud-shelf and flashed
like fire across the ocean, igniting a path of gold where a dark silhouette rose to a fatal rendezvous. And then the water closed over
all, and far below a skull blossomed, growing slowly into flesh and
form, but before Fern could see any clear features white hands
covered it, and it was gone. At the last there came another boat, a
struggling vessel with bent mast and splitting timbers, riding on a
storm beyond imagining. The tempest shook the television set as
if it were made of card; a gust of wind tore round the room,
wrenching at the curtains, snapping the window wide. Lightning
crackled in the gap where the screen used to be. Fern and Will
felt themselves lifted up, they and the house and the hillside
without, as if the dimension in which they dwelled had turned
into a giant elevator, and the only fixed universe was inside the
television. They clung to the bedposts like children on a Ferris
wheel, soaring through the tumult of sky and sea, until they could
see the many-colored flares pulsing like a phantom coronet above
the roof of the clouds, and hear the thunder-drums rolling down
below. And then a hole was ripped in the canopy and a chasm
opened amidst the waves, and there was the ship plunging into it,

and the helmsman was swept away, and Fern knew the glimmer at his throat was the missing key, and she saw the pale arms of the mermaid dragging him to his death. A swift darkness spread across the vision, blotting out even the storm, and a voice boomed out of it as cold and empty as the deeps of space. "It is forbidden to go further back," it said. "The city has been banished from Time and Forever, history and memory. No man shall look on Atlantis again." There was a snick like the closing of a door, and the screen was back in place. The room around them was stationary; house and hillside did not stir. Fern was trembling so violently she did not trust herself to speak.

"My G-God," stammered Will. "My *God*." And: "What *was* that? What did it all mean?"

"It means we're in trouble," Fern said briefly, when she was sure she could keep the quiver out of her voice. She pressed the eject button and replaced the video in the box.

Will was recovering his nerve, too quickly for her taste. "It felt like a rollercoaster ride through the Big Bang," he declared. "I've never been so terrified—never. Wow. Bloody wow. What do we do now?"

"Leave," said Fern.

Will lowered himself over the windowsill, feeling for the topmost rung with an unsteady foot. "Careful," said his sister. She thought she might have been able to open the door with the glove on, but she could not be certain of resealing it afterward, and she did not want Alison to realize anyone had been in the room. Will disappeared from view and she took a last look round, flinching automatically from the mirror, hesitating when her eye fell on the easel. She went over to it and twitched the cloth aside. The area that resembled mold seemed to have grown, closing in about the horse's head: there was a note of panic in its midnight gaze. Fern caressed the surface of the painting with her gloved hand; its mottling altered immediately, coagulating into dark blotches which broadened into rippling bands, the colors flickering and changing like shadows in a jungle. Her fingertips skimmed the stable door, feeling for the lock that was not real; something jolted at her touch, and she began to tremble again, but with another kind of fear, a fear of her unknown self, of the glove that grew on her hand, of the thin current of power that trickled through the very core of her being. She retreated sharply and the cloth slid down over the picture: she would not lift it again. Will's voice came to her from outside: "Fern! Fern!" She pulled at the glove— she thought it was stuck but it slipped off easily. Putting it back in the drawer, she straightened the peacock coverlet and made her exit through the window, pausing to fiddle it shut before she descended the ladder.

"Do you think she'll guess we've been there?" asked Will. He had obviously forgotten his lighthearted dismissal of Alison earlier that week.

"I hope not," said Fern.

They were both relieved when Lougarry returned after supper, stretching out at their feet with the relaxed air of an animal settling down for the night. A huge yawn showed the pointed canines, dagger-sharp and yellow as ivory, but Fern was oblivious, sitting on the floor to treat her healing wounds and for the first time venturing to rub her cheek against the dense softness of the ruff. "Stay with us," she whispered. "Stay tonight. Make me as brave as a wolf. I need courage right now." She didn't register her own admission of Lougarry's true identity. She was thinking: this is what it means to grow up, this is how it feels—to be on your own, to have no one to depend on, no one between you and the dark. Belatedly she began to appreciate how much she had always relied on her father, not perhaps on his strength but on the strength of his position, on the certainties that accompany fatherhood and maturity. She might have run the household but he had empowered her, supported her, obeyed her, kept her safe. And now, America was a long way away. She did not even have a phone number. Mrs. Wicklow and the Dinsdales were good friends, but they could not deal with Alison. She needed a rock to cling to. But the rock had turned into Ragginbone and told her: *Find the key,* and now he had disappeared on some errand of his own. Everything seemed to depend on her, yet she did not know what to do or how to do it. She was quite alone.

"Not quite," said Will, squatting down beside her. She must have spoken her thought aloud. "We are three."

Lougarry turned, and licked her cheek.

Gradually, night enfolded the house, an unchancy night filled with a fretful wind that muttered round the walls, and inside the shifting of ill-fitting doors, the creaking of untrodden boards. Glancing through a window Fern saw the moon ringed in a yellow nimbus, trailing a lacework of cloud. Once again, she heard the motorbike, roaring to and fro on the deserted road. It occurred to her that bikers usually hunt in packs, but this one was always solitary, a pariah maybe, a Black Knight of the highways, armored in leather, anonymous in his helmet. She had never seen him stop the machine, dismount, lift the visor. She had never heard his name. "That dratted bike," Mrs. Wicklow had said once; but she did not seem to know who he was. As if in response to her thought the engine cut suddenly, very nearby. Lougarry rose to her feet, her hackles stirring, showing her teeth in something that was not a yawn. She slipped out of the back door like a swift shadow, returning minutes later even as they heard the bike departing. She had neither barked nor growled—Lougarry was invariably silent—but the danger, if danger it was, had gone. There can't be any *more* people ranged against us, Fern thought, verging on irritation. The biker might be a nuisance but not a threat, inquisitive maybe, but surely not malevolent. She closed but did not lock the door and made cocoa for herself and Will, although it was the wrong time of year, because the drink was hot and sweet and comforting.

"What was Atlantis?" Will asked, warming his hands on the mug though they could hardly be cold.

"I don't really know," Fern said. "No one knows. It's one of those legends that's so old nobody remembers where it came from. I think it was an island, or a city, or both, and it sank beneath the sea. I believe there are archaeologists who connect it with the Minoan dynasty on Crete—you know, Theseus and the Minotaur and the Labyrinth of Daedalus—but although Crete has had plenty of earthquakes it's still there. I have a sort of recollection of reading somewhere that Atlantis was a great civilization aeons before Greece and Rome, and they discovered some terrible secret, or invented the ultimate weapon, and so they were destroyed. However, that could be pure fiction. I've no idea where I got it."

"It's a good story," said Will, "or it would be, if we weren't mixed up in it. So . . . do we deduce that whatever we're looking for must have come from there originally?"

Fern sighed. "I assume so. That seemed to be indicated on the tape."

"It wasn't a tape. It was *real*."

"Virtual reality." Fern's flippancy went no deeper than her words.

"We have to find it then, don't we? Whatever it is. We have to find it before *she* does."

"Yes."

"Maybe we could force the lock on that desk in Great-Cousin Ned's study," Will said pensively. "Or break into the chest in the attic. You must have searched nearly everywhere else."

"This is a big house," said Fern. "It's full of corners and cupboards and crannies and hideaways—not to mention the jumble Great-Cousin Ned accumulated. I've made a start. That's all."

They kicked the subject around in a dispirited manner until their cocoa had cooled. Then they went to bed, staying close on the stair though not hand in hand, leaving Lougarry in the kitchen, apparently asleep.

In the morning, the builder came to collect his ladder. "Well," asked Mrs. Wicklow, "did you get in?"

"We couldn't," said Fern. "The window was jammed as well."

Mrs. Wicklow made a noise somewhere between a grunt and a snort. "I don't like it."

"Nor do we."

They avoided the third floor bedroom now, chary of trying the door again or being overlooked from the window, though there was no one inside to watch them. They felt as if the secrets it contained were so huge they might yet burst the seams of the walls and blow away house and hillside, moor and dale in a sudden gust of power, leaving only a black hole with a single star winking in its depths. When Alison came up on the Friday she no longer looked the same to them. It was she who had spoken the word to hold fast the door even in her absence, she who had worn the chameleon gloves that grew onto hand and arm, she who had used an ordinary television set to look into the abyss. Will seemed to see her witchy qualities emphasized: the narrowing of her bright cold eyes, the dancing lines that played about her smile, transient as water, the rippling quantity of hair that wrapped her like a dim mantle. But Fern thought she perceived something even more disturbing, a hunger that was beyond customary mortal appetite, a desire that outranged all earthly desires, as if beneath the flimsy veneer of her physical exterior was a warped spirit which had long lost touch with its humanity. "I wonder how old she really is?" Fern speculated, observing her deadly pallor, the skin stretched taut over her bones as though her flesh had melted away. "She might be any age. Any age at all." A vision came into her mind of a different Alison, an Alison whose cheeks were as full as her lips, standing in a field of mud with her torn skirt kilted to her knee, gazing with the beginnings of that terrible hunger at a tall house on a far hill. Someone was calling her: *Alys! Alys!* The call echoed in Fern's head: Alison met her regard and for an instant her eyes widened as if she too heard it—then voice and vision were gone and there was nothing between them but the supper table. In the hall, the telephone rang. Fern got there first, thankful to hear her father's greeting, but Alison was on her heels, snatching the receiver almost before she had spoken, her smile a triangle of glitter, her grip on Fern's wrist like a vise. Fern withdrew, frightened by the strength in those lissom fingers, annoyed with herself for her fright. The thought of Lougarry heartened her: the wolf had stayed out of sight since Alison's return but Fern had seen her shadow in the garden and her silhouette atop the slope against the sky. She knew they were not abandoned.

"Sorry," Alison said, coming back into the kitchen. "I didn't mean to monopolize Robin like that, but there was something important I needed to ask him, and then I'm afraid he had to go."

"What was so important?" asked Will.

"It's about the barn. Incidentally, my friend is coming to look at it tomorrow. We'll probably move the boat out then. We have a lot of measuring to do."

"You won't damage the boat, will you?" Will was anxious.

"Measuring," said Fern. "That sounds *very* important."

Alison's stare grew colder than ever, but Fern merely looked ingenuous. She was still young enough, she hoped, to get away with that.

That night, she fell asleep to dream of Alison in the mud-field, barefoot in the dirt, and the one calling her was a gypsy-faced man in patched breeches, but she did not listen: her attention was fixed on the distant house. She raised her hand, and the moisture poured out of the earth and condensed into great clouds, and the lightning fell, striking the gabled roof, and the man was on his knees in the field, but she would not see him. The thunder rolled, and in the next illumination Fern saw Alison's face change, shrinking in upon itself until the bones shone white through transparent skin, and her heart was a red glow pounding visibly behind the webbing of her ribs. Fern woke up shivering, the sweat chill on her brow. She had an idea some noise had aroused her, a thunderclap maybe, spilling over from her dream; but the night outside was still. Then she heard the footsteps in the passage, light steady steps, moving toward the stair. There was no sniffing, nothing to suggest an unwanted visitor. She opened her door and looked out.

It was Will. She called his name very softly, inherently cautious, but he did not respond: as he turned to descend the staircase she saw that his eyes were closed. Just after their mother's death he had developed a tendency to sleepwalk, but it had not lasted long and she had believed he was permanently cured. She followed him, knowing he should not be woken, determined to steer him back to his bed as soon as she had the opportunity. At the first bend of the stair she halted. The hall below should have been in darkness, but a single shaft of light cut across it like a path, and Will moved along it as if drawn by a magnetic pull. The light was not the feeble glow of waning electricity: it was a pale cold brilliance, like concentrated moonlight, and it ran from the door of the drawing room to the stair's foot, where it was abruptly cut off, though Fern could see nothing that might occlude its passage. Within the drawing room there were voices which she could not distinguish. She whispered *Will* but her vocal cords were numb and anyway, it was too late. He had already disappeared through the open door.

She descended a few more steps, meticulously silent, circumspect beyond the reach of panic, though the panic was there inside her, tugging at her heart. But something deeper than instinct told her *this* was the moment, the borderline of danger: whatever was in that room was deadlier far than the night hunter who left no mark or the secrets of Alison's personal sanctum. When she reached floor level she picked her way around the beam of light, letting not so much as a fingertip or a toe intrude on it. The voices were clearly audible now, two of them, one a woman, presumably Alison, though her usual deliberately modulated accents had acquired contralto depth and an edge of adamant, the other a gray, atonal sort of voice, way down the scale, a voice with a judder in it like stone grinding on stone, gravelly about the vowels, grating on the consonants. And in between, answering questions in the dulled timbre of a hypnotic, there came a third. Will. The urgency that gripped Fern was more powerful than fear, more desperate than curiosity. She crept toward the door, dropping to a crouch as she drew near. The back of an armchair a little way inside the room narrowed the beam, casting a shadow that stretched to the hall, and into that shadow Fern crawled, driven by a compulsion beyond courage, any whisper of movement overlaid by the loudness of the voices and a hissing, snapping noise like the erratic susurration of a damp fire. Very carefully, lowering her chin almost to the floor, she craned round in the lee of the chair until she could see what was happening.

Halfway down the long room a fire burned in the unused hearth, a fire without smoke or ash, the crystalline fuel crackling into bluish-white flames and spitting vicious sparks that ate into nearby upholstery. In front of it the carpet had been rolled back and smoldering lines were drawn on the bare boards: a circle within a pentagram, and other symbols that Fern could not make out. She was not certain if the strange cold radiance came from the fire or the sizzling lines. Alison stood outside the pentagram, opposite the hearth, wearing a red wool dress empurpled by the light, so molded to her thin figure that the shallow mounds of her breasts, her rigid nipples, the nodules of her hip-bones were all clearly delineated. There was a blue glow on her face and her streaming hair had a virescent tinge. Within the circle, his eyes still closed, stood Will. And beside the fire, on a low plinth, was the source of the gray voice. The idol. Fern saw the stone lips moving and a pale gleam between widened eyelids. Her reason told her it was impossible, sight and hearing must have cheated her; but although her brain screamed in protest what she saw did not change. Her shock was so great it took her several seconds to tune in to the interrogation.

"Did you try the door to my room?" Alison was asking.

"Yes," Will said. Behind the chair Fern stiffened; her knees seemed to be glued to the floor.

"Could you open it?"

"No."

"Why not?"

"It was stuck," Will said, "and it stung my hand."

"He knows nothing," said the idol. "You're wasting your time."

"I must be sure." Outside the pentagram, Alison paced restlessly to and fro, her dress winnowing against her thighs. "Did your sister try it too?" Will assented. "And with the same result? Good. Perhaps you will know better than to pry in the future."

"He's asleep," said the idol. "Don't indulge yourself."

"What about the key?" Alison continued. "Have you found it?"

Will seemed puzzled. "Which key?"

"Which key are you looking for?"

"The key to the chest in the attic," he answered promptly, "and to Great-Cousin Ned's writing desk."

In her hiding-place, Fern blanched to recall how nearly she had told him, how close they trod to disaster. If Alison were to ask the wrong question . . .

"What do you expect to find there?"

"Treasure," Will responded after a pause.

"What treasure?"

"Great-Cousin Ned's treasure that he brought back from abroad." *Think of doubloons*, besought Fern in the paralysis of her mind. *Apes and peacocks. Pieces of eight. Don't think of Atlantis.* "Pirates' treasure."

"Let the fool go," said the idol. "He's a child playing storybook games. Send him to bed."

"Very well." Alison made a gesture of dismissal. "Go back to your room; sleep; in the morning, you will remember nothing." Will stepped out of the circle, walking toward the hall. Fern stayed where she was. The partial release of tension had left her shuddering, too unsteady to move; she could only trust the looming chair-back would be an adequate shield.

"Now for the girl," Alison said.

"No."

"Why not? She's sly and much too clever for her own good. Do you think I can't control her? A teenage brat? I will probe her brain like soft clay, I will pull out the strands of her thought until her consciousness is void, I will—"

"*No.*" The interdiction was final. Fern, clenching her will to resist she knew not what, felt disaster brush by her yet again. "She's at a dangerous age. If she has the Gift, now is the time when it might be woken. Summon her to the circle, and the touch of power could rouse a response we do not need. Do you want to have to destroy her?"

Alison gave an impatient jerk of her head. "The Gift is rare. Few have it now."

"On the contrary. The seed of Atlantis was scattered wide. There are many mortals who live out their lives in ignorance, not knowing that it is there inside them, dormant, like an organ

whose use is obsolete. Modern Man is limited by his own cynicism. The girl is sensitive against what she calls her better judgment. Don't be the one to teach her wisdom."

"She touched the picture," Alison persisted, "and now the
horse is gone. I must question her."

"The horse was there after she touched it," said the idol, "and
she could not have entered your room. You were careless. Forget
it. We are not here to chase the wind. The excrescence that you
yearn for is a deformity—"

"It took me two hundred years to snare it," Alison raged. "I
will not let it go so easily!" She faced the circle, raising her hand,
crying out words in a language like none Fern had ever heard, a
language as clear and cold as ice, yet vibrant as the voice of fire.
The glow from the perimeter was drawn upward toward her long
fingers, spinning into a cone, released to form a cylindrical column of whirling dazzle. At its center the shape of a horse formed
and faded, translucent as mist, twisting this way and that, fighting
the urge to cohere. The horse in the picture. Fern could make out
dim cloud-patterns on its flank, the tail that drifted like smoke
about its hind legs, the grotesque protuberance on its forehead,
distinctive now it was in motion. A budding growth, maybe three
or four inches long, flaking velvet. A horn.

The rhythms of incantation were jumbled on Alison's lips; the
creature reared and plunged; its neighing scream shook the
house. "Release it!" ordered the idol. "You will break the circle!
Release it!"

Alison's head snapped forward, her grip on light and phantom
slackened: the wheeling scintilla subsided toward the floor. The
outline of the horse shimmered into air.

"Restrain yourself," the idol adjured, the scraping voice heavy
with menace and the sheer effort of speech from that throat of
stone. "You are frittering away power we cannot spare. Time is
running out. Proceed with the questioning."

Fern had almost forgotten her peril, so absorbed was she in the scene unfolding a few feet away. Will's involvement had dwindled to a mere detail: she was concentrating wholly on a dialogue too obscure to elucidate, on phenomena beyond all comprehension. She felt that she had been drawn here for a purpose, perhaps for many purposes, and something more than mere chance had saved them, when Alison interrogated Will. She watched with crooked neck and deadened limbs as an unholy cavalcade of figures materialized within the circle: a cowled woman with vacant sockets, clasping a naked eyeball in her hand, an antlered man with a wicked, laughing face, something that looked like a child but wasn't, and an ancient crone with nails curved like claws, dressed in uncured skins whose pungency wafted across the room. To all of them Alison put the same question: what did they know of the key? The cowled woman and the antlered man were noncommittal: both seemed uninterested, angry at being troubled over a problem which did not concern them. The child that was not a child vanished without speaking. The crone lingered, despite Alison's dismissal, obviously relishing the opportunity to be malicious. She was repulsive beyond the range of normal ugliness: half her scalp was bald and blotched with scabs, the other half sprouted bristling hair; the whites of her eyes were sallow, the irises bloodshot; a single tooth jutted in her lipless mouth. "Your face is going, Alimond," she mocked. "One day, all your powers will not be enough to remold it. In a thousand years or so, you'll be a hag like me. You'll wear your beauty like a dress at the full moon, and a passing cloud will wipe it away. An illusion is fragile: you can't pin it down. The fish won't come so readily to your net by then, ha ha!"

"I abandoned moon-magic long ago," said Alison. "My Gift is stronger than such antiquated skills. I could change your face, Hexaté. For a price."

"A price indeed!" The old crone was contemptuous. "You

always were arrogant, Alimond. I can change it myself, when I want to: my strength is old but not yet rusted. Anyway, I like my face: it's good for scaring drunkards and children. I'll have no truck with the sorcery of the Gifted people. They were better named the Cursed people, cursed down into the deep: their Gifting damned them to a watery grave. Keep your Gift. I prefer my curses. A curse sticks, like damp excrement. Shall I curse you, Alimond? I taught you once, cared for you—"

"Curse away," Alison retorted. "You taught me little and all you cared for was the Gift you deride. When I wouldn't let you control it you cursed me then. I came to no harm. I learned my lessons from Morgus herself, and even she could not rule my mind. Tell me about the key, Hexaté. You must have heard something. The moles and the worms bring all the rumors of earth to your stinking hole."

But the crone's attention had strayed: she was mumbling to herself as if in senility. "Morgus," Fern heard her mutter. "Don't talk to me of *Morgus*. A fat slug swollen with a power she can no longer use. May she rot! Give me the old ways. Give me the sacrifice warm and twitching on the high altar, the throb of power from the planet's heart. Let me taste the blood again, smell the spilt manhood on the wet soil. They do not make magic like that anymore. I have coupled with a billy goat, romped with goblins and satyrs, disfigured the moon, extinguished the stars. What is this key of which you speak? No one ever mentioned a key."

"She's wandering," said Alison. "We'll get nothing from her now."

"She's lying," said the idol. "She wants you to think she has a knowledge you cannot reach. She craves companionship, even yours. Get rid of her."

A flick of Alison's hand, and the crone disappeared. "This is fruitless," the idol said. "The perimeter will not hold much longer, and Hexaté wastes precious minutes in small talk. Summon Caracandal."

For the first time Alison faltered. "He's too strong," she said. "I might not be able to bind him in the circle."

"His power is wasted, burned out: he is nothing more than a man. Surely you are not afraid of a *man*? Summon him!"

Alison lifted her hand in the customary gesture, but the chant of command sounded less clear than before, slurred with uncertainty. The figure which appeared in the circle wore a bulky garment like a coat; his hood was thrown back, showing a shaggy head of hair brindled like Lougarry's fur. At the sight of him, Fern went suddenly cold. "I have come, Alimond," said Ragginbone. "What do you want?"

"You know what I want," she responded. His tone was mild enough but her doubt remained, blunting the edge of her words. "Do you think I haven't felt you watching? Not that it matters: watching is all you're good for now. What have you seen, Brokenwand?"

"I have seen someone taking an axe to sever a spider's web. Very clumsy. I should have guessed it was you. No one else would send a hound that scents blood on the trail of something that has neither blood nor scent. That seemed peculiarly pointless."

"I wanted to deter the inquisitive," she said frostily.

"I will try to remember that," he responded in dulcet accents.

"*You* should be asking the questions," the idol told Alison. "You're bleating like a novice. The hound was a serious miscalculation. A conspicuous hunter draws attention to the trail."

"What happened to it, Caracandal?" Alison demanded. "It does not answer my call."

"Ask Lougarry," said Ragginbone. "If you dare."

"Enough of this!" The luminosity in the carved orbs of the idol appeared to intensify, a glow radiating from within the stone itself, kindling to a flame. "The key. We want the key."

"Where is it? If you have a clue—a trace—tell me, Caracandal. I conjure you—I *order* you—*tell me!*" Once again Alison raised her hand with a peculiar twisting motion, and the veins of light from the rim of the circle streamed toward her fingers. Her fist clenched, grasping the air itself, warping the cone of space that enclosed the Watcher till the buildup of pressure within bandaged him in his own coat, strangling him in his hair, dragging his features sideways. Fern saw the dreadful concentration that fettered his brows, tug against pull, force against force, the struggle not of muscle but of will. Gradually, the pressure was thrust aside: his hair loosened, flesh and feature slid back into place. Alison snatched at the cone but the light frayed from her clutch and dissolved downward; the glinting lines grew dim; the fire sank; Ragginbone towered dark and ominous at the center of the circle, and the last motes of brilliance spiraled slowly around him until they too were gone.

"Not . . . good enough," he said. His breath came short and fast but he stood like a rock, the rock Fern had seen before, solid as Earth. Immovable.

"You have not—the power!" Alison gasped. "You cannot—"

"I do not need power." His voice steadied. "Only habit." He pulled up his hood, and vanished.

The circle blazed back into light; the fire leaped. Fern felt a draft on her face like an icy burn; involuntarily she retreated behind the chair. She heard Alison swear, and the rasping derision of the idol. "Was that well done? You are afraid of him, and he knows it, he trades on it, he takes you by the fear and drags you down into weakness. *He uses your own power against you.* He is an old man with nothing to cling to but his age, crippled in strength, tramping the hills on a quest that is never fulfilled, yet you are afraid of him. You would trap the wild unicorn for its horn, whistle up a hound from the packs of Arawn—yet you are afraid of him. He learned his tricks from a mountebank, he peddled arsenic to a streetwitch and aphrodisiacs to the mistress of a king, he sneaked his way through the centuries, toying with wizardry, squandering his Gift—*yet you are afraid of him*. You would do better to fear me. You have shown me nothing tonight but the depth of your own ignorance. Quench the fire. Clear the circle. It is enough."

"Wait!" she said. "There is one I have not questioned. It may be useless, but . . ."

"Hurry," said the idol. "The fire will die soon. I cannot dally."

This time, the shape in the circle grew very slowly into being, as though coerced from some secure region of invisibility, dredged from an anonymous existence into a shy materialization. It was a squat, dumpy creature less than four feet high, its head sunken onto its chest, a lopsided hump distorting its shoulders, bat-like ears adorning its bald skull, each endowed with independent motion. It stood bundled up in its few rags as if in a motheaten sack, and it hugged itself with many-fingered hands in a pitiful attempt to conceal its poverty and ugliness. Its face was shriveled, its pouched eyes sorrowful and scared. Fern, venturing once more to squint around the chair-back, knew she had seen it before. This was the thing which had skulked in the passage outside her room, after the hound had gone. And with a surge of conviction she knew what it must be. The house-goblin.

"Malmorth," said Alison. "Malmorth the misshapen: is that what they called you? One of a hundred malmorths, hiding in shadows, terrified of your own reflection. Or do you have another name?"

The tiny monster made a whimpering sound in which Fern could identify no words.

"Pegwillen, was it? Is that the name the children gave you—the children you used to play with, all those years ago? What became of the children, Pegwillen? Do you remember? Do you remember who or what you are? Shall I tell you where they went?" An imploring look came into the mournful eyes; a knobbly digit reached out toward her. "They died," Alison said. "A stranger came down the valley with a buzz in his head and a pustule under his arm, and they all died. You were there, Pegwillen, but you could not help them. The cottage was burned with the bodies in it and you were alone. Always alone. And when they built this house you crept in and waited, but the children did not come again. Never again."

The hideous creature closed its eyes, trapped in a terrible memory of suffering. Alison surveyed it without compunction. "What about the man?" she said. "The sea captain who lived here recently. Do you remember him too?" It shook its head, lost in misery. Fern had a brief glimpse of an interminable sentence of wretchedness and desolation, a futile grubbing in a lumber-room of buried souvenirs, searching for something which had long been forgotten. "As you wish," said Alison. "Shall we see what other recollections I can revive?"

The monster stared at her in horror, seeming to quail in upon itself. Its wizened countenance was so full of sadness it appeared to Fern no longer ugly, merely pathetic.

"The man," Alison reiterated. "Did you notice the man? Good. Where did he keep his keys? Did you notice that too?"

"In his pocket," mumbled Pegwillen.

"Which pocket?" Alison's patience was labored. "The average man has many coats, many pockets. Which one did he favor?"

"Whichever pocket he was wearing," the goblin said. Its voice was too quiet for any distinctive tone but at least Fern could hear it now.

"Where else did he put them," Alison pursued, "when not using his pockets?"

"In the desk."

"The writing desk in his study?"

"Yes."

"The desk that's locked with one of the missing keys?"

"Yes."

"Stop this gibberish," the idol interrupted. "The creature is three parts imbecile. You'll get nothing from it but cobwebs in the head. Send it away."

"It might know something," Alison insisted. "It's always been here."

"Dismiss it."

She made a quick, curt gesture, and the goblin diminished into nothingness. The glimmering lines seemed to wane and Fern, restored to a tardy awareness of her precarious situation, judged it was time to leave. But she had knelt too long behind the chair: her cramped legs would not move. Frantically she massaged numb calves. The light sank with the fire, making the shadows less dense, her concealment less sure. Alison was speaking quietly in the unknown language she had used before, perhaps a closing incantation. If she walked to the door she could not miss the figure huddled in the gloom.

And then came a tumult of wind and something rushed past Fern into the room, scattering circle and symbol, springing in front of Alison, crouched low as if ready to pounce. Lougarry's ears were flattened against her skull, her hackles lifted as if charged with electricity, her ragged fangs shone blue in the light of the flaring fire. The silence she carried with her was as palpable as a smell, a physical aura that deadened all neighboring sound. Her voiceless growl seemed to fill the room.

"Get out!" Alison cried. "I did not summon you, demon. Go back to your master! Go!"

"Kill her," said the idol.

For the last time, Alison raised her arm—

But the fire went out, exploding in a dust of sparks, and the wind howled like wolves, and in the sudden blackness the only illumination came from the eyes of the stone idol, still shining with a baleful luster. A small hand reached out to Fern, taking hers, a hand with many fingers of assorted lengths. She heard Alison shrieking in fury, her rage sharpened with fear, the thud of a fall, the curse of the stone, but the tiny voice close by was more distinct. "Quick," it said. "Quick, quick." She was drawn away from the din, through the hall. "Stairs," said her guide, and she climbed after him, her sight readjusting, until she thought she could make out the diminutive figure ahead of her, a bundle of dark in the darkness. "Pegwillen?" she whispered. But as they reached the landing the hand slipped from hers, and the bundle seemed to shrink and blur, and she was alone in the empty passage, standing beside her door.

Inside her room she closed the door, resisting the urge to try and wedge the handle, and got back into bed. She began to shiver with reaction, thinking of what she had seen since she tiptoed downstairs after her brother, an hour, a lifetime, an aeon ago. She had crossed the frontier into another world beyond any further possibility of denial; she might return but reality would never look the same to her.

Sometime later she heard footsteps approaching along the corridor. Not Will again: the feet were shod, the pace measured. They stopped outside her room, waited a while, and then, reluctantly, or so she imagined, they moved on toward the upper floor.

Waking the next morning reminded Fern of those awaken-
ings just after her mother's death, when she had opened
her eyes each day to the realization that the world was
forever different. One of the foundation stones of her existence was
gone, and her environment felt no longer stable; her very spirit
seemed to falter on a cliff-edge, above an unimaginable depth of uncertainty. Over the years she had tried to build a barrier of solid,
everyday things between herself and that abyss: small plans, realiz-
able dreams, material comforters, walling herself in, shutting out not
only the abyss but the view. Now, the walls had fallen in, the wide
world had come close with all its dark possibilities. She felt naked
and afraid, beset by shadows, and yet at the same time curiously
alive, as if a faint current of discordant energy had begun to seep
through her veins, filling her with a fledgling strength, a desperate re-
source. She sat down to breakfast with an assumption of normality,
studying Alison covertly: she looked sleepless and haunted, her lips
pale, her eyes bruised, elfin lines marking the passage of telltale ex-
pressions. "I've seen a stray dog round here," she said to Mrs. Wicklow. "If you see it, chase it off. I won't have a stray hanging about. It
could be dangerous, and it's bound to have fleas."

Under the table, Fern dug her brother with her foot. "Mrs. Wicklow doesn't like dogs," she said, making no attempt to catch the housekeeper's eye.

"Happen I don't," grunted Mrs. Wicklow, but she did not mention Lougarry.

"Are you all right?" Fern asked Alison solicitously. "You look as if you haven't slept well."

"Of course I'm all right," Alison snapped.

Her friend arrived to view the barn later that morning. He was a bronzed, hairless individual with the physique of a workout fanatic and a BBC accent that lapsed into an affectation of cockney with every few phrases. He wore Italian jeans which clung tightly to buttock and thigh and a leather jacket with the sleeves ripped out, lavishly ornamented with studs. Alison called him "Rollo, darling"; he called her dear, dearie, luv, and even ducks. He seemed willing to extend his careless affection to Will and Fern, patting Will's hair with suspicious frequency, but Alison was politely discouraging and although the Capels trooped after her into the barn to keep an eye on the well-being of the *Seawitch* they were soon bored away by the talk of open-plan interiors, multi-level structure, layout, perspective, and feng shui. By common consent they rambled up the hill and found themselves a hummock where they could sit and survey their domain. It was sunny and growing hot: the wind-rippled air was filled with the thrumming of grasshoppers, the honey-drone of a laden bee, a far-off aria of birdsong. Very faintly they heard the bubbling voice of the Yarrow where it tumbled over a low fall. High white clouds chased their own shadows across the upland moor. "It's so peaceful," said Will. "You can't believe in witchcraft and evil up here."

"There is evil everywhere under the sun," Fern quoted, and the gravity in her tone made him turn and study her thoughtfully.

There was a long pause before she ventured somewhat gingerly to broach the subject on her mind. "You were sleepwalking last night."

"*Was* I? I don't remember that. I had this weird dream, though. Really weird. At least . . . I think it was a dream."

"Go on."

"I woke up," Will said, "in my dream, I mean. I felt as if I was awake but I sort of knew I was only dreaming. I suppose it was a relief. Knowing it was just a dream kept it from being frightening. I'd have been scared shitless if I'd thought it was real."

Fern considered taking him to task on his choice of language but was too anxious for him to continue his story. "What happened?"

"I went downstairs and across the hall to the drawing room—"

"Why?" Fern interrupted.

"I don't know," Will responded. "It was just part of the dream. You don't know why you do things in dreams. Anyway, the drawing room was all different—the same room, but much bigger, and the ceiling was so high I could barely see it, and the fireplace was huge, like a great cavern, with a fire burning in it, but the flames were blue and cold-looking. The room was full of a pale light which made everything else look bluish too. That awful stone idol was sitting beside the fire on a kind of dais, only it was enormous, like a statue in a pagan temple, and its eyes were alive, not stone anymore but luminous, like an animal in the dark."

"Did it speak?" Fern asked quickly.

"I don't remember. It's funny: it sounds so terrifying when I describe it but I wasn't terrified in the dream, just numb. I went to stand in the circle in the middle of the room, and the circle seemed to expand, and the walls receded until I couldn't see them anymore. It was like standing in the center of a giant ice rink with a spotlight on you. The fire burned round the edge of the circle, but it radiated cold, not heat. *She* was there too, outside the circle."

"Alison?"

"I suppose so," Will said. "She was like Alison, but different."

"Bigger?" Fern suggested doubtfully.

Will frowned, concentrating on the effort of memory. "Taller," he concluded. "I'm sure she was taller. And more witch-like. The firelight made dramatic shadows in her face, like the hollows in a skull, and her mouth was purple, and she wore a purple dress that changed to blood-color when she moved, and there was a greenish shade in her hair. She was asking me questions, and I had to answer them, although deep down inside I knew it wasn't a good idea." He had been gazing down the valley toward the river, but he turned back to his sister with troubled eyes. "It wasn't, was it?" he said. "The more I think about this, the more I feel it wasn't exactly a dream. Fern . . ."

"It's all right," she said. "Just tell me, can you remember any of the questions?"

"Not really. Except one: she asked me about the missing treasure, and I was going to tell her about Atlantis, only a picture came into my head—pirates with cutlasses in their teeth, and chests overflowing with gold coins, and the *Seawitch* with a skull-and-crossbones flapping at her mast—and I didn't mention Atlantis after all." He added, after a brief silence: "That sounds like a good thing, doesn't it?"

"It was a very good thing," said Fern.

"Did you see me sleepwalking?"

"Yes."

"Where did I go?"

"To the drawing room," said Fern. "I followed you. Everything looked normal size to me, but there was a circle, like you said, inside a pentagram, and a blue fire, and the idol was alive. It *spoke*. And I wasn't dreaming. I wasn't numb. And I've never been so scared in my whole life." The sun shone down on them. The bee bumbled around a nearby patch of gorse. The grasshoppers rubbed their knee-joints together like a frenetic chorus of gypsy guitars. Yet night and nightmare lay as close as a shadow. "We're out of our depth," said Fern. "We need help."

"Gus?"

"No. I think we should leave Alison and her chum to mess around in the barn, and go for a long walk. On our own."

They collected a liter bottle of lemonade from the fridge and Mrs. Wicklow made them sandwiches. "Don't go too far," she cautioned, "and don't get lost. Folks get mazed up on t' moors, specially when t' mist comes down. Pixy-led, they used to call it. Still, it's a fine day and like to stay fine, and Fern here looks enough like a pixy herself. Happen t' boggarts would treat you as friends, any road. What shall I say to Madam, if she asks for you?"

"Nothing," said Fern. "We don't want company. Or fuss."

"What's a boggart?" asked Will, as they climbed the hill-side path.

"I don't know," said Fern, "and I don't want to know. We've got problems enough."

Lougarry was waiting over the brow of the hill, lying so still in the grass that a butterfly had perched within an inch of her nose. The stems bent and shimmered as she rose to her feet, and the butterfly floated away like a wind-borne petal. Fern wondered if, like Ragginbone, the she-wolf possessed the faculty of making herself at one with her surroundings, not invisible but trans-muted, so close to nature that she could blend with it at will and be absorbed into its many forms, becoming grass-blade and wild-flower, still earth and moving air, resuming her true self at the prompting of a thought. It came to Fern that we are all part of one vast pattern of Being, the real world and the shadow-world, sun-light and werelight, Man and spirit, and to understand and accept that was the first step toward the abnegation of ego, the affirma-tion of the soul. To comprehend the wind, not as a movement of molecules but as the pulse of the air, the pulse of her pulse, was to become the wind, to blow with it through the dancing grasses to the edge of the sky . . .

"Fern!" Will's voice was urgent, his grip on her arm imperative. "Yes?"

"Just for a moment I thought—you looked sort of ghostly, as if—I must have been imagining it. Everything is so peculiar right now."

"You imagined it," said Fern.

They followed Lougarry away from the path, over the moorland to a distant height where the bare rock broke free of its green covering and shouldered skyward. Ragginbone was waiting on the leeside, his weather-mottled overcoat merging with the maculation of moss and lichen on the face of the stone. He looked far too warm, swathed in the heavy, coarse material, but he seemed as impervious to sunshine as to rain and wind. "Well?" he said. "Have you found it yet?"

"No," said Fern, "and all is not well." She introduced her brother and they sat down on either side of the old man, suddenly conscious of how thirsty they were after the long hot walk. Fern wrestled in vain with the cap of the lemonade bottle; Ragginbone untwisted it with ease, fingers gripping like roots. Will offered to share their sandwiches. The urgency which had seized Fern earlier, bordering on panic, eased a little in the company of the Watcher. He was her ally, or so she hoped, a dependable adult in an alien world where she felt herself helpless as a child.

"Does Lougarry really belong to you?" Will asked, feeding her his crusts.

"No," said the Watcher. "She belongs only to herself. Being with me was a choice she made, a long time ago. An imprudent choice: I told her so at the time."

"Gus—the vicar—said Lougarry comes from *loup garou*," Will went on. "Is she—*is* she a werewolf?"

He sighed. "Maybe," he said. "Maybe she was—once. Do you

like stories?" Will nodded, his mouth full of sandwich. "Very well. I'll tell you a story. Once upon a time . . . once upon a time there was an enchantress who hunted in wolf-shape in a northern forest far away from here. At first she was careful, avoiding the trails of men when she assumed her animal form, but she became enamoured of the hunt and forgot her caution, and took to slaying even her own kind. Eventually the local people sent for a wizard to help them. The sorcerer who came was very powerful and had recently acquired morality: he saw himself as a dispenser of justice. He bound her in her wolf-shape and told her that thus she must remain, until, as a beast, she had rediscovered her humanity. He ordered her to come to him in a hundred years, and then, if the woman in her was renewed, he would restore her to herself. And so she was driven out of the village where she had lived, and shunned by other wolves who sensed she was not one of them, and for a hundred years she roamed alone in the forest. She ran free until she could run no more, and drank the hot blood until it burned her throat, and when she lifted her voice to howl her loneliness and her loss no sound emerged, for the werewolf is as silent as a ghost. When the time of her punishment was over she went to find the wizard, and he looked into her unhuman eyes and saw a woman's soul."

"Didn't he change her back?" asked Will. Lougarry's chin was resting on his leg; her yellow eyes never blinked.

"He could not," said Ragginbone. "He had lost his power, and no other could complete the spell he initiated. So she stayed with him, at first in the hope that he might find some way to aid her, later—who knows?—out of habit, or even affection. The capacity for affection is the best part of humankind. Of course, if she had killed him, the spell would have been broken. But she was a monster no longer: she chose otherwise." He smiled at Will, who was looking half doubtful, half tragic. "Never mind. It's only a story."

"How could a wizard lose his power?" Fern demanded.

"By over-reaching himself, trying to do something that was beyond his strength. When ambition outstrips ability, that is always a recipe for disaster."

"Could he get it back?"

"Unlikely." Ragginbone gave her a sharp look from beneath lowered brows. "The Gift once spent—or misspent—cannot be given again."

The Gift, had said the idol. *If she has the Gift . . .* "What is the Gift?" asked Fern.

"That's another story," said the Watcher. "I've given you one; now it's your turn. I infer you have a lot to tell."

And so they told him. Fern described the activities of Alison/Alimond, their invasion of her room and what they found there. Will related his dream-sequence, then his sister gave a detailed account of what she had witnessed the previous night in the drawing room. Initially Ragginbone interpolated few comments. "Dragonskin," he said of the gloves. "It has many properties," and "Gadgetry," scathingly, when Fern came to the television set. "A new way of doing an old trick. The crystal ball cubed. Alimond loves to keep abreast of the fashion. Still, she has learned a great deal that I didn't know. A great deal . . ." During the latter part of the recital, however, he was very silent. His eyebrows scrunched together above the lean hook of his nose; his mouth stiffened. When Fern stopped speaking he barely seemed to notice. Thought sat heavily on his face.

"Isn't it time you explained what's going on?" she said at last. "Or we could fall in a pit from not knowing it's there."

"I suppose so." The Watcher uncreased his scowl and looked long at them both. "You know too much for the safety of others, too little to look out for yourselves. I don't like it. You are very young for such troubles, but trouble, alas, is no respecter of youth."

"I'm grown-up," said Fern, forgetting her earlier sensation of ineffectuality. "Anyway, you asked for my help. *Our* help."

"I asked you to find something," Ragginbone conceded. "Instead, you found—"

"Trouble," Will said brightly.

"So be it." Absentmindedly, the Watcher took a pull at the lemonade bottle. For some time he said nothing, while they waited. Fern thought it was like waiting for a flower to open. "Where to begin?" he muttered at last. "Beginnings are hard to trace. The roots of stories go deep . . ."

"Begin with Atlantis," said Fern.

"Ah yes. Atlantis. We know so little of it. Oldest of civilizations, fairest of cities, Gifted, doomed. It is beyond Sight now; its ghosts do not stir. Still, the descendants of those who fled live on, though their numbers now are few, exiles for all time: they preserve ancient documents, never shown to any historian. And rumor is stronger than the strongest prohibition. It was an island in a place that is no more, an arrogant metropolis ruling a mainland empire before the dawn of history. Its power was founded on a curious stone, a globe of rock the size of a serpent's egg. The Lodestone. None knew how it came there, or where its story started. The belief was that it had come from another world—not simply another planet, but another cosmos—although how that belief originated is unknown. Whatever the cause, it responded to none of our physical laws, and the environment was warped around it, and the people who lived there were altered forever. Studying the researches of this century I have wondered if it might have been, not simply *from* another universe, but another universe itself, an entire creation reduced by the final implosion to a sphere of incredibly concentrated matter. That could explain its extraordinary potency."

"That's impossible," Will objected. "For one thing, it would be as small as a pinhead. For another, gravity itself would be distorted around it."

"Gravity may mean two different things in two different worlds,"

Ragginbone pointed out, "and the size of the pinhead depends on the size of the pin. Anyway, that's just a theory. What we know for certain is that the Atlanteans used their power to learn and to teach, to build and to create, to rule, dominate, eventually oppress. The usual downhill slope. They called themselves the Gifted people, and those in whom the Gift showed most strongly were revered, becoming the royalty and aristocracy of the kingdom. The Lodestone affected their genes, and these they spread in the way of conquerors throughout the conquered lands; thus the abnormal strain has been passed on even to the present day. Since the Fall, however, the Gifted have had other, often less flattering, names: witchkind, the Crooked Ones, Prospero's Children."

"What *is* the Gift?" Fern whispered. "What—exactly—is it?"

"Telepathy, telekinesis, telegnosis. The ability to move between Time and Forever, between past and present, between the world and its shadow. A wearisome life and an unwearying body. The Gift can manifest itself in many ways. But you must be aware you have it, you must learn its use. Without understanding and practice it will atrophy, like a superfluous limb. Not for nothing has it been called the sixth finger. It is wise to fear it, folly to indulge it, lethal to abuse it."

"Lethal for whom?" said Fern.

"It was lethal for Atlantis, in the end. They became obsessed with inbreeding, forbidding lawful marriage with foreigners, seeking to produce ever more puissant offspring. Inevitably this went hand in hand with the usual weaknesses of the inbred, disabilities, diseases, even imbecility. There were idiots with the reach of giants, dictators driven by passion and mania. Zohrâne, the last queen, had power beyond conception, but she hungered for more—" Fern recalled suddenly the inhuman hunger she had detected in Alison's face "—for the potential to travel outside the world itself, to pass the Gate of Death yet living, and return unchanged. She was mad, of course. Only the dead may pass; whether the human spirit is reborn here or anywhere is a matter for guess-work and faith: knowledge is not possible. The Old Spirits, those we name immortal, are bound to this world until the end of Time, but mortals must die, even the Gifted ones, and journey blindfold into the unknown. Zohrâne wanted to take that road with open eyes, breaking the first law of Being. She believed that she could use the substance of another universe to make herself a key that would unlock the Gate, admitting her into the dimension from whence that substance came. And so she employed her Gift to destroy its source. She smashed the Lodestone."

"I don't understand," said Will, evidently giving the subject serious consideration. "Surely this Gate you mention is just . . . sort of symbolic; you can't actually *see* it. And even if you could, how did she know the key would fit?"

"Once you have the key you can make the lock," said the Watcher. "Once you have the lock, you can open the door. In a sense you are right, the Gate is a symbol; but every symbol represents a fundamental truth. I will show you the Gate, if you like. It is always near." He stood away from the rock-face and made a sweeping gesture with both hands. Gradually, like a film coming into focus, they began to see an arch delved deep in the stone, and in that arch a door. It looked ancient beyond the count of years, overhung with membranous growths, while species of fungi long lost in evolution clawed at the crumbling lintel. The door itself appeared flimsy, made of ill-fitting boards weathered to gray-ness, the iron ring which should have opened it rusted into immo-bility. Yet there were no chinks between the makeshift planks; no light leaked around the periphery. It was an unobtrusive sort of door in a wall like a million other walls, marked solely by its age; but a magnetism emanated from it that was both a compulsion and a menace. Fern felt herself drawn irresistibly toward it, yet her knee-joints melted with dread at its proximity. "Do not ap-proach it!" Ragginbone admonished softly, and the image slowly faded until the rock was as before. "When the moment comes for it to open, you will know," he went on. "Until then, you may see it many times, or never, it may look the same, it may look different, but you will always recognize it. The awe of the Gate does not diminish."

"What about Zohrâne?" asked Fern, pulling herself together. "*Did* she unlock it?"

"I doubt it," responded Ragginbone. "You have felt its force even when closed; were it to be left open by so much as a crack the pull of Beyond would eventually destabilize the entire cosmos. But we cannot know what really happened. Because of Zohrâne's act, Atlantis has been forbidden to spellbinder and soothseeker. Archaeologists know little of it, and the Gifted cannot look back over the millennia to learn its secrets. Some say it was the shattering of the Lodestone that jarred the fault line on which the island lay; others claim it was the breaking of the ultimate law. Whatever the cause, a great tidal wave overwhelmed the island, and on its back came a storm more terrible than any in the memory of the world. The shape of the continents was changed, mountains became islands, the ocean poured over lowland plains. Atlantis sank beneath the waters, and the seabed opened to swallow it. Not a stone remained, and even the creatures of the deep could not tell where it had been. What became of the key we could only conjecture." He paused, sighed, studied his palm. "Until now."

"*You* found it," Fern said, sudden light dawning. "It *was* you, wasn't it? We saw you on the tape. You were with the alchemist, peering into the smoke." She gave an involuntary smile. "The sorcerer's apprentice."

"Poor Fantodi. He wasn't much of a sorcerer." Ragginbone's eyes had the glazed look of someone gazing far into the past. "And I . . . wasn't much of an apprentice. Too clever for my own good and much too clever for him. Candido Gobbi . . ." He toyed with the name as if it belonged to someone else. "Candido the not-so-candid. Homeless urchin, aspiring mountebank, unscrupulous, immoral, amoral. He grew to be Caracandal, acquired what he thought was wisdom, gambled with the Gift he did not appreciate and lost. Lost respect, power, identity. It is a hard thing, learning to live without the packaging that made up your Self. The hardest thing. What is a sorcerer, without his sorcery? Only a man without a job. They say it is in such nakedness that the true spirit is revealed—but that's the kind of thing people *do* say, when they are comfortable with their purpose in life, and have never been stripped of everything."

"What is Caracandal?" asked Fern. "Is it your real name?"

"It is the name I took in honor of my Gift, as Alison took Alimond. It is the custom."

"Is she very dangerous?" Will demanded.

"Very. The famine that drives her is beyond satiation. The road on which you travel so often depends on how—and why—you first discover your Gifting. In her girlhood she was wronged, and in retaliation she lashed out with a power she did not understand, wielding her newfound ability in hatred and revenge. Her future took shape in that gesture." He looked long and darkly at Fern as he spoke, pondering all that he knew of her. The sunlight showed her face unlined, unformed, petal-smooth, only hinting at the character she had yet to develop. He glimpsed doubt, courage, a budding will, but, he was almost sure, little capacity for rancor. The sixth finger, he thought. If you have it, use it. *Use it.* We have need of power.

"Why did she want to trap the horse?" Fern was puzzling over the recollection.

"It was a unicorn." Ragginbone shrugged. "Presumably she believes in the efficacy of its horn, although the evidence shows it is no more useful than that of the white rhino. But Alimond was born in a superstitious age and she has never really outgrown it, for all her dabbling in modern trends. Unicorns are mutations. The one you saw was probably a windhorse: they are air-spirits, not true animals, and prone to teratogenesis. It has only the transient magic of its kind." There was a pause while he gazed out over the spreading moor, listening to the hum of insect busyness, soaking up the serenity of the summer's day.

When he resumed his voice was altered, softer and yet, by its very softness, alarming, edged with warning—or fear. "It is the idol which concerns me most. I was summoned only in spirit, I could not see clearly beyond the summoner, and Will's perception was affected by the trance in which he was bound, but you saw everything. You were rash, and lucky: Alimond's concentration would have been focused on the circle, rendering her oblivious to all else. As for the idol . . . the idol is a thing of stone: it cannot turn its head."

Fern shuddered, suddenly cold even in the sun's warmth. "Its lips moved," she said.

"That would have been effort enough. It's a receptor: a statue of a pagan deity which can be used as a transmitter by the immortal it represents. Many of the Old Spirits were once worshipped as gods: they hated Man only one degree less than they craved his subjugation. The religions withered long ago and most of the Spirits now sleep, or have dwindled in power, but a few endure, adapting their methods, battening on mortal weakness, finding the shortcuts to men's hearts. You saw three of the lesser ones, Fern, when Alimond called them to the circle: the Hag, the Hunter, the Child. The strongest rarely make personal appearances. They prefer to use receptors, slave-sprites, ambulants—"

"What's an ambulant?" Fern interjected.

"A living being—human or animal—possessed by an external power. Animals are easiest. Humans have higher resistance, but then a human will admit the invader, offered a sufficient incentive, and after that it cannot be excluded."

"That's horrible," said Will. "You mean, someone we *know*—?"

"Possession leaves its mark," Ragginbone said. "The aging process will be arrested, there can be a corruption of the skin, the eyes betray. In the shock of the initial takeover the hair may turn white or gray. There are dangers, too, for the possessor. A Spirit which immerses itself too deeply in a stolen body can lose much of its force when that body is destroyed. But the strongest of the Spirits could control many ambulants, many receptors, putting only a tithe of his thought and his power into each. Like a businessman with a dozen telephone-lines, holding a dozen different conversations at once, or an eight-armed puppeteer, with a puppet in every hand. I fear Alimond has formed a deadly alliance."

"This Spirit," Fern said, "who is he?"

"He is," said Ragginbone, and the lines of grimness set in his face like scars. "That is enough."

"But—doesn't he have a name?"

"He has many names, many faces. Nonetheless, he is one Spirit, one mind. One void that can never be filled. The Lodestone is something for which he has always lusted. I know little of him outside his reputation, I am happy to say, though I once dared to penetrate Azmodel, the Beautiful Valley—the valley in the pit of the world—but once was sufficient: it is not an adventure I wish to repeat. The less you know of him the better. He is oldest of the old, mightiest among mighty: his grip does not slacken, his thought is unsleeping, his hatred is forever. Does that tell you? If Alimond has turned to *him*, her greed has outstripped not only her judgment but her reason."

"If he's so powerful," said Will, "how do we fight him?"

"You don't," said the Watcher. "Neither you, nor I, have that kind of strength. We might just as well try to fight the whirlwind."

It was not an encouraging conversation but just the same, Fern felt encouraged. Back at the house, she looked up the word *telegnosis* in the dictionary. "Knowledge about distant events alleged to have been obtained without the use of any normal sensory mechanism," ran the definition. That night, she dreamed of pain. It was a pain like nothing she had ever sensed or imagined, and it was inside her, in her belly, in the very core of her self, tearing at her, rending her with invisible teeth, wrenching her apart. Her stomach was swollen hard with pain and her thighs gaped and the blood from her torn innards pulsed out between her legs. She thought she screamed but no one seemed to care. "Alys Giddings!" A sharp-faced woman was leaning over her. "You should be ashamed of yourself, making such a fuss. Seven I had and you were the seventh, and never any fuss out of me." And then in the background another voice: "It's too soon. Much too soon." And then the pain flowed away and there was a white naked thing squirming in the phlegm between her legs like a hairless rat, and she picked it up, and a love filled her which drove out even the memory of suffering, so that she wept with love, but when she held it to her breast it would not suck, and its eyes were squeezed shut, and its tiny limbs hung limp like those of a doll. "It's dead," said one of the voices. "Take it away from her"—and then she was standing in a lane somewhere and a man was riding past, and his profile was as fine as porcelain and his long curls shone like gilding in the sun, but he turned his shoulder and would not see her. Her heart was beating hard with the hunger and anger which had come to fill the place where that great love had been. And at the last she was in the field as before, and Fern was Alys and Alys was Fern, and she could feel the mud between her toes, and her heart's glow irradiating her body, and when she gazed into the palm of her hand she seemed to see the planets whirling beneath her skin. Far away was the gabled house, and the clouds rolled over it, and she called to the lightning and it answered her, and her voice was the voice of the wind. She did not see the dark man reaching out to her, only the fair man in the distant house, with the candlelight golden on his sculpted locks. But the candle-flames grew at her summons until they speared the ceiling, and the storm came down to meet them, and the porcelain profile cracked in the heat of the burning. She tasted fire and she tasted blood, but it was not enough. The love that was gone had left a void that would never be filled. Suddenly Fern was afraid, trapped inside so much hatred and emptiness; she struggled to be free but the dream enmeshed her like a cobweb, binding her thought with cloying gossamer, and when finally she fought her way out of it there was only another dream, another layer of sleep.

In the morning she was exhausted, and it was Alison's turn to comment on the shadows beneath her eyes.

"I had bad dreams," said Fern, wondering what her interlocutor would say, if she called her not Alison but Alys. Or Alimond.

It was a strange day. They went to the beach with Gus and Maggie Dinsdale. Alison came too. They might have been ordinary people on an ordinary day out. At low tide broken platforms of rock divided the sands, partly smothered in brown patent-leather sea-weed; the mouth of the Yarrow branched into a dozen rivulets which nudged their way between boulders and tumbled over low ridges of stone, down toward the sea. The shallow waves took on the hue of sand, ebbing from the shore to leave pale threads of foam fraying in the sun. A brisk wind thinned the trippers; the North Sea was icy cold. Despite the chill, Alison swam: men stared at her wispy body and the long hair that wreathed like smoke on the breeze. It looked longer when wet, adhering in rats' tails to her upper thighs. Her red swimsuit webbed her bones like skin.

"You look *almost* like a mermaid," said Fern, remembering her fleeting glimpse of one on the tape.

"She certainly does," said Gus appreciatively. "The lorelei of Teutonic folktales, a spellsinger luring hapless fishermen to their doom. You must know Heine's poem. Have you done any luring lately, Alison?"

"Don't talk nonsense," she said smiling, and the sea-glitter was in her eyes.

Fern turned away, walking toward the water, feeling that bright hard gaze like a cold finger probing her back. There was something at the waves' edge which had not been there before, a piece of tide-borne flotsam, fish-white but not fish, rolling and tumbling onto the beach. A bulbous thing like a head lolled low in the water; limb-like tentacles, knobbled with soft bones, trailed behind it. Fern knew what it was from her dream of the dead child but she would not look closer. Glancing over at Alison she felt a sudden stab of pity, a horror of the immensity of that hidden void which had swallowed both love and loss, a dread of the starved desires which struggled in vain to re-fill it. She found herself wondering how Alison had felt about her Gift, when she knew it could give her everything but that which she truly wanted. Revenge, triumph, conquest must all have appeared meaningless and futile, crumbs to sate the famine of a giant. And with an abrupt flash of insight or inspiration she thought: *That's* why Alison wants to open the Gate. Not for power—whatever she may have told the Old Spirit. For Death. The kingdom of Death—if there is such a place. Even Ragginbone doesn't know what lies across the threshold . . . She seemed to see Alison wandering through a realm of shadows, looking for a cradle where a stillborn soul slept like a curled shoot untouched with green. A rush of terror left her shuddering: megalomania was something she could comprehend, something which might be fought and contained, but a mother's lust for the child that had died in her womb was an obsession beyond reason or measure. And watching Alison, she saw for the first time how deadly she really was.

Involuntarily she looked back at the sea, but the waves were empty: only the white rime of foam lay like spittle on the sand.

They had no means of knowing how, or if, Alison was con-ducting further searches for the key. "Of course, she doesn't realize she's got competition," Fern concluded. "She's sussed that we're looking for *something*, but she thinks we don't know what. As far as she's aware, our minds are still running on pirates' treasure. Under those circumstances she's probably quite happy to let us do some of the legwork. She must reckon that if we find the key we won't know its significance, and she can easily take it away from us."

"I daresay," said Will, "but you haven't found it yet, have you?"

"At least I've looked," said his sister.

It was Tuesday of the following week before Alison left for London. Robin had called twice but although Fern had managed to talk briefly with him she had abandoned any attempt to arouse his dormant common sense. Instead, she hit below the belt, infusing her voice with the wistfulness of childhood, reminding him of the things they had all planned to do together that summer—plans she had deplored at the time without reserve—and maintaining that Yorkshire wasn't any fun without him. After all, she reasoned privately, their current problems, however else they might be described, hardly came under the heading of *fun*. Robin responded with assurances of a prompt return, whereupon Alison took over, expounding fluently on American witch-trials and well-informed friends of hers scattered all over the U.S. whom he must not fail to visit. Fern could only hope that parenthood would win over editorial research. It was on the Monday afternoon, as she was trying to visualize her father, arriving like a bemused knight errant long after the start of the battle, when it dawned on her that there was little or nothing he could do. He might ask Alison to leave, but he was more likely to invite her to stay. And if he came across any unnatural phenomena he would find any excuse, no matter how implausible, to explain them away. Slightly damped by this revelation, Fern quit the studies she had been ignoring for the past hour and walked to the village, technically to replenish their stock of orange juice.

It was on the way back that she saw Alison, deep in conversation. Alison did not see her, and Fern drew aside into the lee of a wall, preferring to remain unobserved. The biker had pulled over close to the verge and Alison appeared to be talking to him at some length. Her manner was curt and authoritative. Only afterward did it strike Fern that throughout their exchange he had never once lifted his visor. Despite the heat, black gauntlets, black leather jacket, glossy leather jeans, and heavy boots so covered him that not an inch of skin was exposed; the helmet hid both neck and hair; the tinted visor masked his face. His machine looked cumbersome but it started at a kick and resumed its balance in motion like a horse getting into its stride. He zoomed off at speed and Alison walked briskly back to Dale House. Fern followed after a prudent interval.

"I saw you talking to someone on a motorbike," she said to Alison at supper on an impulse, scanning her face for discomfort.

"You saw—oh. Oh—yes. The motorbike. He was lost. He wanted the Whitby road. I only hope my directions were accurate."

"She was lying," said Fern later. "He wouldn't ask the way. He's local: we've seen him several times."

The builders arrived the morning of Alison's departure, Rollo and two assistants, taking over the barn. Fern and Will were discouraged from strolling in and out while work was in progress, and the premises were locked when they left in the evening. Rollo's over-friendliness whenever he wandered into the house, particularly to Will, acted as an even greater deterrent. "Who's paying for it?" Fern muttered. "Daddy can't have given more than a verbal authorization."

On the Wednesday she determined to inquire. "They're in Alison's employ," she reported to Will afterward. "That means she's responsible for payment, whatever she may have agreed with Daddy. Of course, he'd never refuse to stump up, no matter how

large the bill: you know what he is. Still, she's taking a big risk. I
wonder why it's so important to her?"

But there was no immediate answer to that.

Early the following morning a very long, very white car pulled
up outside Dale House. The soft top was folded back, the coach-
work was pristine, the chromium unspotted. It looked as out-of-
place on the narrow Yorkshire roads as a shark in a fishpond. The
driver had hair that gleamed like the chromium and wore a pale
silk suit of casual cut which set off his café-crème complexion. At
the sight of him, Mrs. Wicklow's expression grew more dour than
ever, and Will appeared mildly inquisitive, meticulously scornful.
Fern greeted the visitor warily. "If you're looking for Alison," she
said, "she's supposed to be in London. She left here on Tuesday."

"I dropped by on the off chance," said Javier Holt. "I've been
visiting one of our best clients—in Scotland. It was easy to return
this way. I am only glad my associate is so conscientious." His explanation struck Fern as over-elaborate, a little unnecessary. "It
must have been hard for her to tear herself away," he went on.
"The countryside is beautiful, this house clearly atmospheric. I
know how much that sort of thing appeals to Alison. Indeed, she
has told me how she appreciates the opportunity to stay here."

"Has she?" said Fern.

"Are you going to offer me a drink," he murmured, "or just a
cup of tea?" The mockery in his faint smile was only for her.

"Tea," said his hostess, smiling politely in response.

Mrs. Wicklow supplied the required beverage, giving Fern a
look that plainly indicated her readiness to rush to the rescue,
should Javier overstep the bounds of gentlemanly behavior. Will,
having decided the guest was boring, had already disappeared. Left
alone with Javier, Fern was increasingly aware of the faint menace
his presence exuded, the glossy exterior, the dead suavity of manner,

the teasing note that pinked her careful assurance now and then even while she guarded against it.

"*Do* you drink?" he inquired. "You always seem so demure, but I'm sure it's deceptive. You have the poise of a woman and the façade of a Victorian Miss. Most unusual nowadays."

"You know I drink," said Fern. "You've seen me with champagne, at the gallery. You weren't paying attention."

"I beg your pardon." The apology was elegantly insincere. "In fact, I was concentrating on you, not your glass. You interest me. The perfect daughter, managing her helpless father with a mixture of devotion and calculation. Do you ever misbehave, I wonder? You drink, but never too much. You have friends, but not boyfriends. Is that the picture?"

"Maybe," said Fern. "In any event, I don't see why I should show the picture—as you call it—to you, or any other stranger."

"Am I a stranger? Your father and I are involved in a business project together. That must elevate me to the level of an acquaintance, if nothing more."

"You are my father's acquaintance," said Fern, "not mine." She was aware that she had crossed the borderline into discourtesy, but she found it curiously exhilarating.

Javier seemed unoffended, his sleek address tinged only with amusement. "In that case," he said, "allow me the opportunity to progress into acquaintanceship. Had Alison been here, I would have taken her out to dinner. Let me take you instead."

"*Dinner?*" gasped Fern in astonishment. "You mean, in a restaurant?" She had shared fish and chips and takeaway pizza with male contemporaries but had never dined out on her own with any man except her father. But it was not simply her shock at receiving such an invitation which occasioned her reaction.

"Why not?"

"We're in the wilds of Yorkshire," Fern protested. "I don't know that there *are* any restaurants round here. Not serious ones, anyway." As a Londoner, she found it difficult to believe that good professional cuisine could exist outside the Home Counties.

"If that's your only objection—"

"No! I mean—why should you want to buy me dinner?"

"Find out."

Mrs. Wicklow objected at length, on various and delicate grounds; Will was baffled ("Anyone would think you were a real girl."). Fern, however, after her initial surprise, had made up her mind. Caution warned her to be wary, though she was not sure of what: she did not really think Javier would molest or even make a pass at her. She told Will she would use the occasion to pump him about Alison, but in fact she had succumbed to a compulsion that was only half curiosity. She found Javier Holt both repellent and intriguing: the very apprehension he aroused in her was a part of his obscure fascination. She dressed carefully for the outing, uncertain if she was a girl preparing for a date or a soldier girding herself for battle. Most of her best clothes were in London but she had a short black dress, starkly plain, brought to Yorkshire by chance when it was left in the car after collection from the cleaner's, and she helped herself to a cream silk jacket of Alison's that was hanging in the hall. She did not normally borrow clothing, even from friends, but she suppressed her scruples: impromptu dinners called for emergency measures.

"I don't know why you're making such an effort," said Will, watching critically as she applied mascara. "He's awfully old, and he looks pretty dull to me."

"I told you," said Fern, "he's Alison's boss. He may be involved in this business. Anyway, I'm curious."

"Curiosity killed the cat," said Will.

"I'm not a cat."

Javier drove her to an old-fashioned pub in a village whose name Fern never learned. The long white car purred down the country roads while a green evening spread slowly across the sky, chasing the fragile daytime moon. The pub was a squat stone building, thick-walled against the Yorkshire winters, low eaves overhanging windows already yellow with lamplight. Inside, there was a sparsely populated bar and a wood-paneled restaurant with some half dozen occupants. Javier chose a table in the darkest corner and ordered drinks. The waitress lit a candle: the tremulous flame steadied and burned tall between them, elongated by some mysterious updraft into a slender needle of fire. Javier's face, dimmed by its soft dazzle, resembled that of a Byzantine saint, a golden oval, unnaturally smooth, the curved nostrils and almond eyes defined by their own shadows.

"Why did you bring me here?" Fern asked, sampling the unaccustomed gin-and-tonic with would-be nonchalance.

"Why did you come?" he taunted her.

And: "Haven't I seen Alison wearing a jacket very similar to that?"

"Possibly," said Fern. "One cream-colored jacket looks much like another."

"Isn't it a little too big for you?"

"No," Fern replied. "I am too small for the jacket."

He laughed as if he were genuinely amused, but Fern thought she detected a wrong note in his laughter, a subtle discord, as if mirth were a convention to which he subscribed though he no longer experienced any real pleasure in it. The hidden threat that she sensed beneath his polished exterior seemed to her potentially far more deadly than all she knew of Alison Redmond, though she could not have said why. The ironic humor that stirred his mouth, the tiny glints that came and went in his eyes, were as ripples on a mask, treacherous signs of a concealed inhabitant. Her mind teetered on the verge of realization; but the menu was before her, and she must select her dishes, and sip her drink, and make conversation. Mindful of her excuses to Will, she asked him how long he had known Alison.

"Not long," he said, "in terms of pure acquaintanceship. Yet in some ways I feel I have known her all her life, maybe for many lives. I made the shape of a space, and she was there to fill it. I can sense her moods without having to learn them. Nothing she does surprises me." (I wonder? thought Fern.) "Some meetings are endowed with a certain fatality. They are part of something that was always going to happen, a minute but significant detail in a vast inscrutable design. Have you never felt that?"

For some reason, Fern thought of the Watcher. She said: "Such as your meeting with Alison?"

"Or yours with me, perhaps."

The gin-and-tonic was replaced by wine; starters were set before them. Javier savored his meal as a connoisseur, without the relish of pure appetite. Fern paid scant attention to what she ate and little more to what she drank. The burgundy was dark and heavy, clouding her brain with lazy potency. "What is our meeting supposed to signify?" she inquired at last.

"I am not yet sure," he admitted. "The design, as I said, is inscrutable, and it is given to none of us to see far ahead. Too often we must feel our way, blind as moles in the dark; yet even a mole will reach its allotted destination. You are at a time in your development when you must make certain choices. Oh, not courses or college or career: I am talking about something far more fundamental than that. There are many paths laid at your feet, and all are shrouded. You must choose blindly, like the mole. However, we are higher beings than such creepers and burrowers: we can think beyond our instincts, and glimpse fleeting intimations of fate. It may be that you are powerful. You must learn to use that power. I could teach you."

"*Power?*" Her pulse jumped so violently her throat locked; for several seconds she could not swallow her food. "What—what do you mean, power? What could *you* teach me?"

He did not miss the faint emphasis on the pronoun. "You have youth and beauty," he said lightly. "That is a kind of power. Youth, however, doesn't know how to wield its charms, and by the time it has learned they are already fading. I could give you the benefit of my worldly advice."

"Thank you," said Fern, relaxing a little, "but I don't think . . ."

"You don't require a mentor? That is a pity. Instinct is not always a good guide. The young are prone to trust unwisely, to believe wholeheartedly—but you know that, don't you, my demure and sensible Fernanda? You know too much . . . for your age." He switched from lightness to seriousness, from mockery to menace with a swiftness which bemused her. "You would not give your loyalty without due hesitation, without questioning, without examining the alternatives."

"What are you offering me?" she whispered.

"Education. There are so many things in life that even the best university cannot teach you." He might have been referring to the standard lessons of the passage to adulthood. Or he might not.

He changed the subject during the main course, turning to art and literature, asking Fern what she thought of Bosch and Dali, Milton and *Macbeth*. His rack of lamb was rare in the middle and she found herself watching him bite into the meat with elegant precision, white teeth shearing through raw flesh. If she met his eyes there were moments when she fancied the flecks of brilliance were actually moving, radiating out from the pupil with dizzying velocity. ("It's a dragon: don't look into its eyes—") It was an effort to pull her gaze away.

"Macbeth was an interesting character," she said, reckless with wine, "but I thought the witches were silly. Like something out of panto."

"Pantomime is for children," said Javier. "In the artificial world of the theater, children can laugh at Fear. It is a fairy-tale emotion, safe as play. But adults know that Fear is not a matter for laughter. Are you an adult yet, Fernanda? Pantomime makes game of the real world, but the world is not the less real for all that. Do you believe in witches?"

"Of course not," she said; but she was pale.

"Have you never dreamed of riding the wind, chasing the clouds, dancing like a sunbeam on the face of the water? Would you not wish to see the past in an empty mirror—or to hear the music of the stars—to pull down the rainbow—to call up the long-lost dead? You have imagination: use it, give it vitality and force. Turn it into your weapon, a weapon more powerful and more deadly than any of the clumsy engines invented by modern Man. And your beauty, Fernanda: have you considered it? Your perishable youth, your ephemeral bloom. You are as an early flower, a snowdrop before the spring—but you could turn that beauty into a thing of crystal and steel that would not fail or fade, unchanging, untouchable. Think of it—to be always lovely, always loved. Would you not have that if you could?" The lights surged in his eyes, but she avoided them. "Do you believe in witchcraft, Fernanda? Or will you still cling to your Fear?"

"Who are you?" she said.

But she knew. The knowledge had been there in her subconscious for some time, waiting for her to have the courage to confront it. She had known it when she questioned Ragginbone, several days earlier. *The aging process may be arrested . . . the hair may turn white or gray . . .* Behind the mask the temporary inhabitant smiled at her understanding.

"Who are you?"

The restaurant seemed to dissolve around them, and they were in the midst of a wide bare heath. Mist lay in the hollows; a few ghostly trees floated rootless above it. The stars shivered in the bitter twilight. A wind came down from stony heights, cutting her to the bone. The candleflame burned straight and still between them.

His smile shrank, and the paneled walls were back in place.

"I am Javier Holt," he said, with a blandness that was not meant to deceive. "Who else should I be?"

"I've heard your voice before," she said, "but it came from a mouth of stone. I assume that was why you sounded so different. You were less polite then too." She knew she ought to be afraid of him—she should be prudent and silent—but the wine was in her blood and an impulse stronger than wine drove her onward. It was not curiosity but need, a need for certainty and clarity, for an enemy she could categorize, for hard facts, obvious choices.

"You were not called," he said, and his tone was both sharp and soft.

"I came," she responded, "uncalled for."

"Very uncalled for." He forgot to smile, even in derision. "So you saw the rites of the circle. No matter. The Gifted have vivid dreams: let us leave it at that. As for who I am . . . what's in a name? I could be Jhavé and Jezreel, Azimuth and Azmordis, Ingré Manu, Babbaloukis, Xicatli. Does a name tell you the essence of the soul? Can you guess, just from a meaningless label, if I am wizard or demon, Man or Superman? Is a child to judge between Good and Evil, or with a name, a mere word, to set all things in their place?"

"I am not a child," said Fern carelessly, rising to the bait.

"We shall see. Find what you seek, bring it to me—Alison will take it from you if she can, so will others you may have encountered—but I will *not* take it, I will teach you its secrets and we will share in its power—"

That's why he told her not to summon me, thought Fern. He doesn't trust her and he wants to use me in her stead . . .

"Have you shaped a space for me to fill?" she asked abruptly. "Is that the fatality you talked of? Will *I* ever be able to surprise you?"

"Clever words." His lips thinned with brief scorn. "Surprise me? I doubt it. You are trammeled by your fears, unable to break free. You will need courage to choose. To hold power, or to give it away. To acquire vision, or to remain mole-blind." Obvious choices. "The challenge may be too great for you."

She lifted her chin: the sharp movement brought on a momentary vertigo. It dawned on her that she was very drunk. "I don't know," she said shakily. "I must . . . I must think." And: "Please take me home."

He might take her home—he might take her anywhere—but she had no means of escape. She had lost touch with Time and Place. When she looked around she was relieved to see they were still in the restaurant, though the barroom beyond was in darkness and both guests and staff seemed to have vanished. The candle-flame twitched and writhed as the last of the wax was consumed. There was no other light. She could not recall Javier paying the bill, but she supposed he must have done since he was preparing to leave. When she got to her feet the floor tilted. The candle flickered out and she thought she was back on the barren heath, under the icy stars, but Javier picked her up in his arms despite her murmured resistance and carried her to the waiting car.

She did not remember reaching home.

· V ·

ill woke her the following morning, banging on her bedroom door. He came in without awaiting her permission and deposited himself on the edge of the bed. "You were drunk last night," he announced accusingly. "That man had to carry you inside. I was awake; I saw him. Mrs. Wicklow was here too: she said she wouldn't go home till she knew you were all right. She's downstairs now, practicing her disapproving look. You'd better get up."

Fern said nothing, blinking through her headache. Fragments of conversation from the previous evening floated through her reviving consciousness, gradually coalescing into unfinished recollection. Fresh doubts, half-formed questions invaded her hangover, disturbing her few certainties; the throb in her skull made lucid reasoning impossible.

"How did it go with Javier?" Will demanded. "Did he try it on?"

"Did he try what on?"

"*Fern—!*"

"No he didn't. Not in that sense. He tried something, though. I think." She knew him for her enemy but his subtle words had upset her confidence: she found herself wanting proof that

Ragginbone was her friend. Instinct no longer seemed a safe guide. In a sudden nightmare vision she saw herself hemmed in with spidery nets, ethereal strands of treachery and untruth, with no clue how to pick her way between them. "Could you get me some aspirin?" she murmured.

"What did he try?" Will persisted. "Is he part of it—this witchcraft business, and the hunt for the key, and all that?"

"He's an ambulant," said Fern, sitting up cautiously to avoid aggravating the hammer-beat in her head.

"A what?"

"An ambulant. Don't you remember what Ragginbone said? A human being dominated—possessed—by something else. He's got the signs: prematurely gray hair, an unnaturally young face . . ."

"Are you sure?" Will's initial shock was tempered by doubt. "You really were awfully pissed."

"Of course I'm sure. He was the idol. They're the same. He all but told me. He's the Oldest Spirit, the one Ragginbone wouldn't name. The one we can't fight."

"Did he tell you *that*?"

"In a way," Fern said, struggling to arrange her memories in the right order. "He said he could be Jhavé or Jezreel . . . other strange names . . . Azimuth, Azmordis . . . I don't remember the rest. Anyway, it was obvious what he meant. He controls both the statue and the man, he is many people, many ancient gods—one Spirit with many faces. Just as Ragginbone said."

"Azmordis," mused Will. "That sounds like something else he mentioned. A valley or something. But I don't understand why Javier—or whoever—why did he tell *you* all this?"

"He wants to use me," said Fern. "He's another one who seems to believe I'm going to find the key. He doesn't trust Alison. He thinks . . ."

He thinks I have the Gift.

"What?"

"Nothing. *Please* get me some aspirin. Then maybe I'll be able to function properly."

The aspirin cleared her headache but not her head. In her new-found state of indecision, she rejected Will's suggestion that they should go looking for Lougarry and Ragginbone to report the latest developments; she wanted only to be alone, and to sift through the muddle in her mind. In the kitchen, she did her best to reassure Mrs. Wicklow, receiving support from an unexpected quarter. "Said t' wine was too strong for you, he did," the housekeeper conceded grudgingly. "Said as how it was his fault for ordering it, and he should have known better. Very apologetic he was, overdoing it if you ask me. Still, if you say he behaved like a gentleman . . ."

"Oh yes," said Fern, "he behaved."

He turned the restaurant into an empty heath under a frost-spangled sky, but he behaved.

Avoiding Will, she went for a walk, not up the hillside where she might meet unwanted allies but down toward the river. A way-ward path led her eventually along the bank and she sat down on the hump-end of a tree-root overlooking a bend in the Yarrow. A fallen sapling sprawled across the water and a shallow step where the riverbed dropped was bolstered with rocks, dividing the flow into a string of tiny falls. Beyond, the Yarrow ran suddenly dark and deep under pendant trees. Even in the green of summer it was a faintly sinister place, secretive and mysterious, leaf-shadows danc-ing over water-shadows, admitting only the occasional ray of sun-light to strike a spark from the surface of the river. Fern sat there for a long while, mulling over the discussions of the previous evening and her own uncertain conclusions, listening with semi-conscious ears to the chirping and piping of invisible birds and the many notes of the water bubbling over the rocks. Gradually her mind emptied of thought; birdsong and riversong flowed into her; as once before, on the walk to find Ragginbone, she felt herself blending with her surroundings, merging her still limbs and beating heart with the stillness of the trees and the earth's slow pulse. She was leaf and shadow, root and twig: the air breathed through her and the sap of all life ran in her veins. One of the unseen singers alighted nearby, a diminutive bundle of brown feathers with tilting tail and darting eye, as oblivious to her presence as if she were a part of the stump on which she sat. Later, a dragonfly zoomed downstream, a gleam of iridescence borne on whirring wings. Time slipped by unmeasured and unremarked.

It was late morning and the sun was climbing to its zenith when she finally stirred. In the vacant hours her fears and suspicions had not altered, rather they had been set aside: she now knew what she must do. She *had* to find the key. Ragginbone said she must find it, Javier believed she would find it, therefore the clue must be there, waiting for her alone: she could feel it, tantalizingly close, something glimpsed from the corner of her eye, a word she had misread, a question on the tip of her tongue. She remembered Alison summoning the spirits to the circle, her ruthless probing, her impatience, her abrupt dismissals. And the idol's scorn—Javier's scorn—the contempt of an all-powerful entity for the small and furtive. And suddenly, though she did not yet know the question, Fern knew whom she should ask.

Back at Dale House, Rollo and his two assistants had gone to the pub for a lunchbreak. "They've forgotten to lock the barn," said Will. "Let's take a look." But there was little to see. Now the *Seawitch* had been removed the building seemed to have lost its purpose: it was gloomy with shadows, hollow with emptiness, the loft hayless, the stepladder which had once provided access to it missing more than one rung. Planks of pale new wood were stacked against the wall with the frames for ground-floor windows which had yet to be made. There was a scattering of tools, a flurry of wood-shavings. A single ray of sunshine slanted down from an upper casement, a misty band of radiance in which motes of dust described slow spirals. And facing them, a rectangle of protective sheeting covered a tall plaque or painting which had evidently been secured to the brickwork. Mindful of the unicorn which Alison had trapped in a picture, Fern lifted the cover for a stealthy glance underneath. What she saw made her wrench the sheet from its anchorage regardless of caution. The arch was higher than she remembered, perhaps ten feet at the apex, the rusty iron ring looked polished, and flowers, not fungi, overhung the lintel—strangely repellent flowers that resembled speckled fingers and bloodred lips and eyes on stalks. A tiny bronze lizard crawled on the uneven boards. But initially, it appeared unmistakable.

"It's the Gate," Will whispered.

"Y-yes . . ."

"Ragginbone said it doesn't always look exactly the same."

"It ought to *feel* the same, though. It's *meant* to be the Gate—Alison *wants* it to be the Gate—but things aren't always what you want them to be. There's something else on the other side of that door, something . . ."

"It's a painting, ducks," said Rollo's voice behind them. "What they call a *trompe l'oeil*. That's French: deceives the eye. It should be kept covered to protect it from dust and wood-chippings."

"We know what a *trompe l'oeil* is," said Fern, recovering from a momentary shock. "What I don't understand is, why did Alison put it *here*? It doesn't look at all convincing against the bricks—and anyway, it's an *outside* door. Surely she should have chosen an inside one?"

"That's what I told her," said Rollo, his artistic sensibilities clearly stirred. "Have a window, I said. A section of formal garden—moorland in the snow—something like that. Huh! She had her own ideas. I told her it didn't make sense, but she wouldn't listen. Rather obstinate, the fair Alison. An exquisite creature, of course—for a hag." A sideways glance invited Fern's agreement, but she ignored it. "So palely shadowed! so thinly curved!

so porcelain-hard—so latex-soft! Alas, that her natural creativity should be stunted by an equally natural lack of vision. Poor bitch, she'd have told Michelangelo to paint the bloody floor."

"Did *you* paint that?" asked Will, indicating the *trompe l'oeil.*

"I did. To her requirements. Personally, it gives me the creeps."

"You did it very fast," said Fern.

"Nah." Amused, Rollo lapsed into his improbable cockney. "She h'ordered it monfs ago."

Fern said no more, but she looked pensive.

That afternoon, Mrs. Wicklow took a call from Alison to say she was delayed in London and would not return to Yorkshire till Saturday. *Javier's keeping her there,* Fern concluded privately. *She may not know he's an ambulant. It's probably easier for him to manipulate her if she believes her only contact with the Oldest Spirit is through the idol. He's keeping her in London because he wants* me *to find the key . . .*

The dark came late in the long summer evening, the lingering sunset gradually giving way to a green afterglow that hung over the skyline far into the night. Fern left Will in the kitchen and went upstairs early with a glass of milk and a plate of Mrs. Wicklow's handmade biscuits, claiming she wanted to study. Will, bemoaning the lack of a television in a routine manner, turned up the volume on the music center and plunged into a pile of John Buchan novels he had found in Ned Capel's library. In her room, Fern placed the milk and biscuits on the floor not far from the window, climbed into bed, and switched off the lamp. The pallor of the leftover day filled the room with a silvery dimness, softening the boundaries that distinguish one object from another, blending light and shade so that hard outlines were lost and everything was transformed by a gentle unreality. The curtains were drawn back and the plate and glass stood alone and somehow expectant in the edgeless glimmer that still came through the window. Fern sat very still, arms clasped around bent knees. She did not feign sleep, only patience, curbing the urge to whisper or call, summoning him only with the voice of her mind. Whether he would hear she did not know, but she was certain that he would see, and in the end he would come to her. The evening with Javier might have filled her with alarms and indecisions but since then, though she had not yet realized it, she had acquired an unthinking confidence in her own ability: she did not doubt that the shadows would respond to her need. She had been tempted to read with the aid of the bedside lamp but she was afraid even that small, artificial light might discourage her prospective visitor. She could picture him shrinking from the revelation of his ugliness or simply of his actual being, such as it was, an insubstantial thing half-phantom, half-memory, warped with suffering, misshapen in loneliness, blurred over the long centuries by the dim recollections of a twilit imagination. She had touched his hand with its assorted fingers but she had learned to distrust her senses: things were not always as solid as they felt, and the house-goblin, she believed, existed merely as a vague consciousness on the borders of reality, projecting an unsteady image into the penumbra of the living universe.

An hour or more passed slowly and the residue of day was almost gone when she saw it. A single digit, disproportionately long, crooked and knotted like a thin twig, reaching out from the darkness below the window. The shadows there seemed to have clotted into a small hunched shape, a dwarfling crouching out of the lastlight, both skulking and shy, lured by the homely tribute no one had left him for many hundreds of years. Presently, several other fingers joined the first, the tiny hand creeping spider-like toward plate and glass, the extended arm skimpy and knobbled about the elbow. Then the body followed the arm, an awkward, stealthy bundle scarcely visible even to Fern's dusk-adapted eye. She waited until he had sampled both milk and biscuits before she spoke his name. Her voice was softer than the wind's sigh, soft as nightfall, a sound for only a shadow to hear.

"Pegwillen."

For an instant the bundle froze and she feared he would slip away, scuttling back across the frontier into unreality; but he turned toward her and she saw the gleam of eyes long lusterless fixed on her face.

"I was told milk was what you would like," she said.

"Who . . . ?"

She thought he was afraid even to be talked about, to be mentioned in passing, to be looked for or called. So long unwanted and alone . . .

"Someone said it was the tradition."

"The children," he said in his whimper-thin, whisper-weak voice. "I thought the children had come back. Little Nan, and Peter, and Wat . . . always sly, Wat . . . and Joseph who was so noisy, and Tammy who was so quiet . . . I was sure they would come back one day."

"They are playing somewhere else now," said Fern very gently, as if it were a child to whom she spoke.

"The others grew up . . . and then there were more children, always more. But Tammy, and Peter, and little Nan . . . they never grew up. And there were no more children to come after." The Black Death, Fern deduced. That was what Alison was referring to. A whole family, maybe a whole village, wiped out in a matter of days. Involuntarily she stretched out her hand, and presently an attenuated finger slid into the cup of her palm and stayed there.

"They passed the Gate," she said, the words coming to her unbidden. "It was their time."

"Gone," whispered Pegwillen. "Peter, and Nan, my Nan . . . all gone . . ." His sad mumblings merged slowly into the night silence.

"What about the Capels?" Fern asked after a pause. "Three— or four—girls, and a little boy. They came much later, after this house was built. Do you remember them? They must have been children, to begin with."

"Not *my* children." The house-goblin evidently had various categories of childkind. "There were little girls, too many little girls, wearing too many clothes. All frills and curls and fuss. They were always stitching, drawing, baking . . . One of them had her own garden. I made the flowers grow for her, but she didn't see me. They never left me any food. I stole some cake once, but it tasted of sand." Fern smiled to herself. "Their faces got older, but not their clothes. Always girls . . ."

"And the boy?"

"He went away to school. Or maybe he ran away. He was very tall."

"When he came back," Fern prompted, "he was an old man, retired. He'd been at sea. Captain Capel. You remember."

Pegwillen made a faint noise, presumably affirmation.

"He had a dog," Fern went on, feeling her way. "He used to go walking with the dog, over the moors, and along the beach."

The finger she held seemed to flinch, curling into her palm. The word *dog* appeared to affect him adversely. "Sniffing," Pegwillen said. "It came sniffing in the night. It was outside, trying to get in. Then it was inside, in the house. *She* let it in. It looked like a dog, but it didn't *feel* like a dog. Then the other one came, and chased it away."

"The other one? You mean Lougarry?"

"I watched them fight," Pegwillen said, shivering at the recollection. "The other one never made a sound, even when the fangs tore its flank. It ran after *her* dog, down the stairs, into the dark, but I never heard the beat of its paws." One bat-ear twitched back and forward. "Tonight . . . I could hear the boy breathing, in spite of the noise-box. His hands turning the pages. I hear most things. If I listen. Sometimes, I forget to listen."

"You aren't afraid of Lougarry," said Fern, "are you?"

Pegwillen did not answer, but the small nugget of his deformed body seemed to shrink in upon itself, becoming still smaller with an unspoken terror. He's afraid of everything, she thought. Of seeing, and being seen, of newcomers, strangers, intruders, of evil powers, and good . . .

"But you aren't afraid of me," she said.

Pegwillen shook his head. "You were hiding," he explained, "like me. Only you're brave. I'm not brave."

"Yes, you are," Fern said resolutely. "We have to be brave together. Then we can defeat *her*, and she'll go away." In the dimness the sorrowful eyes appeared to brighten for a moment or two; then their gleaming waned, and the tiny hand clasping hers began to fade into insubstantiality. "Don't go," Fern pleaded, suppressing urgency. "I only need a *little* help from you. I'll do the rest. I'll deal with *her*. I promise."

The warmth nestling in her palm became finger once more; the dwindling shadow at her bedside thickened and darkened. "Help?" came the incredulous whisper. "From *me*?"

"Of course," said Fern. "You know this house, you know everyone who lived here, everything that happened. You've been here so long. You know where the captain put the key, the special key, the key he brought back from abroad. Do you remember it?"

"Stone," said Pegwillen unexpectedly. "Stone, and not stone. Sometimes I touch things. I touch them to find out what they are. I touched the key." He gave a curious shudder, not fear this time, mere reaction.

"Do you remember what he did with it?" Fern asked. "Try to remember."

"*She* came," said Pegwillen. "She wanted to know about furniture, and the statue that talks, only it was silent then, and keys. Old keys to old locks. She wanted to unlock doors, poke in drawers. Looking for secrets. He sent her away, but he was worried. I could see the worry in his face. He used to sit in the study, fiddling with the key. A luck-charm, he said, a sea-charm. The key to Davy-Jones's-locker." A flicker of bafflement altered his voice as he jumbled remembered words together. "Then someone came at night, on a machine that roared. Up and down, up and down on the road below. It tried to get in once—a thing in a helmet, with no face—but I made the window fall on its hand."

"Well done," Fern said warmly. "You *are* brave, you see."

She could not tell if Pegwillen was pleased but he continued his story without further prompting. "After that, the captain put the key—all the keys—in his desk. In the secret place."

"Where? Can you describe it exactly?" She sensed a faltering, a momentary hesitation, groped for suitable phrases to reassure him. "I must find the key. If I don't, *she* will. And . . . the captain left us this house, and everything in it. I have the right."

She felt Pegwillen clenching himself in an unaccustomed effort of concentration: the captain—the house—the right—the key. And *her*. Alimond, who called speech from a statue and clawed at his diminutive spirit with recollected pain. *Her*. He looked up, and saw the pallor of Fern's face, far clearer to his dim gaze than he to hers, a face still pure and spotless with the touch of first youth. Doubts vanished, leaving a kind of trust.

"It's behind the drawers," he said at last. "A hole. A slot. When you open the desk, there are two sets of drawers. Three on each side. On this side—" he indicated with his right hand "—the drawers are shorter. The top slides forward, so you can reach into the slot. That side fixed, this side moves. It's a clever desk. A desk for hiding things."

"What about the key to the desk itself?" Fern pursued. "What did he do with that?"

"Took it off the ring," said the house-goblin, "to lock away other keys. Then . . ."

"Then?"

"In his pocket."

"But they went through his pockets," Fern said. "The lawyers—executors—whoever. They must have done. Can you remember what he was wearing that day?"

"Jacket."

"What sort of jacket?"

"His favorite jacket. Old. The one he always wore."

"What color was it? What sort of material? Try to picture it. It's very important. I don't want to have to force the lock on the desk, even if that's possible. Alison would notice—and Daddy would have a fit."

Pegwillen's sad puckered face scrunched still further into a tight little mesh of dimly seen features. His obvious effort affected Fern painfully, yet he did not seem to be afraid anymore. "Wool," he pronounced. "It was made of wool. Thick. Rough to feel. Sort of speckledy."

"Tweed," said Fern.

"Leather elbows," Pegwillen went on. "Hole in pocket. I saw him pull it inside-out to look, and poke his finger through. He said: 'I must give this to Mrs. Wicklow to mend for me. It's a good jacket.' His favorite."

"Maybe," Fern said thoughtfully, "maybe he forgot."

Pegwillen did not comment, waiting in uncertain patience, still clutching her hand. He appeared quite real now, she thought, more goblin than ghost. She wondered if the very density of his being was an act of faith.

"I don't suppose you know what happened to the jacket after Great-Cousin—after the captain died?"

"Given away," said Pegwillen doubtfully. "All his clothes—given away."

Fern heaved a sigh that stretched into a yawn. "It sounds hopeless," she admitted. "I'll ask Mrs. Wicklow in the morning:

perhaps she can help. Still . . . I wonder if you could twist the lock with a screwdriver? Or . . . magic might do the trick. If I borrowed Alison's dragonskin gloves . . ."

"Not magic," said Pegwillen, startling her from a drift of hazy ideas. "Magic can seal and unseal, fix and unfix. But for a lock you must have a key. It is an ancient law."

"Like not crossing the threshold uninvited," Fern murmured. She was growing very sleepy. "*I* see. It's a kind of etiquette. A lot of magic seems to be about etiquette. I like that: it makes things more orderly, somehow. It's nice to think that even the powers of chaos are bound by courtesy if not by physics. Good manners are the one eternal constant . . ." She slid down into a horizontal position and her hand disengaged from his. "Don't forget . . . to finish your milk and biscuits . . ."

In minutes she was asleep.

As so often of late, she dreamed vividly. She was descending a narrow path between high cliffs. The path plunged steeply downhill, broken here and there into uneven steps, some three or four feet in height, but she seemed to be floating a little way above it, borne on an invisible dream-current which swept her along with ever-increasing speed. The path zigzagged and dived, dropping away beneath her into a falling tunnel; above, the cliffs leaned closer and closer together, squeezing the sky to a bright thread. Yet somehow she was conscious of neither vertigo nor fear, only acceptance. And then the thread vanished and she was spinning through a darkness illumined with fleeting gleams of phosphorescence, plummeting faster than a swooping eagle to an unguessable depth. She emerged abruptly into strong light in a valley of rock that seemed to be at the bottom of the world. Her speed slowed to a gentle drift above a chain of terraced pools, some as wide as lakes, stained extraordinary colors by the minerals that contaminated them. One was a pure turquoise shading to emerald, another venom-green, another a clear scarlet, with faint steams hovering over the water at the far end. But every pool was cupped in stone, and precipices of stone walled the valley on either side, natural bastions, topped with sheer cliffs, climbing at last to mountain-ranges too high and remote to measure. The sun was sinking slowly into a cleft of sky directly ahead. A long-legged bird waded in the scarlet lake, drinking the ominous water. It was bigger and brighter than a flamingo, with the beak of a raptor, a glittering crest, and feathers that caught the sun's fire. It reminded her of a picture she had come across in a book of folktales when she was a child. It's a firebird, she thought, a phoenix. I've seen a phoenix— She had long forgotten she was only dreaming. The bird beat its wings, ascending in a swirl of vapor toward the clear air, shedding a glimmer like falling sparks in its wake. She saw no other living thing.

Then abruptly the landscape changed. The lakes were left behind, the valley floor ceased descending and leveled out into sudden fertility. She was in a garden. An impossible jungle-garden, flourishing unwatered, webbed with serpentine trees, mazed with pathways, tendriled with creeping plants. At first it appeared to her merely a labyrinth of convoluted vegetation but gradually she realized its wildness was artificial, the jungle stylized, every curl of every leaf had its own secret significance. There were no birds but many insects, moths marked with the vivid hues that denote poison, spiny caterpillars, hornets with three-inch stings. She saw a mantis as long as her arm and a dragonfly with the head of a lizard. The few flowers reminded her of those growing over Alison's *trompe l'oeil* door in the barn. But it was not till she saw the building that she knew she ought to be afraid. From a distance it looked little bigger than a folly, a circular edifice with many pillars and the fretwork of a broken dome curving overhead. She could not have said why it was frightening but she reached for her elusive fear as a fainting man snatches at consciousness. She was being carried inexorably toward it, and she sensed it was the focus

and center of the valley and inside it something waited which had
called her out of sleep, into dream, and it was too late now to resist. The door grew larger as it approached, towering upward until
it became a vast portal with columns marching on either hand,
and then she was sucked into the temple, and it was huge, bigger
than an amphitheater, bigger than a stadium, and the fingers of its
fractured roof enclasped the whole sky. Her feet touched the
ground; she saw the figures seated round the walls and the single
idol facing her, larger than the rest; but they were all the same.
The lamps were unlit, the sun occluded; in front of the main idol
the hearth was cold. Fiery clouds streaked the sky-roof.

"Come to me," said the idol. "Light the blue fire. It is time.
Time. *Time!*" The voice boomed around that empty place, rever-
berating from a hundred other mouths; yet it was familiar.

"Who are you?" said Fern. Her own voice was a thin slight
sound, like the fluting of a lost bird.

"Do you not know me? I am Azmordis. (Azmordis. Azmordis.)
Come to me!"

And against her will, against her fear, she heard herself echoing: *"Azmordis."*

She took a step forward, and woke up.

The name was still on her lips, the air vibrated with it. She
knew immediately that she was alone in the room, yet she felt as
alert and startled as if she had been jerked from slumber by a cry
of warning or the jangle of an alarm bell. Perhaps it was her own
cry which had roused her, wrenching her from some other place
back into the earthly night. She looked at her clock: the green
glimmer of hands pointed to ten past three. She got up without
switching on the light, located the empty plate and glass and
picked them up, intending to take them downstairs to the kitchen.
She felt restless and uneasy, unable to lie down again and relax
back into sleep. Her dream—if dream it was—still seemed too
close for comfort. Familiar with the house now, she moved easily

down the gloomy passageway to the landing, feeling for the top-most stair with her foot. At the first bend she slowed. There was no sinister shaft of radiance emanating from the drawing room, but nonetheless she thought the hall was not quite as dark as it should have been. With no windows it was normally almost pitch-black, yet as she drew nearer she could make out the shape of the boss on the banister at the stair's foot, and the dim outline of the drawing room door, standing slightly ajar. It ought to be shut; she and Will always left it shut. Of course, Mrs. Wicklow would have opened it during the day, and they might both have forgotten to close it, or not closed it properly, allowing it to creak open a little way, as doors in old houses sometimes do. It seemed to her that the glimpse of the room beyond showed a paler shade of dark-ness, discernible only to the nocturnal eye; but she was not cer-tain. She didn't want to go and look. But she knew she must. Setting down the plate and glass, she stole across the hall.

She pushed the door wider without actually entering the room and saw immediately that the curtains were drawn together, ex-cluding the possibility of a light-source from outside. The hinges emitted a muted groan which sounded very loud in the night still-ness; the door swung back further. She could see the fireplace, like a lipless black mouth, with the twin fangs of the firedogs standing up from the lower jaw. Beside it squatted the idol on its plinth. And there, as she had feared, as she had known, was the origin of that dim pallor, there in the stony eyes that were no longer opaque but showed a translucent glimmer, the crepuscule of some remote unwavering fire, subtle as the wash of starlight from the outer reaches of the Milky Way. "Azmordis," she mur-mured automatically, and the glow strengthened and grew, filtering threads of light from the surrounding darkness and drawing them inward, creating a radiance that was not true light but only were-light, two pale chill flames that could not warm or burn. The stone had waned to a thin film over double cores of dazzle, a fire that came from both within and beyond the receptor, summoned at its spoken name. Fool! Fern cursed herself. You called him. *You* called him. Desperation made her resourceful: she flung out her hand in the gesture of dismissal that she had seen Alison use. "Begone!" she cried, and the archaic word called another from the recesses of memory, a command in an unknown tongue that hissed on the air like a drawn blade. A shiver ran through her that seemed to come from the heart of the Earth or the back of the stars, a shiver of pure power. The two flames shrank, receding over an incalculable distance to unblinking pinpoints; the carved eyes began to cloud back into stone. Fern slammed the door on the room and its occupant and ran up the stairs, stumbling in the blindness of returning dark.

Behind her noiseless paws padded to the bottom step; the yellow orbs of the she-wolf watched her go. You invited me in, said Lougarry's thought. Have you forgotten?

But Fern did not hear.

"By the way," Fern said to Mrs. Wicklow at breakfast, "do you know what they did with Great-Cousin Ned's clothes?"

"Sent to charity," she responded promptly. "I packed 'em up myself. He had some fine suits, old, mind you, but tailor-made, the way suits always used to be. T' new stuff, mass-produced, it's good enough, but t' quality isn't t' same. They don't last t' same, either. It would have been a pity to waste decent clothes. Waste not, want not. There's many in want of a good suit."

I suppose we must try a screwdriver on the desk lock, Fern thought. Or smash it somehow. If only Alison doesn't come back too soon.

"I just kept t' one jacket." Mrs. Wicklow's words intruded on her speculation. "Mr. Capel—your father—said I should take what I wanted, so t' lawyers told me; but I just kept t' one."

"Which one?" said Fern.

"Just an old thing, tweed, for my husband to wear doing t' gar-den. What's got you so interested?"

"I think—" Fern hesitated "—the key might be in the pocket. The key to that desk upstairs."

"Whatever made you think that?"

"It was his favorite jacket, wasn't it? It's a logical place for him to keep his keys." Will, diverted from his cereal, glanced sharply at her. "Well, it might be, anyway."

"Wasn't nothing in t' pockets," said Mrs. Wicklow. "Nothing but a hole, leastways. How did you know that was his favorite?"

"Old men always have favorite tweed jackets," Will improvised, leaping unexpectedly into the breach. "It's a well-known fact."

"Would your husband mind if we looked at it?" said Fern. "The key might—it might have gone through the hole."

"He'll be in t' garden now," said his spouse. "Go down and ask him. Third house from end of t' village."

"Have you had some inside information?" Will inquired as they walked down the road from Dale House.

"I talked to the house-goblin," Fern explained. "The key we want should be in the desk, in a sort of secret drawer behind some other drawers. All we need now is the desk key."

"It's like one of those Russian dolls," Will said. "A drawer be-hind a drawer, a key to a key. We have to work our way through the layers."

After a pause he added: "Shouldn't we look for Lougarry? We might need some backup."

"She isn't around."

"Yes, she is," said Will. "She's just staying out of sight. She has been since Javier Holt came." His sister did not comment and he continued cautiously: "You've been a bit strange since then too."

"I've been trying to understand all this," Fern said slowly. "If you accept it, the next thing is to understand. I don't trust Javier: the Oldest Spirit is too powerful. I couldn't possibly trust Alison:

she's too hungry. But I'm not sure if I trust Ragginbone either: he's harder to work out, and I don't know what he's after. He told me he had no idea what to do with the key, if and when he gets hold of it. That might be true—and it might not. Either way, finding the key won't be the solution. It will only change the problem."

"Then why find it?"

"Because I have to," she said. "I *have* to."

Mr. Wicklow was discovered bent double over a vegetable patch, shirt-sleeved and waistcoated but minus his jacket. His face was apple-red from effort, heat, and high blood pressure, but he straightened obligingly when finally brought to appreciate what they wanted and led them into a greenhouse where a battered hunk of tweed hung from a hook at the back. "T' jacket," he said briefly.

"Thank you," said Fern.

"Check the pockets," Will hissed impatiently.

"Not the pockets," she said. She was feeling her way around the lining close to the hem, pressing the worn silk against the tweed to detect any small hard object trapped in between. When her questing fingers found something her brother saw the change in her expression.

"Is it there?"

"Something's there."

She located the pocket with the hole and maneuvered the object as near to it as possible. Then she pushed her hand through to reach it, tearing the jacket still further in the process, finally extricating a small brass key.

"Eureka!" Will said.

But Fern felt no sense of exultation. Instead, even there, in broad daylight, sheltered from the curious by smudged glass and tomato plants, she experienced a heightened awareness of danger, a feeling that hidden watchers were near, very near, behind the leaves, between the trellises, squinting through chinks in the garden wall. She had a sudden vision of red eyes peering into the smoke to find her, and the groping gaze of something with more than mortal perception, seeking for a peephole through which to spy on her. She had found the missing link, but even as her hand closed upon it she knew that she was too close to her goal, too close for comfort, too close for safety. As once or twice before she was conscious of fear as something outside her, a shadow at her back breathing coldly on her nape. It took an effort of will for her to leave the greenhouse.

"Find what you wanted?" asked Mr. Wicklow.

"Yes, we did," said Fern, glancing round warily for possible eavesdroppers. "It had fallen through inside the lining. I'm afraid I tore the jacket a bit more getting it out."

"Doesn't matter," he said. "I don't keep nothing in t' pockets."

They thanked him suitably and set off back through the village. There were a few people about: a gaggle of tourists with a map, on their way to somewhere else, a brace of hikers, a local or two whom the Capels knew well enough to nod to. Although it was hot a heavy haze bleared the lower sky; it seemed to be creeping down over the moors, enclosing them within a shrinking horizon. Beyond the village the road looked empty and shelterless: the twenty-minute walk home lengthened into a long and lonely trek. The bridge over the Yarrow was still in sunlight but as they climbed higher the haze thickened into a mist which arched above them, fading out the sun, stealing the summer warmth. They moved in a pale, shadowless world, talking rarely and almost in whispers. "Could someone *make* this weather?" Will asked nervously.

"Maybe."

"Who?"

Not the Old Spirit, Fern thought, avoiding his name even in her mind. He wants me to find the key—the real key—and then he'll take it from me. It might be Alison. If she has that kind of power . . .

It was a disturbing *if*.

"Maybe it's just a mist. Hot sun on damp ground. Maybe it has nothing to do with us at all."

"*Is* the ground damp?" said Will.

And, after a few more yards: "It didn't rain last night."

They walked on in silence. The mist drew closer, hugging the verges, obliterating even the spectre of the sun. Even though they knew they could not miss their way they felt disorientated, cut off from familiar landmarks, imprisoned in a white tunnel where time and distance seemed to lose all meaning. The chattering voice of the Yarrow was stilled; they could hear neither bird nor grasshopper. When the sound began it was distorted, so they could not tell if it came from near or far: a whining roar that appeared to be swooping down on them from somewhere up ahead.

"It's that motorbike," said Will.

"Stay on the road," said Fern. "I'm going to get out of sight. I'll meet you at home."

"You'll get lost—"

But she was already gone, veering off the road to their left, leaving the mist frayed into shreds in her wake. An instant later the bike appeared, materializing suddenly only yards away, a dark snarling monster hurtling toward him without braking, without slowing, heading straight for the verge as if Will were not there, blocking its route. He glimpsed the blank glare of the visor, the leather hand twisting at the throttle. Then he flung himself aside even as the bike leaped into the air, clearing the verge, almost taking flight, while he was rolling on the grass half-stunned by the wind of its passage, feeling the heat from the exhaust skim his face. He heard it land without check or falter on the uneven ground and roar on up the slope with a tenacity beyond that of any normal machine. He tried to cry out in warning, fighting for breath: Fern! He's coming! *Fern—*

But Fern had already heard. Climbing the hillside at a run which tugged at her muscles and sent her pulse into a crescendo

she had identified the direction of pursuit, the increased stri-
dency of a lower gear on the ascent. There was no time to realize
it was impossible: over her shoulder she saw the bike emerge
through thinning fog, bouncing effortlessly from tuft to tuft, gaining on her so rapidly she knew any attempt at evasion was useless. She struggled on automatically though a stitch stung at her
ribs, looking neither back nor forward anymore but only down, at
the heather that clawed her legs and hindered her progress. The
bike was almost on her now.

   She did not see the obstacle in her path until she was within a
couple of yards of it. Some instinct made her glance up—the
awareness of a presence, a call in her mind—and there he was.
His body seemed to have coalesced from the mist around him, a
creature of uncertain substance whose diaphanous mane and tail
appeared to mingle with the brume as if the flowing hair did not
end but melted into vapor. The half-grown horn, no longer vel-
veted, stood up in a column of twisted bone, glowing with a wan
luster, the point sword-sharp, needle-fine. The wild dark eyes met
hers with an unmistakable message. She touched the curved neck
and it felt warm and real, summoned the last of her strength ready
to vault onto his back. But somehow she was astride at the
thought, without conscious movement, her hands twined in his
mane, her legs clinging to his flanks. The clamor of the approaching engine was all around them, so the air throbbed with it, and
the faceless helmet was rushing upon her, sleek and streamlined
in its gleaming roundness, terrifying in its anonymity. She knew a
horse could never outstrip a motorbike, but in a flurry of mist and
tail he had sprung away, and the threatening engine faded, and the
shifting fogs swallowed every echo of pursuit, and they were gal-
loping alone in an unseen world. The windhorse ran so smoothly
she was scarcely jolted, though she knew the terrain must be
rugged. She could see nothing of the ground beneath the flying
hooves, nothing of the landscape on either hand, yet she felt their

pace accelerating, faster, faster, until she imagined the turning Earth could no longer keep up and they were borne away on an unstoppable wind toward a region beyond the stars. She might almost have fancied she had strayed into another dream had her sense of reality not been accentuated to the point where she lived every moment with a peculiar intensity. An aeon of time flowed away in a few swift seconds, the mist drew back, and what she saw next was something she would remember all her life.

Hillside and moorland had vanished. She was on a beach, but not the windswept Yorkshire beach near her country home: this was a beach at night, and it seemed to go on forever. The shore stretched ahead of her in an arc so vast that her vision could not compass it; the endless crescent of sand gleamed with a dim sheen as if scattered with crystal dust. To her left, jagged shapes reared up, higher than the highest mountains, wrapped in a velvet darkness which smothered all light. And above and to her right soared a sky so thronged with stars that there was scarcely space for any blackness in between, the nearest clusters too dazzling to look at long, the farther ones still bigger and brighter than any stars seen from Earth, and beyond them remoter constellations like grains of diamond, and the glimmering smoke of whirling galaxies, and the contrails of comets, and fire-tasseled meteors plunging downward into a sea that danced and sparkled with more than reflected light. There was no visible horizon: starry sky merged into starry sea at a distance beyond guess. More than that, the sea itself seemed to be made of stars: the far-off wave-crests flickered with living fire, and the foam hissed on the sand before it withdrew, leaving a spindrift of sparks twinkling and fading in its wake. The windhorse had slowed to a canter, and Fern saw the ebbing water break into a thousand scintilla about his hooves, while a spray like silver fireflies was thrown up behind them. And as she looked down she noticed that the horse himself had become faintly luminescent, and his single horn shone as if tipped with flame. Even her own bare arms had acquired a pearly luster. There was no sound but the waves breaking and behind that, like a distant harmony too complex, or too simple, for the ear to comprehend, came the rumor of an immeasurable universe: the murmuring of infinite waters and the susurration of a billion icy fires. It seemed to her that even the air smelled of stars, a clean, sharp, silvery smell that pricked the lungs with its very purity. Her mind cleared: she forgot the key, the chase, and all the chaos and clutter of her existence. There was only the magic of that ride, and the long line of the beach lying ahead of them, like a thin curving blade dividing the starlit cosmos from the mountains at the world's rim. And somehow she knew that she was the only mortal who had ever been there since Time began, and wherever she went after, the essence of that place of stars would remain inside her forever.

Somewhere far out to sea, maybe ten miles, maybe a million miles, a shooting star plummeted into the water, dissolving into a lake of glitter which broke into vast rings, spreading wider and wider, until at last they reached the shore as nothing more than ripples lapping on the sand. The unicorn quickened his pace once more, and Fern felt the wind of their speed ruffling her short hair, and she saw the flickering limbs below disappear into a blur, and the stars became streaks of light and the sand flew beneath them, and then the beach was gone and she was emerging from the mist onto the upland moor, and there was the scent of summer and a lark rising into an unclouded sky. She dismounted at the top of a slope and saw below her the familiar path down the hillside and the garden of Dale House. The position of the sun told her it must be late afternoon. When she looked round again there was only grass and heather: the unicorn had gone, and of the mist there was no sign.

· VI ·

Will picked himself up after the motorbike had passed, listening to the rising howl of its engine as it mounted the slope, waiting for he knew not what—for the motor to cut, for his sister's scream—feeling helpless and furious and afraid. We should have brought Lougarry, he thought, and he called her name, with little hope, hearing his voice hampered and deadened by the surrounding wall of mist. Then the note of the engine changed, faltering rather than stalling, but there was no cry, no sound from Fern, only the screech of sudden revs, and the altered pitch of a downhill progress. He's coming back, Will concluded, looking in vain for a weapon, a stone to throw, a stick to thrust, anything to shift the rider off balance and bring the machine to a halt. And then there was Lougarry beside him, and he was sobbing with relief, but she did not heed him: she was crouched low with her ears flat against her skull, making her whole body lean and aerodynamic as a missile. The sound of the engine swelled to a great roar and the forewheel appeared out of the mist in midair, as the bike, propelled from a hump in the ground, leaped across the verge back to the road. At the same

140

moment Lougarry sprang. She hit the rider while his machine was still airborne, knocking him sideways, out of the saddle, his booted feet catching at the chassis so that bike and rider crashed onto the road together, with the wolf on top. The wheels still spun, the engine shrieked in protest. Will ran round and switched off the ignition. The biker appeared to be sprawled on the tarmac; Lougarry's bared fangs hung over him, her claws dug into his black leather chest. But the chest caved inward at the pressure and there was only leather beneath her feet, and the studded gauntlets shriveled into vacancy, and the helmet rolled away and rocked to and fro, to and fro on the empty road.

"What happened?" asked Will blankly, but Lougarry only stared in answer, and he could not read the thought behind her eyes as easily as his sister did. "Where's Fern?"

Lougarry moved away from the discarded garments and began to trot up the hill, her muzzle lowered and swinging from side to side. Will followed. When they were some way up the slope the she-wolf stopped, exploring the ground in a circle as though seeking for a scent that was lost. This time, when she met his eyes, he understood. "Where did she go?" he said, questioning himself as much as his companion. "She can't have just disappeared—can she?"

He called her for a while, wandering up and down, with Lougarry at his heels listening for any sound beyond the range of human hearing; but there was no response. Eventually, they went back to the road. The mist was clearing and a passing driver had stopped to examine the motorbike. "Looks nasty," he said to Will. "Can't think where t' lad's got to. Funny thing, him going off like that, leaving his gear and all. Happen he got a bad knock on t' head. Did you see anything?"

"No, we didn't."

"We? Oh—you and t' dog. Impressive-looking animal. Would that be some kind of Alsatian?"

"Sort of," said Will.

At the man's insistence, he helped haul the bike to the roadside—"Otherwise we'll be having another accident"—though he was anxious to get home in case Fern should somehow have returned there. Then the driver went into Yarrowdale to report to the proper authorities and Will half walked, half ran up to Dale House.

But Fern had not come back.

Will spent the afternoon roaming fretfully from room to room, unable to settle to anything or to decide on a definite course of action. "Fern's gone for a walk," he told Mrs. Wicklow. "She vanted to be alerne." Mrs. Wicklow seemed unworried, objecting solely on the grounds that she had made too much lunch—"But there, I daresay you can manage her share"—and had not provided the wanderer with sandwiches. She inquired in passing if they had found anything in Ned Capel's old jacket; Will's answer was carefully casual. "There was a key in the lining," he said. "It could be the key to the study desk. We'll try it sometime." And, changing the subject: "Has Alison phoned? Or Dad?" But no one had rung.

Mrs. Wicklow left early for a shopping expedition to Whitby and Will, his usual appetite seriously impaired, ate only half his lunch and none of Fern's. Lougarry polished off what remained. He did not know whether to take heart from the wolf's demeanor: wild animals were always hungry, he reflected, and even if they felt anxiety it could not be allowed to detract from their first priority. When she had cleaned her dish she slipped through the kitchen door; Will ran after her in time to see her leaping the garden wall at a low point and speeding up the hill, an elusive streak of movement disappearing amongst the heather-tussocks. It was clear he was not meant to follow. He turned back into the house, feeling somehow deserted. He would almost have been grateful for the sight of Rollo and his henchmen; but the builders did not come at the weekend. Upstairs, he spent some while in profitless contemplation of the writing desk, an impregnable hunk of Victorian mahogany which looked solid enough to withstand assault and battery with ease. He fetched a species of skewer from the kitchen and tinkered with the lock, but desisted at last for fear of damaging it so the key would not turn. Then he went up to the top floor and stood outside Alison's room, but the door was immovable, the handle gave him pins and needles, and anyway, he and Fern had learned all its secrets, or so he hoped. Back downstairs, he ventured cautiously into the drawing room. "You know something," he accused the idol, "don't you?" But the idol just sat there, silent as the stone of which it was made. "Jhavé," he said, "Jezreel—" trying to remember the names Fern had mentioned, able to recall only those which resembled Javier. The stone did not stir. Will went out, shutting the door, and returned to the kitchen, where he sat down at the empty table, plunged in depression and doubt.

Fern found him there, when she came down the path from the moors, and through the garden to the back door.

"Where've you been?" he said, greeting her with a relief far removed from his customary fraternal nonchalance. "How did you get away?" Giving her no time to answer, he went on to pour out his own adventure. "Lougarry came—I called her and she came—she stopped the bike. She sprang and knocked it over, but when it hit the road the leathers sort of shrank and the helmet went flying and there was no one there, no one. And then we went looking for you in the fog but I think the scent ran out and Lougarry couldn't follow, so we came back here. I've been waiting for hours."

"Where's Lougarry now?" Fern interrupted.

"She went out. I don't know where."

"She's gone for Ragginbone. Mrs. Wicklow?"

"Shopping. And there's no word from Alison."

"Good. We must open the desk now, before anybody else shows up. When I find the key I'll know what to do with it, but I don't want other people trying to take it from me or influence me. Come on."

Will ran after her up the stairs, thinking that although his sister had always been a decisive person this air of reckless determination was something new. It was as if she sensed instinctively that she had chosen the most perilous option, yet she was resolved to press on regardless, ignoring both instinct and common sense, evading any thought of danger. Will, never the prudent one, knew he must be prudent for her; but she was beyond restraint.

"What happened to you?" he reiterated as they reached the study.

"I met the windhorse," she said. "The one in the picture. He looked more like a unicorn this time. He was faster than the bike." She was not yet ready to talk about the silver beach at the edge of the stars.

"But you were gone so *long*."

Fern was jiggling the key in the desk lock: haste made her clumsy and it wouldn't slide right in. "What were you saying about the biker?"

"He fell on the road," Will recapped, "and Lougarry was on top of him, but his clothes just disintegrated and there was nothing inside. The helmet rolled away—it looked horrible, as if his head had been cut off—but it was empty. I've been trying to work it out. D'you think he could have been another kind of receptor, like the idol—a puppet with no strings, controlled by somebody a long way off?"

"Maybe." Fern sounded dissatisfied. "Not a receptor, though. The Old Spirits use receptors but I'm sure Alison can't—and Alison was controlling this thing, whatever it was. I saw her talking to him—it—in the village. I don't like the sound of it, but—" She broke off as the key clicked home, turning it both ways with an unsteady hand before the lock yielded at last. Then she unfolded the lid and saw the two sets of miniature drawers, even as Pegwillen had described, half-hidden behind a disorder of letters opened or ignored, used envelopes and dehydrated Biros. Fern removed an old ink-bottle and a packet of staples from on top of the right-hand set and took hold of the carved edge, pulling it toward her. It moved easily, sliding forward so the Capels could plainly see the hollow cavity behind the drawers. Will reached out and then drew back, conscious of his sister's tension and the importance she attached to this moment. The light did not penetrate far into the slot; if there was anything inside it could not be seen. Fern explored it by feel; her fingers touched not the cold metal she had been hoping for but paper. For an instant her heart sank. Then she extracted a brown envelope, bulging and awkward with its contents. "Keys," she said on a long sigh. Keys.

There was a big old-fashioned keyring with half a dozen keys, presumably to the various bedrooms and perhaps the chest in the attic. And one other, not made of metal, smaller than the rest and heavier, much heavier. Fern removed it from the ring and for a second it felt so heavy that the weight seemed to be dragging her down, toward the floor, through the floor, down and down into some deep core of gravity; then she closed her hand upon it and suddenly it was light again, a key like any other. "Let's see," said Will, and she showed him, strangely reluctant, as if the mere act of showing was a betrayal of a secret which she alone must keep. It was simple in design, almost crude, yet laden with ancientry, as though the great tides of ocean, the shadows of the treasure vault, the greedy, indifferent or cunning fingers which had handled it, even the cold touch of the mermaid long ago, had all left their sweat, their chill, their mystery, and their darkness encumbering it like barnacles, staining it with years beyond count. To Fern's surprise it felt warm, like a sun-warmed pebble, and it seemed to take heat from her palm, so that presently she fancied its substance began to change, its opaque blandness thinned, and glints of brilliance came and went deep within the stone. This is a fragment of another universe, she told herself, the key to the Gate of Death; and a sudden awe came over her, so that she felt giddy from the hugeness and the power of this little thing, and she and Will and the room appeared to be spinning around it like leaves around the eye of the whirlwind. She looked up and saw the same awe and vertigo in her brother's face, and his hand clutched hers or hers clutched his, until the study grew stable again and the aura of what she held had diminished.

"Do you suppose it affected Great-Cousin Ned like this?" Will wondered at last.

"Maybe it's because we know what it is," Fern suggested, "and it responds to our knowing."

And we respond to whatever it knows, she thought, and the heat of the stone seemed no longer to be drawn out of her but flowing into her, starting with a tingle in her palm which penetrated skin and flesh until it reached her bloodstream and went coursing through her veins in a sudden fiery rush, threading its way through sinew and bone-marrow, so she felt illumined into transparency by the shock of its passage, suffocating from the glow in her chest. She visualized her heart pulsing like an incandescent ruby through the flimsy mantle of her body, even as she had seen Alison's heart glowing in the mud-field of her dream. We respond, she thought; no, I respond. *I respond.* "Are you all right?" said Will. "You look a bit flushed, and your eyes are shining like a cat's in the dark."

"Here," said Fern, thrusting the key into his hand. "You take it. I can't—it does something to me."

Will took it, slightly startled, apparently untroubled by its touch. He slid it into the pocket of his jeans and pulled his T-shirt over it for good measure. "What now?" he said.

I ought to know, Fern rebuked herself. I was so sure that when I found it I would know what to do . . .

And then, sudden and incongruous, the doorbell rang. It was

no harsh electronic trill but a deep chime that resounded throughout the house: ding dong, ding dong. Everyone from the vicar to
Lougarry always used the back door; only Alison would come in
by the front, and she had Robin's key. Anyway Fern, alert for the
sound of her car on the drive, had heard nothing. Ding dong, it
persisted, a summons of ruthless normality, insistent, commonplace. Threatening. Normality could not be ignored.

"I'll go," said Fern. "You clear up here. Shut the desk and lock it."

"What do I do with the desk key?" Will demanded.

"Swallow it," said his sister.

She ran downstairs and approached the front door with trepi-
dation, nursing a slender hope that the visitor, obtaining no response, might already have been discouraged. But the bell rang
again: ding dong, loud in the quiet hall. Conditioned by a lifetime
of good manners, Fern opened the door.

"You," she said.

It was the Watcher. His hood was pushed back and his
brindled hair stuck out in assorted wisps and tufts, like straw on a
scarecrow. Lougarry was at his side. Standing on the doorstep he
resembled more than ever a wandering tramp, vaguely disreputa-
ble, mildly insane, a shaggy man with his shaggy mongrel roaming
the countryside in search of a free supper or a lost ideal. But the
eyes in his thin leather face were bright and shrewd, green in the
late sunshine.

"Why did you ring?" said Fern, taken off guard by the for-
mality of his arrival. "Lougarry always comes to the back door. It's
usually open."

"I cannot come in," Ragginbone said, "unless you ask me."

She opened her mouth to welcome him, and then shut it
again. There was comprehension in his look. Between them, the
threshold marked an invisible barrier, a boundary he could not
cross uninvited. Protecting her.

"What would happen," she asked, "if you just—stepped

across?" She pictured a forcefield, a thunderbolt, instant annihilation. None of them seemed feasible.

"I would have broken one of the ancient laws," he responded gravely. "That would not be tolerated. Retribution would come soon. Even the Old Spirits fear such transgression."

And I invited Javier in, thought Fern, when he came on Thursday. *I* invited him. And now I dare not ask Ragginbone . . . "We have the key," she said, meeting him eye to eye.

"Are you sure it's the right one?"

"It burned me," said Fern. "There was no mark, but it burned me *inside*. It didn't harm Will, though."

"He's too young. Even if he had the Gift, it could not be stirred. The touch of the Lodestone wakes its own power—when you are ready."

Fern ignored the implication. "Would it restore yours," she asked bluntly, "if I gave it to you?"

"It might."

"Is that why you want it?"

"Perhaps." He sighed. "When I was young and hungry I used power for selfish ends, as so many do. Then I discovered the seduction of benevolence, and playing at God to dispense justice and punishment. Only when I was powerless did I try to do good for its own sake—or for mine: who knows?—and by then there was little left I could do at all. I am a Watcher; action is for others. Still, I have dreamed of being able to act again." Unexpected mirth wrinkled his face, twinkled in his eyes. "I am only human, as the saying goes, for all my longevity. What a wealth of meaning in an idle cliché! I am only mortal, desperate, urgent. Spirits have endless ages in which to do nothing, if they so choose, but humans have death to hurry them on. Near or far, the end is always in sight. We have no time to stand and stare. Make your choice, Fernanda. Talking of time, you are wasting yours. If you don't give me the key, what *will* you do with it?"

"And if I do, what will *you* do with it?" she countered quickly.

"I'm not certain," he admitted. "I have always believed that when I had the key, I would know."

"Damn," said Fern. Suddenly she smiled. "That's what I thought, and I was wrong. You'd better come in."

She called Will downstairs, adjuring him in a murmured aside to keep the key hidden in his pocket for the time being, and they all went into the kitchen. Seeing Ragginbone seated at the big wooden table, drinking very sweet, very strong black tea from a stoneware mug, struck Fern as curious simply because she found it so easy to accept: he fitted into the domestic scene as effortlessly as he had blended into the hillside. And Lougarry lay in front of the stove, her chin on her paws and her ears pricked, like any dog who finds the warmest place to couch, regardless of the summer outside. It should have been difficult to credit that this slightly eccentric figure, drinking tea and munching biscuits like an ordinary visitor, had once been a wizard who still retained authority if not power, while his companion toasting her flank against the Aga had hunted as a werewolf in a northern forest and slaked her thirst on human blood. It should have been difficult; yet somehow it wasn't. Belatedly, Fern realized it was she who had changed, broadening her scope to embrace two worlds, the old, safe, hidebound world that would be forever childhood, and the new, terrifying, unfamiliar world of broken rules and illusory enchantment—the world that was teaching her to grow. Now, the two merged naturally, light and werelight, shade and shadow, here in this kitchen where Will kept the key to the Gate of Death in his pocket and Fern related the events of the past few days as if such happenings were part of her normal routine. She started with the process of finding the key then jumped back to Javier, her dream, the incident with the idol. Ragginbone waited until she had finished before he offered any comment. A little to her surprise, it was the dream and the idol which exercised him the most.

"Azmodel," he said. "I feared as much. You saw no one?"

"Only the images in the temple."

His face clouded, as if with a memory both abhorred and desired. "I have passed through the Garden of Lost Meanings when goblin-paw and cloven hoof danced among the leaves, and music thrummed from concealed grottoes. I have stood with the worshippers in the tabernacle, and breathed the fumes of incense and opiate, and seen the blood of sacrifice running over the feet of every idol. Only the colored lakes are always deserted. None can long endure their vapors, and neither bird nor beast will linger there."

"I saw a bird," said Fern, "drinking in one of the lakes. But it was only a dream—wasn't it?"

"Was it? Describe this bird."

"I knew what it was," said Fern, "the way you do in a dream. It was a phoenix."

"Well, well," said the Watcher, inexplicably gratified. "It may have been a sign, and it may not. It may have been merely fortuitous, a wayward illusion. Many have waited there to see the firebird come down to drink, and have sickened on the foul air and seen nothing."

"*I* didn't feel sick," said Fern.

"You were dreaming," said the Watcher, with his customary bizarre logic. "However, there are many kinds of dreams. The Gifted can tune in to the mind and memory of others, often through the medium of sleep. And the powerful can induce dreams to convey messages, to germinate ideas, to communicate, to deceive, to implant a reaction or a command deep in the subconscious. I suspect that is what has happened here. You may have traveled beyond the body in a dream-state or been subjected to an elaborate hallucination—the second is more likely, were it not for the phoenix—but the intent was to program you with a specific response. When you see the idol, you say its name. In our discussions, I deliberately left the Old One nameless: to name him is to summon him, and he has many ears. In naming the receptor, you conjure the Spirit. A bad idea."

"But I tried it," said Will, "this afternoon, when I got back. Fern didn't come and I was pretty desperate. I called it Jhavé and Jezreel; I couldn't recall any other names. Nothing happened."

"You were saved by your defective recollection," said Ragginbone, directing a fearsome scowl at him. "Of all the imbecilic things—to try calling up archfiends because you have nothing else to do. Fortunately for you, the idol represents the one demon-god, and reacts to no other appellation. Try not to be so stupid again: it might be terminal. What we have to do now—" he turned back to Fern "—is to clear the programmed response from your mind. We've frittered away time enough in small talk. You'd better get on with it."

"M-me?" stammered Fern. "But I don't know how—"

"I will tell you," said Ragginbone. "First, we have to find it. Close your eyes, open your mind. Let the light flow in. Empty your brain of thought: let the light reach every corner. Soon, you should see it. It will appear as a blemish, a tiny burl of shadow that the light does not disseminate. Can you see it?"

Shutting her eyes obediently if without much hope, Fern attempted to evacuate any residual thoughts from her brain. The embers of imagination flickered and faded, quelled by the opening void in her head; she was amazed to find she could feel—she did not think that *see* was the correct verb—a kind of illumination entering her from somewhere above, flooding her inward self. And there was the unwanted response, like a fleck of darkness floating on the glimmering landscape of her mind. "Yes," she said. "I see it."

"Erase it," said Ragginbone.

"How?" Her concentration did not relent: she focused on the shadow-blot, trying to fix it in one place. She was filled with a peculiar certainty which she had no leisure to analyze or understand.

"Use the light. Smother it."

Without pausing to think or question Fern opened her mind still further, letting in more and more of the brightness which was not so much a radiance as an irradiation, a light from a dimension of light itself, where darkness could not live. The shadow began to shrink, growing clearer and more dense as she compressed it, until it was reduced to a pinpoint blacker than a black hole. And then she gathered all her strength and squeezed it in a fist of light, tighter and still tighter, destroying it with revelation. Will saw the blood rush to her face and the sweat-beads roll down from under her hair; he said: "Is she okay?" but Ragginbone did not answer. And then her color receded and her head drooped and she said in a wisp of a voice: "It's gone."

"Well done," said the Watcher, and she saw he meant it. "That was a very hard thing to do. So hard, I thought it best to give you no time for reflection or doubt. As I hoped, you have the force I have lost. But it was a lot to chance on hope. The pressure of the dark could have damaged your mind for good."

"Are you telling me," Fern said faintly, "that you weren't sure it would work?"

"Nothing in life is sure," said the Watcher.

Too horrified to answer, Fern could only stare at him.

"It had to be done," he said. "If the Old Spirit were to gain even so tenuous a hold on you, the implications could be appalling. Don't you understand? The immortals cannot use the power of the Lodestone: it is a thing from beyond the Gate, and they are bound too closely to this world. He needed you to control it. Alimond is obviously getting out of hand: she has almost escaped his influence. You, however, are young and malleable, easily tempted, easily managed—or so he thought. He underestimated both your resistance and your Gift."

"*Fern* has the Gift?" said Will.

"Of course." Ragginbone's attention was still fixed on the girl. "Why do you think the unicorn returned to you?"

"I released him from the picture," said Fern. "He was grateful."

"Such creatures do not know gratitude. He came because you needed him—because he loves you. He responded to your power, your youth, your purity—"

"My *what*?"

Under outthrust brows the Watcher's eyes gleamed with gentle mischief. "Don't you know the legend? A unicorn can be tamed only by a true maid. You, I'm quite sure, are a maiden still. Make the most of the association: it won't last." Fern, to her fury, found herself blushing; Will giggled. "Where did he take you?" Ragginbone went on.

"It was a beach," said Fern, still unwilling to speak of it. "A beach at night, under the stars."

The eyebrows went up: for the first time Ragginbone looked unnerved. "Illusion?" he murmured. "Unlikely—the unicorn has no such skill. It must have been truth . . . Yet who has ever seen the silver beaches on the Margin of the World, save in a fantasy, a dream, a crystal gazing far away? It was said the place did not exist outside the realm of story—or if it did, who could ever go there? It seems the question is answered. There is a strange fate on you, Fernanda—or perhaps only a strange chance. But fate or freak, we must tread carefully. There are forces stirring here that I did not expect to rouse."

"What forces?" asked Will.

"Even I don't know everything," snapped the Watcher. "I am several thousand years short of that. Now, will you show me the key?"

Will looked at Fern: she nodded. He lifted his T-shirt and fumbled in his pocket, his face blanching. "It's gone," he said in a pale voice. "It was here—I had it—but it's gone . . ."

"It *can't* have!" Fern jumped to her feet and dragged her brother from his place at the table. "Here, let me look. Pull your pocket inside out. Don't tell me *you* have a hole—" She turned to the Watcher, who sat silent and still with thought. "Could it have been taken by—by magic?" She did not sound convinced of it.

"Oh no," he said, "not *magic*."

"But we're alone in the house."

"Not entirely."

"He wouldn't," Fern said, as comprehension dawned. "He's on our side—"

"He's on no side." Ragginbone stood up, drawing himself to his full height, taller than Fern remembered and infinitely more daunting. His face grew stern: the wrinkles of sorrow and merriment faded, leaving only gaunt bone-shadows and eyes that glittered in their sockets like sunken jewels in a cave. Casual eccentricity slid from him like a veil: for the first time since the circle she seemed to see the true man. "Go and watch for Alimond," he told Lougarry. "Delay her if you can. We need more time. I will deal with this pickpocket." Lougarry nudged at the latch on the back door and was out before Will had moved to assist her. The Watcher fixed his gaze on the entrance to the hall, making a slight but emphatic gesture with his hand and speaking in the language Alison had used to conjure and dismiss, words and rhythms that Fern was already beginning to find strangely familiar. His voice altered with the alien speech, acquiring potency if not power, hardening to the edge of harshness and crackling on the consonants as if the language itself generated an electrical force. The bundle took shape under the direction of his rage, quailing against the door-frame, one crooked fist clasping something pressed into his stomach. In his drawn face all sadness was lost in the distortion of terror.

"Malmorth—" the Watcher began, but Fern interrupted, leaping into the breach with the compunction that Pegwillen always roused in her.

"Don't hurt him! He means no harm. He would never willingly betray us."

"He understands neither loyalty nor treachery. He has forgotten what such concepts mean—if indeed he ever knew."

"That's not true," said Fern. "He's a house-goblin: he's loyal to the people in the house. What did she do to you, Pegwillen? What did she threaten? You can tell me."

The panic that gripped him seemed to ease when he looked into her face. "She summoned me," he whispered. "I had to go. You can't refuse. Even *he*—" he indicated Ragginbone "—can't refuse. She told me—awful things. She said . . . she said she would send a stranger, with the red fever, like before, and you and the boy would go where Nan and Wat and Peter went, and never come back. No one would ever come back. She said she would see to it that I was alone for always. Always. Never able to sleep or forget. All alone here . . ."

"She can't do that," said Fern with unexplained confidence. "She hasn't the power." Ragginbone, his anger arrested, watched her with an expression of curious satisfaction. "That fever was long ago. You can't reanimate the past."

"*She* can," said Pegwillen wretchedly, shrinking into retreat. "She's too strong. Too strong to fight."

"Give me the key," Fern said, "and I'll do my best to defeat her."

"*Could* you?"

"I don't know." Whatever the cost, she sensed she must not lie. "It's always better to try than to give in."

He was in the hallway now, the clutching fist thrust behind him, his other hand almost extended, almost withdrawn, the longest digit uncurling toward Fern. The malformation of his body exaggerated the ambivalence of his stance, so that he appeared to be visibly wrenched in opposite directions, his humpback pulling away from her, his head twisted awry by double confusion. "Pegwillen," Fern said gently, part pleading, part imperative, "give me the key." He made a movement toward her—she was sure of it—there was surrender in his face—

But it was too late. The front door burst open, and Alison came in like a storm, no longer Alison but Alimond, unmistakably and eternally Alimond, her hair spreading around her like a great web, her eyes like slits of broken glass. Will gave an exclamation of horror; Ragginbone, taken off guard, spat out the words of some interdiction he no longer had the power to impose. Fern lunged for the key, but Pegwillen seemed to melt away from her, and Alimond seized his fist and snapped the knotted fingers open with such force they cracked like twigs. "The key!" she gasped, and her breath came short, and Fern saw the energy of the Lodestone coursing through her, even as it had when she herself first held it, and the fire irradiated her veins and throbbed through every muscle, and her head was flung back in ecstasy or anguish, and the red smolder of her heart shone through flesh and skin and clothes. A great shudder passed through her, violent as an earth tremor, and then she was laughing, but though her mouth laughed the sound that emerged was triumphant without joy.

"Release me!" begged Pegwillen. "You promised—"

"I release you," she said, "from the burden of your existence," and she plucked him off his feet and pushed his head into his hump and his legs into his belly, squeezing him into a ball like plasticine, rolling and crushing him until he crumbled between her palms and was brushed away like dust on the empty air. Fern remained immobile, too stunned to scream. "And now," Alimond said, "and *now*, Caracandal—" The Watcher stood tall before her, and in his expression there was a weary courage, pride without hope, an authority now fruitless. The Lodestone had touched her, and she knew no more doubts. "In the semblance of a rock you have spied on me," she said. "I gather you feel yourself akin to such inanimate things. So be it. A rock you have chosen, and a rock you shall remain. *Fiassé! Ruach fiassé!*" She made a motion as if she were throwing something, and a wind tore through the house, a wind that slammed wide any doors in its path, that tugged hair from the scalp and tears from the eye, hurling Will back toward the kitchen table, pinning Fern against the wall. For an instant she saw Ragginbone standing like a pillar of resistance, his coat streaming behind him, then the heavy cloth seemed to be blown into rags, and his body crumpled and tumbled, and he was whirled away like a gust of leaves, and when she looked out of the kitchen window there was a rock on the hillside where he had always sat, a rock that would never speak again. There was no time for sorrow or anger, only desperation. As Will picked himself up an idea came to Fern, a brainstorm born of hopelessness which she knew might lead to disaster. But she must do *something*. She needed to get down the hall but Alimond was in front of her, her attention veering toward her remaining opponents. Lougarry entered through the open door even as she raised her hand. Alimond spun at her presence, her lips flaring into a smile that was all thinness and poison. "So the wolf-bitch has found me at last," she said. "You are too late to help your master. He's a lump of rock on the hill for all time now. Somewhere in the core of the stone his mind knows, his heart feels, but he will not spy on me or curse me again. You should have hurried, whelp: I might have had trouble dealing with the two of you at once. I passed you heading for the road where I left my car but you didn't see me. My hair must have veiled your sight. A fine pair you were to defy me: a broken beggar and his purblind cur. Go now, cur. Flee while you can. *Uvalé! Chiani néanduu!*"

Beside her, the wall cracked. Fern felt the shudder that ran through the house, heard the crunch of rending brick. Now that the witch was distracted she had been trying to inch past her, toward the drawing room, but she stumbled as the floor quaked, grasping the hall table for support. In the tilting mirror she saw the crack issued onto a blackness filled with whirling pinpricks of light which crowded toward the opening, growing larger as they approached, settling into pairs, becoming slanting ovoids of unreflected glow. There were eight—ten—twenty of them, and her heart shrank at the sight. "Lougarry," she whispered, "run. There's nothing you can do. Save yourself. *Run!*" The wolf's forequarters were lowered; the silent snarl curled her lip; her yellow eyes were curiously calm. She did not move.

Alimond's smile stretched out as if it were made of elastic, broadening and thinning, plastered like a red-rimmed slash across the pale frame of her skull. Her flesh seemed to have gone: she was all bones and smile. Her clothing clung as if contracted by suction. *"Uvalé! Lai-rrassé!"* The Rs were a rasp in her throat, the long Ss hissed like a brand on flesh. The first of the creatures was already climbing through the crack while she spoke, a dog-shape fluid as a shadow yet darkly solid, unnaturally thick in the shoulder, its blunt muzzle showing a panting glimpse of wet red tongue and curving jaws. The others poured after it in a mass, an inky cloud, many-legged, studded with eyes, throbbing with the soft, evil growl that Fern remembered hearing before, a single sound from multiple throats. For a moment they halted, waiting upon their enemy; Lougarry stood her ground. "Run!" screamed Will from the kitchen, and "Run!" Fern cried, her voice rising. "Run, Vashtari, run!" The name came from nowhere, from some deep recess in the wolf's thought, and Fern knew, even as she said it, that it was the name of her true self, the woman she had been before her metamorphosis. Lougarry leaped away as if loosed from bondage, out of the house, over the moor, and the black dog-cloud raced after her. There was a minute when the hall was full of hound—flying limbs, flowing muscles, the beat of paws on the carpet—a minute when Alimond gazed eagerly after the pursuit—and in that minute Fern reached the drawing room and flung open the door.

She could not think clearly: she was too numbed by the successive shocks of Alimond's arrival and Pegwillen, Ragginbone, Lougarry wiped out or driven away. The idol waited, a squatting malignance, ugly and implacable. It trembled on its plinth as Alimond closed the crack, the two sides heaving ponderously together, brick locking with brick, plaster re-forming, paintwork more than a decade old washing over the fading scar. Fern acted quickly, too desperate even for fear. When she spoke it was no programmed response: her bell-tone rang through the house in a summons loud as a command. Will ran down the hall toward her; Alimond turned on her heel. "Azmordis," said Fern. "Come to me: I conjure you. Azmordis!"

Alimond cried out: *"No!"* and broke into a jumbled incantation in the other language—a language which seemed to Fern, as her ear grew accustomed, to contain echoes of many better-known tongues possibly descended from it. It's Atlantean, she thought, in the midst of urgency and resolve. It must be Atlantean . . . But Alimond, thrown off balance by the unforeseen, could not get the words right, and behind the blank eyes of the idol the wereglow began, waxing stronger by the second, the cold white gaze of a spirit that knew no warmth. Between the thick lids the stone shriveled to a film, and then it dissolved, and the eyes lived, and the heavy lips creaked with the effort of speech.

"Fernanda," he said, and for a moment she remembered a barren heath, under bitter stars. "You have done well, Fernanda."

He thinks it was the response, she realized. He doesn't know I summoned him of my own accord.

"Alimond."

She did not answer. Her eyes were clenched shut, her features convulsed in a frown of terrible concentration. Her left hand held the key tight against her breast, so tight that the knuckles strained

through her skin and her knotted fist resembled that of a skeleton. Fern could sense the energy pulsating from the Lodestone,
no longer a visible current but a slow buildup of force which
made the very air around them weigh heavy. Will, stealing up behind Alimond, reeled back as though he had been pushed. "You
cannot do it," said the idol. "It is too strong for you to master.
It may aid you, it may not, but it will not accept your rule. You
cannot achieve dominion without my help." But his offer was
meaningless: Fern knew that at once. The Lodestone was a power
source like no other, and Alimond did not need to dominate, only
to channel it. The Old Spirit, Fern realized, had made a fatal
error, a flaw of comprehension perhaps aeons old: he had assumed the Stone was an entity capable of feeling and thought.
But it did not think; it *was*. It struck her that Azmordis saw it as a
rival to be crushed and enslaved—not the essence of an alternative universe, jettisoned by chance into the wrong dimension, but
an actual being imprisoned in the Stone like a spirit trapped in its
own receptor. He should have kept pace with modern physics,
she thought, and the glimpse of such a gap in his wisdom gave
her a brief surge of confidence—then the burden of the air bore
down on her, squashing breath from her lungs, suffocating her
last attempt at hope.

But Alimond understood the nature of the Stone. She was
mortal, she had inherited the warped genes of Atlantis, both the
power and the hunger: the understanding was born in her. What
she held was not only a key but a splinter of the anvil on which
her soul was tempered. The power built in her and around her
until the heavy air became so charged it began to crack under the
pressure, stabbed through and through with chinks of lightning;
her hair lifted of its own volition, spitting microsparks of energy;
her face was sucked inward to cling like tissue to cheekbone and
jaw. "Alimond," said the idol, *"you . . . need . . . me!"*, and the grating of his voice seemed to come from the earth itself, so Fern

could feel the tremor through the soles of her feet; but the witch was not daunted. She thrust the key between her breasts, against her heart, raised both arms laboriously as though hefting a great weight, and then flung them outward, hurling all the force she had mustered at the idol. The air thickened and rippled with power—the stone mouth yawned into a vast hole from which rage screamed like a gale—the eyes bulged as if squeezed from their carved sockets. And then the head started to split, hairline cracks threaded the torso, and with a detonation that stung the air the statue exploded. Flakes of stone sprayed the room, embedding themselves in furniture and plaster; one cut Alimond's cheek, but her flesh was so shrunken it drew no blood. Fern, clamped to the wall, blacked out from the shockwave. The witch, become both activator and conductor, doubled over, shuddering uncontrollably from the might she had unleashed. But Azmordis was gone. With the receptor smashed and Javier far away he had no other instrument to hand. She could work her will unchecked.

When Fern came to herself, perhaps thirty seconds later, Will was crouching beside her, and Alimond was standing over them.

She locked them in the cellar. "I don't care," she told them, "whether I destroy you or not. You aren't important, just in the way." Her grip, as Fern had noticed before, was vise-like. She dragged them across the hall and thrust them down the steps, securing the door behind them. Will was too shaken to resist, Fern had not yet thrown off her faintness.

"In any case," said her brother, "she could have used magic against us. We can't fight that."

"No, but . . ." Fern was still struggling against the giddiness in her head. "I think . . . I think she may have overtaxed herself. Ragginbone was right: she has a tendency to go to extremes. She didn't have to be quite so . . . melodramatic, just now."

"Melodramatic!"

Sitting on the cellar floor, Fern tried to clarify her reasoning.

"Crushing Pegwillen—sealing Ragginbone in a rock—sending the hellhounds after Lougarry: all that was overkill. I mean, she didn't have to get rid of Pegwillen at all: he was no danger to her. And with the others, she could have done something *quieter*. She's vengeful, immoderate: it must have drained her. She wasn't expecting to have to deal with the idol as well. And now . . . she'll need everything she's got to open the Gate. That's why she didn't harm us: she doesn't want to waste her strength. She's afraid to end up like Ragginbone, exhausting her power till she has nothing left. She'll have to take a breather before trying to use the key. That gives us some time."

"Time to do what?" Will asked.

"Get out of here," Fern said, slightly surprised at the demand.

"And then?"

"Leave out the difficult questions," his sister said with a wavering smile. "Let's just get out first."

The cellar offered few methods of egress. The door was immovable: they had heard Alimond ram the bolts into their sockets. There were two small windows under the vaulting, level with the ground outside, which were just within Will's reach if he stretched up, but no other exits. "I was in a house once on the south coast where there was a secret passage in the cellar," Will volunteered. "Smugglers used to use it."

"I don't know if there was any smuggling done round here," Fern said vaguely. "Anyway, we haven't got a secret passage. You'd have found it before now if we had. It'll have to be the windows."

With some difficulty, since it was both heavy and awkward, they maneuvered the wine-rack under one of the windows. It juddered across the uneven flags and the bottles it still contained rattled ominously; Fern favored removing them, concerned about possible breakages, but Will insisted they were vital makeweight. Even with the rack in position, scaling it proved harder than expected. Will made the attempt, claiming he was the more agile;

Fern gave him a leg-up. It took several false starts, savage exhortations to his sister, and a vocabulary she did not bother to censure before he had scrambled on top, and all the time they sensed an undercurrent of growing urgency, a compulsion close to panic tugging them onward. They had no respite to grieve for Ragginbone and Pegwillen, no thought to spare for Lougarry. They must get out, do something, though what to do, or how, they did not know. If they didn't stop Alimond, no one would: there was no one else left.

The rack teetered perilously as Will lurched toward the window.

"It doesn't open," he said.

"Break it," said Fern.

Well versed in TV thrillers, he took off his T-shirt—a complicated maneuver on top of a wine-rack—wrapped it round his arm, and punched at the glass. But the glazing, though old, was obstinate; after several blows he had achieved nothing but bruised knuckles and a sense of furious irritation. "I can't get enough swing," he told his sister. "Pass up one of the bottles." With a silent apology to her father, Fern complied. An instant later there was a crash which she hoped Alimond would not hear, a pattering of falling glass, and an overwhelming smell of vintage Corton. Will cursed fluently as his naked chest was doused in wine.

"Come on!" said Fern. "If she missed that she must be in the barn; that means she's started."

"The *barn*?"

"The *trompe l'oeil*: remember? All that talk of conversion was just a cover: she's fixed it up for her occult activities. That's where she's going to try and open the Gate. You've got to get out, and then let me out. Come *on*!"

But it took Will some time to clear away the broken panes, and the framework was too stubborn for his efforts: eventually, he was forced to wriggle through a gap perhaps a foot square, into the uncut grass at the side of the house. He failed to see the clump of nettles in his immediate vicinity and whipped back a hand already stinging into an angry scarlet. Had he been a little bigger and broader in the shoulders, he would never have managed to get through. As it was, when he finally unbolted the cellar door to release Fern he was a gory sight, smeared dark red with burgundy, streaked with drying blood where he had nicked himself on the glass, grass-stains and earth-stains over all. She hugged him, regardless of the wine, and after a moment he hugged her back, both of them untypically demonstrative.

"She's not here," Will said, meaning Alimond. "You must be right: she's in the barn. What do we do now?"

"What we can," said Fern, and there was a shiver in her voice as if she were on the edge of tears, but she had released him and turned away before Will could see her face.

Outside, a lingering sunset heralded the end of the long summer's day. Attenuated shadows slanted eastward across the valley; Ragginbone's rock was almost invisible against the dark mass of the hill. Fern glanced quickly away from it, her heart shrinking. It seemed to her a lifetime since she had opened the door to him, many lives since she and Will had gone down to the village that morning to find the key to the desk. It was as if a single day had stretched out into an infinite spool of time, and she was trapped within it like a mouse on a wheel, desperately going nowhere. Nightfall might bring an ending too fantastic to imagine.

The barn was bisected with shadow, the roof and small high windows still golden in the sunshine. Nothing could have looked less like a sorcerer's fane. It resembled a Victorian painting of rural England, a deserted building dozing in the mellow light against a green background of valley and hill. It was only when they reached the barn door that Fern felt the familiar sense of oppression emanating from it, as if the rustic scene was indeed no more substantial than canvas, and behind it a darkness waited which the light could barely contain. She tried the great door, very gingerly for fear of alerting Alimond, but although her hand did not react it was obviously locked from inside. When she bent down to peer through the keyhole she could see nothing, though she thought she heard the echo of Alimond's voice, chanting what might be an incantation. "We have to get in," she told Will.

He grimaced. "The window?"

"Mm. My turn this time."

They had no leisure to go in search of a ladder, so Will stood on one of the more stable kitchen chairs and Fern scrambled awkwardly onto his shoulders, supporting herself against the barn wall. When she finally managed to stand upright she was comfortably on a level with the window. The glass had long gone, and she put her hand through a vacant pane to feel for the latch. Alimond's chant was clearly audible now; also a faint hissing, a breath on the edge of sound, like the exhalation of a fire but far softer. The frame was stiff: when Fern pulled it outward, involving some perilous balancing as she tried to squirm out of the way, it made a rasping noise which brought her heart into her mouth; but the witch continued oblivious. Fern remembered Ragginbone saying something about the total concentration required for maintaining the circle; emboldened, she clambered over the sill, landing on the floor of the hayloft with a thump which went equally unremarked. She brushed off a few wisps of straw and leaned out of the window. Will was looking up at her.

"Okay?"

"Okay."

"What are you going to do?" The difficult question again.

"Try and get the key back." She didn't look hopeful. "Listen: there's no point in your waiting here. Go down to the village, fetch Gus; he might be able to help."

"D'you think he could cope with Alison?" Will said uncertainly.

"Not really. But we need some support, and he's the best option."

"Good luck."

She smiled in acknowledgment, a curious, close-lipped smile which, he thought, made her appear suddenly much older, no more his teenage sister but a woman grown, a stranger. Then she was gone. He leaned against the wall for a minute, straining to pick up any whisper of sound, but the barn remained silent. Then he set off for the village, his walk breaking into a run, wondering as he went what on earth he would say to Gus.

Inside, Fern stole to the edge of the hayloft and knelt on the floorboards to look down.

The first thing she saw was the *trompe l'oeil*, uncovered now, the details of flower-tendrils and basking lizard indistinguishable in the gloaming. It stood at the hub of a wide semi-circle which ran from wall to wall, its perimeter drawn in flame, beyond it not a half pentagram but a rayed star with many points. Alimond was positioned inside the boundary this time, a difference which Fern appreciated by instinct. She was binding herself in her own invocation—a hazardous proceeding—if anything went wrong she would be caught in the vortex of catastrophe, unable to escape. She had changed into the red wool dress and her face and arms gleamed ghost-pale in the gloom of the barn. The last light of the sun leaked through the westward window, splashing the farther wall with a hazy patchwork of gold; there was little other illumination. The fire-lines gave off only a faint glow, too muted to reach Alimond. Her long hair had dulled to the color of shadow; the hue of her dress was as somber as an old bloodstain. Her left hand was closed tightly on the key, her right described a series of sinuous, almost boneless movements, as if the member had acquired its own insidious identity, and the fingers writhed and undulated with serpentine skill. Fern, staring too long and too hard at those darkly seen indicta, found herself sliding into a state of mesmerism approaching a trance. She forced her brain back to alertness and focused on the outpouring of Atlantean, trying to pick out a word here and there for later use. As the chant progressed slivers of light flickered into being between Alimond's fingers and leaped toward the door, playing across the painting like will-o'-the-wisps, igniting random fragments into glimmering visibility. Seeing the witch totally immersed in her practices, Fern began to edge toward the broken ladder. The sudden extinguishing of the late sunshine brought her to an abrupt halt. She realized that the sun must have dipped behind the hill, leaving the barn entirely in shadow. Only the fire-lines remained, a penciling of brightness floating as if rootless in the vacuum of the semi-dark. There was a moment when it seemed to Fern that the wall of the building had thinned into transparency, and both circle and star were complete, and the Door stood alone at the center like a portal into nowhere.

She found the top of the ladder more by touch than sight and started her descent, moving softly out of habit. When she came to the missing rungs she lost her footing and slithered the rest of the way down, but Alimond was beyond hearing. Her incantation was rising, soaring to a crescendo, and her voice grew with the litany, so that for a minute Fern thought it had become many voices, as if a whole chorus spoke through her mouth. There was a noise like scalding steam and a barrier of flame sprang up from the periphery of the circle, enclosing Alimond and the Door in a translucent cylinder whose marbled fires shone dimly blue, shot now and then with flickers of angry yellow. The barn wall had vanished and Fern could plainly see the other side, curve interlocking with curve in an unbroken circumference, the many-rayed star glinting beyond. That can't be right, she thought suddenly, bewilderment stirring in some recess of her mind. The Gate of Death is supposed to open on another dimension. If it's outside the world, it *must* be outside the circle. Whatever she's opening, it isn't the Gate . . . Forgetting all animosity she tried to cry out in warning, but as in a nightmare she made no sound. Alimond's many voices climaxed on a single word which turned the fires all to silver, and silver lightnings rippled through the flame-curtain, and both word and light came tumbling earthward like a dying fountain, diminishing into glancing echoes and a falling foam of sparks, and the boundaries were shrunken back to mere lines of brilliance, but set in the Door was a keyhole which shone with a light of its own. Once you have the key you can make the lock, Ragginbone had said. Once you have the lock, you can open the Door. Alimond stepped up to the threshold and, unclosing her left hand, looked down at the key. A tiny lizard scurried over the slats and disappeared into the circle. Abandoning the last of her caution, Fern ran to jump over the fire-lines.

But the circle was sealed, and she had not been called. The power hit her like a forcefield, sending her sprawling to the floor. She got up again, battering on the air as if it were a dungeon-wall, screaming she knew not what; but Alimond was deaf and blind. She leaned forward and inserted the key into the lock. For an interminable second Fern saw her poised thus, the serrated line of her profile knife-edged with light, her long white fingers curling like tentacles round the precious object. "Rozalyn," she murmured, and Fern knew it was the name of her stillborn daughter, and she was Alys Giddings again, the long-lost peasant-girl starved of love and motherhood for all time. Then she turned the key. There was a quiet click, soft as the fall of a pin, in that instant the only sound in the whole world. Immediately, Fern was aware of an indistinct shape in the circle beyond where the wall should have been, standing so close to the Door it might have been a phantom reflection of Alimond, shadowing her every movement. The key shivered into non-existence even as the Door opened. Fern found she had fallen to her knees; she picked herself up and ran around the star till she was almost behind the witch and could see past her into the widening aperture. Alimond straightened and froze.

The Door had opened onto a vast chamber that seemed to

Fern's dazzled gaze to be lined entirely with gold. After the darkness of the barn she could make out few details, only a glimpse of space and a light like a molten sunset on gilded pillars and shining floor. And opposite Alimond, her rigid stance exactly imaging that of the witch, was a woman with a golden face, not unlike hers but immeasurably more beautiful. Her black hair was twisted into a column on top of her head; her clothes clung and shimmered. In her right hand she held a knife from which the blood still dripped, in all that golden vista the only red. Atlantis, Fern thought, as the truth dawned. This is the Forbidden Past. Zohrâne, like Alimond, tried to unlock the Gate of Death, and like Alimond she was cheated. The key called to itself. All they've found is each other. The two women stood, and stared, and did not move.

Fern shifted her position, straining to see more of the background. She thought there were other people waiting outside the circle, tall figures in robes with a metallic luster. And on the floor behind the priestess-queen there was a crumpled, fallen thing the size of a child, its cheek pressed into a scarlet pool. Fern went suddenly cold. "Death," Alimond said, and her voice was altered almost beyond recognition, husky with confusion. "Where is Death? I wanted *Death*."

"Have it," said the other, though Fern realized afterward that she had spoken in Atlantean. Fury distorted the beautiful visage—the fury of an obsessive balked of the ultimate goal, an all-powerful dominatrix denied the last gamble of power. She hurled the knife to the ground and raised her hand in a gesture similar to one of Alimond's but far more assured, careless with practice, reckless with force. The witch, benumbed with failure, did not seem to register the threat. But before Zohrâne could utter the lethal words the golden hall went suddenly dark. Little noise filtered through the Door but a muted groundswell of sound had been gradually encroaching on Fern's hearing, and now it grew to a rushing, booming roar that obliterated not only speech but thought. A huge shadow stretched across that shining world, chasing the last of the light. Through the murk Fern glimpsed blurred images of panic; Zohrâne looked up, over her shoulder, and in the glimmer of the fire-lines a fear showed on her face where no fear had dwelt before, unfamiliar as ugliness. Too late, Fern understood. This was Atlantis—Atlantis at the End. *Shut the Door!* she told Alimond, crying not with her voice but with her mind. *For God's sake—shut the Door!* But the witch's mind was empty, a vacant hollow where even desolation had moved out. The ground heaved like water: a seismic ripple raced toward the Door, shaking it loose from its frame, bursting the bounds of the spell, scattering circle and forcefield. The floor of the barn bunched and split; Fern barely outran the tremor as she reached the exit, wrestling with lock and bolt, flung outside on the crest of the earthquake as the building shuddered free of joist and hinge. And then the sea came, sweeping away both witch and witch-craft, exploding from the barn in a gigantic wave which picked Fern up and sent her rolling over and over like a pebble, down the hillside into nothingness.

Part Two

The Door

✦

⋅ VII ⋅

Someone was choking, someone very close by; she could hear the coughing, retching noises, feel the horrible tightness of asphyxia in her lungs. There was a rhythmic pressure on her chest and Will's voice calling, calling her out of the warm darkness, nearer and nearer to unpleasant reality. And then her vague apprehension crystallized and she knew it was she who was choking, she who struggled and gasped, vomiting sea water in a great rush onto the grass. "She'll be all right now," said Gus Dinsdale, who had evidently been giving her artificial respiration, "but we've got to keep her warm." She wondered what Gus was doing there, when surely she must be in Atlantis. Then she recollected that a long time ago she had asked Will to fetch him, but she couldn't think why. Something to do with Alison—no, not Alison, Alimond. Alimond standing in front of the Door with the light of another time on her face. As memory came flooding back Fern tried to sit up and saw she was lying on the hillside in the early dusk: she was not sure quite where but it seemed to be some way below the house. The chatter of the Yarrow sounded very loud and near. She started to shiver convulsively, wet clothing and dripping hair increasing her discomfort. Gus wrapped his jacket around her, lifted her in his arms, and carried her up the slope.

"It looks almost like there was some kind of flash flood," he said. "Will and I saw it on our way to your house—a great cascade pouring down the hill, sweeping away everything in its path. Your barn seems to have been completely destroyed. One moment it was like Niagara Falls, and then it was over. Quite extraordinary. I never heard of such a thing in this part of the country before. You were lucky: we found you wedged against a tree. It probably saved your life. If you'd been washed into the river . . ." He left the sentence unfinished. "Maggie's at Dale House," he went on. "We'll have you warm and comfortable soon."

Back in the kitchen, swathed in several towels and clutching a hot-water bottle, Fern sipped cocoa generously laced with brandy while Maggie Dinsdale scrubbed potatoes to add to the stew Mrs. Wicklow had left in the oven. "Now," said Gus, "are you going to tell us what's been going on here? Will comes rushing over in a fearful panic saying Alison is up to something and you are in trouble, and when we get here either there's a flash flood or a water main explodes—only as far as I'm aware there isn't a water main on that spot—and we find you half drowned draped round a tree-trunk. I'd like an explanation."

"Where *is* Alison anyway?" added Maggie. "She's not in the house."

"She's in the sea." Fern shivered again, though not from cold.

"The *sea?*" said Will, Maggie, and Gus with varied degrees of surprise and bafflement.

"The flood may have been pretty strong," Gus elaborated after a pause, "but she couldn't have been carried that far. Still, we'd better inform the police, if you think she's missing. They'll find her soon enough. They'll be wanting to look into this business, anyway. And we ought to get hold of your father. What's the matter?"

"Not the *police!*" Will was horrified.

And: "Daddy'll call soon himself," said Fern. "He moves around a lot: I don't have a current number for him. Please—please don't worry him. He worries awfully easily."

"What's wrong with the police?" Gus was looking suspicious.

"Nothing," said Fern, digging her brother with her foot. "It's just—"

"I think you'd better tell us exactly what happened here."

"I can't," said Fern. "I don't—I don't remember."

"Well, what was Alison up to?" Maggie asked reasonably, turning to Will. "Or don't you remember either?"

"You wouldn't believe the truth," Fern said simply, "and I'm too tired to lie. Don't pester Will: it isn't fair. Couldn't we just leave it that I don't remember?"

There was a silence that lasted long enough for her to know she had made her point. Then Gus said quietly: "I'm good at believing things, you know. It goes with my job. Try me."

"All right," Fern sighed. "Alimond—that was her real name— she came here to find something. Something Great-Cousin Ned picked up abroad."

"An antique," supplied Maggie, nodding her understanding. "I always thought Alison was a crook."

"Don't interrupt," said her husband. "Go on, Fern."

"I suppose it was an antique," she said. "It came from Atlantis. That's about as antique as you can get. We found it first but she took it from us and locked us in the cellar, and when we got out I sent Will to find you. I'd climbed into the barn through one of the upper windows: I had to try and stop her."

"Stop her doing what?" asked Gus.

"The thing we found," said Fern, looking anywhere except at her audience, "it was a key. It was supposed to be the key to the Gate of Death. Alimond had made an image of the Gate in the barn, a *trompe l'oeil*. I think she wanted to find the soul of her stillborn child. She used magic: she was a witch. But it wasn't the Gate, it was only a Door, and when she opened it all she found was Atlantis, the Forbidden Past, and the tidal wave coming to engulf the city. I tried to make her shut the Door but her mind had gone and I couldn't reach her, I couldn't break the circle, and I felt the earthquake coming and I ran to get out, and then the water hit me and I don't remember anymore. I really don't." She shifted her gaze, meeting Gus's eyes. "That's all."

"I never liked her," Maggie declared at last.

"You've *got* to believe us," said Will. "My Science master says there are millions of other worlds—with other rules—and time travel is feasible, at least in theory: it's been *proved*."

"I'm not saying we don't believe you," Gus said soothingly. "I saw the flood, after all. And I don't imagine your sister is on hallucinogenic drugs, nor has she shown any previous signs of being a chronic liar. But we *will* have to call the police. Meanwhile, I think I need some of that brandy too."

The police came, admired the barn, which was now a three-sided ruin, and went, promising to look for Alison Redmond by daylight. Maggie served the stew. "Are you sure you'll be all right?" she reiterated several times. "We could stay here for tonight. Or you could come back with us."

"We'll be fine," said Fern, and "I'll take care of her" from a resolutely mature Will.

The Dinsdales left them to their supper and walked slowly down the hill, arm in arm. "What do you make of it all?" Maggie asked. "Was she inventing, or suffering from some kind of delusion, or—?"

"She wasn't lying," said Gus. "People who are in shock don't lie."

"It couldn't be schizophrenia, could it? She's such a sweet girl; it would be awful. But they say it's mostly young people who get it, and she might have had some kind of paranoid fantasy, and set up that flood herself."

"Impossible," said Gus. "For a few seconds there were literally tons of water pouring down the hill. It was like . . . like a tidal wave."

There was a long pause. "You know," he went on, "I sometimes think mankind is dangerously arrogant. We do a few sums, and then claim we have the universe off pat. We measure the spaces between the stars, and declare them empty. We set a limit on infinity. We are like the occupants of a closed room; having worked out everything within the range of our knowledge, we announce that the room and its contents are all that exists. Nothing beyond. Nothing unseen or unknown, incalculable or ineffable. This is it. And then every so often God lifts the veil—twitches the curtain—and gives us a glimpse, just a glimpse, of something more. As if He wishes to show us how narrow is our vision, how meaningless the boundaries we have set for ourselves. I felt that when Fern was talking. Just for a minute I thought: This is truth, there's a world beyond all the jargon of unbelief."

"But you can't *really* believe her," Maggie insisted.

"I believe in God," he admitted. "The modern Church is skeptical of His powers, but we used to believe God could do anything. Right now, I'm ashamed of the hesitance of my faith. If God can do anything, anything is possible. For the moment, at any rate, I intend to keep a *very* open mind."

"**T**hey didn't believe us," said Will.

"Of course not," said Fern. "It doesn't matter." She pushed her stew aside and sat staring at nothing very much, trying to assimilate the events of that endless day.

"Will you tell me about it?" Will asked. "Properly, I mean. In detail."

"I was just thinking . . ." Of Lougarry. Of Ragginbone. Of poor helpless treacherous Pegwillen, screwed into a ball like plasticine and blown away like dust. Of Alimond, cheated by her own invocation, confronting Zohrâne through the Door in mindless bewilderment and despair.

Will was silent, reading something of her thought in her still face.

"How did you guess what Alison was after?" he asked eventually. "What you said, about the soul of her stillborn child: how could you know that?"

"I dreamed of her once," said Fern. "No, more than once. But in this dream I *was* her, I knew how she felt, how she hungered. Then that day on the beach it came to me. She was very . . . unbalanced." Her expression altered, tainted with a curious sadness. "Poor Alimond. It must be so terrible to feel that way. Starved—empty—desperate. And then, when she opened the Door, to find even the key had failed her . . ." After a pause, she continued with a slight effort: "I've been wondering if—if it was her Gift which helped to unbalance her. Ragginbone said the people of Atlantis became warped from inbreeding, but he can't know for sure. Supposing it's the Gift itself which affects you."

"Ragginbone had it," said Will, "and he's normal. In a peculiar sort of way. I mean . . . he was."

"He lost it," Fern reminded Will. "And he seems to have done some pretty strange things when he had it."

"He said *you* have it," Will persisted, rather doubtfully.

"Perhaps."

"Well, then. You're the most normal person I know. You're *boringly* normal." His grin was intended for reassurance.

"I used to be." She didn't smile. "This summer, I've felt so many things I never felt before. As if my—my equilibrium—my internal balance was no longer steady but teetering this way and that like a seesaw. I don't know myself anymore. There's a new person growing inside me, a Me with whom I'm barely acquainted. I don't *know* myself but I sense, I understand—sometimes I understand things I don't *want* to understand. I suppose this is how a caterpillar feels when it's turning into a butterfly. Only I'm not sure what I'm turning into. Maybe some vivid poisonous moth. Like Alimond." And she concluded, with rare openness: "I'm scared. I'm scared of *myself*."

There was a knock on the back door, light yet sharp; the panels seemed to quiver at the touch. The invading sound fell into the following silence like a single pebble into a motionless pool. The Capels, their nerves already on the stretch, froze.

"Who is it?" Fern demanded, her tone a little shrill.

"Can we come in?" said a familiar voice—a voice that had them both on their feet, Fern tripping over her dressing gown, Will pouncing on the latch. And outside in the dark stood Ragginbone, flesh and blood and swirling coat, the pointed hood pushed back from his scarecrow hair, Lougarry at his side. Her pelt was scuffed, her tongue lolling. The bones showed in her heaving flank, as if she had run herself visibly thinner in a flight beyond hope or help, until at last her pursuers had flagged and failed, sucked back into the pit from whence they came. "Death breaks the spell," said the Watcher, smiling a smile with many wrinkles. "Have you forgotten? I think it's safe to deduce that Alimond is dead. I would have called earlier but you seemed rather busy, and my friend here has only just returned. Now, what about some tea? And then you can tell me everything."

They talked far into the night. Lougarry, having lapped her way through two bowls of water and disposed of all the uneaten stew, lay down in her usual place, listening with cocked ears though her head slumped and her eyes were closing with exhaustion. Will thoughtfully produced the brandy and poured a lavish measure for Ragginbone; Fern absentmindedly poured another, smaller one for herself. "You showed great courage," the Watcher told her when she related the events in the barn. "It is dangerous to interfere with even a minor incantation: it can misfire with disastrous effect. But to intrude on something on that scale—"

"I couldn't get in," said Fern. "The air was like a wall. I wasn't brave: just useless."

"You were brave to try," Ragginbone insisted. "Maybe that was why you survived. Magic may appear to be a mindless force, like electricity or the wind, but its use touches on powers from before the count of Time, the unknown and unknowable forces that monitor the fate of all worlds. The fact that you lived through this indicates a pattern, a small but essential strand in the greater pattern in which we all have a part."

"Javier spoke of a pattern," said Fern.

"We are not unalike in some things," Ragginbone conceded. "The Lodestone brought men closer to the Old Spirits, not simply in terms of our abilities but also in our vision of the cosmos. That is why the Spirits both loathe and lust after it. The unearthly powers would be theirs alone without it. They must have watched the downfall of Atlantis with triumph but also with awe: the forces unleashed were stronger than any they could wield. You caught a glimpse of that storm on Alimond's phantom tape: legend says the waves were higher than mountains and the air-spirits were blown out of the skies and the Nenheedra himself, the great Sea Serpent, woke from his unending sleep and reared out of the heaving waters to hunt."

"Are there really such things as sea serpents?" Will interjected, torn between cynicism and wistfulness.

"There was only one," responded Ragginbone, idly topping up his brandy. "The greatest of all living things. Long ago he hatched, in the dawn of Time, an Old Spirit who took a physical shape to outdo the earliest monsters and feast upon all creatures of flesh. The land could not bear him and he wound his giant coils through the oceans before the continents were fixed, sleeping the long sleep of snakes in the deep between his gargantuan meals. But the longer the snake, the longer the sleep, and one day he woke after an agelong slumber to find the monsters gone and the world changed. His own size defeated him: there were few creatures left big enough for him to eat. Only the great whales, and they sang lullabies to maze him—"

"Is *that* what whales sing for?" said Will. Fern merely looked skeptical.

"So he hunted less and slept the more," concluded Ragginbone, quirking an eyebrow at her, "until at last he sank deep into the seabed, and roused no more. They say that long cleft in the midst of the Pacific was formed by the greatest of his coils. Of course, it is only a legend. Still, most legends germinate from a seed of truth and feed on the imagination of Man. We need our demons: they are symbols, overblown maybe, often exaggerated, but effective. They offer simple confrontations between Good and Evil. War, famine, and pestilence are much less straightforward."

"You mean the Sea Serpent *isn't* real?" queried Will, becoming confused.

"Who knows?" said Ragginbone unhelpfully. "What is Reality?"

"What I don't understand," Fern interrupted, "is what happened to the key. When Alimond had turned it in the lock it just disappeared. Where did it go?"

"At a guess," said the Watcher, "once in the lock it connected with itself, and as the Door opened it moved into the Past. You cannot have two aspects of one object in the same zone of space and time. Therefore, when the key Here moved into There, it became the key There. It hadn't disappeared, it was just on the other side of the Door. It's what's called a time trap. That's why, if you journey into the Past, you must be very careful never to coincide with yourself. It can happen to people too."

"I'll remember that," said Fern.

"The Door was destroyed," Ragginbone continued. "Atlantis was destroyed. The key must have wound up at the bottom of the sea. That's where it was found."

"What happened to the bits?" asked Fern.

"The *bits*?"

"Of the Door. Are they Here, or There?"

"Does it matter?" shrugged Will.

"I hope not," said Ragginbone, but he was frowning.

The conversation drifted on into silence; the level sank in the brandy bottle; Lougarry let her eyes close completely, though her ears remained alert even in slumber.

"Would you like to stay the night?" Fern offered hesitantly, unsure if the invitation was appropriate. "We have plenty of room."

"Thank you," said Ragginbone, evidently a little surprised, "but I don't think so. I've lost the habit of sleeping under a roof. Caves now, caves are different. More natural. Lougarry will be here, if you feel nervous."

"We'll be all right," said Fern. "Anyway, Pegwillen will come back now, won't he? With Alimond dead. I know you didn't like him, but it felt right for him to be here. He *belonged*."

"Not anymore," said the Watcher, hovering between grimness and a reluctant pity. "Death can break a spell but it does not restore life. Alimond turned me into a rock; the house-goblin she simply exterminated. These delicate shades of vindictiveness! She wanted me to know my fate and suffer accordingly, but with Malmorth she didn't care. She tore his slight spirit from its semblance of a body and hurled it into Limbo like an unwanted rag. It—he—cannot return. Don't mourn for him. Ultimately, it was probably a relief. Misery and loneliness had eaten at his mind for too long."

"I'm glad Alison's dead," said Will after a minute or two. "She deserved it."

"I suppose so," said Fern.

When she finally went to bed, reeling from a sudden blast of tiredness after a day whose length might have been measured in centuries, she found herself glancing with fading hope into corners and shadows; but there was nothing there. The house seemed to have lost the essence of its personality: now, it was just a stack of rooms. The corners and shadows held no more secrets. The house-goblin was gone, and the witch was gone, and the key to Death and Time was lost forever.

In the morning, Fern picked a bunch of wildflowers and put them in a jam jar on the kitchen windowsill.

Not to mourn, she told herself, but to remember.

They found Alimond later that day, floating in the Yarrow where the river ran dark under the trees. Her hair, caught in a net of twigs and weed, matted the surface of the water like thick colorless algae. The young constable who helped to haul her out was inexperienced in the matter of dead bodies; he had to sit down and duck his head between his knees. Even his older companion said it gave him "quite a turn," not so much the bloating and bruising of the face or the slime that drooled from the open mouth but that dreadful vacant stare, as if those eyes had looked into an emptiness more terrible than any vision of Hell. At the inquest, a pathologist confirmed that she had drowned. Formal identification was provided by Rollo, his studded leather traded for a jacket of mauve-gray silk which he clearly believed appropriate, his mock-cockney accent not in evidence. Gus Dinsdale described the so-called flash flood, and Fern, looking as youthful and vulnerable as she could manage, pleaded memory loss. The coroner was kindly; Robin guilt-stricken. (He had returned from the

States in a rush despite Fern's careful downplaying of the whole affair and now blamed everything on his own wanton absence.) Fern was profoundly relieved that Javier Holt did not put in an appearance. She was almost sure that he would come, one day soon, and although Alimond was dead and the key out of reach still she feared him, a lingering irrational fear that she could not reason away.

Afterward, Maggie Dinsdale found her husband curiously thoughtful. "I had a word with that chap from the path lab," he said. "He didn't mention it in his evidence—he was obviously puzzled and presumably didn't wish to complicate things—but apparently Alison drowned in *salt water*." He paused. "She's in the sea, Fern said. *In the sea* . . ."

For no particular reason, Maggie shivered.

The funeral was held in London. Robin went, Fern declined. She was relieved to note that with Alimond's death her hold over Robin had evaporated so completely he seemed slightly bewildered by his own recent behavior—a bewilderment, however, that was easily swallowed up in the overreaction of his conscience. For a short while he became so protective that Fern found herself plotting distractions to keep him away from Yorkshire. "We'll go down to the south of France for a couple of weeks," he informed his children on his return from the funeral. "I had coffee with Jane Cleary: they've invited us to the villa. She was really shocked when I told her about this business. You'd like to go, wouldn't you?" His gaze latched hopefully onto his daughter. "You were never very keen on Yorkshire."

But Fern returned a noncommittal answer. Even though their adventures seemed to be over, she was reluctant to let go. Ragginbone was still in the vicinity and Lougarry continued to patronize the kitchen. "She belongs to this local guy," Will had explained to his father, tip-toeing through the truth. "He's a bit eccentric. We look after her sometimes." Robin, who felt he ought to be a dog-lover even when he wasn't, accepted this without further question, patting her cautiously from time to time and wondering why her yellow stare made him uncomfortable. It was all of a piece with the other factors which contributed to his inner discomfort, many of which seemed the more disquieting because he could not specify what they were. "You do *want* to go to France, don't you?" he reiterated, almost pleading. Will said: "Yes, of course" much too enthusiastically; Fern, apparently lost in abstraction, said nothing at all. He knew from other parents that teenagers were habitually abstracted, it was a teenage state of mind: they mooned after boyfriends or girlfriends, agonized over spots and exam results, wrapped themselves in a fog of alienation which might be the result of drug-taking or might be merely hormones. But Fern had never been that kind of teenager. Fern, envious acquaintances had opined darkly, was too good to be true. Sooner or later she would go off the rails.

"You are all right, old girl, aren't you?" he inquired awkwardly.

"Yes, Daddy. Of course I'm all right."

"You're usually so keen on going to France."

"I'm just not in the mood, that's all." She's upset because of Alison, he thought. That's what it is. She probably blames herself. "I like it here," Fern went on with the flicker of a smile, shattering illusions. "Don't worry, Daddy. I expect I'll feel differently in a week or so."

"Saw Javier Holt at the funeral," he resumed after a minute or two. "I gather he took you out to dinner when he was up here." Vague suspicions reared their half-formed heads at the back of his mind.

"Yes, he did." Fern infused her voice with mild boredom although her stomach clenched.

"What happened?"

"We went to a pub somewhere. It was all right really. I didn't think they'd have any decent restaurants round here. It just goes to show."

Robin appeared to relax a little. "Oh, I don't know," he said. "Yorkshire food—roast beef—pudding—it's famous."

"The menu was French," said Fern.

"Javier said he'd be passing through here in a day or so," Robin pursued. "On his way to Scotland. Said Alison had some stuff here belonging to the gallery—pictures she'd borrowed, I think it was. Anyhow, he's going to pick them up. Thought that chap Rollo took all her things, myself."

"Yes," said Fern, "he did. I helped him pack."

"That's what I told him," said Robin. "Still, he's coming anyway."

Fern and Will had entered Alimond's room the day after her death. The door handle no longer resisted them; inside, the carpet was faded and the fixtures and fittings had reverted to their former moth-eaten condition. The peacock bedspread looked tawdry and out-of-place. Lougarry padded in after them, her hackles stirring. "Well," said Ragginbone from the hallway, "what are you going to do with all this?" His gesture indicated the books, the videotapes, the paintings, the familiar box on the bedside table.

"I suppose we ought to burn her magic things," Will said. He did not sound very keen. "I wonder if you could re-tune this TV set for ordinary channels?" He toyed with the remote control, producing various types of crackle.

Fern grimaced. "Paranormal service will be resumed presently."

"You ought to keep the important items," Ragginbone insisted. "The box, the gloves, some of these books. Most of it's rubbish— Alimond had a taste for pointless gadgetry and the general bric-a-brac of ritual—still, you never know. There are a few bits and pieces which might be interesting."

"None of it belongs to us," said Fern. "She must have made a will. It belongs to her heirs."

"The only proper legatee for a witch is another witch," stated the Watcher.

"So?" Fern was defiant.

"One may show up. Someday."

In the end, whatever Ragginbone considered essential went into Fern's wardrobe, on the top shelf at the back. She herself appropriated one of the pictures, driven by a peculiar compulsion, hiding it under her bed for safe-keeping and sandwiching it in a pile of reserve blankets. She expected to sleep badly, haunted by the concealed arcana in her room, but her slumber for several nights now had been unbroken, and her dreams beyond the reach of memory. Will had kept the television set after Rollo declared it broken.

And now Javier was coming, as Fern had anticipated. As she had dreaded.

"What do you think he's after?" Will asked the following morning. Mrs. Wicklow was dusting in a ubiquitous manner while Robin attempted to conduct business by telephone; the younger Capels had wandered outside to put themselves out of earshot.

"Whatever he can get." Fern shrugged. She decided it was important to present at least the appearance of indifference.

Their stroll carried them in a circuit of the wrecked barn; Will, who had picked up several fragments of what he insisted was Atlantean debris over the past few days, was carefully scanning the grass. The tarpaulined shape of the *Seawitch* lay round the back, well clear of the wave's passage. As they approached it Will gave an eager exclamation and crouched down, reaching for something on the ground that seemed to be running away from him. When Fern gazed into his cupped palm she saw a tiny crab no bigger than a thumbnail, its fragile carapace tinted some translucent shade between gray and green and gold. She brushed it with her fingertip, feeling the nip of fairy claws.

"It's over a week," she said. "How could it still be alive?"

"It came from the *Seawitch*," Will volunteered. "Maybe it felt at home on the hull of a sunken ship."

On a mutual reflex, the two of them went over to the covered prow and lifted the tarpaulin. And stared—and stared—in blank astonishment.

For the carved figurehead which Will had so diligently cleaned was festooned with seaweed. It hung down in long streamers, glossy as patent leather, beaded with pods and clotted here and there into knots and tangles. The wood of the ship's side was damp, not rain-damp but sea-damp, smelling of ocean, glinting with salt-crystals where it had begun to dry. New limpets clung to the planks; startled antennae waved from the seaweed-tangles; diminutive snails, gaudy as flowers, studded the hulk. Something which might have been an eel slipped from a crack and slithered away into the grass.

Fern was the first to recover the use of speech. "This is ridiculous," she said.

"The flood didn't go this way," said Will. "And anyhow—!"

The ship might have been hauled off the seabed just ten minutes ago.

"There's something strange going on," Fern concluded rather unnecessarily. "We ought to tell Ragginbone. He *might* know what it's all about." Experience had slightly dented her confidence in the Watcher's omniscience.

But although Lougarry came at a call a request to be taken to Ragginbone was met with an unmoving stare. "He's never there when you want him," Will complained. "What's the point of a wizard who has no power and can't even be on hand when he's needed?"

"He'll be back," Fern said, determined to be positive. "I hope."

They tugged the tarpaulin back into place, like conspirators concealing the evidence of a crime. They felt irrationally guilty, hiding a secret they did not understand yet which already seemed to be their business and theirs alone—a secret which must be safeguarded from the prying eyes of the well-intentioned. They were restless all that day: their adventures had been unpleasant and often terrifying but the possibility that they might not be over filled both Capels with a nervous excitement akin to anticipation. At Will's insistence they spent the afternoon exploring, following the route of the flood down the hillside and along the valley of the Yarrow. Will, enthusiastic to the point of obsession, searched the ground like a detective hunting for clues; Fern wandered along the riverbank and eventually sat down in the spot she had favored before, losing herself in speculation. Almost out of habit, she began to tune in to the rhythms of her environment: the timeless reverie of the trees, the exhalation of the wind, the agelong heartbeats of the deep earth. The bubbling voice of the stream was like a few snatched notes from a greater music, the distant sea-music whose echoes she had heard on the beach at the Margin of Being; and as she listened her thought was carried away and away, back to the legendary shoreline where Imagination and Reality meet, and she smelled the star-smell like distilled silver, and breathed the air that had never been breathed before, and heard the foam hissing like fire upon the sand. *Where* did that beach exist? she wondered. Or had it been spun out of magic for the duration of a dream and the need of a moment, bounded by the scope of her own fantasy? Was it a place in the imagination of God, or only of Man? But surely the whole world was simply a place in the imagination of the Creator—a fortuitous accident or a divine inspiration, according to your state of belief. Man himself was born of a spark in the ultimate Mind; God had burgeoned from a spark in the mind of Man. Who had first imagined Whom? Her thought spread in endless circles, like the ripples from the fall of a star into a limitless sea, until at last they touched upon the riverbank, and she was sitting under the trees in the late sunshine, and a bird was whistling somewhere nearby. Will joined her shortly after, carrying part of a huge shell in whose broken whorls the music echoed again, faint as a sigh.

"I've been looking for you," he said. "Where have you been?"

"Somewhere," she said vaguely. "Or nowhere. This is beautiful."

"It's a pity it isn't intact."

"Keep it anyway. It comes from Atlantis, after all."

She stood up to leave but as they turned Will's foot seemed to be caught. He bent to free it and saw there was something twisted round his ankle, something snake-like, camouflage-colored, gleaming wet. Something that tightened like a noose on his leg and pulled him back toward the river. "Fern!" he cried. "What is it? *Fern—!*" She seized a fallen branch and began to beat the serpentine limb just below the coil; its grip loosened but a second came slithering out of the stream, feeling its way through the leaf-mold, and she dodged only just in time. Will yanked his leg free, gasping with fright. Fern pounded furiously at the tentacles; as they slid back into the water she leaned over the bank and looked down. The Yarrow was not deep; slanting rays of sunshine would pick out pebbles and clumps of twig on its bed. But the sun was too low now and the rising dusk filled the shallows. Fern craned forward, forgetful of danger, peering into the dimness. Her face was a yard from the water when its substance seemed to change. The riverbed opened up into an abyss deep as midnight, huge swirls of weed came billowing toward the surface and a half-seen shape sank swiftly into the murk, many-limbed, amorphous, blurring quickly into shadow. Fern drew back, grabbed Will's arm, and dragged him away up the hillside at something close to a run.

"What did you see?" he asked her when the slope slowed their pace.

"I don't know," she said, "but whatever it was, it shouldn't have been there."

That night, she *did* dream. She was floating in that strange, out-of-body state she had experienced before, following the line of the Yarrow down the valley toward the sea. Trees leaned across her path, their branches trailing seaweed whose long ribbons rustled and stirred as she passed through. An enormous fish brushed the surface of the water: Fern thought it might be a pike but then realized it was a swordfish. As she emerged from the river-cleft above the sea her feet skimmed the wave-peaks, breaking the water without a ripple, foam-scuds blowing through her. She plunged down into a greenish twilight, her speed accelerating until she seemed to be rushing through the depths faster than thought: the great tides of ocean flowed over her. She had swift glimpses of undulating forests and sunken mountains, stalky eyes peering from chasm and crevasse, a long defile of blue lobsters marching across the seabed, the steel-trap mouth of a cruising shark. But the visions and the dangers had barely time to leave their imprint on her mind before they were swept away, lost in the wheeling vastness of the seas. When she slowed down she found herself drifting over a coral reef. The water around her appeared to be shot with silver, until she saw she was in the midst of a huge shoal which turned on a shimmer and dived, vanishing into a dimension of blue. Beyond, she saw a garden, a surreal garden with waving clumps of spaghetti and macaroni-beds and swimming tubes with flower-heads and gaudy fish fanning like blown petals over all. A basking stone pounced on a stray shrimp before settling back into inconspicuity. A large grouper coasted alongside her, its thick purple lips drawn down in an expression of perpetual disapproval. She wondered if it could see her. But it veered away and she was gliding on toward a rocky overhang beneath which the coral had grown into shapes strange even for a submarine garden: long thin branches laid end to end; an unexpectedly regular ladder-formation of stems; a hollow sphere, sea-smoothed, gleaming through the dim water like bluish ivory. It took her a moment or two to realize what it was, and perhaps because she was dreaming she felt no horror, only curiosity. An anemone blossomed in one empty socket; minute polyps had already begun to stake out the fallen jaw. It seemed to Fern a good place to leave your remains, where the ocean could recycle them and tiny lives could batten and thrive on the discarded leftovers of one departed life. She extended an insubstantial hand to touch the brow-bone in an inexplicably necessary gesture of acknowledgment.

And it began to change. The coral-polyps melted away and the anemone retreated into its sack, shriveling into non-existence. The skeleton re-formed, lost fragments of humerus and sternum solidifying out of nowhere, sprouting internal organs that appeared to have coalesced from the very plankton which had fed on them, finally mantling itself in a creeping growth of flesh which washed over the exposed anatomy like rising tide. Even as she withdrew her hand, he was whole. He. He was young, only a few years older than herself— Too young to die, thought Fern—naked but for the rag-ends of unrecognizable garments. He had obviously not come to rest there naturally: his clothes were weighted with stones, his eyelids with shells; strands of weed were braided in his dark hair. His face was pale in the sea-glimmer, and peaceful, and somehow familiar. (It was only later that it occurred to her he was beautiful.) And on a chain around his neck hung the key. Oddly enough she did not remember Alimond's tape of the past, and her fleeting impression of the boat foundering, and the mermaid, and the drowning man. It was as if fate had drawn a blind in her head, screening out anything that might get in its way. Memory nagged at her, telling her there was something she had missed, but her conscious thought focused solely on that elusive familiarity, trying in vain to pin it down and put a label on it. She was sure she had never met him before and yet . . . she knew him. And gradually her frustration grew into a slow anger that he was lying there serenely dead, somewhere in the ocean waters thousands of years ago, when he should have been alive and real and Now. The emotion poured through her like wine into a clear glass, giving her color and substance, hardening and defining her. The dream shrank from her increasing reality, the grotto receding into a blue disc at the end of a lengthening tunnel until at last it was swallowed up and, fighting oblivion, she struggled through layers of darkness into awakening. When she opened her eyes she was still angry, although it took her several minutes to remember why.

In the morning, there was still no sign of Ragginbone. Will went into the garden before breakfast, calling for Lougarry, but she did not come. An air of unease hung over the house, unsettling even Mrs. Wicklow, who had arrived early for a projected shopping expedition to the supermarket in Guisborough. "There's been strange goings-on," she said, "since that flood business. People seeing things that didn't ought to be there. Of course, boys get worked up, over-excited, and then they imagine anything, from beasties to boggarts, but Mr. Snell, he's not the type to go seeing things."

"Who's Mr. Snell?" asked Fern, and "What did he see?" from Will.

"He lives just up t' road from us," Mrs. Wicklow explained. "Walks his dog every evening, down t' beach if it's fine. He come by yesterday on his way back when we was in t' garden: he was in a right pother, pale as dough, and the dog shivering and yapping away. Mind you, it's a nasty little creature: once bit a child. We asked him what was t' trouble and he said he'd seen something on t' beach. Wouldn't say what it was. Well, we thought it was all just boys' stories, but Mr. Snell . . ."

Fern and Will abandoned breakfast, murmured a passing excuse to their father, and headed for the sea. The beach was popular in summer but recent bad weather had kept tourists to a minimum. As they walked, a thin veil of cloud drew over the sun and the wind turned chill. Down on the shore, the dull light washed everything with gray; a solitary beachcomber picked his way along the waterline, but there was no one else around. The Capels left their shoes by the steps and wandered down to where the foam-swirl poured over low rocks and fanned across the sand-flats. They paddled through the ebb and flow of the waves, searching with their eyes for anything unusual or alarming; once, Will flinched from a thick strand of weed that looked, for a moment, like the tip of a tentacle. Passing the beachcomber with a brief "hello" they soon found themselves alone. The mouth of the Yarrow was a long way behind; ahead, sea and shore drew together, squeezing the beach against the crumbling cliff of rock and impacted mud. And across the sand, there were tracks. Fern and Will bent over them, initially more baffled than afraid. They saw pronounced indentations running in two parallel bands, up the beach toward the cliff: the distance between the most widely spaced marks was more than three feet. Gradually a picture formed in their minds. It was a picture with few specific features but it included a great many legs, spiky, single-clawed legs that all scuttled in unison, like a cross between a lobster and a wood-louse. Only bigger. Much bigger.

The rising tide sent a wave sprawling up the beach which spread itself thinly across the sand, eroding the imprints to dimples. "We haven't got long," said Fern. "We could get cut off here."

But Will was already following the tracks to where they vanished under a large boulder. He dropped to his knees; coming up behind, Fern saw him peering into a hole beneath the stone. It had obviously been silted up but *something* had scrabbled away at the entrance, clearing an opening that was low but broad enough to swallow the tracks, a narrow crack into utter blackness. Will said with a marked fall in enthusiasm: "I suppose I *could* try to crawl in . . ."

"*No,*" Fern said, rather more firmly than was strictly necessary.

She seized a handful of his T-shirt to emphasize her point. He did not attempt to break free, only sinking down to sand level, keeping a short distance from the slot. Then she felt the T-shirt pull as he inched closer.

"Will—!"

"I just want to take a look . . ."

A second later he shot backward, almost knocking her over.

"It's in there," he gasped, "whatever it is. I saw—eyes. Moving about. Only they weren't synchronized. They moved separately, like—like two eyeballs, just floating around in the dark. What do you think—?"

"On stalks?" Fern suggested.

"It's from Atlantis, isn't it?"

"I think we should get away. Now—"

The claw shot out so fast that if Will hadn't already begun to reverse he wouldn't have stood a chance. Even in that one brief appearance they registered every detail. It resembled the pincers of a gigantic crab, huge chunks of armor-plating with the ragged edge of a badly sharpened saw. The ancient shell was crusted with barnacles and coral-polyps, weed-smeared and sea-stained. But it moved as if it had been oiled, and the snap of those pincers closing had the iron impact of a guillotine. Will's leg was within millimeters of being sliced in half—but even as Fern yanked him backward the claw withdrew, disappearing into the dark beneath the rock.

Will swore.

His sister did not bother to admonish him. "Come on," she said, maintaining her grip on his T-shirt.

"But—supposing someone else finds it?"

"They won't. The tide's coming in. It'll go with the tide."

"Are you sure?"

"No."

They did not slacken their pace until they had retrieved their shoes and were walking up the road to the village. Will stopped at the vicarage to consult Gus's ample library for any background information on primitive crustaceans. Fern returned home to find the house empty and a note on the kitchen table telling her Robin and Mrs. Wicklow had gone to Guisborough. She prepared coffee and toast to make up for the breakfast she had missed and then allowed the one to go cold, the other soggy, while she lost herself in fruitless speculation. Dale House felt curiously bleak deprived of the goblin's furtive presence and the solitude began to be oppressive. When she heard a car on the drive, she started up without thinking and ran to open the door.

But it wasn't her father's Audi which had pulled up outside. This car was long, and low, and gleaming white. The driver unfolded himself from the front seat with pantheresque grace and came toward her, the familiar knowing smile shadowing his mouth. His hair shone like a steel helmet. Fern drew back into the hall, starting to close the door, but slowly, too slowly. She knew he was an ambulant, a manifestation of Azmordis, oldest of spirits, all-powerful and all-hungry—but he was also a social acquaintance, her father's friend, and the lifelong habit of courtesy made her hesitate.

"Are you going to let me in," he said, "or shut the door in my face?"

And of course she could not. Even now, knowing what she knew, she had to play the game, fulfill the demands of good manners. "I beg your pardon," she said. And: "Was I expecting you?"

"Oh, I think so," he responded, stepping over the threshold. She wasn't sure if he closed the door or if it closed itself after him, the Yale lock sliding into place with a soft terminal snick.

"I told your father I would be around one day. Where is he, by the way?"

"He's out," Fern said reluctantly. "He'll be back soon"—and as she spoke she realized that somehow Javier knew she was alone, had known before he came, choosing his moment, relying on her weakness and the reflexes instilled by her polite middle-class upbringing.

She thought: Etiquette can be lethal . . .

"You might offer me coffee," he suggested. She was conscious of how tall he was, and felt even smaller than usual.

"I might," she said, "but it's gone cold."

"Heat it up."

He followed her into the kitchen. She put the coffeepot on the hob and waited, resenting her passive role, striving to conceal both tension and fear. The next move had to be his. She had found the key, and lost it; she had summoned his presence into the idol, and it had been destroyed; she had tried to prevent Alimond opening the Door, and had failed. Now, every move had to be his.

"What happened to Alison?" he asked.

"You must know. She made an image of the Gate, and unlocked it, but it wasn't what she expected. It wasn't the Gate of Death. It was a Door into—somewhere else."

"Where?"

"Atlantis." She could think of no good reason to withhold the information. "Zohrâne opened the Door *there*, and Alimond opened the Door *here*, and they found—each other."

"You were present?" queried Javier.

"I watched. I wanted to stop her, but I couldn't break through. The circle was too strong."

"So how did she drown? She *did* drown, didn't she?"

"Oh yes." Fern shivered, maybe at the recollection, maybe at the proximity of Javier. "The Door opened on the End, the fall of Atlantis. The sea came through and we were swept away."

"Yet you survived . . ."

"Luck, I suppose."

"In magic," said Javier, "there is no such thing as luck. What became of the key?"

"Guess."

She went to pour the coffee but he grasped her by the shoulder, swinging her round to face him. His gaze seemed to pass through her eyes, probing into her mind, seeking the weak spot, the pressure point, his mark. Riding on instinct, she thought: He mustn't know it's gone. Better to tell him the truth now, and then he won't peer too close if you have to lie . . . She said: "They both had it. Zohrâne in the past, Alimond in the present. When the Door opened, the two keys were in one time zone, so they must have . . . fused. It was in Atlantis when the flood came. No one can get it now."

He released her with what might have been a sigh, his face blurring as the spirit behind it shifted its concentration. There was something almost obscene about that slackening of expression, as if the flesh had momentarily loosed its hold on his bone structure. A wave of unreality hit Fern. She clutched thankfully at the coffeepot, pouring with unsteady hands, finding relief in an ordinary action. When she turned to Javier again, his features were back in place. Normal service was resumed; over coffee, he made desultory remarks, mainly about Alison. Uncomfortable silences intervened.

When he had finished he set down his cup with a curious deliberation, as if it were the tiny gesture that completed a ritual. Or initiated one. "By the way," he said, "do you have my picture?" It might have been an afterthought, an extra detail of no particular significance. But it's important, Fern concluded. He thinks it's important, so it must be. All those questions about Alimond were just a preliminary, perhaps even a smokescreen. *This* is why he's here. "You may remember it," he went on. "I believe you admired it once. *Lost City.* A colored etching by Bellkush, rather unusual. It's—quite—valuable."

He wants me to feel like a thief, she deduced. He thinks that will divert me from any dangerous speculation. But all he knows is that *Alimond* had the picture: he can't be sure I have it . . . "I remember the one," she said. "Why should it be here?"

"Alison had—borrowed it," he said. Fern caught the faint hesitation. "It was not at her apartment. And she never went anywhere without pictures; it was an idiosyncrasy of hers."

"I can't recall seeing it," Fern said, frowning as if in concentration.

"Are you sure?"

She didn't see him move, but suddenly he was holding her wrist. The yellow pinpoints came and went in his eyes; his grip was like a manacle. This time, his gaze strove not to probe but to mesmerize, dulling her wits, draining her of self and certainty. His mouth curved into something that merely resembled a smile, devoid of all warmth. Thus he had smiled in the restaurant, when the walls had vanished, and the icy stars glittered above a barren heath . . .

The kitchen grew darker. The ceiling seemed to be low overhead, the windows narrow. Where the hob had been there was an empty firepit, choked with a mess of cold ashes. Straw blew across the floor . . .

And in the opposite corner, on a rumpled palliasse, two small shapes were huddled under a blanket. Shadows covered them. She did not want to look but she could not help it: she thought she could make out an arm—a child's arm—crooked at an unnatural angle, the underside disfigured with what appeared to be black pustules. The shapes lay very still. The smell of death filled her lungs and turned to nausea in her stomach.

There was a movement outside, the flicker of torches in the twilight. She knew there should be shouts but she could not hear them, only the hiss of flame eating at walls of wattle-and-daub, and the sudden crackle of burning thatch, and the scurrying feet of mice running to and fro, to and fro, finding no way out. She remembered Pegwillen, his playmates lost to the plague, the cottage razed. Insects were dropping out of the roof; the air was dim with smoke. The child's arm twitched in the heat with a brief illusion of life.

"Where is my painting?"

And now all she could see was the eyes—Javier's eyes, Azmordis's eyes—bright with reflected fire. In the tiny recess of her brain that was still cold and clear she thought: Not yet. Don't say anything yet. This is the past, it was over long ago, it isn't *real* . . .

He forced her wrist outward, thrusting her hand toward the flames.

"Where is my painting?"

"Rollo took it!" she gasped. "He took all Alison's things. He must've taken it—"

Her eyes were watering from the smoke; she hoped they weren't actual tears. The blur of moisture temporarily blinded her. She was able to wrench herself free of his hold, and something clattered, and when she could see the fire was gone, and the cottage, and coffee was dripping down the oven door, and the metal pot clanged across the stone flags.

"Dear me," said Javier mildly. "You seem to have knocked over the coffeepot."

They went upstairs so he could see Alison's room, and on the way down, simulating indifference, she watched him opening doors and peering into cupboards. The search was cursory; he was evidently convinced of her ignorance. His thumb-mark was still in her mind, numbing her power of resistance; he did not need to push too hard or probe too deep. A part of her still belonged to him, or so he thought. She hoped he was wrong.

When Will got back, the white car was driving away.

He found his sister sitting at the kitchen table, her chin on her hands. She was trembling slightly from reaction but her voice was steady enough.

"Don't worry, I'm all right. He wanted the painting. The one I kept."

"Did you give it back to him?"

"No."

"But it's his, isn't it?" Fern did not answer. "What on earth have you done to the bread? It's burned black."

"Is it?" she said. She felt suddenly weak. The loaf had been left next to the hob, close to the point where Javier had thrust her hand. It was a charred mass. "I—it was an accident—"

Will was beside her, looking anxiously into her face. "Are you sure you're okay?"

"Just," she whispered. "Only just."

Lougarry arrived about half an hour later, nudging the back door open with her nose. She did not lie down in her accustomed place by the stove but stood in the midst of the floor, her tail on the twitch, fixing them with an insistent stare. Will was trying to describe some of the more improbable monsters he had encountered in Gus's books, but he abandoned the subject, turning thankfully to the she-wolf. She did not respond to his welcome, merely waiting. The twitch of her tail might have indicated impatience.

"She wants us to go with her," he said.

"About time," said Fern.

Lougarry led them over the moors to the rocky height where they had met Ragginbone once before. They were very close before they could see him, the earth-and-stone colors of his coat melding him with his background. "Aren't you warm?" Fern asked on impulse.

He laughed, pushing back a heavy sleeve to reveal an arm all bone and sinew, knotted and gnarled like the limb of a veteran oak, jutting veins twining muscles petrified rather than softened with age. "I rarely feel either heat or cold," he said. "There's little enough flesh left on me for that. The temperature has to get to extremes before I sweat or shiver. In any case I find, with longevity, that I've grown to disregard such things. I weather the seasons like a tree or a stone, drawing closer to nature's more durable features, becoming that which I resemble. Fleshly vulnerability would be rather out-of-place in a man of my years."

They sat down with their backs to the sun-warmed rock. As Will related recent events the Watcher's face grew thin and hard with concentrated thought. "It's Atlantis, isn't it?" Will said. "It's sort of leaking through into the present day. Because of what Alison did."

"It's the sea," said Ragginbone. "The ocean is an entity with a spirit—a *mind*—of its own. Once it was untamed and free, its deeps uncharted, the breeding-place of mermaids and monsters, invariably hostile to the land-born mortals who sought to bestride it. But times changed. Men learned to ride out its tempests and harvest its wealth, and the sea grew accustomed to them, if still distrustful. With reason. We reaped where we did not sow, without gratitude or understanding. We probed into its inmost secrets, polluted its waters, devastated its creatures. And now . . . sea calls to sea. The boundaries of Time are broken: it can reach into the Forbidden Past and summon monsters to work its revenge." He added, almost as an afterthought: "You are near the coast here. And rivers and streams, rainfall and dew, they are all part of the great Water which dominates the earth. It is a Mind which we alienate at our peril."

"Are you sure?" said Fern. "Couldn't the manifestations be— well, haphazard?"

"They could," Ragginbone admitted. "But the sea lives. The planet feels. It is something we ignore too easily. Still, whatever is happening, it must be stopped. The crack in Time will widen the more the past forces a passage through, and what will follow we can only conjecture. Time is there for a purpose, to keep things in order. Once you change chronology you change history. The past could eat up the present, the crack could spread, fracturing the other dimensions, the very universe might collapse inward. Or the impact could remain localized. A dogwalker beside the river may be taken by a giant octopus, a leviathan may sink a fishing-boat near Whitby, a mermaid may be beached in Robin Hood's Bay. None of the options are particularly healthy. We must do something."

"What?" asked Will, baldly. "Our efforts at doing something haven't been very successful so far. Whenever one problem is out of the way we find ourselves with another. Javier was there this morning, threatening Fern. She won't say what happened, but I know he frightened her."

"The Old Spirit is to be feared," the Watcher said grimly.

"He was after that picture," Will continued. "The one Fern liked. She told him Rollo had it—Alison's camp friend in the leather gear. Does it matter?"

"It might," he said. "Fernanda . . ."

But Fern was abstracted, wrestling with a puzzle of her own. "I thought you said it was feasible for the Gifted to travel into the past," she interjected. "Without the Door, without all these rami-fications. These dreams I've had . . ."

"That's different," said Ragginbone. "You can explore another person's memory, and you can travel in spirit, as long as your body remains in the present, anchoring you in the right point in Time. The range of the spirit is limited only by imagination. It's when you take your body with you that you're in trouble. There are ways, without leaving the Door open, but they are perilous. Many have tried it, few returned. As I told you, if you meet yourself you are lost. And if you enter the past physically, it will absorb you, you lose track of the present: that is history's defense mechanism. I did it once . . . only once. I thought the need was great enough. It was the coming back which drained me." Briefly, lines they had not seen before netted his face, the handwriting of pain.

Fern said eventually: "All right, so . . . we know the Door is open. The Door into the Forbidden Past. It's been washed away, but the opening is still there, and it isn't just a standard flaw in Time, it's a kind of rupture which could spread if it isn't sealed. Could we make a new Door, the way Alimond did, using a *trompe l'oeil* and magic, and then close it?"

"Not without the key." Ragginbone's voice was faint, as if he were being slowly drawn back from some faraway place in his mind. "The power of the Lodestone unlocked it; the power of the Lodestone must lock it again. That's why it's so hard to close. And the key is in Atlantis. For good."

"Couldn't—someone—go there in spirit," said Fern, "in a dream—and find it?"

"The spirit can only be a witness, never a participant," said Ragginbone. "I thought I'd made that clear. To participate, you need to *be there*. In any case, Atlantis is Forbidden, even to dreamers. You would have to make the journey as your Self, your whole Self, going back through the Door that is not to the last days, back to the moment when the Door opened, stealing the key despite flood and tempest, rebuilding the Door in order to close it. The dangers are too obvious to enumerate. In any case, it's probably impossible."

"How could you go back through the Door to a point *before* it opened?" Will wondered, frowning.

"I told you it was impossible," said Ragginbone. "However, the crack is widening. If your purpose was fixed, your heart brave—

there are powers that respond to such things. So they say. And magic exists to break the rules."

"Could *we* do it?" said Will. "Go back—to Atlantis?" Eagerness crept unawares into his voice, and his eyes grew bright.

"*You* couldn't," said Fern crushingly. "You're too young—and you don't have the Gift." She had grown rather pale, like someone who sees an abyss opening in front of them, and fears to be sucked over the edge. "Even if you got the key, even if—somehow—you survived the tidal wave, you'd need power to reinvent the Door. And the Door is your only chance of getting back."

"That is another difficulty," Ragginbone sighed. "I fear—the Door must be locked *from the other side*. The key has to remain in the past. It was found on the bottom of the sea: remember? If you try to change history, you will surely perish. There is a natural flow in the progress of the universe, what the frivolous call a Current of Events. Go with the flow, and it will go with you. Try to redirect it, to alter what *has been*, and you will be overwhelmed. Magic breaks the rules of Science, but not the ultimate Laws of Being. If you went back to Atlantis, and by some elasticity in the zone of the probable you managed to obtain the key and lock the Door, you would have to stay on the wrong side of it. And there might be no way to return."

"You'd have to trust in Hope," said Fern. "Is that it?"

"No," Ragginbone replied shortly. "Hope needs something tangible to sustain it. You would have to rely on Faith. Only Faith can endure in the teeth of the evidence."

The Capels walked home in the late afternoon to find a vaguely anxious Robin being soothed by Mrs. Wicklow in the kitchen. "Just as I told you," she said as they came in. "*They're* all right. Children don't think you might be worrying: they just go their own way and then look all injured when you want to know where they've been. Anyhow, they had t' dog along to take care of them. I wasn't too fond of her to start with, but I reckon she's not one to get lost, even on t' moors, and no one's going to give 'em any trouble when she's around." Lougarry had risen sufficiently in Mrs. Wicklow's estimation to acquire gender, Fern noted.

After supper she went early to her room, leaving Will and her father to argue over the mysteries of mah-jongg. The picture under the bed seemed to draw her: she wanted to take it out and study it, losing herself in that postage-stamp panorama of a city she had never seen, roaming sunlit street and shadowy alley in search of some unknown goal, neither the key nor the Door but something else, something she would not recognize until she found it, or until it found *her*. She resisted the urge, burying herself under the covers, craving sleep, afraid to dream.

She awoke hours later, with the realization that she must have slept after all. The rectangle of window behind the curtains was just beginning to acquire a tinge of gray and a few birds were piping in the dawn. Her mind was very clear. She could remember no dreams but while she slept her doubts seemed to have rearranged themselves and a necessary resolve had taken over, not dismissing fear but putting it in its place. She got up and dressed, thinking in passing that her clothes would be all wrong and she didn't speak the language, yet curiously confident that somehow these details would be taken care of. Then she took the picture out from under the bed.

· VIII ·

It was Will who found she had gone. He had woken early with a vague feeling of wrongness, as if, only seconds before he opened his eyes, the entire world had slipped on its axis by a fraction of a degree, leaving everything slightly misplaced. Instinct told him he had missed something essential; if he had surfaced barely a moment beforehand he would have seen it—whatever it was—but now he was too late for all time. A horrible foreboding settled on his stomach. It was much too early for any sane adolescent to think about getting up unprompted but after a brief attempt at a lie-in he scrambled out of bed, pulled on a dressing gown, and headed automatically for his sister's room. When she did not answer his knock he tried the door and went in. The sight of the vacant bed was disproportionately shocking; after all, he told himself, there was no reason why Fern, too, should not have risen prematurely, maybe gone for a walk. There was no need to feel this awful black panic. Then he saw the picture.

She had propped it up on her dressing-table, in front of the mirror. Will, who had not looked closely at it before, found his gaze drawn inward until it was enmeshed in that tiny nest of details almost too fine for the human eye to distinguish. For an instant he imagined that microscopic vista was alive: he glimpsed the turning of wheels, the pacing of feet, the undulation of assorted robes, all on a scale so small it reached his brain as little more than a garbled message, magnified by some trick of his fancy into a fleeting reality. He rubbed his eyes, and the impression was gone. But it had been more than enough to alarm him. He raced downstairs and out into the garden, shoeless and wearing only pajama-bottoms under his dressing gown, calling for Lougarry. He might have run across the moor in search of Ragginbone just as he was if the she-wolf hadn't leaped the low wall and come bounding to meet him. "She's gone," he said, dropping to a crouch on a level with her yellow gaze. Unusually, she licked his face, as if to steady him. "I think she's gone into the past. There's this picture—it was Alison's but Fern kept it. I hadn't realized what it was, the drawing is so minute, but when I looked just now it was a city, like Atlantis might have been, and it was *moving*. Fetch Ragginbone. She can't manage alone. We've got to help her." Lougarry licked him again, fixing him with her strangely calming stare. Then she turned, sprang back over the wall, and vanished up the hill toward the moor.

Indoors, Will dressed, fidgeted, wandered into the kitchen to burn himself some toast. Ragginbone arrived in less than an hour but to Will, shoveling successive pieces of toast-shaped ash into the rubbish-bin, the waiting seemed interminable. They mounted the stairs very softly, hoping not to disturb Robin. "Ah, *that* picture," said the Watcher, bending to examine the etching. "I should have studied it more carefully. Stupid of me. Still—who knows?—maybe it's for the best. The Door is open: even without such a clear passage, she would have found a way. There is always a way, if the heart is sure." He straightened up, massaging his back, as stiff as the oak-tree he sometimes chose to resemble. "Well, there's nothing we can do now. She's gone where we can't follow. I'm afraid we're condemned to wait."

"Wait?" Will's face flushed with unexpected anger. "Just *wait*? B-but—we could go after her, we could help—"

"No," Ragginbone said quietly. "We haven't the Gift. I've lost it, and you have yet to find it, if it is there to find. We must stay here."

"But the Door's open!" Will said. "I can feel the picture, pulling me in. I can *feel* it—"

"Maybe. But the key calls only to the Gifted. Even if we were allowed to pass we would have no chance of achieving the task, less than none of getting back. And we might be a burden to your sister. She has chosen to go alone because she knows she can act best alone. She showed that in the barn, for all her failure. She has courage, and steadfastness, and luck. What could we give her which is worth more?"

"But it's impossible!" Will insisted. "How can she find the key under a tidal wave? How can she lock the Door when it no longer exists? And you said yourself she won't be able to get back. It's *impossible.*"

"Magic is impossible," said Ragginbone.

They went back downstairs to the kitchen and the Watcher dosed Will with sweet tea and prepared impeccable toast. "When will we know?" asked Will. "I mean, if she's going to get back—somehow—*when* will she get back?"

"That, I fear, is the crucial question. When you travel physically in time, there is nothing to hold you to the present, so the moment of your return can be rather imprecise. Although you maintain a certain sympathetic link with the time zone from which you came, it grows more tenuous the longer you stay in the past, and it tends to ignore specific hours and minutes. You might reappear an instant after your departure, even though you had been gone a month. Or a week later, or a year. You might miss the present altogether, and land in the future. It's all somewhat haphazard."

"You're really cheering me up," said Will. "I'm beginning to realize why Fern didn't always trust you."

"You should never trust anyone completely," said Ragginbone, smiling a half-smile which snaked up one side of his face. "Unpredictability is a vital aspect of intelligence."

"I wish you'd stop being clever," Will grumbled. "Look, there must be *something* we can do. I can't just sit here . . ."

"You could pray," said the Watcher.

When Robin came down to breakfast Ragginbone had gone. "Fern went out early," said Will, wearing his customary insouciance as if it had shrunk in the wash. "She said she might be gone all day. She took some sandwiches." He felt the sandwiches made the story more convincing. Anyway, enough toast had been burned to account for several slices of bread. His father would not have noticed any discrepancy but Mrs. Wicklow, when she arrived, undoubtedly would.

Robin digested this information along with his desultory breakfast. "Is your sister—" he fished for words "—is she, well, you know, *all right?*" Will looked genuinely blank. "I mean, not in love or something, is she? All this mooning about—going for walks by herself—she's never acted like this before."

"Of course she's not in love," Will said scornfully. Fern, his tone implied, had her failings, but falling in love was not one of them. "She doesn't moon, either. She's just . . . thinking a lot. I expect it's her age. Anyway, people are different in the country. In London, when you go out, you go *to* somewhere: to the cinema, to the shops, to see your friends. In the country there's nowhere particular to go *to* and we don't have many friends yet, so we go for walks. You should be pleased. It's awfully healthy."

"You must be dreadfully bored," said Robin, with a revival of his chronic guilt. "Maybe we could invite some of your friends down—"

"Oh no," said Will, adding hastily: "There isn't much point, is there? Not if we're going to France soon."

"Didn't think you were very keen," Robin said, accepting the reprieve with mistrust.

"Well, I don't know." Will shrugged, vague before his time, switching moods with teenage unpredictability. "I daresay it would be a good idea. When Fern gets back."

"Gets *back?*" Robin jumped. "How long is this walk going to take?"

Several millennia, I should think, Will said, but to himself. "I mean, I'll *talk* to her when she gets back. Don't be silly, Dad."

Quelled, Robin subsided into a silence punctuated only by his tea, departing presently to read a proposal, study some color-plates, and resort, inevitably, to the telephone. I wish he would go to London, Will thought, sighing over the paradox that his father's presence, so desirable while he was absent, was now the bane of his life. I wish he would stop worrying. I've got enough to worry about, without having to worry about his worrying. I hope to God Fern's okay . . .

I wonder if that's a kind of prayer, hoping to God.

Just before lunchtime, a shout having elicited no response, Robin went looking for Will to summon him downstairs. He found his son in Fern's room, staring at the picture on her dressing-table. Will started when he walked in, placing himself in front of the etching, but he was too slender to obscure it completely. "Haven't I seen that at the gallery?" Robin exclaimed. "It must be the one Javier was looking for. *Lost City*—he mentioned it at the funeral. Fern must have stumbled on it after all. I'll give him a call this afternoon. He said he'd be in York this week, visiting clients or artists; I've got the number somewhere. At least that's one thing off my mind."

"No!" said Will. "I mean—it can wait, can't it? What's the urgency?"

"Javier wants it back," said Robin. "It doesn't belong to us, you know. What's the fuss about?"

"I like it," Will said desperately. "I—I'd like to keep it. Fern likes it."

"I suppose I could make him an offer . . ."

He carried the picture downstairs, depositing it on one of the armchairs in the drawing room. "Rather unusual," he remarked, "a colored etching. Complicated process. Looks sort of ghostly, doesn't it? What's that bit in the middle?"

"That's supposed to be the city," Will said. "It's done awfully small: I don't know how he managed it. Don't stare at it so hard, Dad: you're going cross-eyed."

"Funny thing," said Robin. "Almost thought it was moving. Some kind of visual trick, I imagine. Clever stuff." As he turned away his gaze skimmed the room automatically, and the mild anxiety-lines on his brow deepened. "Where's that statue gone? The one Fern hated so much? Hasn't put it in the cellar, has she?"

"Well, no," Will faltered, groping for a suitable explanation. "I'm afraid . . . it got broken."

"*Broken?* But it was solid stone!" Will, unable to think of any further elaboration, remained prudently silent. "It was an antique," Robin went on. "Probably pretty valuable. How on earth did it get broken? I know Fern didn't care for it, but—"

"Alison did it," Will said flatly. "I don't know how, but she did it. The carpet must still be littered with the chips."

"Are you sure it was Alison?" Robin said. "I won't be angry if . . . well, not very. So long as you tell me the truth . . ."

His son responded with a frigid stare. "I'm sure."

"Sorry," Robin said awkwardly. "I just don't understand . . . Did she drop it, do you know? Mind you, even if she had, the floor's carpeted, and anyway—You did say it happened in here?"

"I think so," said Will, distancing himself from the incident. "So Alison told us."

"I suppose there could have been a flaw in the stone," Robin mused. "One of those invisible cracks that goes suddenly when it's struck in the right way. Or rather, in the wrong way. Still, it would have to be struck pretty hard . . ."

"Let's have lunch," Will said, taking his father firmly by the elbow. "Or it will get cold and Mrs. Wicklow will be offended."

"It's a salad," said Robin.

"Then it'll get warm."

Afterward, while Robin telephoned Javier Holt, Will slipped out of the back door and went in search of the Watcher.

"**I** don't like it," Ragginbone said when he heard Will's news. "You should have hidden the picture."

"You didn't suggest it before," Will said indignantly.

"I expected you to act intelligently without a prompt," Ragginbone retorted with casual unfairness. "Well, it may not be too late. You said the ambulant is in York. How long would it be since your father called him?"

Will hunched a shoulder. "Not sure. A couple of hours at least. Maybe more. You said you'd stay in the vicinity, but—there's a lot of vicinity around here. This was the last place I looked." They were sitting on the bank of the Yarrow, close to the spot where the thing had come out of the water. "Why did you come here?"

"I was waiting," said Ragginbone.

"For Fern?"

"For anything. For a sign, good or bad. Come." He got to his feet. "We must go back to the house. We have to conceal the picture; if necessary, we must destroy it."

"What exactly are you afraid of?" Will asked.

But Ragginbone was already striding up the slope toward the road.

The afternoon was intermittently cloudy with a breeze that took the heat out of the sun: swift shadows dipped and rose over valley and hill, switching the landscape from radiant to somber so rapidly it was as if you could actually see the world turning beneath a motionless sky. Will had a fleeting vision of himself swept along in the hectic rush of Time while his sister was left far behind, cut off on some remote shoal of the past where light and life would never come again. Being young, he needed reassurance; he had not yet learned to confront the irrevocable without fear. He clutched at

Ragginbone's sleeve, but even as he started to speak they reached the road, and the strengthening wind blew his words away.

Ahead they saw the pale gleam of a car turning onto the driveway. Sunlight flashed off the chromium in a sudden stab of fire.

"That's him," Will said, forgetting his wider anxieties.

"Ah," said Ragginbone, "but whom?"

The front door was shut when they got there and they lost precious seconds running round to the back. At a word from the Watcher, Lougarry had matched her pace to theirs. Mrs. Wicklow glared in astonishment and disapproval at the stranger invading her kitchen, with his weather-wizened face and his scarecrow garb. "William!" she said—always an indication of severity—"I don't know who this is but your father—"

"He's a friend. Where's Javier Holt?"

"Oh, *him*." One object of disapprobation temporarily displaced another. "He's in t' drawing room, packing up a picture I think. Mr. Robin left him to it and went back to t' study—"

But Will, stranger, and dog were already clattering down the hall. Mrs. Wicklow followed them; they heard her calling for Robin even as Ragginbone threw open the drawing room door, murmuring a hissing word in Atlantean by way of insurance. The room was empty. The picture leaned against the chair-back as Robin had left it but the glass protecting it was shattered as if by a blow, spider-cracks webbing out from a focal point at the very center, and the paper itself had been ripped from top to bottom, the irregular tear gaping to show a section of the image was missing. The Lilliputian vista of the city had been completely obliterated. "What's he done?" said Will. "Now Fern will *never* get back—"

"She could not have returned by that route anyhow," Ragginbone said with unnatural calm, tipping the picture forward to examine the reverse, which was still intact. "Nor could he."

"What do you mean? Where is he?"

"He has gone after her," said the Watcher. "Or after the key. Into the past."

The entrance of Mrs. Wicklow with Robin on her heels cut short any further explanations. There were confused questions, bewilderment (Robin), suspicion (Mrs. Wicklow), stammered introductions. "This is Mr—" Will began, and then stopped, conscious that Ragginbone was clearly an ineligible name for a respectable inhabitant of the real world.

"Watchman," said the old man, borrowing from the title Fern had bestowed on him.

"Lougarry belongs to him," Will added. "At least, she belongs *with* him."

"If he's t' Watchman," said Mrs. Wicklow *sotto voce*, "happen she's t' Watchdog. But who are they watching? That's what I'd like to know. If you ask me—" she turned to Robin "—there's a lot going on here that you haven't been told, and I think it's time you were." By "you," it was apparent that she meant "we."

"Exactly," said Robin. "To start with, where the hell's Javier?"

"He's gone," said Will baldly.

"His car's still there." Robin glanced out of the window.

"He did not take his car," said Ragginbone with peculiar emphasis. "He seems to have vanished—into thin air. We know he did not leave via the back door: Mrs. Wicklow would have seen him. He did not leave via the front door: Will and I would have seen him—after all, we saw him go in—and he would have taken his car. In short, he did not leave at all. He has simply—vanished."

"Impossible," said Robin. Mrs. Wicklow looked skeptical. "People don't just disappear like that. Perhaps he's nipped down to the cellar . . ."

They looked in the cellar. For good measure, they checked upstairs as well. It took some time to establish the total vacancy of the house.

"He ain't here," Mrs. Wicklow conceded at last. "That's definite, even if nothing else is." She gave Ragginbone a look at once dour and darkling. "I need a cup of tea."

"I need a drink," said Robin.

"How are we going to explain this?" Will hissed in Ragginbone's ear.

"We don't," said the Watcher. "People will find their own explanations. They always do."

"I suppose I'll have to inform the police," Robin was saying, pouring his recently acquired duty-free Scotch. "Rather embarrassing, I must say. Man gone in a puff of smoke, so to speak, and in my house. Police are bound to think it's a bit suspect. I mean, he can't just—dematerialize."

"These things happen," said Ragginbone, accepting Robin's slightly hesitant offer of whisky. The senior Capel was wondering if his son's unlikely friend might be a former businessman or academic, fallen on hard times due to a serious alcohol problem. "The world is full of unsolved mysteries. However, calling the police at once would be a little hasty, I think. After all, Javier Holt is an adult: you are not responsible for his well-being. And what disappears must reappear—somewhere. He may return."

"There's the car," said Robin. "Can't just leave it there."

"Why not?" said Ragginbone.

"I don't like it," Mrs. Wicklow said after he had left. "What they call unsolved mysteries is mostly just tall stories on t' telly, but when all's said and done, people don't just vanish. Particularly nasty slick types like that Mr. Holt. They're t' sort who always pop up when you don't want them to."

"All the same," said Robin, "he's gone, hasn't he? Just— well—gone."

"**I**f Javier has gone into the past," Will asked Ragginbone when they were alone, "does that mean the Old Spirit has too?"

"Not entirely," said Ragginbone. "It's a little more complex than that. The Old Spirit already exists in the past, remember; he could not risk returning to a time where he might be brought face to face with himself. Using an ambulant guards him from that danger, or so he must believe. In any event, the Old Spirits seem to have avoided Atlantis: they feared the power of the Lodestone. However, as far as I am aware he cannot control an ambulant in the past from his position in the present—the puppet is too remote from the puppeteer. It is an interesting situation. The ambulant must be more than merely a vessel after all: its will is his, its spirit is his; its soul is dispossessed, but its brain must retain a degree of operational independence. To achieve that, I imagine he would have to put a certain amount of his native strength into it."

"You mean, it would be very strong?"

"Maybe." The hint of a smile teased at Ragginbone's mouth. "But if the ambulant was lost, *he* would definitely be weakened."

"How does that help Fern?"

"It doesn't," Ragginbone admitted. "She is beyond our help." If there was a faint emphasis on "our," Will did not catch it. "But should the ambulant be destroyed or unable to return, that might help us here. Azmordis would have—mislaid—a little of his core power. That would be all to the good."

"I don't care about that," said Will. "I care about Fern."

"Continue to care," said Ragginbone. "Who knows what love can do? The immortals affect to despise it, calling it a fleshly weakness, but we who are human prize it above all things. The love of family, the love of friends, the love of lovers. We like to believe it can endure when all else withers. Dearest of vanities. Maybe—"

"Leave out the philosophy," Will snapped. "I'm not in the mood."

Ragginbone smiled, and was silent.

It was the longest afternoon Will ever remembered, even longer than the one he had spent waiting for Fern to come back after the chase with the bike. Ragginbone headed up onto the moor—"The wind will blow the philosophy out of my head"—and Will went back to the river, but it was empty of shadows. The sun, racing through drifts of cloud, kept pace with the wheeling Earth as though the day refused to be left behind. As is always the case when you have time to kill, Will thought of several things he could do and decided, for various reasons, that all of them were ineligible. His watch had broken some weeks ago and when he returned to the house he felt rather than knew that it was growing late. The afternoon was still golden, the wind had dipped: it was very hot. Javier's car stood in the driveway, the unlikely relic of an improbable venture: for an instant Will pictured it standing there forever, glistening, waiting, always unoccupied, always unclaimed. I suppose Javier took the keys with him, he thought bitterly, briefly diverted. What use are car-keys in the past?—And then: Dad will be really worried about Fern by now. What do I tell him?—She's just popped over into another dimension for a while. Not sure when she'll be back—Oh *shit*. Ragginbone could have been more use . . .

He went in through the kitchen door. Mrs. Wicklow had evidently been persuaded to go home. (Will was sure it would have taken persuasion: the housekeeper had long decided—with some justification—that the Capels required far more of her attention than Great-Cousin Ned.) The clock, which was slow, told him it was five past seven.

His father was in the hall.

And in the end, it wasn't difficult.

"Where's Fern?" Robin said. There was no fear in his voice and no uncertainty, only the dreadful blankness on the far side of anxiety.

"She's gone, Dad," he answered. "Like Javier. Just gone."

Gone.

⋆ IX ⋆

She had been climbing the stair for a very long time. She could not remember being at the bottom of the stair, or how she had come there, only climbing endlessly upward. Her legs were not tired. The stair was erratic, sometimes twisting this way and that, sometimes coiling in a spiral, yet her goal was always ahead of her, the tiny bright rectangle of the exit, a casement or a door, not far above but never growing any larger, though she knew she must be getting nearer. Walls went past on either side of her, dim openings, great pillars half ruined or only half imagined, passages to nowhere, archways soaring into nothingness. There were gossamer nets which might have been spun of stone, window-glimpses, chinks of a sky whose color she could not quite make out. The light was soft, the shadows pale. The air was neither stale nor fresh. She was not out of breath, but after a while she realized that she did not seem to be breathing. She tried to remember what came before the stair, and why it was so important that she should reach the top, but her brain was blurred, her purpose forgotten. Memory had shrunk to a crowded miniature even smaller and more distant than the one ahead of her, a vivid microscene in which pattern and detail were no longer visible. She kept going. She could not think of any alternative. No time passed; all Time passed. Then she was at the top of the stair, and there was the exit, not a remote crevice but a low doorway under a brow of stone. She stepped out into the sunlight.

Into the Past.

She was standing on a mountainside above a city. She could see broad avenues fanning out from the base of the slope like the rays of a star, criss-crossed by other streets both wide and narrow, forming a jumbled mosaic of roof and wall and pavement stretching unbroken toward the horizon until all features were lost in the haze of distance. Far beyond there might have been a suggestion of amber fields, the dark flames of trees, thin lines of verdure marking the passage of invisible rivers, but she could perceive no clear details. The main thoroughfares might once have been laid out to a pattern, but time had long since submerged the original design in the labyrinthine wanderings of lesser streets, which had sprouted from the principal system as naturally as tendrils from the branches of a vine. Some of the buildings were well spaced out, porticoed and colonnaded, surmounted by towers, domes, cupolas, divided by squares and crescents, gardens and fountains; others huddled together under crooked eaves, hiding the narrow slots of alleyways and cul-de-sacs. The mountainside faced nearly due west and the city was drenched in sunset light, shadowed in bistre and umber, a golden city sprung from the imagination of Man when Everest was a sand-dune and Stonehenge merely a pebble on the beach, a city already ancient when all else was young. The vastness and wonder of it held her as though entranced: never in her short life had she even dreamed of such a place. This is Atlantis, she told herself. I am in Atlantis. And as she stood and gazed there flicked into her mind an image of another city—of gray walls looming like cliffs, geometric towers of crystal and iron, roads cleft like gorges between monstrous buildings, the breath of acrid fumes and the ceaseless snarl of shining vehicles with no visible means of propulsion. She pushed the horror away, baffled by her own eccentric fancy. It was as though something in her mind had slipped, and the image had found its way through the chink, imprinting itself on her thought. The weakness frightened her. The shock of her arrival—the impact of the vast and unimaginable metropolis—must have temporarily overpowered her. She tried to clear her head but it felt light and curiously fuzzy, as if a fog had seeped in, veiling something in her subconscious which should not have been there. Flashes of memory came and went like a picture drifting in and out of focus. She pulled herself together and looked round to see precisely where she was.

The mountain was in fact a volcano, long extinct, which stood at the southernmost tip of the island. On the seaward side a lava-delved fissure in the rock had been eroded by the hungry tides to create a deep channel spanned only by a waveworn arch of stone, while within the ancient crater was a natural harbor, sheltered from every storm, its waters green and still. The Atlanteans had ringed it with wharfs and jetties and ships of all kinds were moored there: fishing boats, pleasure boats, longboats, triremes, quinqueremes, slavers, and traders. Hollowed in the mountain walls surrounding the port were quayside markets, taverns and caverns, murky storerooms curtained with nets and hazardous with coiled ropes, anchors, fishing spears, and harpoons. A tunnel, facing north, led to the main gates of the city, which could be closed and sealed, in the unlikely event of an assault, not to protect the town but the harbor. But she had not come that way. Somehow, she must have found one of the few hidden stairs, narrow, dark, and precipitous, which burrowed through the mountain, winding upward to emerge on the outer slopes through unobtrusive doorways whose significance was long forgotten by both neighbors and passersby. Here, the mountainside had been molded into terraces and the pillared homes of the wealthy looked out over the lower city, while paved roads not designed for horse-drawn traffic looped or zigzagged their way down to the plain. Below and to her left she saw the huge dome which she knew must be that of the temple, inlaid with gold and reflecting the last fires of day with a brilliance to outdazzle the sun. The Atlanteans had no fortifications, she noted, thinking of the wooden walls of Géna and the stone walls of Scyre. But then, they saw themselves as the first bastion of civilization in a world still primitive; secure in their dominion and the power of their Gift, they feared neither invader nor pirate. And for a few minutes she was daunted, seeing the splendor of their city. What could she hope to achieve here, alone and unaided, a stranger from far away on a desperate quest to perform a Task that could not be done?

She was suddenly aware that she was very tired. Perhaps that was why she felt so peculiar, defeated before she had begun, with her mind playing tricks. She had arrived earlier that afternoon on the argosy from Scyre: she could remember gazing upward in awe as they rowed under the ocean-made bridge, and seeing the encircling cliffs open out around them, and tying up at the docks, and how the solid ground had rocked and heaved underfoot after so long at sea. It couldn't have been much more than a couple of hours ago, yet the images seemed strangely distant, like childhood impressions revived thirty years on, their colors grown richer and their details fainter with the passage of time. Storybook pictures, elusively unreal. She had no recollection of locating the stair nor of her climb in the dark, except that it had seemed interminable. Yet during that period something had happened to her: other memories, other thoughts had invaded her brain, creeping into the secret places where she could not find them, lurking in her subconscious waiting for an unwary moment when they could emerge. She could *feel* them there, an alien presence, potentially terrifying, stirring at a word. *City*—the alarming visions returned, but now she glimpsed a pavement thick with hurrying figures, and rain streaming, and small portable canopies carried on sticks, red and blue and black, striped and patterned, bobbing and jostling like spiked flowers dancing above a moving current of people. Clouds slid behind a building that appeared to be made out of transparent tubes, lit from within by an evil white glare. She pushed the chimera away, back into the fog from whence it came. Perhaps this is how insanity feels, she thought in horror. Like something hiding in your head. She needed sleep. She would be all right, if she could only sleep. She found her way down the mountainside via long flights of steps that carried her from one swoop of the descending road to the next. At the bottom, the ground leveled out abruptly. A wide throughway circled the volcano, much used by horses; slaves who seemed to have no other job were clearing away the droppings. They wore heavy iron collars and the scars of old whippings mottled their bare backs. She crossed the road and was soon walking down another street, heading vaguely toward the temple. She was so tired now she could barely lift her gaze from the paving and when she halted she swayed on her feet. People stared at her barbarian clothes, her pallid skin, the hair cropped close after a bout of lice picked up in Scyre. (She had been lucky it was only lice: they said you could catch every disease in the world in Scyre.) She stopped at a wine-shop to ask for an inn, her impure Atlantean betraying her northern origin. The man there told her to take the next turning, or maybe the next; she was sure she would get lost, but moments later she was standing before an archway with above it the familiar laurel-bough which meant "Strangers Welcome" anywhere in the empire. She went in, and a woman whose kindness belied her brusque manner showed her to a room on an upper floor and insisted on helping her to bed. "Nothing to eat, thank you," she murmured. "Later . . ." She rolled over and tumbled instantly into oblivion.

She awoke in the small hours with no idea where she was or, more frightening still, *who* she was. She thought the window should have been a tall rectangle with a gray lightness filtering through loosely hung drapes, but she knew that was nonsense.

Her mother's cabin had no windows, no drapes, only the fire dying slowly in the hearth and the red glow shrinking inward on the fading embers. She should have been at sea, in the tent-like structure near the stern erected for paying passengers, staring through the open flaps at the unwavering stars, rocked in the cradle of the wide wild ocean. But the floor beneath her bed was solid, unmoving, and only a few strands of night leaked through the shutters screening the double arch of the windows. I'm in Atlantis, she reminded herself at last, picking the pieces of her identity out of a jumble of conflicting images. Atlantis. The realization filled her with an unexplained sensation of panic. She sat up for a while, listening to the sounds of a city at night: the rumble of isolated wheels, horse-hooves tapping on paving, shouts, footsteps, silence. Something was missing—a murmuring rumor, like the hum of bees around a hive, a background noise which was associated with the word *city* in the depths of her subconscious—but she could not think what it was. Eventually she lay down again and slid slowly back into sleep.

It was much later when she woke again, still stupid from slumber, and tottered over to open the shutters. The sun was high and hot. She made use of the pot provided, filled the earthenware basin from a tall ewer, and washed her face and hands. Then she dressed, wishing she had more suitable clothes. Her close-fitting breeches were designed for mountain climes, unstitched to the thigh and laced tight against calf and crotch, the leather cured into suppleness and thinned by long wearing. In Scyre, she had replaced her boots with sandals and her tattered skins with a loose shirt of undyed cloth which managed to be simultaneously yellowish and grayish, but she was still much too warmly clad. Her purse was strapped to her belt under the shirt; she hoped she had enough money. "You will not need it," the Hermit had said, "once your Task is complete," but his gaze was fixed on the stars and he rarely glimpsed the pitfalls of practicality. The man sent to be her guard and guide had carried a small bag full of coins, but both he and his wealth had been lost overboard in a storm during the sea-crossing. Now, she could not even recall his name. "You are chosen," the Hermit had informed her in front of the whole village. His face was withered but his eyes shone brighter than sunlit rain. "It is written on the sky and whispered in the wind. I have been watching and listening a long, long time, and now the message is clear. You need only courage and a true heart. If help is required, it will be found. You are nominated by Fate, and she, of all people, does not allow her choices to be proven wrong." Nevertheless, inns cost money, fares must be paid, and even Fate needs a little support. The elders of the village had donated some of their personal treasures, and these had been sold in Géna to provide her with funds. One or two had been extremely reluctant: they had a low opinion of Fate and none at all of the mad old man who lived alone on the mountain harkening to voices no one else could hear. But: "The village is honored," said the Eldest, and that was that.

She found the breakfast table in the courtyard, under a tree dusted with blossom. The inn was neither large nor luxurious but a fountain played there and in an adjacent bathhouse several of the guests were sharing a sunken pool; she would have liked to join them but in her northern home, climate and modesty forbade casual nudity. It occurred to her, inhaling the mixed scents of flowers and baking, that she had not smelled a midden since she arrived. Géna had the inevitable reek of too many people living too close together and in Scyre when it rained the streets ran with liquid filth, but the ship's captain had told her Atlantis enjoyed a drainage system which kept the roads clean and the air sweet. She thought it strange she had not noticed such unnatural freshness the previous night. But she had been so very tired, tired beyond exhaustion: she was still not sure why. The sundial showed her it was past noon. Too late for breakfast. She helped herself to new bread, curd cheese, and olives by way of lunch and sat down to eat at leisure, absorbing the tranquility of the courtyard and the general strangeness of her surroundings. The fountain rose in a slender spire of water, empowered by she knew not what, above a carved stone bowl that never overflowed; the tree-shadow spread like lace across the paving; at one point, the sound of a drum or gong was carried from somewhere in the city, a throb so deep it seemed to come from the ground itself, like the first note of some profound subterranean disturbance.

"What was that?" she asked her landlady, who appeared shortly after.

"The drum in the temple."

"What does it mean?"

The woman shrugged. "It is a warning. There is a ceremony afoot. The temple precincts are sacred: during such ceremonies, ordinary citizens are forbidden to enter there—though few of us would wish to. Still, rumor, they say, is a seed carried on the wind: it has no need of a legitimate eyewitness. The recent sacrifices break every law."

"But I thought the Atlanteans worshipped the Unknown God," said the girl. "I was taught He prohibits sacrifice."

"No god rules in Atlantis," said the woman, thinly. "That was always our boast. Now, it is our curse."

"Who *does* rule here?" asked the girl, sensing, even as she spoke, that she should already know the answer.

The woman looked at her with lifted brows. "From where have you come," she said, "that you have not heard of the Queen of Queens?"

She blushed, feeling stupid. Of course she had heard of Zohrâne, the hereditary queen: who had not? She was about to say *I have seen her* but she bit back the words, knowing that was impossible. It must have been a picture she was remembering, a picture or a statue, of a woman with a golden face and a stiffened column of hair, throwing up her hand in a gesture of power and rage. The recollection troubled her because she could not pin it down.

"You want to be careful," the landlady went on. "We have become wary of foreigners. Once," her tone grew scornful, deriding both herself and her fellow countrymen, "once we welcomed all comers, secure in our inborn superiority. Now, we fear the misbegotten fruit of our loins, our unacknowledged grandchildren and great-grandchildren, mongrels who may return to steal our empire and our Gift. A necessary paranoia, so they claim. But you should be all right. You are too pale to be a half-breed."

The girl smiled politely, returning to the more important issue. "Why does the queen need sacrifices?"

The woman hesitated. "There is a report that she seeks to rule over Death itself," she said at last. "Presumably the sacrifices are to draw him hither, so she may assert her authority."

She will try to open the Gate of Death, had said the Hermit. She wants to pass beyond the world and return yet living, in violation of the Ultimate Law. It must be stopped. If the Gate is forced and the Wall of Being breached, all life could be sucked through. In this cause she will destroy the Lodestone and uproot the earth. *It must be stopped.* Her Task. Desperate and impossible. *You have been chosen. The blood of Atlantis flows in your veins . . .*

When she had finished her meal she left the inn and made her way to the temple.

The city was paved throughout, mostly with the lion-colored stone which evidently predominated in the area, only a few alleyways and sidestreets showing the sallow earth beneath. It's all golden, she thought, the roads, the houses, the pillared arcades, the dirt underfoot. Even the people. The Atlanteans were tall, neither thin nor fat, their complexions varying between ochre and olive, their hair every shade of dark, from mahogany to the purple-black usually produced by henna. The men were often bare-chested, girdled about the waist with belts, sashes, and chains, their loose trousers tied in at ankle or knee, their short sleeveless jackets made of leather, or knotted thongs, or silk stiffened into rigidity by heavyweight embroidery. The women seemed to favor long trousers rather than dresses and were wrapped in veils so diaphanous as to be almost invisible, tinted to the hue and pattern of flowers, jasmine-pale, iris-streaked, orchid-spotted. They must bathe frequently, she thought: the smell as she passed close to them was of perfume, not sweat. She could feel them staring at her after she had gone by. Foreigners appeared as noticeable here as the deformed. Even the slaves, mainlanders from the conquered kingdoms often generations in servitude, had grown to resemble their masters. There were none of the pigs and goats she had seen rooting in rubbish heaps in Géna or the rats which had teemed in Scyre; instead, cats abounded, many of them yellow as the city, others striped and dappled like their jungle cousins with large ears and elongated faces. Tiny bright-colored birds ventured through windows and pecked at tables for crumbs, and long-legged dogs in jeweled collars followed master or mistress, disdaining to sniff at the roadside flotsam. On the principal streets, sweepers removed the rubbish on a regular basis.

When she left the inn the temple had seemed very near; she could see its gilded dome arching above the surrounding buildings. But gradually she realized this was the effect of its size: from the mountainside it had appeared merely huge but on ground level it was immense, an architectural prodigy which might have been constructed by giants rather than men, its soaring hemisphere polished with sunlight, stabbing the eye with pure flame. The houses in its immediate vicinity looked huddled and shrunken, drawing closer together as if in awe of their overpowering neighbor. She turned off the main thoroughfare and found herself in a maze of narrow streets which evidently constituted a kind of market. Here, the very shops were jostling each other for space; awnings straddled open-fronted stores while more secretive emporia lurked behind curtained doorways and rustling blinds. There was the clinking of coins, the flashfire exchange of rapid bargaining, the leisurely drawl of the skilled, the whisper of furtive deals. Everything edible or wearable, useful or useless seemed to be for sale. Briefly, she forgot her goal and wandered in a trance, bathing her senses in a kaleidoscope of new impressions. A motley of aromas flowed over her: the hot-brown pungency of spices, the flower-and-musk of oils, the sting of vinegar and pickles, the reek of a molten cheese. People sidestepped her, a passing cat looped her leg. And then she was standing still, and Atlantis faded, and the nightmare city returned, its gray towers dwarfing market and main street, the image rushing over her in a vast surge of rumbling, skirling, juddering noise . . . She closed her eyes, and felt the soft touch of the cat against her calf, and heard its mewing voice. When she opened them again, there was the cluttered precinct, and the rickety pattern of awnings, and a woman at a nearby counter was asking her if she was all right. "Yes," she said, "yes, thank you." They gave her a drink made from lemons, cool in the heat, and refused any payment. Take care, the woman said, there are pitfalls here for strangers. The girl smiled and moved on.

And then at last she emerged onto the wide promenade circling the temple, and the great dome reared immediately above her, its apex lost behind the arc of its own horizon. It was raised above street level, looking down on the city, ringed by a roofless colonnade whose marble pillars loomed like the trunks of headless trees. Many steps ascended toward it, cloven at intervals by shadowy gullies where dim posterns closed off the netherworld of cells and cellars, chambers and catacombs which lay beneath. People were seated here and there on the steps or strolled in the colonnade, but every entrance was guarded and crossed spears barred unauthorized worshippers from gaining admission. She did not approach any of the doors, walking instead around the outskirts seeking a more unobtrusive means of ingress. At one point an elevated walkway, supported by a row of arches, joined the temple to the upper storey of a neighboring building, probably a stables. She studied it for sometime, absorbing everything in the vicinity. A beggar was sitting under one of the arches, cross-legged, his bowl in front of him. His hair, snarled into elflocks and discolored with the city dust, hung over his face; the same dust adhered in patches to his skin, making his limbs appear piebald. His clothing was brief and ragged. A cracked water-jar stood beside him but he did not touch it, immersed maybe in some drug-soaked dream, or locked in the stasis of despair. Drawing nearer, she saw he was quite young. It might have been fancy but at the sound of her footstep she thought his gaze flicked upward for an instant, and a gleam of alertness scanned her face.

The advent of a vehicle caught her attention: a chariot pulled up beside the adjacent building and an ostler came out to unharness the horse, leading it through the broad entrance. The passenger followed; the charioteer sat down to await his return. They're going through to the temple, she thought, glancing up at the covered walkway. There were two guards by the stables but they had neither breastplate nor spear, only short swords. One of them had removed his helmet to scratch his head. As she watched, the beggar, apparently aroused by the arrival of the chariot, twitched into action, tottering toward the guards as if on a reflex, his bowl extended and the untouched water-jar dangling from his right hand. One of the men said something contemptuous, the other rattled his discarded helmet in mockery. And then the beggar let fall his bowl and, moving with sudden speed, shook the water-jar so that a small object flew out, hitting the first guard on his bare torso, dropping to scutter across his sandaled foot. He screamed. The other stood just a moment too long with his jaw hanging and helmet in hand; a swift kick caught him in the groin and he doubled over, reeling to avoid the thing on the ground. Then the beggar was through the door and inside the stables. The two guards, one groaning, the other yelling, lurched after him. The passersby, including the charioteer, seemed content to spectate, giving the creature from the jar a wide berth. The girl approached cautiously. It was a scorpion, longer than the span of her hand, its carapace sculpted in bronze, its tail curled into a question mark. Presently, it went one way and she the other, slipping quietly and unremarked into the dimness of the stables.

She ducked into one of the stalls to avoid the ostler, pressing herself against the warm flank of its occupant, who watched her with an incurious eye. When the man had moved on she made her way through a gloom thick with horse-smell and straw-tufts till she came to a wooden stair. At the top, she found the hayloft on her right; on her left, a passage leading to the walkway. She judged the chase must have taken the same route perhaps a minute or two ahead of her; with luck, any guards posted to this particular entrance would have been diverted. The walkway was cool after the stable, sunlight filtering through a latticework of stone to lie like a net along the floor. The door to the temple was open and unmanned. Everything was very quiet. She stepped through, peering from side to side, seeing no one. Where the beggar and his pursuers might have gone she did not know, but it hardly mattered. Inadvertently, he had aided her; now, she had no further interest in him. Her Task preoccupied her to the exclusion of all else. Yet she had no real idea what she was meant to do.

She was standing on a gallery which ran round the entire circumference of the temple under the rim of the dome. Inside as well as out, the enormous vault was overlaid with gold. Indeed, the whole interior seemed to be golden, leafed and gilded, molded and wrought, the marble pillars yellow-veined, the gallery dipped in amber shadow. Below, light was admitted through many tall slender windows draped with sheets of gossamer which glistened with a fugitive sparkle. Wraith-like flames hovered over vessels of oil, blurring the atmosphere with the hint of smoke.

There was the scent of lemon and sandalwood and other things she did not recognize, a dark-gold perfume, potent but diffuse. She guessed there must be louvres somewhere round the perimeter of the dome, since the air, though still, was not stifling. She sensed that here in the temple was the nucleus of the city, the pure element of all that was Atlantis, its golden heart not so much a symbol as a raw manifestation of wealth and glory and undisputed dominion. Not a place to worship a deity but a hallow to deify the worshipper. The Unknown God was too far removed, distanced by His very Incognito: here, the Atlantean lords raised themselves in His stead, wielding unearthly powers, striving always for more than their Gift had to give. She felt them doomed, though her fear had neither cause nor shape, yet still she found the temple awesome and beautiful beyond all other works of Man. Even the mad dreams of Zohrâne seemed suddenly to touch something deep within her—the yearning to outreach her grasp, to dare against fate, to break the Laws that cannot be broken. For such is the essence of human nature: from the moment Lucifer rebelled, we have known him for one of us.

She pushed aside her treacherous empathy, moving to the balustrade, looking down into the belly of the chamber. The vast floor stretched away below her, perhaps five hundred feet from wall to wall, its mirror-surface reflecting the gold of the ceiling as in a lake. Engraved on it in lines spider-thin yet very clear was a huge mandala enclosing a rayed star or sun, and within that several hieroglyphs or runes whose meaning she did not understand. At the center stood the altar. It was a piece of plain rock, unadorned, smoothed maybe by the sea, its shape irregular; no doubt it had some significance of which she was unaware. Its top was slightly hollow and on it rested a black globe the size of a serpent's egg. As her gaze reached it she felt its pull, so strongly that her heart thumped and her breath grew short. And suddenly she realized that the golden temple, even the city itself, was little more than a decorative receptacle for this one deadly thing, a glittering corolla around a seed of infinite power. Even as she stared the force emanating from it seemed to intensify, as though responding to the surge within *her*: the air throbbed with it, and the chamber trembled like a mirage, shivering on the borderline of existence, and only the Stone was real. She groped her way along the gallery until she found a stair, descended in a stumble to ground level. The force compelling her on was so strong she thought she crossed that wide floor in two or three steps. Then the altar was before her, and she had laid her hands on the Lodestone.

It was not a stone, she knew that at once. To call it a stone was merely a title of convenience: it felt and looked a little like stone only because it was harder than hard, heavier than the whole planet, but the heaviness was inside it, not weighing it down but drawing it into itself. It was neither alive nor dead; it had Being without Consciousness, power without purpose. It was a ball of matter so dense there might have been entire worlds crushed within it, and she shuddered at its touch, even as that touch disseminated through her body like the fallout of a shooting star, burning her with a thousand sparks that illumined but did not destroy. Her hands became transparent as the fire in her veins glowed through the filmy layers of her skin. With a fascination beyond horror she saw her bones shining like phosphorus, and the multiple sinews that knotted and bound them rippling like threads of living silk. Then the burning faded, and her hands clouded into normality, and the Lodestone released her, leaving her swaying as if she were faint or drunk. The echo of a door slamming somewhere below barely revived her sense of danger. She half ran, half staggered across the floor to the cloister beneath the gallery and collapsed at the base of a pillar, huddling into the golden shadows.

The woman entered a few minutes later. She walked across the sheer marble with the rustle of soft-shod feet, the fluid pacing of limbs both sinuous and strong. Her beauty was the beauty of the leopardess, a black-and-gold deadliness, yet the poise of her head on the curving slenderness of the neck had an unnatural liquidity, for all its regal arrogance: when the man behind her spoke the turn of her chin was snake-like in its suppleness. Her hair was not stiffened into a horn this time but piled in a thick mass of twists and coils, tiny gems lurking like insects in its inky abundance. Her long veils were yellow as pollen, draped around hip and shoulder and trailing like flower-dust in her wake. Jewelry tinkled faintly as she moved. The girl knew her at once: Zohrâne Goulabey, last scion of the Thirteenth House, High Priestess of the Unknown God, Queen of Atlantis, Empress of the World—or as much of the world as had already been sucked into the far-flung net of the ruling island. Those who had kept count said she was almost a hundred and fifty years old, though her face had a metallic smoothness and her figure retained the gloss of a body in its prime. It was rumored she had poisoned her elder brother when she was only eight to secure the succession, disposing of her father, the Wizard-King Pharouq Goulabey, before she reached twenty. Her mother, the legendary beauty Tamiszandre, had died of a surfeit of griefs not long after. Zohrâne had never been seen to weep. She did not wed, vowing to admit neither man nor child into her heart, that no one might come close enough to kill her. Instead, she surrounded herself with bodyslaves, changing them frequently, executing any who roused her to affection. Her advisers hated her only marginally more than she hated them. Studying her, even from a distance, the girl sensed a familiar ugliness exuding from her for all her physical perfection, a rapacious emptiness that would devour life itself to feed its hopeless need. It was something she knew she had encountered before, and the recollection unsettled her, partly because she could not pinpoint its source, but also because of the nebulous fear which accompanied it.

The man who followed Zohrâne was as tall as she and appeared considerably older. His head was shaved; heavy bracelets clasped his biceps, looking more like armor than ornament. His sleek torso was woven with muscle. He must formerly have been extremely handsome, but an accident or infection had crêped and bubbled the skin down one side of his face, and partial healing had caused it to tighten, distorting the symmetry of his features. A latent menace hung round him like a miasma. "They are all here," he was saying. "I have them in the antechamber. They complain, but in whispers: they fear even the walls may retain their mutterings and replay them to your ear. They have made their own subjection."

"Of course," she said. "When I first took power I offered the twelve families a choice: to subject themselves, or to be subjected. There is always a choice. They took the way of pomposity and self-importance, of indolence, cowardice, greed. They thought to cling onto dignity in bending to my will rather than breaking themselves against it. The great houses were shorn of their greatness ages before, little men living on the reputation of the dead. They tell themselves their own interests are best served serving me. That way, they can be comfortable with servitude."

"You need them," he reminded her.

"I need their heritage, the power that sleeps inside them. The strength they have become too nervous or too wary to use. They are the descendants of those who first touched the Lodestone and were forever changed by it. Its potence endures, in their blood, in their bones. I will draw it out, bind it together. It will be enough."

"Are you sure?" The sudden neutrality of his tone betrayed an insidious hope, lurking behind his superficial allegiance. The puckered eyelid gave his sidelong gaze a twist that was coldly malevolent.

"Nothing is sure." Zohrâne smiled. Beside her, his natural menace was diminished, a weapon as slight as a jeweled paper-knife. "Are you afraid, Ixavo?" They had drawn close to the altar now. "Are you afraid of the Stone?"

"You will destroy it?" His furtive utterance was magnified by the space into an enormous whisper.

"I will remake it."

"It will resist destruction."

"All things resist destruction, according to their capacity. Rocks, pebbles, diamonds. Unity is instinctive to being. It doesn't matter." She flung the words over her shoulder like scraps to a beggar, turning to face the Lodestone.

"It will hear you."

"It cannot hear, nor see, nor feel. It is nothing but a lump of crude power. A lump. I hear, and see, and feel. I can break this lump like ordinary rock, and reshape it to my own requirements. I have no fear of a lump, a rock. Have you?" She placed her hand on it, and the girl seemed to see a shudder flow up her arm like a current of hidden flame, jabbing at her brain. She thought: Zohrâne has lived too long in its aura, reached too far into its core. The power has turned her mind. Her reasoning is merely the cunning of madness; she wears her residual sanity like a veil.

Worst of all, she realized, Zohrâne was without fear, and fear is the braking system of intelligence.

"Touch it," the queen said to Ixavo. "For fifteen years you have been the Guardian. Have you never touched it before? Are you really so weak, so incurious—as stupid as the herd-animals we call citizens? I thought more of you, Ixavo. There were times when I believed you might merit my enmity."

There was a long pause, a pause with many layers: tension, hesitation, thought.

"I touched it once," he admitted unwillingly. The watching girl sensed his resistance and the memory of horror. "It burned me. I felt the burning shoot up my arm and melt my face. It was like the fire of the gods. Another time—I might burn away."

"The *gods*." Her contempt was scalding. "What do I care for gods? The Unknown has always been content to remain that way, and as for those petty spirits who call themselves deities, at least here in Atlantis we have had the sense to scorn their worship. The

Gift is beyond their fabled powers. I will take that Gift and absorb it so that it cannot be Given again. The so-called gods shall fade to legend in my shadow. I shall cross from world to world, through Death and back, outside the range of any immortal. Godhead will be my stepping stone."

"What do you want?" he asked slowly. "You rule half the earth. What remains unconquered? An empty desert, a barren mountain range, a few primitive peoples living in caves and mud-huts. Why put yourself to so much trouble to subjugate such as those?"

"You don't understand." Once again, she stretched her hand toward the Lodestone, not touching but as if exploring its hidden magnetic field. "I had thought more of your intellect. Ruling is a detail: I want to *be*. To be last and always, alone and supreme. To have *no limits*. The whole Atlantean empire is a child's playground when compared to the measureless realms that lie beyond the Gate. I *will not* be confined to a solitary planet, a single cosmos, the routine boundaries of life and death. I shall triumph over them all. Ruling is a chore, but triumph is forever sweet."

"And then?" said Ixavo. "When you have triumphed. What then?" Even at that distance, the girl read the comprehension behind his heavy inscrutability. The queen was mad and he knew she was mad, yet he would do nothing to thwart her. Possibly he feared her too much; possibly he was planning to use her, hoping to reap some profit from the backlash of her rashness.

She did not answer the question; her mental focus had clearly moved on, leaving the subject behind. "It is nearly time," she said at length. "Are you sure the others will be ready?"

"They will be ready."

"And the sacrifice?"

"Yes."

"He must be young and strong. The *nymphelin* this morning was beautiful, but he walked with a limp. I will not be seen thrusting the city's rejects at Death's portal as though in mockery of my own ends. Give me the cream of Atlantean youth. Take the sons and daughters of the twelve families: the power is in them, let me drain it with their blood."

He did not react: he had evidently been around her too long. He may even have shared her tastes. "That would be . . . unwise, Highness. As I said before, you need their support."

"For this ceremony only. After that, they will be dross."

"Then start the ceremony. After that . . ."

But his doubt did not touch her. Her insanity had narrowed and intensified her perception, concentrating it within the parameters of her own ambition. She looked at Ixavo and saw his reservations, schemes, evasions, lies, as if he were a crude, obvious creature whose most secret passions would be too predictable to command her interest. He would follow her, she believed, like a jackal in the hope of carrion, the lesser predator trailing the greater, saving private dissent for private expression. She despised him for that transparency, for the banality of his plotting, for the ease with which she could control him: yet contempt was so much a part of her normal emotional range that she was barely conscious of it anymore. He was a useful tool: the rest was superfluous. She had chosen him because he was the son of an Atlantean commander killed abroad, brought up by the priests of Hex-Âté in the forbidden city of Qultuum and therefore, despite his questionable religious background, uncommitted to any dissident factions in Atlantis itself. She had seen evidence that he possessed a certain power, but he used it rarely and she had dismissed it as a weaker strain of the Gift, too negligible to signify. Knowing herself all but omnipotent, she included him in her general abhorrence of lesser beings without feeling the need to consider him a threat.

The girl, immobile in her inadequate hiding-place, caught a fleeting glimpse of Zohrâne's mind, a chink of awareness opening unwanted in her thoughts, and shrank from its total lack of humanity. The ceremony was plainly due to start any minute and she knew she ought to leave, or at least remove herself from the participants' line of vision. But although the Guardian departed Zohrâne remained, standing by the altar and gazing at the Lodestone as though wrapped in a trance of gloating. Her hands roamed over it in a caress without actual contact, framing its outline in her gestures; a secret smile curved her closed lips. Almost she seemed to make love to the Stone: though she did not touch it again her gestures were sensual, even lascivious, while her expression misted into a half-drowned look bordering on ecstasy. The watching girl thought with a curious detachment: She is going to destroy it because she thinks that is the way to absolute domination. Like a besotted man strangling the paramour who teases and torments him, believing thus to possess her utterly. But afterward the beloved has gone beyond possession, and all he has is remembrance. Maybe this is what I am supposed to prevent. But she had no idea what to do, or how, and she sensed instinctively that it was too soon, her moment was not yet. For now she must observe and be unobserved. And despite, or perhaps because of its effect on her, that strange bonding with an ultimate power source, she felt that it would be better destroyed. It was too strong, too hypnotic, too terrifyingly purposeless to be left among greedy, desperate mortals: the very lust of it was a corruption. Broken, its power would disseminate, maybe vanish altogether. Let Zohrâne shatter it—if she could.

Minutes later, the queen fell back from the altar, her rapture fading into the steely stillness which was the essence of her beauty. She drew her veils around her, encasing herself in a skin of yellow gossamer, revealing details of her anatomy formerly blurred, and walked swiftly toward the side door where she had come in. The girl got to her feet and began to run through the cloister, back to the stairs leading up to the gallery. She was farther from it than she had realized; commune with the Lodestone must have disorientated her. A priest coming through the main entrance saw the flicker of movement and shouted for the guards.

There were too many within call. She saw she was cut off, doubled back, and within seconds was writhing in the grip of strong
arms sheathed in leather and bronze. She ceased to struggle when
she saw it was no use, standing very still, staring stonily at her
captors. "What do you want done with him?" asked the captain.

"Her," said the priest. "Take a closer look. Ixavo will want to
examine her, but not now. There isn't time. Throw her in the cell
with the other. I have to start the drum."

They took her away, holding her firmly but not painfully, evidently confident she could not escape. Down a gloomy stair, and
into the convoluted passages beneath the temple. The drum began while they were on the stair, the same sound she had heard at
the inn but far louder, a deep rhythmic boom that made the walls
vibrate. Even the soldiers were disturbed by it. It was a noise that
got inside a person's head and pounded against the sides of the
skull, a noise that loosened the very ligaments binding the joints
together. When her teeth stopped shaking the girl found herself
being thrust through a low door into darkness. The door closed
behind her, sliding into its familiar groove with the thud of stone
settling on stone. Bolts scraped; a key clicked and rattled. Then
silence, the dense, furry, clinging silence of warm stale air in a
small space, torn with the harsh rasp of her own breathing. She
sat down slowly on what felt like solid rock, leaning against the
wall. She could see nothing but the blotches of residual light on
her retina dwindling into a void. As her panting eased she heard
the soft hiss duplicated, somewhere close by, an echo in an echo-
less room. The hairs rose on her neck. Then she remembered.
The other, the priest had said. "Hello?" she whispered. In the
dark, she found it automatic to whisper. "Are you there?"

"Of course," said the dark, prosaically. "Where would I go?" It
had a reassuringly normal voice, cool but not cruel, its sarcasm as
gentle as a feather-edged knife. Her fright gradually lessened.

"Who are you?"

"Myself." There was laughter in the answer, and certainty. "Strangers first. Who are you?"

"You're a stranger too."

"Not as strange as you."

"How do you know?" she demanded, mildly indignant.

"I saw you—briefly—when they pushed you in here. And earlier. Outside. You're no Atlantean. Your skin is fair and your eyes are pale and your hair is the color of dying leaves. You're a girl by the walk and the voice, although your body looks like it isn't quite sure yet. I don't recognize your accent. So who are you?"

The beggar, she thought, annoyed with herself for not catching on sooner. Curiously, his uncomplimentary words did not trouble her. She was concentrating on her own identity: even as she reached for it, it seemed to fragment, dream interfacing with reality, pieces of her self floating away leaving gaps filled with unfocused memory. "My name is Fernani," she said, but she wasn't certain. Somehow, it didn't sound quite right. "Some people call me Fern." That was better. *Fern* belonged to her: it fitted like a well-worn glove.

"Where are you from, Fernani? And what are you doing *here*?"

"I come from a village partway up Mount Vèz in the Viroc. North of Géna—"

"I know where the Viroc is: I've seen maps. You're a long way from home."

"I wanted to see the world," she said, avoiding any hint of defiance.

"You won't see much of it in here."

"You're good at stating the obvious, aren't you?" She thought it was time to fight back. "It's your turn now. Who are *you*?"

"Rafarl Dev. Some people call me Raf. I'm a different kind of stranger." She could hear the mockery turned inward, on himself.

"What kind?"

"A half-breed. A bastard. A traitor by blood, a freak by inclination. An inborn outcast. Don't you know the law here?"

"Of course not." The landlady at the inn had talked about it, she remembered.

"I thought everyone in the empire must be interested in the city which rules them?"

"The Viroc is a long way away, as you said. I'm just an ignorant provincial."

She heard the ghost of a laugh in the darkness, a ghost as warm as friendliness. "Obviously. You're an ignorant provincial, I'm an arrogant urbanite. I apologize. For all my doubtful status, I still think like an Atlantean. We believe our city is at the center of *all* worlds. I suppose that's why the twelve families were so upset when they found the Gift cropping up among those from less se-lect regions. It dawned on them that they were spreading their tal-ents with their seed, so about four hundred years ago marriage with foreigners was made illegal. It didn't do much good, of course. The bad habits of the ruling classes are well-known. But when Zohrâne took power she started ordering cross-bred infants to be butchered at birth, often with their errant mothers. A few slipped through the net. My mother is of the House of Dévornine: her kin would not let her be so casually slaughtered, though my fa-ther was hunted down like a dog. They married her to a dullard of pure Atlantean stock and my mother forced him to accept me: it was her condition for agreeing to the arrangement. She told me the truth when I was old enough to understand. A few years later I ran away and since then I've lived rough. I go home once in a while for a fancy meal and a soft bed. And her. She gives me money which I ought to refuse, but I don't. The scapegrace son— only they would be unlikely to let me reform, even if I wished it."

"Are you really a beggar?" she asked.

"So you noticed me."

"You made yourself noticeable."

The ghost laughed again, something between a gasp and a

sigh. "Necessity. I had to get in here. I'm a beggar when it suits me. A beggar for a whim, a thief at need, a pirate whenever I can steal a boat. A parasite battening on a city of parasites, which has half the earth as its host."

"It's a beautiful city," she said.

"*Ara-yé.* It's beautiful and corrupt. I love it and hate it. That is the double curse of my heredity."

"Why did you want to get into the temple? It doesn't seem to have done you much good."

"I can leave when I want to." He sounded dangerously unworried. "If I'm gone too long, a contact outside will send a message to my mother. The Dévornines rank third of the ruling families, and my illegitimacy is still unofficial, no matter how badly I choose to behave. The priests would not dare offend her. But I shouldn't need her assistance. When the ceremony is over, I'll find a way to make the guard unbolt the door."

"How?"

"Call him. Tell him there's a hole in the wall, or the previous occupant left a handful of coins on the floor, or whatever. Pique his curiosity. Arouse his greed. The average intelligence of the temple guard is not high. When he's distracted, I'll try to knock him out. You can probably help with the distraction."

"Thanks," she murmured. If help is required, had said the Hermit, it will be found. This is my help, she thought, suddenly sure. That's why I'm here.

There was a silence, already vaguely companionable. The temple drum had stopped long since and no sound came from above. "How will you know when the ceremony's finished?" she inquired.

"Guesswork. They don't usually go on much more than an hour."

"You still haven't told me why you're here."

"Three days ago, the street patrol picked up a friend of mine on some minor charge. Probably false. Uuinoor's honest: he doesn't have any versatility. I learned last night they brought him here. He'll be in another cell somewhere around." She heard him shifting his position, restless with waiting. "If I don't get him out, he'll join the queue for sacrifice."

"So might you."

"No risk of that. I told you, I'm a Dévornine."

"Before they caught me," Fern said, "I overheard a conversation between Zohrâne and a priest. She called him the Guardian."

"Ixavo. How did you manage that? You must have crept in quietly after me . . ."

"I'm naturally unobtrusive."

"What are you doing—an ignorant provincial—sneaking into the temple to eavesdrop on the queen of the civilized world? It savors of spying, but you don't look like a spy. In any case, Zohrâne's few remaining enemies are all Atlantean."

"I'm not a spy. I wanted to see the temple, that's all. The rest was chance." She took a deep breath to steady herself. "You're in danger. More than you know. Zohrâne told the Guardian specifically to target the twelve families. Apparently she wants the calibre of sacrifice improved. She said the last one was a *nymphelin* who limped. She thinks the Gate of Death will open wider for the healthy and highborn."

The ensuing pause felt wrong, as if the very darkness tightened. "Limped?" said her cellmate. His voice had gone suddenly cold.

The pause stretched out for several heartbeats.

"I'm sorry," Fern whispered.

Since her arrival in Atlantis she appeared to have acquired a new level of insight into the emotions of others, almost as if the barriers that isolate the individual mind were breaking down, and she was receiving messages from the naked dimension of the spirit. It had happened with Zohrâne when, for a few seconds, she had peered into the starving void of her soul—a void that reminded her of someone else, though she could not quite recall whom. And now it was happening to her in the dark, with a man she could not see. She sensed the abrupt pang of grief taking him off guard, the clenching of a complex inner pain. There was a remote quality to his grief, and the pain seemed to be associated more than anything with failure, one of many failures, as if he saw his life unfolding in an endless pattern of deeds unachieved, friends let down, enemies he could not or would not defy. Under the veneer of light-hearted fecklessness, mockery, and self-mockery, she seemed to see him examining himself through a distorting lens that made his very soul ugly. She became so involved in his pain she felt her own heart stabbed in sympathy.

"It must have been this morning," he said eventually. "They're not usually so hasty. I was finished before I started." Pause. "Not much of a hero, am I? Turning up too late to rescue someone who's already dead."

Another pause. This one threatened to extend itself indefinitely. Fern rushed into speech, groping for the right words with which to string her ideas together, only half certain of what she wanted to say and too impetuous to be afraid of saying it wrong. "Nobody's a hero all the time. A hero is just an ordinary person who does something exceptional, not a rare breed, whatever the law of Atlantis may claim. We're all ordinary: you and me and Zohrâne and . . . and the priests and the guards and the slaves. And if we try, and fail, and still try, and go on trying—if we're lucky and hopeful and occasionally brave—we sometimes manage to pull it off. Heroes aren't born or made, they make themselves. There are probably lots of heroes who never do anything heroic. It doesn't matter. Failing doesn't matter. What matters is trying again." The words ran out and she found herself panting from the torrent of them, slightly stunned at an outpouring which seemed to have come from nowhere in her mind.

There was a silence through which she could not see.

Then: "I thought you were a child," he said. "A runaway waif come to seek your fortune. But you talk . . . as if you were a thousand years old."

I am unborn, said her thought. Many ages unborn. She flinched away from the nightmare in her head, clinging to memories that seemed to shrink in the darkness while the horror grew and reached out toward her . . .

"Fernani?"

"Just Fern," she mumbled.

"How old *are* you?"

"Sixteen." That was something she was sure of, a solid fact to hold on to in a maelstrom of doubt. Sixteen.

"Uuinoor was nineteen," Rafarl said after a while. "He always seemed much less."

"Did you know him well?"

"Not really. His sister is a close friend of mine—his twin-sister. At least, she was. She was the one who asked me to help him. You can save my brother, she said. Only you. You're a Dévornine."

Fern said nothing for a few moments. She was conscious of a feeling she had rarely experienced before, a feeling sharp as a needle, bitter as bile. It fermented inside her like a kind of emotional contamination, discoloring the whole spectrum of her spirit. *His sister is a close friend of mine* . . . She was afraid to speak in case her voice betrayed her. Stupid, she admonished herself furiously. Stupid. You barely know him . . .

She tried to picture how he had looked, the beggar under the arch, but her blurred recollection seemed to have little to do with the man in the dark.

"Uuinarde thought I could persuade my mother to use her influence," Rafarl was saying, "but she refused. She said it wouldn't do any good. I was angry, so . . . I tried this. An idiotic impulse, no time for proper planning. I knew she'd never fail *me*, however she felt about my friend." Fern felt rather than heard the sigh that followed, brushing her cheek like a zephyr. "I wasn't really being heroic, or even brave. Mostly, I was just enraged."

"Well, you're going to have to be heroic now," Fern said, recovering herself. "I told you, Zohrâne ordered the Guardian to take the children of the twelve families. He didn't like it—I should imagine he's prudent rather than compassionate—but he'll obey. You'd be ideal. A half-breed means a half measure. Half obedience, half defiance, depending on whose side you're on. We need a stratagem to get out of here. And it had better be more effective than your last one."

"We?" The ghost-laugh returned, shaking his tone.

She thought: Danger excites him. Whatever he says.

"You may as well rescue *somebody*," she said.

They sat for a while unspeaking; she could sense his concentration, possibilities weaving, knotting, unravelling in his mind. The dark thickened around them, as though drawn and focused by his thoughts. She felt a growing pressure weighing down on her. "The ceremony should be over soon," Rafarl said eventually. He sounded curiously breathless.

And then: "What's happening? I feel as if . . ."

". . . as if we're suffocating," said Fern, her voice constricted to a whisper.

It had been cooler underground, away from the sun, but the temperature must have crept up without their noticing and now the heat was becoming oppressive. Fern could feel the sweat gathering under her short hair and trickling over her temples and down her neck. When she touched her face it was wet.

"There's something . . . going on up there," said Rafarl. "Maybe . . . a fire." She heard him rise and move to the door, thumping on it with his fist. "Guard! Guard!" No response. *"Tarq-morrh . . . gniarré!"* Both words were outside Fern's vocabulary but she thought she could hazard a guess at their meaning. "Either he's not answering . . . or . . . he's gone . . ."

"It's not a fire," Fern said as realization dawned. "It's Zohrâne. She's trying to—" She broke off, making a conscious effort to inhale. Breathing was no longer something her body could take care of by itself. The air pulsed in her ears like blood. She was vaguely aware that Rafarl had slid to the ground beside her: his leg touched hers at the thigh, his shoulder nudged her shoulder.

"Trying to what?" he asked.

"To break . . . the Lodestone."

"What?"

"She's using the twelve families . . . concentrating their power . . . turning it back on its source . . ." Haltingly, Fern tried to explain something she did not fully comprehend herself. Even as she spoke she registered a new sound carried from above, a sort of thrumming boom, like the distant hum of a swarm of bees in an echoing cave. She realized after a minute or two that it must be the drumskin in the temple, vibrating in the buildup of power. Its shivering note seemed to swell as a bizarre accompaniment to whatever was transpiring above them. The sound was not so much loud as pervasive: it resonated from floor and ceiling and walls, and the air trembled with it. Covering her ears did no good: it was already inside her. She had given up trying to talk and Rafarl's protest was swallowed up, compressed into a fading gasp. The heat closed around them like a fist, squeezing the last droplet of perspiration from their bodies. She felt his arms move to encircle her and she clung to him in response, locking her hands across his back, seeking not shelter but mutual protection, as though their combined strength might somehow shield them from the relentless escalation of the spell. Her sweat-soaked breasts were clamped against his unfamiliar torso; she sensed his strained breathing as his rib cage heaved in her embrace. *You have the Gift.* Was it the Hermit who had said that? *Use it.* And instead of resisting the power she reached into it, toward the Stone, her untried ability waxing as it renewed contact with its matrix. She stretched out with her mind, laboring to enclose them in a cocoon spun from the very force that bore down on them. Her breathing seemed to ease, but she wasn't sure. The clasp of her arms grew stronger than a band of steel.

And then it snapped. There was a crack that split the air and stabbed like lightning deep into the ground. Her skull rang with something that might have been sound or light or both; for a hideous second her brain appeared to be flying apart, fragments of memory, thought, self spewing in all directions. What happened to her body she did not know. There was an instant of struggle, then blackness swallowed her. When she recovered consciousness she was doubled over and her mouth tasted of vomit. "You were sick," said Rafarl. "On me."

"Sorry."

He was still gripping her shoulder, pulling her into a sitting position. She put her hand in the wetness on the ground and swore in a language she could not remember.

Close by, a crevasse had opened up in the darkness, a right-angled shaft of reddish pallor. The light-source was weak, but after so long in the gloom of the dungeon it seemed dazzlingly bright. "It's the door," Rafarl supplied. "That . . . earth-tremor— whatever it was—must have jolted it loose. I think the bolts have ruptured." He stood up, dragging her with him. "Come on. On your feet. This is our chance to get out."

The door was heavy, the hinges damaged. They both had to shove before twisted metal finally succumbed and the whole stone slab keeled outward and thudded into the passageway. "That'll bring the guards," Rafarl muttered; but no one came. A torch was guttering in a wall-bracket; another had shrunken to a red smolder. Fern tried to recall from which direction she had come but could not.

"This way," said Rafarl.

"Do you know where you're going?" she inquired after a couple of minutes.

"No. And if you want to come with me, you won't ask."

Around a corner they found the jailer and one of the guards. There was blood and froth on their lips and dark patches under their skin as if from bruising or internal hemorrhage. Fern was glad of the poor light so she could not see them clearly. "Whatever happened here," Rafarl asserted, "it killed them." He took the key-ring from the jailer's belt and at every cell door they came to he knocked and shouted, but there was never any answer. The note in his voice grew slightly more desperate with every hopeless call. At the last he unlocked it anyway, fumbling with several keys until he found the right one, thrusting the door open only a foot or so before he drew back. Fern saw a shadow crossing the light, shaped like an arm. "They're dead," he said. "They're all dead." Briefly, she shared his nightmare of returning above ground to find Atlantis itself a city of corpses through which they would wander aimlessly, uncertain what to do with their leftover lives. "I wonder how we survived," he speculated. "Maybe our dungeon-walls were just a little more solid than these. Strange. I never thought I'd be grateful for the security of the prison-cell which held me." The ghost-laugh, real enough in the dark, failed here, but not because of the torchlight.

It wasn't the walls, thought Fern. It was me.

But she said nothing.

The next door they came to was different. Not a cell door this time: taller, broader, metal-plated, inlaid with the Atlantean sun-star in some sort of copper alloy that looked bloodred in the torch-light. There were bolts at top and base: it unlocked to the largest key. The chamber beyond was invisible in the darkness, but Fern sensed height, depth, space. A smell reached her that she knew she had never smelled before, yet somewhere in her genes, in the ancient, unforgotten places of her race-memory, it was familiar. Her skin crawled. Rafarl took a torch from the wall-bracket in the corridor and stepped across the threshold. She followed him.

The room was vaulted: shadows fled from arch to arch and

skulked behind the pillars. Round the walls there were things she had seen once before, things with spikes and bars and chains, in an antique castle—she could not remember where—long ago and far away, but those had been age-blackened, rusted with disuse; these were sharpened, scoured, polished. Used. There was a brazier on one side but it had been overturned, perhaps in the aftershock of the spell. Ash sifted across the floor. To her left, the torch-glow glinted back from many edges of light: an array of knives laid along a bench, knives of every shape and size, straight and curved, broad and slender, hooked, corkscrewed, double- and triple-bladed. All scrupulously cleaned, shining in the dark. *Loved.* In the center of the room was a table of stone, a rectangular slab approximately the length of a man. Straps were positioned at judicious intervals; lamps stood at each corner, so angled that, when lit, their overlapping beams would cast a shadowless glare across its surface. Its very emptiness drew her, filling her eyes, filling her mind. She thought: It's all so *clean.* And: Where does the smell come from, if it's clean? But she knew the answer to that. The cleanliness was only superficial, a purification that could never penetrate beneath the skin. But the smell, the smell was old and strong. It had sunk deep, deep into the stone, into the roots of the shadows, into the sinews of the walls, permeating to the very core of the room. There were other things there too, sounds, sights, waiting under the silence and behind the torchlight. Cries and whispers, the memory of blood. She stood and listened, afraid of echoes she could not hear. When she glanced down, she saw her hand locked in Rafarl's. He too did not speak, only moving the torch so the shadows swiveled, leaping from nook to nook. She thought of the gilded sanctum above, the germ of power at its heart, now shattered by Zohrâne in her lust and envy. This is Atlantis too, she told herself. This is the underbelly of the city. The flipside of the coin. Without it, the temple, the palaces— the whole metropolis—would not exist.

Apart from the spilled brazier, the chamber was intact. As if there was something here that resisted destruction, a terrible negative force. "They say," said Rafarl, "this room is directly below the altar. It must have been at the epicenter of the spellshock."

And: "It's empty. Anyway."

"Is it?" said Fern.

When they left, he stopped to re-lock the door. Keeping people out. Shutting something in.

It was a few minutes before they spoke again.

"Your friend didn't die there," Fern said at last. "Sacrifice is quick." (She hoped it was.)

"I have lost many friends," said Rafarl.

The stair to the upper level was unmanned: the guard at its foot lay in an ungainly sprawl, as still as a gargoyle. "Perhaps Zohrâne is dead too," Rafarl said, hesitating.

"No, she isn't," Fern said, suddenly sure, although she could not have explained why. "Let's take a look."

"But if she *isn't* dead—"

Fern, however, had already slipped past him and was cautiously pushing the door open. When the gap was wide enough she slid through; Rafarl, reluctant and slightly surprised, followed her.

The first thing Fern saw was the crack in the dome. It ran from the far wall almost to the apex, a jagged line fraying here and there into hair-thin fractures, gaping abruptly at one point to show an eye blink of sky. Splinters of masonry were scattered across the immaculate floor, curling flakes of gold leaf, a drift of dust that glittered faintly even in shadow. A thin ray of sunshine had negotiated the crack and slanted across the chamber, falling just short of the vacant altar. The fragile rune that it drew on the marble outshone the mandala and turned all the gilding to dross. She did not know why it took her so long to register the bodies. They were sprawled in a broken circle around the tabernacle: most had retreated to the cloister or been flung against the pillars, but a couple lay closer to the center. Near at hand, someone was groaning. They have the Gift, Fern remembered. They won't all be dead. "That's my uncle," said Rafarl without audible regret, indicating one who made neither motion nor sound. She glanced quickly at her companion, absorbing brief details of his profile, the bump in the straightness of his nose, the concave line of his cheek. There was a fresh bruise along the bone, relict maybe of his arrest; she couldn't see his eyes. This was the beggar who had looked at her so slyly, the man she had come to know in the dark. The traces of her vomit smeared his clothes. She shivered at the touch of something at once unknown and inexplicably familiar.

A noise from the heart of the chamber drew them from their separate reflections. Beside the altar one of the bodies was pulling itself upright, clutching at the stone. The bright vein of sunlight dimmed anything just beyond its reach even more than objects at a distance and the figure was consequently unclear, though a darkness fell about it like loosened hair and yellow cobwebs clung to its limbs. Its movements were clumsy from weakness or pain and they could hear the rasp of its breathing echoing round the vault. It had not noticed the newcomers: its whole attention was centered on something gripped in its right hand. Stiff-legged and unsteady, it hobbled toward the sunlight. The head was bent forward, the fingers slowly uncurled. The beam of radiance fell on an open palm and an odd-shaped fragment cupped within it. At that range Fern could not hope to see what it was but still she knew. She thought she had always known.

The key.

✦ X ✦

"We have to go," Rafarl said. "Now." Fern nodded, allowing him to draw her back into the shelter of the cloister. As she retreated she noticed something embedded in the nearest pillar, a wedge-shaped chip of black stone the length of her thumb. The marble was cracking around it, tiny fault lines spreading visibly outward. The Lodestone, she thought. There must be pieces of it all over the place. But the key—the key is the core . . .

"We must get it," she muttered, pulling away from him.

"Get what?"

"The key. I don't know exactly how she did it—some form of telekinesis—but when she smashed the Lodestone one piece of it took the shape of a key. Probably the piece at the heart. She will use it to unlock the Gate of Death."

They were talking softly now as some of the prone bodies began to struggle to their feet. Others lay very still. One of them, Fern saw, had a fragment of the Stone protruding from his chest like a featherless dart. It had entered him with such force it must have split the breastbone: most of the fragment was buried in the wound, blood welling sluggishly around it.

254

"Death comes to us all, even the Gifted," said Rafarl somberly. "Why rush it?"

"You don't understand. When we die we leave this world. We don't know where we go: another place, another cosmos . . . *else-where*. We aren't *supposed* to know. But if Zohrâne can open the Gate while she still lives she believes she can defeat Death, and come and go between worlds as she pleases. That's forbidden. It would be like—" she tried to remember the Hermit's words "—a breach in the Wall of Being. Life itself would be sucked into it. It would be the end of everything."

"How do you know all this?" Rafarl demanded. "The people here are afraid of the queen, but they wouldn't help her if they knew they were committing suicide. As for Zohrâne herself, she's probably mad, certainly evil, but never stupid."

"She's blinkered," said Fern. "It's part of her obsession. I've come across it before."

"That's a lot of experience for sixteen years."

"Look, are you going to help me, or—or just *talk* about it?"

But the burgeoning quarrel had no chance to progress. A detachment of guards arrived, fortunately through another entrance. Zohrâne, closing her hand upon the key, summoned her reserves of strength and began to give orders in her customary imperative manner. The surviving representatives of the ruling families leaned on each other for support or crouched over their motionless companions. Fern saw Ixavo sitting propped against the base of a column with his head bowed; she was a little surprised to find him still alive, remembering his aversion to the Stone. When he looked up the light fell on his disfigurement and she thought it must have been aggravated by the release of unnatural forces: the diseased area appeared to have both spread and constricted, giving an ugly twist to his mouth and screwing one eye into a leer. There was something about him that she found especially disquieting, something Zohrâne had missed, something inexplicably *wrong.* It troubled her more each time she saw him, as if her mind were screaming a warning that her ears could not hear. But whatever it was, she was unable to pin it down, and Rafarl was gripping her arm, drawing her away. She did not resist him now. He peered round a side door and drew back hastily, dropping to the floor, dragging Fern with him. "Play dead," he hissed. "They won't notice two more corpses." The second clutch of guards was on them even as she froze.

But they were lucky. The newcomers marched straight across the cloister into the center of the tabernacle. Zohrâne was already leaving, delegating to Ixavo, now on his feet, the task of clearing the devastation. He seemed to have recovered very rapidly. Listening to his voice as he issued instructions and cracked out commands, Fern was distracted from their immediate danger. She heard a flaw in its timbre which she felt, irrationally, should not have been there. It was a voice that might once have been smooth and pleasant to the ear were it not for the grating note that made it at once soft and harsh, a crack in the bell that corrupted its whole tone. She wondered if the affliction of his skin had also infected his vocal cords, destroying both beauty and sound.

"When I give the word, we run," whispered Rafarl.

They moved at just the wrong moment. Ixavo turned: across a wide arc of floor his eyes met Fern's. His face stilled, his lips parted on a word she did not need to hear. A lance of silence reached out toward her, binding them together in an instant of stasis. The word he had only breathed echoed in her mind. *You.*

They ran.

Behind her, Fern heard the thud of pursuing feet, Ixavo's cry: "The girl! *I want the girl!*" The order caused some valuable confusion: Fern's short hair and leather breeches meant the foremost guards slowed, looking in vain for a girl to arrest. Rafarl, hearing the chase falter, was quick to capitalize on their doubt. "She went that way!" he said, indicating to the right along the colonnade as the guards issued from the exit. Then he grabbed Fern's hand and raced down the steps, pulling her with him. They had gained useful seconds, but not many. It would not take their pursuers long to realize their mistake and come pouring after them. Across the encircling roadway Rafarl dived into the market precinct, twisting and dodging through the narrow streets with the lightning certainty of a weasel in a rabbit warren. A couple of guards, ignoring the ruse, were still on their heels, but Rafarl had the knack of hooking his foot around table-legs and the supports of stalls as he passed, precipitating an assortment of wares into their path. Even as they fell back Fern heard the hue and cry of the others rushing to join them. But the civilians showed little enthusiasm for the hunt: storekeepers rounded on the guards over their spilled merchandise, strident voices were raised in argument, irate citizens dammed the torrent of pursuit, apparently without deliberate intent. Rafarl plunged through doorways into the midst of discreet deals whose participants barely gave the fugitives a second look, up stairs, out of windows, over roofs. Fern saw another door ahead of them, an arched door in a stone wall, a door like all the rest. Rafarl, still in the lead, dropped from roof to balcony, from balcony to terrace, seized the handle, thrust his shoulder against the planks. Unvarnished planks, bleached almost white and peeling from the heat. A gecko scurried across the lintel. The chill that brushed Fern's nape reached beyond the surface of memory, far down into her mind. She shrieked a warning, clutching his arm and yanking him away just as the door gave. They tumbled backward onto the terrace. The door swung out over empty space.

The building beyond had either collapsed or been partially demolished: there was no floor, only a sheer drop to the sewers below. They picked themselves up slowly; under the city dust, Rafarl's cheek had paled to khaki. "How did you know?" he said. "You couldn't have seen anything." She shook her head. She had seen only the gecko, and the peeling plankwork. But the gecko had gone, and the door was solid wood, roughly carved. She could not explain it.

They had no time to talk. Rafarl negotiated another window, ducked through entrances and exits, up and down one street or many. Fern followed in trusting confusion. The chase was left behind, bogged down in a morass of indignant citizenry, mazed with alleyways and passageways. After a while, Fern realized they were in another part of the city altogether. The streets grew wider, the crowds more sparse. The flow of carts, chariots, and phaetons that had monopolized the main thoroughfares was here reduced to a trickle. Arches opened onto secluded gardens, spilling over with flower-scents, musical with falling water. They stopped in a small square at the center of which a gaping dolphin vomited into a circular basin. Fern sat down thankfully on the lip but Rafarl jumped into the pool and dipped his head under the cascade, washing the dirt from his face and hair, drenching his whole body in blissful coolness. His ragged clothing clung to him like skin: she saw hard swellings of muscle and brown gaps of flesh, satiny with youth, as yet untouched by rough living. She wished she could follow his example, but she felt too shy and she knew her leather breeches would stiffen in the wet. At last he straightened up, shaking back his locks in a shower of bright droplets that spattered her arms and legs, turning toward her so that she saw him properly for the first time since they met. He was dark as bronze, golden as the city. His hair dripped down his back in a tattered mane, cut unevenly or not at all. Sharp bones drew his cheeks into leanness: above them his eyes were crystal-brown, water-clear. "Well?" he said, possibly reading too much into her examination.

She averted her gaze, splashing her face and neck. "Join me," he said.

"I can't. These clothes . . ."

He grimaced at the leather, evidently taking her point. Then

he cupped his hands under the fountain, offering her a drink before it spilled. She lapped from his palm like a kitten, managing
little more than to moisten her tongue, suddenly laughing, as suddenly serious. When he laughed she noticed there was a tooth
missing in his lower jaw, giving him something of the look of an
urchin rather than an adult of twenty or so. "Raf," she said. She
had not given him his name before.

"Fern." He traded name for name. He was studying her with
the same attention she had accorded him, seeing a slight barbarian stranger, boyish yet unlike a boy, curiously poised in her awkward garb. She looked as pale and delicate as a flower, as cool as a
northern breeze, yet he sensed in her a resolution as strong or
stronger than his own, a core harder than diamond. And behind
her green-veined eyes he glimpsed a shining well of thought, a
knowledge far beyond her sixteen years, at once alien and incom-
prehensible. "I'd almost certainly have been killed falling through
that door if you hadn't stopped me," he said. "And in the temple
dungeon . . . we survived. We survived when so many others died.
I am enough my mother's son to know that can be neither luck
nor chance. You have the Gift. The Atlantean strain in you must
come from far back, yet it's there. It has to be." He waited, but
she did not respond. "Why didn't you tell me?"

"I heard it could get me into trouble here," she said at length.
"Your people are jealous of their inheritance. Am I supposed to
trust you?"

"Don't you?"

"Yes."

"Then why—?"

She looked down at her hands, plucking absently at the hem
of her shirt. "I don't know. The Hermit near my village said I had
the Gift—you say I have it—but I'm not sure. Sometimes I feel it
so strongly . . . and sometimes there's nothing there. Maybe I'm
just afraid. Afraid of having it, *using* it—afraid of doing harm. I

don't mean I'm afraid of the authorities *here*. I expect I ought to be, but I'm not; I don't seem to have time for that. Ever since I arrived, I've been so *confused*. My head seems to be in a muddle, full of thoughts—images—I don't recognize; I don't even know how they came there. The strange thing is, when I'm in danger—when I feel the power, when I get too close to Zohrâne—that's when my mind is clearest. There's something I have to do . . ."

"You *are* a spy," Rafarl said flippantly.

"No. I was sent . . ."

"By whom?"

"The Hermit . . . I think. I don't know. I don't know. But you're going to help me: I'm sure of *that*. That's why we met."

"Well, I'm not," Rafarl said, not mincing his words. "I won't get mixed up in some mysterious mission when even the emissary knows nothing about it. It all sounds too much like religion to me. I don't believe in religion—*any* religion: it's the stupidest excuse for trouble mankind has ever come up with. Anyway, I'm giving up trying to help anyone: I'm obviously not much good at it. I have enough problems trying to help myself."

He expected her to argue but a rare frown puckered her forehead: she was evidently still preoccupied with her own bewilderment.

"What will you do now?" he asked her.

"I haven't decided."

He produced a sigh which she did not seem to hear. "You'd better come with me."

They left the square and made their way toward the mountain, crossing the peripheral road and climbing the slope via one of the many paved footpaths which scrambled from terrace to terrace, zigzagging between steep flights of steps. The sun was very low now and an isolated cloud, the shape of a pointing hand, extended an endless digit out of the west. Long shadows lay across the city. The softness of evening wrapped the gardens on either side of the path; occasional trills of birdsong rose from cultivated thicket or cloistered tree. Through all the adventures and terrors of the day the wonder of Atlantis had remained with Fern, a constant counterpoint to every incident, every emotion, and still she gazed at her surroundings with wide eyes, as if trying to impress each new detail in the shifting files of her memory. Somewhere at the back of her thought there was a lurking certainty that one day she would be gone and Atlantis lost to her forever, but although more desperate concerns preoccupied her attention, whenever they could be set aside she concentrated on the sights and sounds of the most beautiful city in the history of the world, so that its image might endure in her mind long after the reality had vanished. She had a sudden vision of herself at some time in the future, standing in a strange room by a rectangular window, looking out on a landscape that had nothing to do with the Viroc—it was odd how difficult she found it to remember her home—and she knew she was thinking of Atlantis, straining to recapture the scenes that passed too quickly even now. The afternoon had been long but not long enough, the hours had stretched out to encompass a jumble of excitements and fears, and had raced by before she could catch hold of a single moment and appreciate it at leisure. The sky appeared too vast for the sun to make the crossing in only a day, but dusk came swiftly in the tropics, and already its blood-orange disc was sinking into the haze along the horizon, while the purple cloud-hand seemed to thicken and spread above it, unfurling many fingers, pressing it down into oblivion. Looking up ahead in the lastlight, Fern saw marble walls blushing with more than sunset, low round domes peeping over them, the topmost plumes of trees with crimson leaves. "What is that?" she asked Rafarl.

"The Rose Palace. Pharouq built it for Tamiszandre, because she didn't like the old palace in the lower city, but he died a month after it was completed, and she would not live there anymore.

She spent the rest of her life in a house by the sea, a long way from here. Now, it's Zohrâne's principal residence."

"It's beautiful," said Fern.

"It's high up," said Rafarl. "She likes to look down on her subjects."

He turned off the path to the right, leading her through a wicket gate into a grove too dim for her to see clearly. And then they were ascending some steps up to a veranda, and there were windows onto lamplight and a doorless arch with a curtain that swung and glittered. Crystal beads tinkled as they passed through. A woman sitting alone on a sofa sprang to her feet with a cry.

"Raf! Oh, *Raf!*"

She hugged him; he responded cautiously, evidently disconcerted by so passionate a welcome. *"Mié—!"*

"I'm sorry, dearest—I know you hate fuss—but something so dreadful has happened . . . Your uncle Rahil—"

"I know."

"You *know*?"

"We were in the temple. *Mié,* I want you to meet a friend of mine."

"Is this the little *nympheline* you told me about?"

"No," said Rafarl. Too bluntly, Fern thought, but the returning pang of unwanted emotion had no time to linger. The woman had moved toward her with an outstretched hand and a smile at once warm and elusively wistful. She was little taller than Fern and slender to the point of thinness, large-eyed, bird-boned, impossibly fragile about the wrists and ankles. Her dark hair hung loose: paler threads gleamed here and there as if it were woven with moonlight. Her sun-sheltered skin was ivory-fair and so fine the veins showed blue beneath it and shadows marked it like a bruise. Instead of the usual trousers she wore a long dress which covered more of her anatomy than was customary, made of some dull silk, the color of dusk. A single veil, so insubstantial its hue could only be guessed, clung around her as if of its own volition, perceptible as hardly more than a blurring of her falling hair and a haze over the sheen on her robe. No jewelry adorned bare arm or throat and her features were untouched by the cosmetics favored by most Atlantean women. The smile lit her face like spring in a faded garden.

"This is Fernani," said Rafarl. "Fern, this is my mother. Cidame Ezramé Dévornine." In Atlantis, Fern knew, women of high lineage kept their kin-names if they married a man of lower rank, and had the right to pass them on to their children. The abbreviation Dev, which Rafarl used, was discretionary, perhaps because of his illegitimacy.

Disdaining more formal greetings, Ezramé clasped Fern's hand between both of hers. "Why, you're just a child," she said. "From the north, I think. What are you doing here in our city? I fear . . . it could be unfriendly to you."

"I haven't found it unfriendly," Fern replied.

Rafarl interrupted. "It's a long story, and would go better with food. We're starving. I could do with a bath too."

"Of course, dearest," said his mother, and to Fern: "Forgive my impatience. I am a little distraught today . . . Rahil is—*was*— my only brother. We had not been close for many years—" Rafarl muttered something inaudible "—but we grew up together, he was my family. There was always a remnant of affection between us. This has been a great shock."

"I should go," said Fern, acutely uncomfortable. "You must want to be alone with your son."

"Not at all," Ezramé responded with her swift warm smile. "I didn't mean that you were unwelcome: on the contrary. Rafarl, believe me, would show less sympathy than you. He and his uncle were never on good terms."

"We weren't on *any* terms," Rafarl remarked in an aside.

"Come with me," Ezramé said to Fern. "I expect you'd like a

change of clothes, wouldn't you? Those breeches must be horridly uncomfortable in the heat."

Fern murmured a further protest and was thankful to be ignored. The Cidame led her to a disrobing room, swathed her in a towel, and then left her alone in the bath chamber. "Raf can wait till you've finished. I know northern customs are different from ours." Fern immersed herself in the warm water up to her neck, luxuriating in a pleasure unknown in the Viroc. But the Viroc seemed impossibly far away, her whole childhood as remote and illusory as a fairy tale, the memories mere transparencies slotted into the back of her mind. She had not thought of her home for some time: indeed, she hardly thought of it at all. She tried to remember her own mother, and an automatic picture came into her head—a taciturn figure with a thick plait of hair—but it was strangely artificial, frozen into a woodcut: she wasn't even sure what color the hair ought to be. Ezramé Dévornine, a woman she had only just met, a foreigner, an aristocrat, seemed not just nearer but infinitely more real, reminding her of a tenderness she had long forgotten, something which had no place in the saga of her village in the mountains. The inchoate fear returned, nibbling at the edges of her thought, but she disregarded it. There was nothing she could do about it, nothing she needed to do: she had only to follow her fate and trust that the stars which had sent her knew their business.

She got out of the sunken bath and wrapped herself in the towel again. In the dressing room, clothes had been laid out for her: loose trousers of pale green gauze, gathered on the ankle, silver sandals, a bodice stitched with seed pearls. And the inevitable veil, patterned with faint leaves like the ghost of a vanished woodland. She was uncertain precisely what to do with it but settled for draping it shawl-like around her shoulders, while behind her the electricity caused by the friction of silk on silk made it cling close to her legs. "You look lovely," said Ezramé, coming to find her. "How fortunate you're so small: my things fit you almost perfectly. The trousers are probably too long, but it doesn't matter."

"You've been so kind," Fern began, suddenly shy to find she was wearing her hostess' clothes; but Ezramé brushed aside both gratitude and gêne.

"The veil isn't quite right . . . here, that's it. Long ago, they say, it was worn for modesty—it is still traditional to cast it over your head in public, at least on ceremonial occasions—but Atlantean women scorned to hide their beauty, and the veils grew thinner, until they became little more than a fashionable accessory. Some, however, are rare and valuable."

"Like yours?" Fern asked.

"This is an heirloom," Ezramé admitted with a slightly rueful smile. "It was made by my ancestress, Phaidé Dévornine, who was the most Gifted of our line. Legend says it will protect the wearer. It cannot be stolen or lost, only given to another. I've noticed myself how the patterns seem to shift and change, but that may be because the design is so large and complex, so I am always finding new things in it."

"Do you have the Gift?" Fern said, and then wished she had not; from Ezramé's expression, the question was too personal.

"A little," she said at last.

"But—" Fern hesitated, seeing the weariness and sorrow of ordinary aging in her face.

"I do not choose to use it. I desire neither power nor long life."

"I see," Fern whispered, and she did.

The three of them sat down to eat in the salon overlooking the garden. The windows were shielded with gauze screens to keep out the insects; within, a galaxy of candles filled the room with flickering gold. This is how I shall remember it, thought Fern, pushing aside the thought of the stone chamber beneath the temple. Always golden, by day and by night. I shall remember when it

is long gone . . . And suddenly she shivered, though the evening
was warm. Rafarl, also bathed and changed, looked her over critically but offered no comment. A slave brought them dishes of rice
speckled with sultanas and herbs, vegetables cut or carved into
exotic shapes, fish in its skin and fish in its shell. "Your stepfather
will not be back," Ezramé told her son. "These days, he prefers to
spend his nights elsewhere. No, dear one, don't protest. I too prefer it: you know that. Besides, it gives us an interval to talk." She
had been informed of her brother's death by the servant who had
escorted him to the temple; no official notification had been received and she had been refused permission to tend his body.
Rafarl told her the rest: his own incarceration and meeting with
Fern, the conversation she had overheard between Ixavo and
Zohrâne, the breaking of the Lodestone and the devastation they
themselves had witnessed. As he spoke Ezramé bowed her head
in her hand. "I do not know whether to feel joy or regret," she
said. "The Lodestone has been the cause of so much that is evil,
yet it is not—*was* not—evil in itself, or so I understand. Evil is
made by men, not stones. Its power founded our city and our empire, but I fear we are self-corrupted. And without the source of
that power, who knows what will happen to us?" She lifted her
goblet but did not drink; her eyes were full of shadows. "I feel . . .
I feel in my heart this is the end."

Rafarl reached out to touch her; the teasing note in his voice
was very gentle. "Because the past has been dark you expect the
future to be darker," he said. "The roots of Atlantis go deep, *mié*. I
doubt if even the shattering of the Lodestone can shake them.
Anyway, Fern here can outdo your forebodings: she believes
Zohrâne's ambitions could destroy not only the city but the whole
world. She thinks she's going to prevent it, and I'm to help her,
which is rainbow-chasing . . ."

Curiously, Fern was unaffected by the flippancy of his attitude: instinct told her that mockery and self-mockery were the weapons he used to disarm his feelings of guilt, frustration, futility. His mother, equally intuitive, listened to the words rather than the tone. She was looking at Fern with a steady gravity which ignored all attempts at jest. "How did you get here?" she asked.

"I'm not sure," Fern said, responding to candor with truth. "I remember a sea-voyage, on the argosy from Scyre, but the recollection is so vague, like something in a story. Reality started yesterday—" she could scarcely credit it was only yesterday "—after I landed. There are times when I almost feel I just . . . *arrived*. Out of nowhere. That's the most frightening part. Out of *nowhere*."

"There's a worm in your head," Rafarl said lightly, "eating your brain." It was a slang phrase for the onset of madness.

"I know," said Fern, recognizing the sense if not the idiom. "I've wondered about that myself."

"Nonsense!" said Ezramé. "You fell from the stars: I suspected it all along. Are you not star-pale, white as the young moon? Please don't argue: my mind is made up. You know, I too lived briefly in the north, many years ago—my father was a consul— and there was a flower growing there that I always loved, *nevelinde* the natives called it—" she pronounced it never-linda "—the snowbell. You remind me of that flower. It was very small and very delicate, but it came long before the spring, braving the winter snows. I thought it was the strongest and most valiant of flowers. It doesn't grow here: our climate is too warm. We have only those opulent blooms which like an easy life."

"My mother is fanciful," said Rafarl, and his smile was wry.

"You're kind," Fern told her, and her smile was not.

Later in the evening, a servant returned who had been out to glean information, the same who had accompanied Rahil Dévornine during his fatal attendance at the temple. Ixavo had circulated a description of a girl, he reported, his gaze avoiding Fern. The temple guards were combing the streets for her and her associate, bribing any who would take a bribe, threatening those who would not. "They couldn't come here!" Ezramé protested.

"They might, Cidame," said the man. "Who would gainsay them? Only the queen can overrule the authority of the Guardian, and in this affair, why should she? She has made it very plain that she has no respect for ancient lineage . . . even her own."

Ezramé turned to Fern. "You'll have to leave," she said. "I'm sorry: I had hoped you could stay here tonight; but it's too dangerous. My son will take care of you." Rafarl raised one eyebrow, followed presently by the other. "Keep those clothes; they are not in the official description. Cover your hair with the veil. I'll have Aliph pack up some food and a waterskin: Raf can carry it. If there's anything more I can do—"

"There is one thing." Fern was hesitant. "The inn where I stayed last night—I was expecting to go back, so I didn't pay my bill." She felt in her purse, which she had pinned to her waistband. "I've got some money here . . ."

"Keep your money: I'll see to it. Tell me which one it was and Aliph will go round there in the morning."

"If the world is going to end," Rafarl said dryly, "what does it matter?"

"You shouldn't die leaving your debts unpaid," said Fern.

It was deep night when they left the villa. The moon was just off the full, a fat, smiling, yellow moon which outshone the neighboring stars. Tangled shadows made walking hazardous. Only a few scattered lights illumined the mountainside, but in the city below the streets were picked out in flambeaux, doorways spilled radiance, unshuttered windows shone from dark buildings like golden tesserae in a mosaic of darkness. "I have heard Atlantis called the Jeweled City," Fern said softly. "Now I know why."

"Mistranslation," said Rafarl. "Not the Jeweled City: the City of Jewels. The name isn't metaphorical, it's factual. We've dragged the mainland rivers, mined out the mines, pillaged the treasuries of little kings. We're overloaded with precious gems. The nobility no longer wear them: they think it's vulgar. Here, diamonds are commonplace."

"Is that why your mother doesn't wear any?" Fern inquired suspiciously.

"No." He paused, apparently selecting a trail in the uncertain night. "She doesn't like them, that's all. She wears only the ring my father gave her."

Avoiding the public paths, he found a route down the slope through private gardens, descending from terrace to terrace via narrow flights of steps or a scramble down a crumbling wall or uneven rock-face. Fern hid her qualms, following Rafarl with a confidence she did not possess, fumbling for purchase on steeps she could barely see. On a couple of occasions they had to jump, once into a clump of shrubs from which Fern emerged scratched and battered, once more than fifteen feet onto a close-cropped lawn. The landing left Fern stunned for several seconds. But: "You're all right, aren't you?" said Rafarl, and she was, determined that where he could go, so could she, without faltering or complaint.

They crossed the ring-road at the bottom of the steps as quickly as possible and plunged into a bewilderment of back-streets. The buildings drew increasingly close together, hiding the moon. Here and there, through a gap between jostling roofs, Fern saw the dome of the temple away to their left, like the rim of a planet rising into a blue-black universe. Her sense of direction was poor but she guessed they must be some way east of the inn where she had spent the preceding night. This was an area given over to street-bars and snack vendors, skulking taverns, anony-mous doorways emitting the throb of jungle drums where sinister wardens vetted all comers. Women lounged on corners with their lips tinted purple or blue, many of them showing bare breasts under the obligatory veil. Rafarl turned into an archway so dark that its guardian could hardly be seen except as a pair of huge shoulders heaving themselves out of the gloom.

A voice like gravel said: "They're looking for you, Dev."

"I know."

"You and a girl." There was a glint as eyes swiveled in an unseen face.

Rafarl ignored the implicit question. "Do they know my identity?"

"No. Only the description. *We* know. That dodge with the scorpion . . . you've used it before. A giveaway."

Rafarl did not comment. "Is Ipthor in?"

"Probably."

The shoulders moved aside; Rafarl stepped forward into almost complete blackness. Fern, behind him, grabbed a fold of his loose shirt. "Stairs," he warned her. She felt her way down the irregular treads which twisted dizzily deep into the ground. At the bottom, Rafarl thrust another door open and she found herself following him into a wide chamber. It was very large but low, as if the weight of the city, pressing down from above, was gradually compressing the space between ceiling and floor. The ceiling in question was coved, dipping at intervals to meet squat pillars; the walls were enlivened with gargoyle-carvings. Many of the monsters held colored lamps in their gaping mouths, or candles in translucent vessels: the light these emanated was multi-hued and erratic, making separate caves of green and scarlet and magenta, leaving some corners—the room contrived to have many corners—in darkness. Several musicians were playing in a remote alcove, a soft background rhythm consisting mostly of thrumming strings and drumming fingers. Rafarl roamed the chamber, peering into the shadows, stopping at length beside a niche where two men were sitting close together, rolling dice.

"Ipo."

One of the men gathered up the dice and dismissed his companion with a quick jerk of the head. "Sit down, Raf. I've been expecting you." Rafarl sat on the bench opposite him; Fern perched on the end. Ipthor gave her a swift glance that might have been cursory but was not. What little light reached them was greenish and unsympathetic, washing the warmth from Rafarl's skin, highlighting the slight roughness of pockmarks or old scarring on Ipthor's sunken cheeks. He was darker than Rafarl, yellow as drab, and his whole face appeared concave, as if he had been punched by a huge fist early in life and all his features had been driven inward. His eyes were crooked and set in a downward slant, making his expression seem both sly and sad. His clothes were ragged but he wore golden ear-rings and there was the glint of commonplace gems on his fingers. The winnings from recent gambling were stacked at his elbow; Fern automatically suspected the dice were loaded. "I hear you're in a lot of trouble," he remarked conversationally. "The guards came here—"

"Here?"

"Only out of politeness. In a street search, it's considered insulting to overlook anywhere. The captain was suitably respectful. He turned over a few shadows, swatted a barfly, apologized to the management in the same breath. He has some bad habits he wouldn't want his colonel to hear about." Ipthor grinned nastily. "But then, so has the colonel, only his are more expensive."

"Will they come back?"

"Né. They know we know you—they know we know they know—but they won't push their luck. Nor should you." His gaze slid briefly toward Fern. "I said the *nympheline* would get you into the *morrh-dhuu* if she could."

"Different girl," Rafarl said shortly.

"Prolific, aren't you?"

"Leave it. Ipo, we need to get out, lie low for a while—"

"So I see." Ipthor chewed thoughtfully on something which might have been tobacco. "The *Norne* is at her mooring right now and my uncle will be drunk for at least a week. How about piracy on the high seas? You've always said that's what you wanted. And there's a dozen of us ready to follow you."

"No." Fern heard, rather than saw, Rafarl's grimace. "I can't go for good."

"Your mother?"

"Mind your own business."

"Too many women in your life, if you ask me," Ipthor opined.

"I didn't."

"So what have you got in mind?"

"Somewhere. What I need is to leave the city—now. Quickly and very quietly. There's blood money on offer and plenty who don't object to the stain on their hands. Even here. You know that." Ipthor gave a grunt which might have been assent. "It has to be the secret way. Tonight."

"It'll cost you."

Rafarl produced a small leather pouch and tipped a coil of dull glitter onto the table. Fern opened her mouth to comment and closed it again without speaking.

"Your mother's jewels. Well, well. Did you pinch this or did she give it to you?" Rafarl didn't answer. "And what makes you so sure you can trust me?"

"I'm not," he retorted, scooping up the necklace and replacing it in the pouch. "Payment on delivery. Lose me, you lose your fee."

Ipthor spat out his tobacco and laughed.

They left the city via the sewerage system, through a darkness smelling of feces and rustling with rats. Fern had sufficient experience of cities to be accustomed to such odors, but still she shrank from the putrid water that licked at her feet. There was nothing she could do about her clothes. Already she could feel her gauze trousers growing clammy around the ankles from splashback. This, too, is the fairest of cities, she thought. The bowels of Atlantis. And suddenly she felt she was beginning to understand it: a gilded powerhouse ruling an empire of the despised, and the mentality of a people who believed instinctively in their own superiority. Here, all the ugliness was below ground, hidden away in tunnels and catacombs. Out of sight, out of scent. The sewers, the dungeons, the torture chambers. The stainless streets and shining domes sprouted on top of this noisome labyrinth like roses on a dung heap. Let the mainlanders wallow like animals in their filth, the Gifted people were made of finer clay; they had lifted themselves far above their own excrement. But it's still there, thought Fern. Atlanteans are no different from other men. We all shit: it's the great common denominator. And if you ignore it then the shit will accumulate and accumulate, until the whole world is defiled. Vaguely she detected in the attitude of Atlantis the beginnings of a deadly trend, but how it would evolve or where it might lead she could not remember, though she thought she ought to know.

"You're lagging," said Rafarl, looking back. "Try to keep up."

Ipthor's torch flickered and smoked some way ahead. Fern ran a few steps to catch up with them and almost lost her footing when something wriggled from beneath her shoe and vanished into the slime. There were other things in the murky stream which did not wriggle, drifting sluggishly or wedged on an unseen snag, things with matted remnants of fur or peeling scales, invariably gnawed and incomplete. On some a trace of blood still showed dimly red. The passage gradually widened and the noxious flow grew correspondingly swifter and deeper: floating objects were now carried past them instead of being left behind. Once, Fern saw a jagged ridge, several feet in length, just breaking the surface, and somewhere in front of it a pair of eyes that stood out of the water all by themselves. "Keep well to the side!" said Rafarl. Ipthor quickened his pace.

Fern had no idea how long the journey lasted. Eventually they halted at the bottom of a vertical shaft soaring upward into utter blackness. A ladder-like system of grooves was cut into the rock, with metal spikes, rust-smeared, alternating on either side. Ipthor slotted his torch into a wall-bracket. "You'll have to do without light," he said. "I need both hands." He removed his shoes and began to climb; Fern, at Rafarl's instigation, followed him, her sandals hung by their straps around her neck. She did not ask the height of the shaft or how long it would take. As she gripped the first spike her fingers looked very puny, her arms surely too slight to sustain her body-weight for more than a few minutes. She hugged the rock wall, clinging on with her toes, concentrating on achieving a rhythm of progress. She felt Rafarl move up close behind her, so close that once, when she flagged, a supporting hand was pressed into the small of her back. The torchlight dwindled below them into a circle of sooty orange, shrinking slowly to the diameter of a coin, thankfully obscured by their intervening limbs. Ahead—well ahead by now—Ipthor scrambled up the rock-face like a lizard; she could not see him but she could hear his rapid movements, the occasional gasp or oath as he stubbed a toe. Now and then he dislodged a loose chipping that bounced off her scalp or shoulder. With the sounds of his ascent gradually receding above her and the light retreating below she succumbed to the illusion that she was suspended in a limbo of darkness, always climbing, always still, going nowhere. It reminded her of some incident in the very recent past—an endless stair, dream-like archways, walls and pillars insubstantial as vapor—but although the memory seemed so near and so vivid that she was sure it must be important, she could not quite catch hold of it. She was desperately grateful for the proximity of Rafarl, encouraging her without

words, impelling her on by his very presence. She did not speak at
all. Possibly she was afraid her voice would let her down.

And then the noises above ceased; there was a long pause, a
scraping groan like the sliding of a bolt in a rusty socket, the creak
of an old hinge. A disc of vague pallor appeared, gray against the
dark, quickly broken by the silhouette of Ipthor, crook-legged and
nimble, more insect than reptile. Fern climbed faster. It was only
when she was finally outside, gulping the wholesome air like a
parched nomad at an oasis, that she found her limbs were shaking
from the effort and her fingers, cramped from clutching the
spikes, would not immediately uncurl.

"Where are we?" Rafarl demanded.

"See that road over there? That's the eastward road to the Bay
of Lhune. It crosses the coast road about a mile from here. Where
are you headed?"

"I'll know when I get there. Here—" He tossed the pouch to
Ipthor. "Thanks."

Ipthor tugged it open, automatically checking the contents.
"Diamonds!" he sighed. "Diamonds are for desperation. Ixavo
would have paid in hard currency. Five hundred *phénix* apiece, no
less. Or so I was told."

"You should have taken it," Rafarl said lightly.

"*Ara-yé.*" The evil grin danced and fled. "Too late now."

He disappeared back into the shaft, pulling the trapdoor shut
behind him. Fern sat down on a milestone which announced they
were three leagues out of the city. "We've got a long walk ahead,"
Rafarl told her. "Put on your shoes."

The night was growing old; they had been many hours underground. The sky over the eastern horizon was already starting to
lighten: Fern could see distant mountain shapes emerging to the
north, maybe part of a volcanic chain with the natural fortress-
harbor of Atlantis as an isolated outpost. The broad valley-plain
lay between, perceptible in the gloaming merely as fields of shadow

stretching away and away, with few trees and only a single gleam of water far off, reflecting the moonlight long after the moon had set. The paved road marched across the landscape with the resolution of its builders, straight as a rule. "We must reach the crossroads before dawn," said Rafarl. "After that, we have to get out of sight." They set off along the empty road, listening for horses' hooves and the rumor of pursuit, hearing only the zither-music of the cicadas and the call of a night bird, flying home before the onset of morning.

They reached the coast just short of noon. Turning north at the crossroads they had gone only a short distance before Rafarl chose a faint track on the right which meandered uncertainly through the pale grasses, petering out close to an abandoned farmstead. But Rafarl had found another path, even if it was not the one he was looking for, keeping in the lee of any available trees, descending at last into a gully where the thread of a river gurgled half-heartedly in a bed of cracked mud. They had followed it, screened by the banks, until the ditch became a cleft and the languid water gathered itself together for a final sprint and poured in a slender fall down a low cliff toward the sea. Fern and Rafarl clambered down beside it, drinking from the pool below, which was clear if not particularly cold, before skirting the sand and crossing a stony promontory to the next cove, and the next. They had traveled perhaps another mile when Rafarl alighted on the destination he sought. It was a shallow cave, its entrance almost hidden by a rock-fall, evidently cut off at high tide since damp weed sprawled on the threshold, but within the floor sloped upward and the sand was powdery and dry. Fern sank down on it, exhausted from a long day and a longer night, dizzy from walking under the relentless sun. She was too tired to eat the food Rafarl proffered, too tired even to bathe or wash the filth from her clothes. She curled up on the sand with her head on a weed-cushioned boulder and fell instantly into sleep.

When she awoke, the first thing she heard was the sea. The familiar sense of dislocation ensued, but this time she thought that outside the cave there was a shoreline of silver, and fiery waves spreading their sparks upon the sand. She felt no panic, only a singing in her blood and a moment of hopeless struggle, as she snatched in vain at a long-lost image, too precious to forget, too magical to remember. And then she came to full awareness, and saw there was daylight beyond the cave-mouth, and all the details of their escape from the city returned to her, driving the fleeting impression back into the realm of fantasy.

She got to her feet and went outside, into the apricot glow of early evening. The tide had retreated since their arrival and the falling sun stretched her shadow out before her on the sand, impossibly tall and thin; beyond it, the leisurely rollers drifted ceaselessly inshore, crumbling into gold in the last rays of day. On the headland to her left she saw the white pillars of a house, partially concealed by a cluster of trees. But she could see no sign of human occupation and even at that range she thought a section of the roof was missing. Rafarl was nowhere about but his clothes were drying on a rock and the small pack his mother had given him still lay on the floor of the cave. She decided to follow his example, rinsing her things in a pool and then spreading them out beside his. The advancing shade of the ridge would soon eclipse them but it remained very hot, though the air was fresher than in the city. She ran down the beach and plunged in among the golden waves, tumbling over and over in water almost as warm as her bath of the previous night. Then she swam out farther and watched the dancing sunfire dying around her and a pale mauve twilight spreading swiftly across the vast discus of the ocean.

"Fernani!" came a call, and there was Rafarl, standing at the water's edge with the foam frilling his ankles, naked but for a brief loincloth secured with a thong about his waist, his arms, legs, shoulders flushed to copper in the sunset. He raced into the sea toward her and she knew a sudden spasm of panic, or something like panic, realizing she too was naked, and she turned and dived like a seal, but too late, too late, he caught hold of her and they were sinking down together, down into deeps of blue in a chaos of tangled limbs and spiraling bubbles. And then he must have pushed off from the sea-floor because now the rush was upward to emerge in an explosion of spray and light, and Fern was gasping for the breath she had not had time to take, half furious, half laughing, and Rafarl's arms were around her, and her breasts against his breast.

Slowly now they swam ashore, and lay side by side in the shallows with the fallout of breaking waves swirling around them. He opened her mouth with his tongue, and her body seemed to awaken at his touch, even as at the touch of the Lodestone, but this was a different kind of burning, more heat than flame, closer to the dark heart of Earth, a magic of this world and not another. Her mind floated away and she was lost in her senses, and her resistance was merely a fleeting hesitation, and there was a stab like a knife-thrust deep inside her, stab on stab, thrust on thrust, but the pain turned all to sweetness, and the tears of the sea tasted salt on her lips. Her Task was forgotten; the broken memories which eluded her, the destruction of the Stone, Zohrâne's madness, the key—gone and forgotten. There was only Now. The sun had vanished long since and a purple dusk drew over them like a cloak. And still the sea, untiring, surged and sank, surged and sank, against the island shore.

Later in the night they returned to the cave and slept a while, out of reach of the rising tide. Before dawn they got up and swam out toward the sunrise, and the morning came sparkling across the water to meet them. A couple of thin cloud-wisps straddled the horizon like wide-winged birds, fire-bellied in the advent of day. "Once," said Rafarl, "men would have believed they *were* birds, the albatrosses who were the messengers of the Unknown God, bringing Him news of all that passes in the world. Now, we believe only in ourselves. All else is fairy tales and nonsense." Fern wondered if the edge in his voice was scorn or regret, and if he himself knew what he really felt.

"Which aspect of nature would you worship," she asked, "if you could make a god for yourself? The sun? The moon?"

"The sea."

"What about Love?" she teased him.

"Love is not meant to be worshipped," he retorted. "It's meant to be enjoyed. Anyway, it's the business of men, not gods."

Back on the beach he inquired, idly: "Where did you learn to swim so well? The Viroc mountains are a long way from the coast."

The Viroc? For a few seconds, her mind was a blank. The *Viroc* . . .

"I expect there were lakes," he suggested, disturbed by the sudden emptiness in her face.

The lake came into her thought as if at his bidding, a blue-green spit of water between snow-capped heights, cold as a glacier. "Yes," she said, "there was a lake. It was freezing, even in summer. I suppose . . . I must have learned there. Anyway, I thought everyone could swim. It's natural, like running. You don't have to learn to run."

She ran along the sand to prove it, and he chased her, and there was no more talk for a while. Afterward she thought: I have no memories anymore. The package of images she had been carrying around with her seemed to have faded; her hovering confusion had ceased. She existed only in the moment, caught in a teardrop of Time, without past or future. Strangely, it did not trouble her. She was pillowed on Rafarl's chest, their limbs interlaced; the beat of his heart was loud in her head. She thought: I am his lover. They had made no promises, no vows; this was an interlude which might end with the next sunset or ebb with the changing tide. Yet she knew, with a certainty that belongs only to the young, that this was for always. Whether she had a year, or a week, or just a few hours, she would make it last forever.

"We can stay here till the hunt loses interest," Rafarl murmured, echoing her thought. "A fortnight maybe. Or less. The temple hierarchs must have other problems to concern them."

"What will we eat?" asked Fern pragmatically.

"Fruit. Fish. Each other." He bit her arm, gently. "I've been wondering . . . Ixavo almost seemed to recognize you. Have you met before?"

"No." Doubt made her brusque.

"It's you he wants, not me. I'm just an accessory. Why?"

"I don't know."

Abstractedly, he stroked her hair. "There are too many things you don't know." And, after a while: "They say the Gifted can see beyond knowledge. Maybe that is how he saw you—in a basin of moonlight, in the smoke of a spellfire, in the eye of his mind."

"Maybe," said Fern; but she didn't believe it.

Around midday they climbed the headland to the deserted house. "This is where Tamiszandre spent her last days," Rafarl said. "No one comes here now." It was a still, sunlit place, filled with a tranquility that felt like sadness. Around the back an orchard had run wild, sending exploratory branches through the stricken roof, beginning the invasion of the courtyard with questing offshoots and saplings that elbowed the paving-stones aside. They plucked silver and golden peaches and ate them on the terrace overlooking the sea. Here, too, the garden was taking over, insidious tendrils snaking round the pillars and miniature creepers, goblin-fingered, working on the demolition of balustrade and walls, finding a roothold in every chink and cranny. Divided from the continent since the ending of the Age of Ice, Atlantis had inevitably evolved its own ecosystem, with flora and fauna unlike their mainland cousins. The radiation-field of the Lodestone had stimulated or enhanced each variation, and now the island gloried in a thousand kinds of uniqueness. Rafarl told her the names of those flowers he knew: the pale, diminutive bloom with the bloodred heart called starwound, the clusters of yellow paramour hanging from every rafter, fantassels, speckled fairyfoot, deadly venomel. Birds as small as butterflies and butterflies as large as birds came to sip at the copious supplies of nectar. Coral-pink swans with black beaks, nearly twice the size of their mainland relatives, flew overhead: the *phénix* of Atlantean coinage. Somewhere high up they saw an eagle, with a wingspan that dwarfed the swans.

When they had eaten their fill they helped themselves to water from the well and some cooking pots from the neglected kitchen and went back to the beach. Rafarl took his hunting knife and disappeared in search of dinner, returning sometime later with an assortment of shellfish. They cooked the mussels and crabs over a makeshift campfire but he taught Fern to eat the oysters raw, though she was never entirely convinced by the delicacy. "I couldn't find much else," he said. "All I saw was a manta-ray flapping off into deeper water and a patrolling shark. And this used to be such a good spot for fishing. Usually, I take a spear—I wasn't sure how I'd fare, with only a knife—but in the event, it didn't matter. Something's wrong here—the very denizens of the sea are fleeing our vicinity. I don't understand it." He was scowling as he spoke, evidently perturbed. His temperament appeared often mercurial, his customary flippancy and cynicism interspersed with unexpected flashes of gravity, light underlaid with dark, weakness veined with strength, rashness, carelessness, folly flecked with the glints of true courage: all contradictions. Yet Fern sensed in him, amid the tangle of character and anti-character, of positive and negative energies, a fiber of steadiness, as yet undeveloped, almost invisible, like the stealthy glimmer of a seam of gold in a tin-mine. She thought: I love him, he won't fail me. It was the logic of youth, optimistic, defective; but still she was sure. She would have staked her life on that certainty.

She said: "Maybe it has to do with the breaking of the Stone."

"Is that supposed to reassure me?"

"No," said Fern.

They slept little that night, making their newfound love like people for whom the world is running out. Fern did not think of her Task, not because she had abandoned it, but because she felt it would present itself for her attention when the moment was right, and until then she had an intermission, a suspension of hostilities, given by whatever gods there were. They lay in the cave while outside the tide rose and fell, and she thought that in this life and maybe in all lives she would remember that love sounded like the sea, and the beat of her heart was waves on a beach, and she would hear its echo in the nucleus of every shell.

· XI ·

In the morning, *she* came. She came to the cave-mouth because she knew it and stood there in the early light, as slender as Fern but much taller, with hair that fell to her knees. Her skin was dark without a tan, greenish-ochre; her slanting eyes were neither green nor blue but the aquamarine that lies in between; the fall of her hair was dead straight and dead black, without any gleam of a lighter shade. She was angry with the rage that has no reason and no rationale, a firework that spits and crackles, singeing anyone in the vicinity. Fern identified her at once and the too-familiar pain returned tenfold, gripping her in a vise of silence.

"I knew you'd be here," the *nympheline* said. "I knew I'd find you, skulking in a cave like the coward you are. Running. Hiding. That's what you're best at, isn't it, running and hiding? I showed you this place: it isn't yours to skulk in. Bury yourself in the sand like a worm! Crawl in the coral like a sea-slug! Go and skulk somewhere else, somewhere I can't find you, somewhere I can't see you and hate you! You ran away and left him to die. *You left him to die!*" Tears were leaking through the fury, misting her bright eyes. Fern drew aside, pulling the veil around her nakedness,

283

more from diplomacy than modesty; but Uuinarde ignored her completely.

"He died before I got there," Rafarl said. "There was nothing I could have done." Even at the dawn of history it sounded like a cliché; Fern felt him grow tense with self-disgust.

Uuinarde didn't hear, didn't care. "You promised me you would save him!" She was crying openly now, sobbing with pent-up grief and frustration and hurt, choking on her own misery. "You gave me your word—the word of a Dévornine! Word of a recreant—a bastard—a mongrel! I offered to *love* you—"

"You never loved me."

"I would have loved the man who saved my brother! But all your oaths, your brave declarations meant *nothing*. When it came to the crunch you didn't think of him or me: you thought only of your own skin. You just ran—taking the nearest woman with you. Not even a woman: a foreign half-girl—an outsider—a nobody. I would have given you *myself*—"

"I didn't want a trade." Rafarl's tone had sharpened. "You didn't need to whore yourself for your brother's sake."

"*Whore* myself? You—you—*scum*! Guttersnake—*fourgané*! *Ourunduuc!*" She flung herself toward him, a sudden knife in her hand: the blade shone bright and thin. But there was no intention behind the attack. Rafarl had wrested the poniard from her before Fern reached them and Uuinarde threw herself against his shoulder, weeping like a rainstorm. Rafarl comforted her with routine gestures, looking both reluctant and inadequate. Fern's jealousy flared at the sight, and burned up in a minute, and was gone.

When the storm was over Uuinarde was persuaded to sit down and accept a drink of water, daubing her face with the corner of her veil. She was unrepentant, but the initial fervor had gone from her rage, leaving her sullen and resentful. She was one of those for whom the cruelty of an unexpected bereavement is too much to deal with, and in consequence she was desperately looking for someone to blame, someone accessible, near at hand, not the remote faceless figures of the powers-that-be. Fern surveyed her with a certain abstract curiosity. Under the influence of the Lodestone mutations were commonplace, she knew: *nymphelins* were the result of one such quirk of nature. She was vaguely aware that they were supposed to be able to store oxygen and control their heart rate in a way that allowed them to stay under water for far longer than the norm, though they were still basically human, unlike the mermaids of fishermen's tales, who were reputed to have small gills hidden behind their ears as well as air-breathing lungs. Fern thought: I should have known it was she who found this cave. It's the kind of hideout only a *nymphelin* would find. She brought Rafarl here, and he—brought me. She wondered if it was important and came to the conclusion, rather surprisingly, that it wasn't.

Rafarl had sat down beside Uuinarde and was listening to a further tirade on his shortcomings, this time *sotto voce*, evidently meant for his private ear. "If you really think your brother's death is my fault," he responded, stung to a maddening evenness of tone, "you should have betrayed me to Ixavo. That way you could have obtained revenge and made a profit on the side."

"Blood money!" Uuinarde spat out the words. "Just because you're beneath contempt doesn't mean I am too." She flung a sulky glance at Fern. "Why is *she* here, anyway? Why doesn't she say something? She just looks at me in that cold fashion like a fish on a slab. Make her go away."

"Leave her alone," said Rafarl, and the corner of his mouth twisted into a smile that was only for Fern. "She hasn't injured you."

"She's the one they're looking for," Uuinarde said. The anger and the petulance faded from her face, leaving it vividly pensive. "They're saying in the city that the Lodestone itself is broken—that it resisted Zohrâne's will, and broke because it would not bend, and the Gift is gone forever. And Ixavo is searching for a foreign girl, a girl who came at the breaking of the Stone, a girl who is not a girl, not a boy, not a woman. He says she has come to destroy us."

"Do you believe him?" asked Fern. "He sent your brother to the sacrifice."

"What do you know of my brother?" Uuinarde snapped back.

"I have a brother of my own." She spoke without thought: there was no brother in her pictures of the Viroc, none in the official record of her life. Yet she could see him in her mind: fair-haired, clear-eyed, candid, enthusiastic. Will.

"Do you believe Ixavo?" Rafarl repeated Fern's question with more than a trace of scorn in his voice.

Uuinarde made an involuntary movement, half shrug, half shiver. "Of course not. But there is something in the air—a feeling—a smell. A smell of endings—of unimaginable change—a doom hanging over us like a great shadow. People talk of fleeing the city but it's only talk. They stay because they must, because they feel part of this doom that we cannot see. Everyone goes about their business the same but it's unreal, like a play where you know something is going to happen soon. Something terrible. The animals are nervous: dogs howl, cats scratch. And the fish are leaving, I saw them on my way here, huge shoals swimming away, all together like a living river, and crayfish marching along the seabed, and crabs scrambling after. I saw sharks and porpoises, scorpion-fish and angel-fish, side by side. Even the tiniest things, the wisps of jelly and gossamer tentacles, even they are going. And behind them the waters are empty, like a graveyard."

"What does it mean?" Fern demanded.

Uuinarde met her gaze with eyes that looked far away. "The Sea is angry," she said. "When I touched the rocks I felt the whole island tremble in fear. The fish are going to safer shoals. The Sea is coming. Soon, it will be here." Her focus altered; she asked Fern with sudden simplicity: "Are you the spirit of the Stone? Did you emerge in the moment of its breaking—to save us?"

"I'm supposed to save . . . something," Fern said. "But I didn't come from the Stone. It has no spirit, only power."

"She fell from a star," Rafarl offered, quoting his mother.

"What's Zohrâne doing?" Fern pressed the *nympheline*. Her moods changed like weather; the clouds and the lightning had vanished; now, she was all mist and bewilderment.

"I don't know," she said. "She's in the temple all the time, planning something maybe, arranging a new ceremony. The guards will let no one near, not even those of the highest rank. Only the senior priests. There is a rumor the Families are conspiring against her, but everyone knows it is too late. She doesn't care. Morbis the street-seer says she has drawn all the power of the Stone into herself, she is glutted with power, and she will spin the world on her fingertip, and toss it into the firmament like a juggler's ball."

"Impractical," commented Rafarl.

"When is this new ceremony?" Fern inquired after a minute or two.

"Tomorrow. At midday. There will be many sacrifices; the temple will run with blood. Already there is a strange nimbus about the broken dome, as if a light other than the sun is on it. A light from the ending of the world." A tremor ran through her slender body; Rafarl frowned.

"Will *you* go?" he asked.

"Perhaps. I could follow the fish, to calmer waters where it's safe." She added bleakly: "I have nothing to stay for now." She stood up in a swift, impatient movement, went to the cave-mouth. "The tide is going out," she said. "Too far out. Look."

They joined her. Sure enough, the sea was shrinking, retreating faster and farther than they had ever seen before, leaving in its wake a flotsam of drying weed, broken shells, and the carcasses of countless creatures too small to name. Rocks lifted up their heads which had never felt the sun. "It is the End," said Uuinarde, and a shadow touched them, though the sky was cloudless. The beauty of the little cove was gone: it had become a place of decay. The departing water exposed a seabed unsightly and somehow unwholesome in its nakedness. "I shall follow the fish," Uuinarde said, but she sounded uncertain. She removed her veil and tied it around her waist; underneath, she wore only a short dress or tunic of some thin material that clung. Her feet were bare. She walked out toward the shrunken waves, paused to look back. (Never look back, say the legends. To look back is death.)

"I wish you luck," said Rafarl.

"There is no more luck." The wind blew her voice away from them. "It has gone with the tide."

"*Ré vidéva,*" Fern called. Till we meet again.

"I doubt it," Rafarl said when the *nympheline* had disappeared. "She will follow the porpoises. Uuinarde had no loves, no ties but her brother."

"Maybe," said Fern. "You loved her, didn't you?"

Rafarl sighed. "I thought I did. For a while."

"And now?"

His mouth was wry. "I don't know if I love you. But I know I never loved anyone else."

Back in the cave Fern dressed quickly, tossing Rafarl his outer clothing. "How long will it take us," she asked, "to get back to the city?"

"We're not going back. I told you, we lie low for a week or two, until the hue and cry has died down. I'm not changing the plan because a grief-crazed nymph says the world is ending and the tide has gone out too far. It will turn in due course; it always does. If the sea starts playing rough we can climb up to the house: we'll be above any storms there. The city is too dangerous for us now."

"The danger doesn't matter," said Fern. "I have to be at that ceremony tomorrow. Something is going to happen there which I have to prevent, or change: I'm not sure what but I'll know when the time comes. Uuinarde was right: this is the End. This is *an* end, anyhow. Afterward . . . I don't know. Are you coming?"

"No," Rafarl said bluntly. "You're not going anywhere either. You'll get lost without me."

"I'll manage." She was strapping on her shoes, apparently unperturbed.

"You *won't*. Forget all this nonsense about fate and doom. There's nothing you can do. Zohrâne is the most powerful sorceress in history: the demon-gods of the mainland avoid her, the earth-spirits crawl from her sight. Even if you were able to attend the ceremony you'd be helpless against her. She'll brush you from her path like dust, blast you into eternity like a feather—"

"Feathers ride the wind," said Fern. "They're too light to blast. Anyway, I didn't say I'd be challenging Zohrâne."

"You won't get the chance. You'll be arrested as soon as you set foot in the city, the guards will throw you in a dungeon, and Ixavo will interrogate you until you're too dead to answer. You'll achieve nothing, and you'll probably get yourself killed in the process. I don't intend to help with that."

"Of course not." Her demeanor was quiet, acquiescent, taking him off guard. "You've helped a great deal already. Thank you. I have no right to expect any more."

"Is that all you can say?" He was on his feet, shedding cynicism, his stubbornness cracking against her resolution. He looked at her with wild eyes; a tentative finger explored her cheek. "You don't even know the way."

"I'll walk south and west till I find a road. Then I'll follow the road till I can hitch a lift. I'll get there. It doesn't signify if I'm arrested. At least they'll take me where I want to be."

They argued for another twenty minutes before he gave in. Or rather, Rafarl argued, expending passion and energy in vain; Fern merely maintained her position. At last he said: "All right. All

right. I'll take you back to the city, but that's all. After that, it's up
to you. I'm not getting involved in some impossible crusade just
because we made love on a beach."

"Look at the beach now," said Fern as they left the cave. A rising haze bleared the sun; dead things were blistering on drying
sand. The scent of rottenness was carried from the naked seabed.

"The tide will turn," said Rafarl with somber optimism. "The
luck will turn."

"Yes," said Fern, "but when?"

They could not re-enter Atlantis by the secret way through
the sewerage system since the route was impossible without an
expert guide. Instead, Rafarl proposed to take the open road, if
not in an open manner. Leaving the coast along the river-passage
they had used before they crossed the arid plain, passing an occasional solitary farmstead set in a patchwork of poorly irrigated
fields. Rafarl would wave to the farmer if they saw him; if not, he
would scout round, checking the stable, until eventually he found
what he wanted. Transport. Ensuring the owner was nowhere
about, he harnessed the horse between the shafts of the cart and
drove off, with Fern perched on the seat beside him. "Where do
you think the farmer might be?" she inquired nervously, peering
about her.

"No idea. Gone to market on his other horse, perhaps. Or
simply having lunch. I suppose you want to leave him some
money?"

"Well . . ."

Generously, Rafarl did not push it.

He negotiated the winding paths among the fields till they
came to the coast road, then urged the horse to a trot as they
headed south. At the crossroads they swung west toward the city.
"Get into the back," Rafarl ordered. "If we meet anyone, you're
much too conspicuous. The official description of me would
probably fit several thousand Atlanteans, but foreigners are few

and far between and your fairness is distinctive. Cover yourself in straw and sacking and if I say so, get your head down." Fern obeyed without complaint. It was not a comfortable way to travel but she could appreciate the necessity. As they reached the first houses it became essential for her to lie down and remain concealed all the time, so she could see nothing of the metropolis, assimilating their progress only by the growing volume of noise—the vibration of wheels on the flagstones, the clacking of hooves and the cracking of whips, the background rumor of feet hurrying and voices chattering, murmuring, bawling . . . Even without the view, she discovered it felt like coming home. Rafarl stopped at last at a livery stable where he stalled the horse, theoretically for collection later. This time, Fern did not trouble herself unduly about the bill. She sensed it was no longer relevant.

"Which way is the temple?" she asked.

"Are you set on this?"

"You know I am." Now that it came to the point, she wished she wasn't. But even if her heart failed her, she could not change her mind.

"Left outside, second right . . . Forget it. I'll take you there." And, as they emerged onto the street: "Draw your veil over your hair."

They walked along in silence, that silence just before parting where everything has been left unsaid and it is too late now to say it. Fern felt as if her stomach was full of words, words burning to be spoken, but her lips refused to unclose and the words remained inside her, seething, like a bad case of indigestion. Much too soon, Rafarl said: "Here we are." And here they were. Soldiers paraded up and down on the circular roadway. The steps were bare of onlookers. The damage to the dome was invisible from where they stood yet Fern sensed the intrinsic weakness like a flaw at the epicenter of the city. It recalled to her something she had seen somewhere else, another temple maybe, a far smaller dome gaping open like a mouth, more sky than roof; a valley of rock; a garden of illusions. But the memory, like so many others, belonged to that part of her mind which was shut off, and she could not pursue it to its origin. She only knew that it was evil.

She looked round at her companion and found that he was looking at her, and as look met look there was an instant when their eyes locked, and would not be released. His brows were drawn together in a line of brooding; his smile was the wrong way up. "Well?" he said. "Are you really going through with this stupidity?"

"I have to."

He shrugged painfully, wrenching his gaze from her face. "You're on your own."

She did not watch him walk away. Now the moment was here she didn't want him to know how afraid she was. Her heart was thumping so hard with fear she felt actually sick. But she knew what she had to do.

She stepped out from the shelter of the side street onto the exposed promenade. There was a guard captain nearby, identifiable by the horsehair crest on his helmet. She went straight up to him.

"I've come to see Ixavo," she said, surprised to find her voice quite steady. "I think he's been looking for me."

They took her beneath the temple, down into the dark. She knew where they were going, although she did not recognize the twists and turns of the passageway. Underground, she lost her sense of direction. But it didn't matter. She knew. There was a guard outside the metal door in a different uniform from his fellows, a black tunic with the sun-star emblazoned in scarlet on his chest. The captain conferred with him at length. Fern did not listen. She was thinking: I need more time. Time to work out what to do, to feel her way, to respond to the intuition which had driven her thus far. She tried to come up with a plan, but she had never had a plan. The guard seemed unwilling to interrupt the proceedings beyond the door. Thought ebbed with her courage, leaving her empty. Her legs felt weak. She was almost thankful for the strong arms of the soldiers supporting her.

Rafarl had been right. Why, why had she come here?

Futile. *Futile.*

And: I'm such a coward. Such an awful coward . . .

The guard turned and pushed the door a short way open. A bright light filled the gap. After the gloom of the subterranean corridors, it appeared almost as bright as day. (She remembered the lamps around the table.) There were no groans, no screams. Only the sounds of small movements, and a dreadful patient quiet. The guard had gone inside. They waited. The quiet reached out into the passage: her captors stood like statues, the officer ceased to fidget. And then came the noise. Not the kind of noise they had been expecting but a thin, fluttering thread of sound, magnified and distorted by the unseen chamber. On the other side of the door, someone was whispering. The words were inaudible, there was just the soft, persistent, probing trickle of a voice that seemed to have no vocal cords and no lips, only breath and tongue. Meaning emanated from it like a smell. They listened, both soldiers and prisoner, riveted by an obscene fascination.

The screaming came later.

Fern tried to cry out but her throat clenched. No! Please no! and *Don't let it be me!*, hating herself for her selfishness, her cowardice, her fear . . .

The guard emerged and shut the door, cutting the scream to a murmur. She did not register what he said but the captain gave an order and she was propelled down the passage, her legs scissoring into a weightless stride. They passed the cells, many still useless from seismic damage, entered another corridor, opened another door. A door of polished wood, with no bolts. Inside, the soldiers relaxed their grip. To her relief, Fern found her knees did not give way. They were in what was clearly a private apartment. She looked around, scraping herself together, forcing horror and shame out of her mind: she needed the space to think. These must be the living quarters of the Guardian. The room was not merely comfortable but luxurious: the chairs were deeply cushioned, the walls hung with velvet tapestries. There was no natural illumination but a wheel of candles was suspended from the ceiling and lamps burned in every embrasure, making the shadows thin and translucent, faded by overlapping zones of light. Too much light, she thought. Ixavo entered after them, dismissing the guards. He wore the cream-colored robe standard for prelates outside the hours of ceremony with a heavy sundisc, emblem of the Atlantean empire, on a chain about his neck. His disfigurement seemed in some inexplicable fashion to be etiolated by the light, its angry redness dulled, its pitting and puckering irradiated almost out of existence. Instead, she could distinguish only the substructure of his bones, the molding of statuesque features.

He did not look surprised to see her.

"Sit down."

She sat, too quickly, her limbs still unreliable. He was scrutinizing her face; she hoped it did not betray her.

She said: "There's a lot of light in here."

"I like to see what I'm doing." He must have detected her shudder; the hint of a smile spread his mouth. "Did it disturb you, back there? You need not trouble yourself; it had nothing to do with us. I merely supervise: it is a part of my duties. If interrogation were left exclusively to me, there would be less noise and more talk. Much more talk. The mind is infinitely more vulnerable than the body." Somehow, she was not particularly reassured. "The methods here are regrettably crude. Unfortunately, that sort of thing is a necessary wheel in the primitive machine. Pointless now, of course, but it has to go on. Zohrâne expects it."

She underestimates him, Fern thought, returning scrutiny for scrutiny. She sees only the man on the surface, the shallow plotting and commonplace ambition, but all that is as superficial as the blemish on his face. There are layers underneath, deeps beyond the shallows. And looking into his eyes—almond eyes that glittered with their own light—she fancied for a millisecond that she glimpsed something else behind the screen of personality, a capacity for darkness, a void that lived and hungered, so huge that her mind flinched from it—

"Drink this." The personality was back in place. His voice was all smoothness, with roughness under the smooth. He handed her a goblet of clouded glass filled with wine the color of blood.

She sniffed, but did not drink. An image enveloped her thought, excluding the recent past: a room with many tables, a candleflame thin as a blade, a man with a halo of steel . . .

"It won't harm you," he said.

"I'm not thirsty."

"Wine is not for thirst." He raised his own goblet in a toast; she set hers down. "I knew you would come," he said, "in the end. I have been waiting a long, long time."

Time seemed to change as he spoke its name, bending out of shape, out of rhythm, curving round to encapsulate them in their own miniature cosmos. The past was coiled around the future: the present was an isolated moment, belonging nowhere, trapped at random in a maze of inverse reflections.

"More than fifteen years," he went on. "The rip was widening. History moved over a little too far to accommodate me." Fern made no response, sensing his expectation, understanding nothing. "Fifteen years treading softly around the leopardess. She sees only what I permit, uses me—when I give her leave. A disagreeable necessity. She cannot be used. She has gone too far into madness."

"I noticed," said Fern.

"Did you?" His tone sharpened. "When?" And again: "Drink your wine."

"I . . . am not . . . thirsty."

"How long have you been in the city?"

"Two—no, three days." She had a feeling the question was not as casual as it sounded. Time still seemed to be on hold, as if it had lost track of the way forward. On the wheel, the candles neither dripped nor shrank. She could not hear any rumor from the city above and suddenly she was afraid it was no longer out there. There was only a barren heath, under cold stars . . .

He said: "You should have come to me before. Why did you run?"

"I ran because I was chased." She was groping her way through the enigma of their exchange, sensing it was vital to feign comprehension. Whatever she knew of him was hidden, some-where behind the phantoms in her head, but an awareness be-yond memory alerted her to perils she could not see. "Anyway, I didn't come to Atlantis to find you."

"What choice do you have?" A ripple of submerged irritation disturbed his expression. "You cannot close the Door without my help. Zohrâne has had it made in effigy, up at the Palace, with pan-els of gold and fungus of agate and a lizard on the lintel studded with emeralds. The first version was in lignum vitae, but she re-jected it as too mean. As if Death could be dazzled by her extrava-gance! It will be brought to the temple tomorrow and erected in the place of the vacant altar. The ceremony will start at noon. Zohrâne will open the Door; it is fated. She is driven by the impatience of mortality, blinded by the arrogance of Man. An Alimond magnified in power, multiplied in obsession. She will destroy everything—for a whim. Forget Caracandal: he cannot aid you here. Only through me can you obtain the key and restore the balance."

Alimond. Caracandal. The names spun in her brain.

"How?" she demanded warily.

There was an infinitesimal change in his manner, a barely perceptible relaxation. "You admit that you need me?"

She nodded slowly, untrusting, baffled to find the enemy on her side.

"It is a heavy burden," he said gently, "for one so young. Drink your wine."

Automatically, she lifted the goblet. But questions intervened, staying her hand, and some element in the aroma deterred her, recalling things forgotten. "What is your plan?"

"It's unwise to fix on a definite scheme when we can only guess what will happen. When the Door opens the flood will come, we know that much. But the temple is raised above ground level; the foundations were laid with the Gift; it should stand a little while. Anyway, I have power enough to protect both of us for the short time that we need. You will be concealed on the gallery: when Zohrâne has begun her invocation I will join you. No one will notice me then. Once the great wave has passed, the tabernacle will probably remain under water. We may require the services of a *nymphelin* to dive for the key; I will arrange for a suitable arrest. Also a boat, a light *carrarc*, to be tethered in the walkway which connects the main building to the stables. Records made by the exiles indicate the island was not overwhelmed immediately—" his use of the past tense confused her still further "—so we should have a brief lull in which to reach the mountain. Then we can get to the Rose Palace."

"The Palace?" Fern was coasting, attempting to assimilate his certainties. The flood—the drowning of Atlantis—the ultimate End . . .

"Didn't you hear me? There are two Doors. As the Door is duplicated, so the spell will be duplicated. Sympathetic magic. The second Door will be near enough to pick up the vibrations of the spell and focus the excess power. Of course, we cannot be absolutely sure—this is something that has been done once and once only—but our hope depends on it. The Palace should be above the initial flood level. There, you can lock the Door." And he concluded, as if in reassurance: "Your Task will be completed."

"And then?" Fern said quietly. It was the first time she had contemplated Then.

"There are secret ways through the mountain to the harbor. I have a sea-going vessel moored there; the ancient crater will shield the port for a while. We can sail clear of the cataclysm and ride out the storm. At the oracle of Hex-Âté in Qultuum we will find a way back."

"Back?" said Fern.

She knew at once she had made a deadly error.

"Don't you wish to go back?" He was staring at her with peculiar intentness, his gaze narrowing. In the midst of each whirling iris the pupil opened onto nothingness.

She struggled to blank out perplexity, desperation, doubt. Whatever happened, he must not see the panic of her ignorance. He had shown her the means to achieve the unachievable, yet her fear was redoubled. She feared the wall in her mind, the dark behind his eyes, the scent of the wine. "Why do you need me?" she asked, fishing for a diversion. "Why not use the key yourself?"

"It is not for me." His voice grew curt. "You must know that. Its very touch all but destroyed me."

"What shall I do with it," she persisted, "when the Door is locked? Shall I cast it into the flood?"

"Do not speak such folly, even in jest. The key is the kernel of the Lodestone, the seed of unearthly power. It can give you your heart's desire."

"And you?" said Fern bluntly. "What's in it for you?"

His control was fraying. "Without my help, you will gain *noth-*

ing. You fumble your Gift, your courage is tentative, your imagination blunders. Do you want to stay here and rot? Did Caracandal deceive you so easily? *There is no returning without me.*"

Help will be found, had said the Hermit. This is my help. The way back . . . Caracandal . . . Alimond . . . Not back, but forward. I am unborn, ten thousand years unborn . . . *Who am I?*

Ixavo bent over her, his hands enclasping hers, raising the goblet. "Drink your wine."

There was no draft but the candleflames shriveled and the lamps died. All the light in the room was gathered into his eyes, circling and circling the two black holes that seemed to expand even as they snared her gaze, drawing her down, down into the abyss. Zohrâne's emptiness was famine and greed, bounded by her lost humanity, withered into the dregs of a soul; but this was the real thing, the Pit, enormous, inhuman, implacable as eternity . . .

It's a dragon: don't look into its eyes—

For an instant, a splinter of time, fire rushed into her mind, filling her with remembered terror. Then it was gone, and the wall was back in place.

She broke the handclasp with an effort that drained willpower, not strength. The wine-cup fell and shattered, spilling its contents on the floor.

"*I* will decide," she said at last, emphasising the pronoun. "I don't need the wine."

"Decide then."

She had a feeling he was puzzled, as if, in the invasion of her consciousness, he had been reaching for something he could not find. He sat down in the chair opposite, disposing his limbs with peculiar deliberation. Fern saw the stony muscles coiled in his arms, meshed across his torso. She thought: He could have coerced me, he might still, yet he refrains. He can only try psychological manipulation. Perhaps the use of force invalidates my choice. She mistrusted his protection, suspected his guidance, feared him as she had never feared Zohrâne. But he had insight where she had only instinct, he *knew* what she only dreaded. Uuinarde had said: The Sea is coming. Ixavo talked of a giant wave, of certain annihilation. The beautiful city—the temples and palaces, sewers and slums—the people she had come to know there: Ezramé, Ipthor, Rafarl—all doomed. The choice was no choice. She must do what she could.

Help will be found . . .

"All right," she said. "I agree."

He held out his hand, but she would not take it.

"This is not a bargain," she said. "Just fate."

"So be it." He slipped the chain over his head, unhooked the sundisc, and tossed it aside. Then he hung the empty chain around her neck. It felt like a slave collar. "For the key."

She stood up, encouraged to find she still could. "I have to go. I'll return in the morning."

"You go nowhere." His tone was as heavy as the slamming of a door in a sepulchre.

"I have things to do—"

"Warning the fortunate few? A waste of time and breath. Or perhaps you want to say farewell to your vagabond friend? Let him go. He is dead, little one, many ages dead. They are all dead. Why trouble yourself? We are the only living people here." His smile ate into her soul. He went to the door, called the guards. "They'll fetch you food, if you're hungry. I'll have you brought here an hour before noon tomorrow. Sleep well. There's nothing else you can do."

She thought he would have given her a candle if she had requested one, but she was unwilling to betray so much weakness. In the dark of a solitary cell, despair lay in wait. She summoned what few resources she had to resist it.

That was the worst time. They brought her food which she did not eat, water which tasted of dust. Then they left her alone. By Ixavo's orders she had been provided with some cushions and a blanket as well as the pot which was standard issue. On entering the cell, she had had a moment to take in a few details before the door was shut and the light extinguished: unlike the dungeon she had occupied with Rafarl, this one was not delved in natural rock but lined with stone blocks, set in mortar, with the additional luxury of a grating in the floor through which the pot could be emptied immediately after use. Fern tugged at the grating but was unable to lift it: the iron fretwork had been drilled deep into the surrounding stone. Defeated, she sank back on her heels, brushing against the cushions. She lay down to rest her head and wrapped herself in the blanket, more for comfort than warmth, though there was no comfort to be had. In the lonely dark the passage of time altered, becoming no longer continuous but a shapeless limbo where she floated in stasis, reaching in vain for minutes and hours to hold on to. She lost track of her own body, feeling it meld with the blackness until only by touch could she maintain contact with her outer self. And as she lay there her grip on her inner self gradually slackened, and she was swamped by the all-pervading night.

She never knew when she crossed the boundary into unconsciousness. It was a transition from darkness into darkness, slow or swift, she could not tell. She opened her eyes on sunlight and a green hillside, green as the valleys of the Viroc, furred in patches with the misty purple of heather. There was a house below her, a strange gray house with a steepled roof and tall chimneys, unlike any house she had seen before. The windows were shutterless and seemed to be filled with glass. She started to go down to the house but a wolf rose out of the grass beside her and gazed at her with yellow eyes. *I must go,* she said. *They're waiting for me.* She had no idea who *they* were but the compulsion was growing, pulling her onward. The wolf did not move. *I must go,* she repeated, but she seemed to be rooted to the ground. The house was so near she was seized with a fury of frustration and need. She struggled to move her feet . . .

It is not permitted, said a voice beside her, and there was the Hermit, only he didn't look like the Hermit anymore: he was thinner, or fatter, younger or older, and instead of an assortment of ragged pelts he wore a curious garment like a coat, with a pointed hood shading his face. *This is not your time.*

But I must go! she pleaded.

You cannot. His tone was stern. *History will not be cheated. Go back.*

Back . . .

The dream changed as image melted into image in scenes too rapid for the mind to retain. When the pace slowed everything was blue. She was drifting through a blueness lanced with silver; it was vaguely familiar and after a while she realized that she was under the sea, gliding through a shoal of bright fish in the subaqueous light. There was a coral reef below her, a horned forest full of waving shadows, and she was peering into every cranny, brushing aside tresses of weed, touching sea anemones to close them. It came to her that she was searching for something, though she did not know what, and a great dread was on her that she might find it; but she found nothing. And then the reef dropped to a dim plain of sand, and there was a wreck ahead of her half sunken into the sea-bed, a wooden ship which might have been a fishing vessel but for the prow carved in the form of a woman. As she drew nearer she saw it was Uuinarde. Her black hair broke free of the carving and fanned out in the current, and her dead face was turned toward Fern, and her eyes were full of sorrow. *But you left,* said Fern. *You went with the porpoises—*

But Uuinarde was gone and the tide turned and the water

shrank into pools and puddles of slime, and all around her the sea-floor was drying in the sun. Very small and far away she saw the cove where she had stayed with Rafarl, and the rocks hiding the cave entrance, but in between was a great space of mud, littered with dying things. There were fish flapping helplessly from side to side, and writhing worms, and the feeble snapping of tiny claws. She began to walk toward the beach, picking her way through the carnage, but suddenly she was assailed by an overwhelming sense of wrongness: she should not be there, she had gone long ago, she ought to be in a prison cell, with a cushion against her cheek and the hard floor pressing her body. With a vast effort she tore herself away from the wasteland of the disappearing sea, and then she was back in the dungeon, and her eyes opened on darkness.

She lay there wondering why she had gone to so much trouble to wake up, when waking was so bleak. But her brain recoiled from further slumber, dwelling instead on the meeting with Ixavo, and the terrifying doubts and questions it had raised. She thought of the huge tragedy he had foreseen so indifferently, and the fact that he talked about it as if it were already in the past, ages past, and Atlantis itself was only a fragment of history, and there was nothing to be done, nothing worth doing, except to retrieve the key and complete the Task. Yet she knew the Task was not important to him as it was to her: he wanted the Lodestone, or what was left of it, to control it, to exploit it, maybe through her. She was *his* key. Somehow, she had to prevent that. He had drawn her into an unholy alliance, shown her how to act, offered her his aid—bound her to his service. But she would not be so bound: she must find a way to use him and cheat him, even as he sought to use and cheat her. He had said: *We are the only living people here,* relegating Atlantis and all its citizens to a vanished graveyard; but she refused to accept that. She would fight for the people she cared for. She would fight to save them, to salvage the key and close the Door and defeat Ixavo. But the enterprise appeared vast and impossible, and she was alone in the dark, and suddenly she felt horribly young, and hopeless, and afraid.

A long time later, there was a light. She saw it on the ceiling, an unfocused mesh of faint radiance traveling across the cell, shapeshifting as it moved. Yet because it was there she knew there *was* a ceiling, and floor and walls, and the blackness was no longer amorphous. The light was coming through the grill; she realized someone was passing below with a torch, and she knelt and peered down, and saw the flicker of flame, and an enormous pair of shoulders spread beneath. "Hello?" she called. "Who is it? Can you help me?"

"Fernani!" The voice was Rafarl's. "Where are you?"

"Here."

The shoulders stepped aside; the torch was raised; she felt the sudden draft of heat on her face. Then she made out Rafarl, looking up at her. "I'm locked in a cell," she said. "There's a kind of grating in the floor but it won't budge. Can you get me out?"

"Why don't you use the Gift?"

She hadn't thought of that. Somewhat pessimistically, she tried to concentrate on the criss-crossed ironwork, willing it to break; but her will felt ineffectual, her faith half-hearted. "It's no good," she said. "I haven't had enough practice. It only seems to work when I don't have time to worry about it—mostly when I'm in danger."

"You *are* in danger," Rafarl pointed out.

"Not *immediate* danger," said Fern.

Rafarl consulted with his companions—one of them sounded like Ipthor—then turned back to her. "Hold on," he said. "We'll come and find you. When the Lodestone broke the aftershock opened up new passageways: Ipo says we can get through from here into the catacombs, and thence to the dungeons. Do you know your cell number?"

"No," she said, "but it's right beside a stair, close to the apartments of the Guardian."

"All right. We may be a while: we'll have to get the keys from the jailer. Hold on."

And with that they were gone.

She sat down and waited. The best part of a century went by in a pitiable state of anticipation and suspense. She had given up all hope several times when she finally heard the bolts sliding back. And then there was Rafarl, and she was stumbling through the door and clutching him in something between an embrace and a stranglehold, and behind him Ipthor was looking amused, and the shoulders, last seen manning the entrance to the basement club, lifted the torch for a better light on the situation. "Are you hurt?" demanded Rafarl, alarmed to find her so overtly demonstrative. "What did they do to you?"

"Nothing. Nothing. I'm fine." To her astonishment she found she was weeping, uncontrollable tears streaming down her face. "I'm so glad you came. So glad . . . " And, smudging the tears with her hand: "Why did you?"

He grimaced. Scowled. Shrugged. "Does it matter?"

"No."

"This is Gogoth."

The shoulders gave a grunt of acknowledgment. Fern looked up into a broad face, olive-dark, with the nose spread widely across its flat surface and eyes compressed into slots between cheekbone and brow. There was a fading slave-brand on his left temple in the shape of an owl. The *th* sound at the end of the name, rare in Atlantean, gave it an uncouth ring. But Fern, torn between relief at her escape and the renewal of urgency, had no time to be daunted. Even as they ran down the passageway, stepping over the unconscious jailer, she was pouring out the gist of Ixavo's revelations—the imminence of doom, the tidal wave, the fall of the city. She had expected incredulity and skepticism and was surprised when Ipthor took her side. "There is an uneasiness, a buildup of pressure: you can feel it when you're underground. I think we should go. The *Norne* is waiting. I'll get the others together. Meet us on the wharf."

"You don't really believe this." Rafarl's protest lacked conviction.

"The water is low in the harbor; on the east coast the tide has not come in. You don't have to be a priest to read the omens. It might be nothing more than freak weather conditions but when it comes to my own skin I like to be very, very prudent. If Atlantis falls, I intend to be somewhere else." His unpleasant grin flashed out for a moment. "Just as well I didn't take that reward. The *phénix* may be on the verge of drastic devaluation. It would have been a shame to sell my honor for a handful of scrap metal."

"What honor?" said Rafarl absentmindedly.

"You're a better sailor than any of us," Ipthor persisted. "We'll need you. You have the ear of the sea-gods: hence, no doubt, your penchant for nymphs. If it starts blowing a tempest you're the only one who'll be able to handle the boat."

"If," said Rafarl. "This is all ifs. I must see my mother. If—if she'll come—"

"Women are bad luck on board ship," said Gogoth.

"Women are bad luck anywhere." Ipthor made a wry grimace.

"*And* Fern," Rafarl concluded, his tone sharpening. "I won't go without them. If you think women are bad luck, try sailing without a captain. That's worse."

Ipthor nodded; it was Fern who demurred. "I can't leave till after the ceremony," she said. "There's something I have to do."

"Your mission," said Rafarl. "I wondered when we'd get back to that."

There was a short silence. "Very well." Rafarl turned to Gogoth and Ipthor. "Go down to the harbor, get the boat ready. Lay on water and food: we may be some days at sea. I trust you to enlist a suitable crew: the usual gang, I can't take more. What about your uncle?"

"I suppose we ought to take him with us," Ipthor conceded. "It is, after all, his boat. Honesty is not a priority for me, but when he sobers up he might be useful. I'll peel him off a taproom floor and sling him in the hold."

"All right. I'll meet you at dawn. I'd rather not risk negotiating the channel in the dark."

They had re-entered the sewer now and were standing at the junction of two tunnels; water thick as grime sucked at their feet. Gogoth and Ipthor disappeared in one direction; Rafarl and Fern took the other. Presently they came to a shaft, much shorter than the one they had climbed before, which brought them out in a narrow yard between high walls. It was deep night and Fern could see little but a glimpse of the waxing moon above and a glimmer beyond the opening into the neighboring street. She followed Rafarl through the gate back into the shadows of the city.

The villa was in darkness when they arrived. The arch leading onto the porch was secured with a blind of wire mesh; the ground floor windows were similarly protected. Rafarl, undeterred, went to the second from the end, and after some judicious fiddling the blind slid upward. "I have an arrangement with my mother," he explained in a whisper. "Ludicrous, isn't it?—all this. My stepfather's idea. He's too mean to pay for a private guard and too paranoid to leave anything open. He must be home tonight. My mother never locks up." They shinned over the low sill and slithered to the floor. With the exclusion of the night breeze the room was airless, muffled in gloom. Rafarl felt for the candle and tinder-box Ezramé always left on hand. In a moment, Fern saw a glancing spark, and then his hand was cupped to shield a tiny cone of flame from the draft of movement. "This way." He led her through to the vestibule and began to ascend the stairs. A noise from above brought him to a halt. Ezramé emerged at the top, her loose night-robe pulled on in such haste she was still tying the strings down the front.

"Raf?"

"*Mié.*"

"Downstairs. Don't wake your stepfather."

Back in the salon, she lit a lamp and fetched wine herself, not wishing to disturb the servants. Most establishments had household slaves to whom they were less considerate, but Ezramé disapproved so strongly of this practice she had been able to carry her point with her husband. "Why did you come back?" she said, the welcome in her looks, not her words. "The city is too dangerous for you now. Indeed, I fear it is becoming too dangerous for us all. The temple guards go where they like and take whom they will. They went to the House of Mithraïs—the oldest of the ruling houses—" the footnote was for Fern's benefit "—they took the youngest son, though his mother wept and pleaded. He's ten years old. *Ten.* I can't bear to think of it. What does Zohrâne hope to achieve, apart from the enmity of her subjects?"

"She doesn't care for that," said Fern. "She is going to open the Gate."

"The Gate?" Ezramé looked puzzled.

"The Gate of Death." Fern turned the goblet between her fingers, looking at the wine, at the wall, at nothing. "I have seen Ixavo. He knows more than she thinks. He knows *me.* He offered me help—after a fashion."

"I said he knew you." Rafarl threw her a suspicious look. And, with an edge in the question: "What kind of help?"

Fern gave a slight shrug. "Help on *his* terms. He wants to use me—and I need to use him. After the Gate is opened the Sea will come; it will fall on the city in a great wave, destroying everything. Ixavo has the power to protect me. I have to meet him in the temple and get the key. Then we go to the Rose Palace. The mountainside should be above the water, for a while. There's another model of the Door there—he calls it the Door, not the Gate, I'm not sure why. Zohrâne had a second made because the first wasn't rich enough. Ixavo says in magical terms it's the same thing, and I can close it, and lock it, and fulfill my Task. I can't refuse. It's the only chance I have."

"And then?" said Rafarl.

"He'll get me off the island on a ship he has prepared. He wants the Lodestone. The key is the core. But he can't touch it himself, for some reason. He thinks to control it through me."

"You'll allow that?"

Fern shook her head.

"How will you prevent him? On his ship, in his power, what can you do?"

"Throw myself in the sea, if it comes to that. If I can't think of anything better." Unexpectedly, she smiled.

Ezramé watched them in silence, not understanding but saving her questions, too wise to interrupt. Rafarl got up and paced the room, kicking an obstructive footstool from his path. "You're really set on this idiocy, aren't you? I suppose there's no point in telling you to forget the business with the Door and come with me now?"

"No point." Her voice was very quiet.

No one said anything for several minutes.

"So this is the end." It was Ezramé who spoke at last. "The end of Atlantis. I've felt it coming—I've felt it for some time—but now it's here, it's soon, it's real . . . Strange, it's almost a relief. The doom that lies ahead of you, sensed but not known, vague and formless as a shadow—that is perhaps worse than the doom you can see clearly, no matter how terrible or how close. Do you know when—?"

"We leave at dawn." Rafarl was curt, not looking at Fern.

"Oh no," Ezramé said gently. "Atlantis is my home. I have

been here too long to go now. I have loved it and loathed it, ignored its beauties, done too little to combat its evils. There have
been many moments when I felt trapped in this city as in a cage
of gold, but I chose that cage, it would be wrong to abandon it.
Even now. You are young, your choices are not made. You can sail
away, find kingdoms of your own, build anew. I am too weary of
my life for all that."

"Don't talk that way." Rafarl sat down beside her, took her
hand. "I won't leave without you."

Fern moved away, feeling she would be an intruder in their
dispute. Low voices reached her: Rafarl passionate, deriding,
imploring, Ezramé regretful and very calm. At length Rafarl
looked round. His face was bleak and set. "What about you?" he
asked Fern.

"I told you, I have to complete the Task. I'll go with Ixavo."

"I don't understand what this Task means," Ezramé said with
a revival of anxiety, "or what it is you have to do, but you mustn't
trust Ixavo. The corruption on his face lives but I have often felt
that the man inside is dead, an automaton motivated by some external power. Whatever force he uses, it is not the Gift. He comes
from Qultuum, the dark city, where natives still worship ancient
earth-spirits with pagan rituals. Oh, I know we in Atlantis have no
right to superiority now—the House of Goulabey has dragged us
down to the level of barbarians—but of one thing I am sure,
Zohrâne worships no power but her own. Even the Stone which
was its source she has destroyed in her jealousy. Ixavo—"

"I don't trust him," said Fern. "I *need* him."

"So you said." Rafarl's manner was unpleasant. "You *need* me,
idiot. If you go with Ixavo, you're finished. Why can't you bring
yourself to *ask* me?"

"Ask you what?"

"To wait for you."

"You can't," said Fern. "The others would never agree to it."

"I'll make them agree. Ask me."

"If you go now, you'll be safe. If you wait, the storm will come. The Sea has no mercy." And she shivered as she said it.

"*Ask me.*"

But she was silent, troubled by forgotten hauntings, knowing only that she could not ask him to risk his life. Her own seemed of little account now.

Ezramé rose, touching Fern's arm. "There is an empty bedroom at the back of the house," she said. "You can sleep there for a while. My husband will not know to bother you. Save your decisions till morning."

There were two couches, but they only used one, lying together in a fierce embrace, making love without words, for words meant conflict. Rafarl fell asleep immediately after but Fern lay wakeful for a long time. In the dark before dawn she slept at last, a sleep without rest or refreshment, slipping straight into a zone of fractured dreams. She was back in the city, the city of her nightmares, with its hard gray streets and cliff-like buildings, and that background of noise that she had once missed without being able to pinpoint what it was. But in the dream, she knew. In the dream, she knew everything. The city broke up, sections of it peeling away like paint from a frieze, and other images followed, too many to remember, skittering across her sleep like mayflies. She tried to hold on to them, knowing they were telling her something important, something she needed to learn, but her mind would not retain them. And then the rapid scene-changes came to a halt, and she was in a dark room full of tables (Why *tables?* she wondered afterward), and there was a candle in front of her, and beyond the flame she saw Ixavo's face, no longer disfigured, a golden face framed in an aureole of silver. He smiled in a way that made her afraid, and the candleflame grew until it was as tall as a spear, and opened out, and then the room was all fire. She was surrounded, imprisoned, her hand was in the flames, Ixavo held her wrist so she could not draw back, and she saw the flesh charring and flaking off her bones. There was no pain but she knew it was true because she could not feel that hand anymore. She struggled frantically, screaming the silent screams of nightmare—and woke to find herself trembling, the sweat already chilling on her skin. The darkness was a shade paler; the only sounds were a bird calling out in the garden and the gentle rhythm of Rafarl's breathing. Her hand had become trapped under his body, causing a temporary numbness. She extricated it without disturbing him and waited for the feeling to return, thankful for such a mundane explanation of the dream-horror. She did not dwell on the rest. The night was ebbing, and she curled her limbs around her lover, pressing her breasts against his back, desiring only his warmth and his nearness for whatever time remained to them.

As soon as it was light Rafarl got up, washing and shaving with unaccustomed deliberation. Fern watched, sitting on the couch, naked under the single sheet. "I'm going down to the harbor," he said. "The *Norne* will be ready. You still won't ask?"

"No."

They did not say goodbye.

Ezramé found her sitting there, dry-eyed and cold. She wrapped her in the priceless veil, heirloom of her house. For all its fineness it was as warm as summer. "I want you to have it," she said. "What you have to do is obviously very dangerous. It may have some power to protect you."

"But *you*—"

"I do not need it now."

At breakfast, Fern ate little, though she knew she should be hungry. Conversation was brief. Rafarl did not return; his stepfather, too, had gone out. Ezramé's presence warmed her as the veil and the summer could not. "I don't want you to be alone," Fern said, meaning, at the end.

"Aliph will stay with me. He has been with my family for

twenty years. I have spoken to him. I told him to find a ship, but he would not."

"Maybe we should warn other people."

"They would not believe you—or if they did, they would still remain. It is hard to tear yourself from your roots."

There was a pause while Fern sipped a drink made from lemons and other, more exotic fruits, the fruits of Atlantis, which would never grow again.

"What does *Norne* mean?" she asked, for something to ask. The morning loomed in front of her like a wall, a wall with no gate, save the one she had to close.

"It's a kind of witch," said Ezramé. "A witch of the sea. In Atlantis, there are a hundred words for *witch*."

A witch of the sea. Fern saw a carved prow from which the paint had almost bleached, the skeleton of a hull now high and dry. The familiarity of it was like an ache in a tooth long removed. She would have been afraid, if she had had the time. But there was only a little time left.

She finished the blended juices slowly, trying to savor the taste—the taste of Atlantis—to hold it in her memory for always. But it is all but impossible to remember a taste, and it had evaporated from her mind almost as quickly as from her mouth. She wanted to hug and kiss and cling, but she and Ezramé just sat, face to face, no longer speaking, hand clasping hand.

It was well before midday when Fern said: "I have to go."

✦ XII ✦

The drum was beating in the temple for the last time. There was a gray haze creeping up from the rim of the sky, tarnishing the sunlight; the gold of the city—of marble and stone, painting and gilding—was dimmed. The strange nimbus which Uuinarde had remarked around the fractured dome had become more noticeable: its fiery luster was blurred as if by a thickening of the air, an imperceptible pollution, its resplendence disseminated into a corona that had the tincture of dust. Up on the mountain there had been a freshness, the hint of a breeze, but in the streets below the atmosphere was that of a sealed room, stifling and curiously tense; every breath tasted of dirt. No one had stopped Fern on her way to the temple, for all her fair skin and alien countenance. Phaidé Dévornine's veil wrapped her like a film of shadow; she could almost imagine it had the faculty of rendering her, not quite invisible, but somehow unobtrusive. The temple guard had let her pass, and she had arrived unhindered at the Guardian's apartment. Ixavo found her there when he came to change for the ceremony. "You escaped," he said, and for an instant his face was blank, as if he did not know how to react, or what expression to assume.

"Of course."

His features shifted, hardened, becoming vulcanized into their customary aspect. "Yet you keep to your bargain. That is wise. At least you have the intelligence to realize there are no alternatives."

"It wasn't a bargain," she reminded him. "I keep to my fate."

And now the throb of the drum was dying, and for Atlantis time was running out, the city's agelong lifespan shrunk to little more than an hour, the minutes and seconds trickling steadily into eternity. Fern crouched in the amber gloom of the gallery, screened by the balustrade, close to a stair. "I have arranged for the arrest of a *nympheline*," Ixavo had told her. "One of my personal guards will escort her to you. He will see she is secured, so she cannot attempt to escape." The last note of the drum was still vibrating faintly in floor and walls when the man came, leading the *nympheline* on a short chain. Her head was bowed; long black hair hung forward over her face. When she looked up and the curtain parted her eyes were neither green nor blue but a sea-color in between. She did not speak; nor did Fern. The guard fastened the chain round one of the supports in the balustrade, seemed to hover on the verge of saluting, and then left.

"You've changed sides," said Uuinarde, low-toned by instinct. They could hear people gathering below. "You betrayed us."

"I'm on no one's side," said Fern. "I have something to do. I'm trying to do it. That's all."

And: "Why didn't you go with the porpoises? You could have been far away."

"I am an Atlantean," she responded. "This is my home." Like Ezramé, Fern thought, and she wondered where *her* home was, reaching for memories of the village on Mount Vèz, but all she could picture was the house in her dream in the prison-cell, the strange gray house with the steepled roof and the eerie windows reflecting sky. A house she did not even know.

"Can you undo the chain?" asked Uuinarde, extending her wrist, weighed down by the heavy manacle.

Fern tried, but without success. "Ixavo will do it," she said. "He'll release you, when the moment comes. He has a task for you too."

"I won't help him!"

"You won't *be* helping him," said Fern. "You'll be helping me."

She thought Uuinarde would object, but there was no more leisure for talk. It seemed to her right that the nymph should be there, a falling-into-place of the jigsaw-puzzle of destiny, and after her initial protest Uuinarde herself appeared to accept it, and the two of them drew close together, peering through the balusters down into the heart of the tabernacle. The drumbeat had started again, not the great drum this time but a soft tattoo, rhythmic as a pulse, finger-tapped on the tabor by a pair of acolytes standing on opposite sides of the chamber. The priests were still taking up their positions, one at each point of the engraved sun-star. They were chosen from the most Gifted, those who would have been called holy, if holiness had been current in Atlantis. Many were related to the twelve families, having taken to the priesthood for further advancement and prestige. Their heads were shaved like Ixavo's and their split cloaks embroidered so thickly with metallic thread that the folds hung rigid, like strips of wood. They faced the center of the circle, where formerly the Lodestone had rested on its altar.

But the ancient altar was gone. In its place stood a door, a door without a wall, erected in grotesque isolation in the midst of that vast floor, duplicated by its own reflection, like the lone gateway to a vanished palace, marooned in a standing pool. But the water was hard and did not ripple, and the Door was set under an arch of quartz, with strange growths of jasper and agate on either side, fungoid creatures whose jeweled eyes squinted from toadstool heads, grasping the frame with many claws. The Door itself was black, but the panels were inlaid with obscure hieroglyphs in red gold, the handle was a single ruby, and a tiny reptile encrusted with green stones glittered on the architrave. There was no keyhole anywhere on its surface. A monument to insanity, thought

Fern, a nightmare fantasy in gilding and gems, extravagant and crude, ultimately banal, the brainchild of a witch-queen with the taste of a barbarian conquistador. The Gate of Death, or so Zohrâne had claimed, a gate from world to world, from Life to Immortality. But Fern had seen that Gate on a rooftop terrace, had felt its awe and its horror, and she knew Ixavo was right, this was a Door, only a Door, though where it led she could not guess. *She will try to open the Gate of Death,* had said the Hermit, but the memory of his instruction faded, and she seemed to hear another voice, clear but very far away, saying "Things are not always what you want them to be." It came to her that this was her own voice, in some other place or time, but she had no idea to what she referred, no respite to wonder or fear. Two thurifers entered the chamber below, walking at a measured pace, bearing vessels of burning oil from which scented fumes drifted toward the gallery. Behind them came Zohrâne. She wore an ankle-length dress of a silk almost as fine as her veils, glittering as if sprinkled with crushed diamond. Every detail of her anatomy was visible under the shimmer, the tumorous breasts with nipples black as grapes, the red jewel in her navel, the triangular shade of her pubic hair. Long drifts of gauze, tinted with the hues of sunset, orange and vermilion and rose, flowed behind her like a comet's tail. The hair on her head was stiffened with gum and twisted into a tall conical structure, like a horn, secured with gold wire, a style Fern recognized, though she did not know from where. Possibly it had some ritualistic significance. A faint patina of gold overlaid her eyelids and cheekbones; her mouth was like polished metal. The key hung on a thread about her neck. Ixavo followed her at a suitable distance. He did not look up at the gallery but assumed a position near to the adjacent stair. The thurifers also drew aside: Zohrâne alone stepped into the sun-star and stood facing the Door.

Certain preparations had already been made, Fern guessed; she could just distinguish a line of grayish-white powder describing a

circle inside the star. No, not a circle, a semicircle, closed off along
the diameter that included the threshold of the Door. Zohrâne
made a sweeping gesture and spoke a single word, and the line
crackled as if taking fire, flickering into a glow, so she was divided
from her assistants by an arc of flame. The engravings on the floor
also started to pulsate with an elusive radiance, a phantom glimmer
that came and went as though at the mercy of an erratic power-
source. The priests began a low chant in which Fern could identify
only the noun *haadé*, a reverential term for death. As the chant
grew in volume she began to be conscious of the terrible potency of
language, the sense that a name spoken is a summons and more
than a summons, an act of creation, for a word shapes an idea, an
idea shapes belief, and belief shapes the world. The temple was
filled with belief, a rising tide of belief, building in force like water
behind a dam, and Zohrâne stood in the center controlling it with
fluid gestures, her rippling fingers leaving brief trails of light on the
air. Her lips moved in an invocation at first inaudible but which
grew with the momentum of the ceremony until the murmur had
become a crescendo, drowning out the priests. "*Haadé! Haadé ai
zoïna!* Death for the living! Unlock the Gate, open the Way! *Uvalé!*
Open to the key—the key—the key!" She held it up, and light
leaped from her hand onto the Door, a snake of light that writhed
and danced across the toadstool faces, the claws of agate, touching
them with an obscene animation. The background litany changed,
becoming deeper and stronger; the semicircle parted. Many hands
plucked a slight figure from the shelter of the cloister and thrust
him within the perimeter, which closed behind him, sealing him in.
He was very young, perhaps eleven or twelve, nearly naked. He
looked this way and that in confusion and fear. Fern's grip tightened on the rail. Zohrâne let the key drop against her breast and
seized his shoulder, pulling him effortlessly toward her, her supple
fingers tensed into steel. She raised her other arm: a knife appeared
in her grasp where no knife had been before. The boy shrank and

seemed to cry out, but his voice was overwhelmed by the rising clamor of the incantation, the pent power was released, and a curtain of flame hissed upward and boiled against the dome. Through a blue haze of fire Fern saw the knife fall—the knife unsheathed from air and nothingness—saw the blade buried deep in the boy's chest. But the knife was real, and the flesh was real, and the tongue of blood that licked across the floor was red. The spell peaked on a word Fern did not recognize, and Zohrâne bestrode the body, shuddering with an orgasm of power, and the fires silvered and sank, but now the Door was set in a wall, thick as a shadow, and beyond lay a darkness not of Atlantis, and the circle was complete.

She didn't need to kill him, thought Fern, somewhere in the stillness at the back of her mind. She knew she had never seen killing before. *She didn't need the sacrifice. She was feeding her ego, not her Gift . . .*

And there was the keyhole, as she had known it would be. A ray of white light sprang from it like a lance, roving the chamber, dwindling to a notch of brilliance. Zohrâne bent over the child, pressing her mouth to his forehead for a long moment in something that only resembled a kiss, as if she sought to suck not his life but his death. Then she straightened, grasping the key, wrenching it from its thread. "I'll be back," Fern whispered into Uuinarde's ear. "I must *see* . . ." Her footfalls on the stair barely ruffled the all-embracing silence. She found herself beside Ixavo, but it did not matter. Zohrâne was stooping, sliding the key into the lock. It turned with a tiny snick, impossibly loud in that vacuum of noise. And as the queen pulled open the Door, Fern, hiding in the cloister almost directly behind her, the veil drawn instinctively over her face, was one of the few to see what she saw.

A woman. Attitude for attitude, shock for shock, she seemed to mirror Zohrâne. She might almost have been a specter of the queen's own death, that Death which she wished to cheat and defy: waxen-cheeked and haggard, skeleton-thin, her dim hair leached of all color. And in her eyes Fern thought she glimpsed the same hunger, the same emptiness, before all was lost in the blankness of absolute bewilderment. She wore a dress of some unknown material, more opaque than Zohrâne's but equally clinging, dull red like old blood. Behind her there was only a dark in which the completed fire-lines of sun and circle floated like star-trails in the void. This is no other world, Fern told herself, inexplicably certain. One witch has found another: spell has turned on spell, seeker on seeker. There are no loopholes into eternity. Zohrâne's back was toward her but she could see the tensing of her muscles, the involuntary tightening of her grip on the knife. And at the same moment she was conscious of a swelling sound, beyond the silence, a noise that would have filled her with new panic had she not been concentrating wholly on the Door. She took a step forward, heedless of discovery; thought she heard the woman speak. And over her right shoulder, for a fraction of a second, she saw someone else. Someone outside the perimeter as she was outside the perimeter, white-faced and desperate, peering through into Atlantis. She froze.

"Fool!" The admonition came from Ixavo; he was grabbing her arm, wrenching her away from the sight. "Don't you know not to look? Run!" They were on the stair even as Zohrâne dropped the knife, raising her hand. The clamor now shook the chamber, a great rushing, roaring din in which all individual sound was lost, filling the world. Darkness reared above the dome; the sun was blotted out. As they reached the gallery Ixavo was already shrieking an enchantment too primitive for speech, a gibbering of animal voices from the aeons before language was invented. He flung Fern down beside Uuinarde and towered above them, his face distorted from the utterance of sounds not meant for human throat, sounds more sensed than heard against the onslaught of noise from outside. And then the Sea came, falling on the dome with all the weight of the five oceans, crushing the gilded roof like sugar glass, and the gold and the beams and the black water were crashing down on them, and terror fled and panic, and there was no more circle, no more ritual, no more time . . .

Fern's arms were around Uuinarde: the *nympheline's* face was buried in her shoulder. She looked up, and saw Ixavo had drawn on the sea itself to shield them, encasing them in a great bubble, a skin of water tugged this way and that by the pressures without, wavering, flexing, bulging. Ixavo's own features seemed to be pulled and pummelled as he struggled to keep the membrane intact. She felt the quiver in the ground itself, the cracking of supports below. The gallery floor began to sag; Uuinarde's head jerked back with a scream she could not hear. Ixavo had no strength to spare for the earthquake. But Fern was already groping with her mind, without hesitation or thought, reaching down into the very foundations, clenching rock on rock, holding the shuddering pillars with her willpower, her Gift, her belief. Her ears closed out the sea's howling: she was exploring deep in the Earth, feeling for the quickening heartbeat of the planet, fighting to get a grip on rending stone and the jolting of plate against plate—*No!* Ixavo's warning seared through her brain. *Don't spend your strength! You cannot do it! Focus your power here—only here—* Reluctantly she let go, withdrawing into the cell of their immediate safety. Below, she sensed a chasm tearing through the temple floor, felt the pouring sea boil in the updraft of escaping gases. But beyond the fragile protection of the bubble she could see only the seething dark.

Long after, the waters sank. It might have been another dawn, another age. The bubble burst; welcome air rushed in. Fern found she was still holding Uuinarde, and the *nympheline* still clung to her: they looked at one another, too devastated for tears, and did not let go. Ixavo leaned on the balustrade. Effort had drained most of the color from his skin, leaving it darkly sallow; only his disfigurement stood out like an open wound. The breath rasped from his lungs, his voice rasped. Fern was visited by the thought that he was enduring beyond normal human capacity, not holding on but held, in the grip of some Other who used him, drove him, consumed him without compunction. "Come," he said at last. "This is a respite, not the end. Not yet. The key." He bent over the chain, unclipping the mechanism which released the shackle. Uuinarde watched as if he and the manacle and the wrist it held were utterly divorced from her. "What did you see," she asked Fern, "through the Door? Was it Death?"

"Maybe." Fern shivered at the memory.

"She saw *herself.*" Ixavo's grin was empty, like the grin of a skull. "It was folly. Had you set even a finger or toe across the threshold, you would have been lost. You know that."

Do I? thought Fern. What do I know?

But the question was huge and ominous, and she feared the answer.

"Dive," Ixavo told the *nympheline.* "We want the key. The key Zohrâne used to unlock the Door. It's down there—somewhere. Get it."

Beneath the gallery the water still surged, heaving with debris, sucked into whirling currents by the rifts and tunnels below. They saw spinning beams, sections of roof, clotted lumps of clothing, a hand drifting like a starfish. "No swimmer can live in that," said Uuinarde.

"You're a *nympheline,*" said Ixavo. "Try."

"How will I find something so small?"

"By looking for it."

"Is it important?" she asked Fern.

"Yes."

"More than life?"

"More than life."

Uuinarde nodded; her face grew set. She folded her veil into a sash, winding it across her chest and round her waist. Then she climbed over the parapet, slid into the water, and was gone.

She emerged some minutes later, clutching one of the supports against the swirl of vicious eddies. Her hair clung to cheekbone and brow; there was blood on her lip; her hands were empty. "I'll help you," said Fern, knowing herself helpless, swinging a leg over the rail.

"Don't be stupid." Ixavo pulled her back. Uuinarde recovered her breath, and dived again.

She was gone longer this time, breaking the surface at last on the wrong side of the chamber, struggling from pillar to pillar to return to her starting point. The shell of the temple still stood, roofless under a cloud-driven sky, broken portions of the gallery jutting here and there in precarious isolation. It resembled a cauldron filled with obscene soup: leakage from the sewers was already finding its way into the mixture; regurgitated flotsam jostled for space before being dragged down again; monstrous bubbles rose at the center, exploding like blisters on the face of the water. Many released evil-smelling gases; one spattered blood. Not far from their unstable peninsula the wall was starting to split as the torrent sought to escape, flood meeting flood. Uuinarde, running out of pillars, negotiated the remainder of the circuit with increased difficulty. As she drew nearer, Fern saw the red of new bruising on her arms and jaw, the filth dripping from her hair.

"Have you got it?" Ixavo's eagerness bordered on frenzy.

The *nympheline* shook her head, too exhausted to speak.

"You must come out," said Fern. "Rest."

"No." Ixavo was inflexible. "The earthquake may return at any moment. We mustn't linger." Fern thought he would have kicked the *nympheline* from her handhold if he had not managed to recall how much he needed her. "Find the key. Then we can all get out."

Uuinarde took a few ragged breaths, looking up at the other

girl. Fern noticed she never looked at Ixavo now. Her eyes were slits of emerald-blue in a face streaked with slime, distorted with rubescent blotches. Then she pushed back her hair and plunged once more under the water.

She had been gone only a little while when it began again. This time, the noise came from below, the shifting of unwieldy rock, a rumble in the belly of the earth. New crevasses opened up: the sea at the heart of the chamber was sucked down while the current around the edge accelerated, spiraling into a whirl-pool. The precipice on which they stood jolted free of the wall, balancing only on a couple of unsteady columns and a stab of power from Ixavo. Uuinarde surfaced some distance away, grab-bing hold of a passing hunk of cloth, bloated with trapped air. It was impossible to see if there was a body attached. The flow car-ried her past Fern too swiftly for her straining hands, spinning the *nympheline* into orbit around the vortex, pounding her with hurry-ing debris. She submerged—reappeared—transferred her clutch to a broken beam which bobbed and rolled in her grasp. Fern saw that she would be swept by again even farther out of reach. She twisted one end of Ezramé's veil around her arm, unraveling the other over the maelstrom, blown on a breeze of thought or faith, a ribbon of gossamer almost too slight to be seen. But the *nymphe-line* caught it and it held, strong as a rope, and Fern and Ixavo drew her to safety, though he cursed her for her obvious failure. She did not respond; her mouth was shut hard. Only when she had struggled over the coping did her lips part, ejecting some-thing into Fern's cupped palm. "The key!" Ixavo said, and his face gloated, yet he shrank from it. Fern did not thank Uuinarde— they had gone beyond thanks—only their fingers entwined for a moment; the *nympheline*'s were slimed from the unclean water. Then Fern hung the key on the chain around her neck and Ixavo swung her across the gap, onto an uneven ledge protruding from the wall along which she could scramble to the exit. Behind her, there was the sound of tearing marble, sharp as a report, as the Guardian relaxed the grasp of his power. He leaped for the ledge, abandoning Uuinarde. Turning, Fern saw her tumble to her knees on the tilting platform—saw the columns snap like celery-sticks— saw the segment of gallery slide into the water and vanish in a gulp of muddy foam. There was an instant of expectancy, of frantic hope; but she did not re-emerge. She hadn't even cried out.

"We don't need her now," Ixavo said, thrusting Fern onward.

She was too stunned to answer.

Outside, much of the walkway had collapsed but the *carrarc* was there as promised, pitching on the water below, the painter knotted through the leftover fretwork. Something stronger than luck must have kept it there. Ixavo sprang down into the boat: it tipped and ducked but did not capsize. Fern allowed him to lift her in; she had no choice. The ruin of Atlantis stretched on every hand. The waters were subsiding slowly now, funneled into turbulence down narrow streets, spreading into calmness in the wider areas of squares and avenues. The effect was that of a vast lagoon from which topless edifices, shattered pediments, piers and pillars jutted like fantastic rock formations. The upper storeys now stood clear of the waterline, many of them minus one wall or several, bare rafters spanning the empty roof-space like fleshless ribs. Occasional cataracts poured from crevices and window-slots where the water had been temporarily contained, but most of the devastation was still, wrapped in a deceptive quiet. Sea and storm had withdrawn after the first assault and were recharging their energies before returning to finish their work. Steered only by Ixavo's will the *carrarc* slipped through the lake, skirting island buildings, avoiding the man-made reefs below. Great quantities of wreckage drifted past, matted into rafts or piled into pyramidal structures like huge icebergs of rubbish. There were other things among the flotsam, things with hands, limbs, hair, but Fern tried not to look at them. A cat which had survived somehow mewed from a promontory: they saw no other living creature. Massive clouds were stacked above the horizon but the falling sun found a chink to peep through, like a prisoner peering out between the bars of his cell. Low rays ranged across the desolation, turning the brown waters to murky yellow. Overhead, an inky sky sagged toward them, pregnant with the tempest to come.

When they reached the mountain they saw the earthquake had opened a wide ravine in its flank: the villa of the Dévornines was gone. A slice of the palace had been hacked away, exposing three-sided rooms, the caverns of vaults unaccustomed to daylight. They left the boat and ascended the slope to the palace entrance. Here, there were people about, though very few. An old woman sat on a step mumbling to herself: when she saw them, she pulled her veil over her face. Two youths, possibly servants or slaves, begged Ixavo for orders, but he brushed them aside. "Go where you will," he said. "It will do no good." There were soldiers at the palace gate but they merely stared at the intruders; their spears lay on the ground.

"What of the queen?" asked one.

"She's dead," said Ixavo. "I am her legatee."

After that, they shrank from his path. He moved through the corridors with long strides; sometimes, Fern had to run to keep up. She was thinking: They are all gone. Ezramé, the faithful Aliph, Uuinarde . . . all gone now. The world that remained seemed raw and barren, an existence without meaning. She adhered to her purpose because that was all she had left. Walls of rose-tinted marble unfolded around her, doors and passages hemmed her in, forcing her too close to her protector. It was beautiful, one of the most beautiful palaces ever built, but she stalked through it unseeing, uncaring. Eventually they came to a door that was chained and fettered as if Zohrâne had feared it might escape. Ixavo made a noise like the groan of a quake itself and the chains clattered to the floor, the fetters peeled away from the panels . . . Beyond, there was a long room which had once been longer, cloven by the

ravine, filled with the dying sun. Fern blinked in the sudden brilliance. But even as they entered the light faded, smothered in the
creeping advance of the storm, and the dazzle shrank to a filament
that cut a semicircle through the dark, and at its center was another door, the Door, and it was open. It was far plainer than the
version Zohrâne had used in the ceremony, its wooden surface unadorned, its framework bare of jeweled fungi. The lizard that scut-
tered across the lintel glittered like a dart of green fire; but it was
real. The opening was narrow, masked by the Door itself, so Fern
could not see what lay on the other side. The keyhole shone with a
glow that came from nothing in the room.

"Don't try to look!" said Ixavo, reading her thought.

The circle barred her way, but she knew what to do. *"Uvalé!"*
she ordered—Open!—and the line broke, allowing her through,
reconnecting behind her. She was immediately conscious of being
sealed within the boundaries of the spell, united in a perilous rela-
tionship with the Door and whatever lay beyond, closer to that
Beyond—the Beyond she must not even see—than the room outside the circle. Ixavo was not merely excluded but distanced: she
felt herself contained in a solitary pocket of power, yet in some
way it encompassed a potency and a potential far larger than the
exterior world. She had never learned the words of any incantation
but it was unimportant; what mattered was certainty and belief.
The right words would be whatever she chose to say. *"Fiassé!"* she
cried. "Be!"—and in Atlantean the verb has a far deeper meaning
than in lesser tongues, it was the command of creation, the summons that conjured substance from the void. The circle flamed
and sank, the Door trembled. She thrust it shut, very cautiously,
sensing that it must not swing too far, remembering Ixavo's warning: *Had you set even a finger or a toe across the threshold* . . . She
murmured the word of closure into a falling silence, the same silence she had heard earlier that day in the temple. The two moments seemed to blend in that quietus: many doors became one

Door, the broken circles one circle. The torn edges of Time drew together. She inserted the key in the lock, felt it turn smoothly, without effort. There was a familiar click—the sound of a pin's fall, of atom colliding with atom—and the world was whole again.

She removed the key, hanging the chain once more around her neck. When she turned, she saw the circle waning to a glimmer, and the figure of Ixavo, no longer remote, a looming threat outside a barrier that was nearly gone.

"Come," he said. He did not tell her she had done well or ill. She sensed the fever of his impatience as a tangible aura.

"Where?" she demanded. He ignored the question, seizing her arm to propel her in his wake. Instinctively her right hand closed on the key, drawing resistance from the Stone, feeling his grasp slacken, though whether because of her will or as a tardy gesture of tact she was not sure.

"The treasure vault," he said. "There's an underground passage down to the harbor. We must hurry. Do you want to wait until the whole mountain rears up to bury you?"

He moved toward the door where they had entered; she followed, knowing he was right, fearing his rightness, his practicality, his urgency. But even as he passed through a shadow arced and fell—there was an ugly thud—his body folded, disintegrating into a sprawl along the floor. In the momentary paralysis that ensued Fern saw the gash sliced across his naked scalp, the spreading discoloration around dented bone. An onyx vase rocked on its side close by, its circular base sharp-edged, dipped in red. Fern looked up and met Rafarl's eyes.

"I've killed him," he said. Possibly it was an effect of shock that his tone sounded clipped, devoid of inflection.

What was there to kill? Fern wondered.

But all she said was "We must hurry," picking up the dead man's words, stepping over the thing that had been a present menace only seconds before. "He said there was an underground passage from the treasure vault—"

"It'll be locked."

Fern, however, was already running down the nearest stair. At the bottom, they found earthquake damage had chipped the foundations and loosened the joists. Doors were shaken from their frames, bolts unfastened. In a string of interlinked vaults three of the palace soldiery, deprived of the restraints of authority, were smashing locks, wrenching open chests, breaking into cupboards. One of them drew his sword on the newcomers; then let it drop. "Help yourselves," he said. "There's plenty for all." His face shone with a greed on the edge of despair—the wallowing in riches that will never be spent, the grasping at a dream in the instant before awakening. He plunged his hand into a chest and lifted it out dripping with coins. A second man was rummaging through a heap of sacks and leather pouches; one split, leaking a puddle of gems that flashed and glittered on the murky floor. He upended another, and a shower of rubies, blood-dark, streamed through his fingers. These were the jewels the Atlanteans had rifled from the hoards of a thousand mainland kings—royal heirlooms, holy symbols, stones blessed and accursed: an emerald torque might have been the wealth of an entire tribe, a single diamond the purchase price of a kingdom. And all had been stored in the dark, unseen, forgotten, fire and ice, legend and malediction, piled like rubbish in a heap, secret as a sewer, commonplace as muck. What were ordinary jewels to the Gifted monarchs, who had the Lodestone under their hand? And Fern felt automatically for the piece around her neck, seizing Rafarl's wrist when he hesitated, casting a wanton eye over the treasure they had to leave behind.

They found the entrance to the passage in a corner, shoving a heavy chest out of the way in order to gain admittance. It was unlit, but Rafarl appropriated a discarded lantern from the unobservant looters. The floor sloped down a short distance before breaking into steps. The sidelong beam of the lantern showed them walls of natural rock curving into an arched roof, snail-tracked from the transit of ancient moisture, riven from the subsidence of endless droughts. Wider fissures were presumably the result of seismic activity: at one point they had to leap a chasm more than five feet across, landing precariously on the crumbling stair below.

"So you've done it," Rafarl said as they groped their way down into the dark. "The crusade crusaded. Your Task tasked."

"Mm."

"Was it worth it?"

She paused for a moment, stared at him. "I don't know. I don't suppose I ever will."

They went on. For some time neither of them spoke. She did not ask him why he had come back, for the second time, against his judgment, against his word. He had come: that was all that mattered. In her heart, or wherever the truth of her soul was subsumed, she had always believed he would.

"What about the others?" she said at length. "Will they wait for you?"

"They'd better." His voice was grim, essaying in vain for a note of amusement. "They won't make it without me. I'm the only one who can manage the ship in a storm. Ipo knows that: he's no fool. His decision will rule the rest."

"And he said he'd wait?"

"No. He damned me for a stubborn imbecile and said he'd go." She heard the ghost-laugh she remembered from the prison cell, shaking the lantern-beam into an arabesque. "I hope he lied."

"I hope so." She caught his hope and held it close. "He's your friend, isn't he?"

"Of a kind."

After a pause, she inquired: "Why did he make you pay for

guidance through the sewers? Wouldn't he do it for friendship's sake?"

"That's different. It's a question of principle. He's the only one who really knows those tunnels. To lead people through for nothing would be to cheapen the secret of his knowledge. Nobody values a service which they get for free."

Fern said nothing, unconvinced.

She knew she had traveled one of these subterranean passages before, on the day of her arrival, and it ought to worry her that she had no memory of such a journey, no recollection of carrying either torch or lantern; but it was too late now for minor anxieties. Even the confusion in her head seemed trivial now. In front and below she saw the paler slot of an opening, not daylit but filled with a lighter gloom, gray against black. They emerged at the back of a store, apparently untenanted, fumbling between suspended nets and tumbled lobster pots toward the exit. Outside, it was dim with nightfall or stormcloud: lamps and cressets flung a ragged glow across the quayside, light flickered on dark water. There were people on the wharf, drunken mariners looking for ships, fleeing citizens offering preposterous sums for their fare to the mainland, a smattering of beggars and thieves who took their charity or snatched their purses, only to enjoy a final taste of meaningless prosperity. "We should have picked up some of those jewels," said Rafarl. "It would have made Ipo feel less of a mug for waiting."

"If he's waited," said Fern. "Here—" she pulled him to a halt "—take this. I don't need it now." She drew off the chain, hung it around his neck. Her smile shivered. "There is no jewel in Atlantis worth more."

"You may need it," Rafarl protested. "Besides, I have no Gift to use it."

"You have now," said Fern. "My Gift to you." She felt that this was significant, symbolic or essential, a part of some greater plan which she could not see, only sense. The Hermit had read fate in the stars but the stars were obscured now and she must read without light, by touch. "It might help you—or protect you."

"What about *you*? Don't you need help and protection?" There was sarcasm in his voice, a mockery born of bewilderment and emotional quandary.

"I have your mother's veil," she remembered, taking it off as she spoke, binding it round her as Uuinarde had done. She did not mention the nymph or her death: it was too near, too painful, too pointless.

They hurried along the quay, almost running now, past uncoiling cables, unfurling sails—the shouting and the pleading, the orders and the panic—looking for a boat that might have gone long before.

In the corridor of the Rose Palace, the body of Ixavo lay inert on the floor, a snake of blood winding down its neck and across the pristine marble. Presently, the broken head jerked up, the open eyes focused. Awkwardly, like a puppet controlled by an invisible and unskilled puppeteer, it got to its feet.

The *Norne* was there. The mainsail was unsheaved, trailing from the yard, swelling and sagging in the erratic wind which scurried round the harbor. Random gusts hustled those vessels still at their moorings, flaring or extinguishing every unshielded lamp. The rigging vibrated with an uneasy music, a pervasive hum rising to the whine of a hundred banshees. Waves slapped at the jetty, breaking into gashes of spume. Ipthor was waiting in the stern: yellow teeth gleamed in his smile, brighter than his eyes. Beyond him Fern saw the shoulders of Gogoth and a dozen unknown faces—faces wan as tallow or tobacco-dark, hook-nosed or broken-nosed, hairless or stubble-jawed, one very old, one very young, marked with fear, bravado, slyness, rashness—but all watchful, all, in that instant, watching *her*. "So you found her," sighed Ipthor. "Passengers are paying for deck space in unstamped gold, or with the signets of their ancestors, or the jewels of their wives. Someone offered me an emerald as big as my fist: I would have accepted it, but I think it was glass. Must we take her along?"

"I've paid," said Fern, curiously unperturbed, and: "She's paid," said Rafarl. "The ransom of Atlantis would not cover the price of her fare."

"Not funny," snapped Ipthor.

"Not a joke," said Rafarl. He swung Fern down into Gogoth's arms, vaulting across the gap after her. A handful of would-be refugees, seeing them embark, hastened along the wharf to join them, but the motley crew had already sprung into action, unanimous if not coordinated, unexpectedly competent. Mooring-lines were jettisoned, hands seized the oars, impelling the *Norne* toward open water. A woman on the quayside was holding out a small child, infant or toddler: Fern reached out to her, responding mechanically, only to be restrained by Ipthor. "No," he said. "We can't take the extra weight."

"A *baby*?"

"They should get to high ground. They'll be safer there."

"Would you have taken him," she accused, "for a necklace of diamonds?"

"Of course. I could always throw the brat overboard. Don't be stupid: he's better off where he is. Our chances aren't good." He added, pointedly: "We left it too late."

They were well out into the harbor now. The sheer walls of the prehistoric crater reared up, an encircling barricade against any invasion, though no such eventuality had been feared for many long centuries. The pool of sky above was obliterated, lost behind all-smothering cloud: the stars were asphyxiated, the moon drowned. The only light in the whole world seemed to come from their own lanterns and the lamps along the receding wharf, their tattered glimmer initiating a brief, futile struggle against the overpowering dark. The *Norne* felt suddenly very alone. The few ships riding at anchor out in the bay skittered nervously in the wayward surges of a sea normally calm and still. No one else was preparing to leave. As Fern stared back toward the quay she saw a tall figure materialize and stand close to the edge. She could distinguish little at that range but she thought the head was shaved. "Raf!" she called. Her tone was barely above a whisper but he heard—heard and recognized the note of not-quite-panic, compelling as a scream. He passed the helm to a companion and joined her, Ipthor at his side. The figure on shore was moving now at something between a swift walk and a kind of gliding run. Its legs swung so fast they appeared almost to blur. He turned onto a wooden jetty where a galley lay in wait, an ocean-going bireme with its oars shipped and single sail bundled against the yard. They saw him spring down onto the deck, saw the mooring-ropes unloop from the bollards, the double row of oars extruded and dipping into the water. The ship crawled away from the jetty like a huge millipede. Cressets flamed in prow and stern: a ruddy glow cupped the hairless skull of its solitary occupant. "There must have been slaves already chained in the hold," Ipthor said uncertainly, and: "He's dead," said Rafarl. "I killed him. You saw he was dead."

"The spirit that drives him isn't human," Fern said. "There's something else in there, something . . . darker. Very old. Very strong. Empty. Evil is always empty. It isn't finished with him yet."

She added: "It doesn't need slaves, only oars. It has a power beyond the Gift."

"How fast can he go?" asked Rafarl, but the question was answered for him as the galley accelerated toward them, thrusting a phosphorescent wake through the water. He was back at the helm in a few strides, using the vocabulary of the street to exhort his crew to greater effort. Fern turned to watch him for a moment— just a moment: his hair flaring in the wind of their passage, the shirt whipped around his thin back. A moment to hold on to, to fill her eyes forever. She said to Ipthor: "Tell him—," but she could think of nothing for him to say, nothing but goodbye, and that was the one thing she wanted to leave unsaid. This was their third final parting, and she knew it was final indeed, but she had no time to think about it, no time to hurt.

"What can *you* do?" Ipthor said, sensing her resolution, his expression torn between doubt and skepticism.

"I'm the one Ixavo wants. You know that." He wants the key. But by the time he knows I haven't got it, it should be too late.

"You'll be killed."

"It doesn't signify," she said impatiently. "Not *now*." There was a world of meaning in that *now*. Not NOW. Here at the end of things.

She swung her leg over the gunwale. He removed the knife from his waistband—a big ugly knife, notched and re-sharpened, serviceable and mean—and thrust it into hers. No more words passed between them. She did not look back at Rafarl—all the stories say, you must never look back—only smiling at Ipthor, in the millisecond before she jumped. She thought: This is my friend—thoughts are far swifter than speech—and then the water rushed over her, colder than before, and when she resurfaced the *Norne* was some distance away, entering the channel under the bridge of stone, and the bireme was almost on her, the plunging oars dangerously close. She tried to evade them but the ship was too near: even as the blades lifted clear of the water she was swimming beneath them, under a canopy of oars, and in a moment they would come crashing down on her—but the canopy was raised, and in a few strokes she was at the stern, and Ixavo threw her a rope and hauled her up while she clung on with sliding hands, smashing ankle and knee against the side of the ship.

"I knew you'd come to me," he said. His physical deterioration had affected his voice: the grainy tone had become a scrape, and there was an echo behind it as if it were resounding in some vast hollow space. "I called you, and you came."

She had not heard him call, even in her mind. She tried not to look too closely at him but she could not avoid seeing the caked blood running down from his scalp and the way his disfigurement appeared redder and angrier, perhaps inflamed, as if the very flesh had boiled, bubbling against the bone. He turned, striding for'ard; his lifted hand loosed the huge sail; the ropes grew taut and thrummed; the oars, briefly eluding his control, slipped in the rowlocks. It was as if the entire ship were a living organism and he was the brain commanding its musculature and its motion. Yet he was clumsy, his attention distracted by her presence. As they passed under the bridge the *Norne* was already well ahead, breasting the wild sea beyond. Ixavo had lost interest in pursuit. She realized that the more power was transmitted through his mind, the less he seemed able to think. As if the strength that drove him was destroying his physique, overloading his cerebrum. From the back the slash in his head was all too visible: his skull looked misshapen around it and the ripped skin was peeling away from the wound, but very little fluid oozed out. She thought she could see the pale glint of bone in the gap.

The sail filled; beyond the bridge sky and sea opened out. The waves were rising, their spines curving upward and then sinking down again like restless monsters circling the ship. Great siege-towers of cloud were advancing out of the east; a long drumroll of thunder attended them, battered to and fro across the sky like an echo in a narrow gorge. Livid flashes played around the summit of the clouds: double-pronged lightning stabbed below. One struck the massive natural arch behind them: there was a rending crack, and the bridge that had stood since Atlantis was made plum-meted seaward, vanishing in a soaring sheet of spray. The shock-wave, rushing athwart contrary currents, swept them on; in front she glimpsed the *Norne* again, lifted on its keel, teetering on the crest of a breaker. She had grasped the ship's side to maintain her balance but Ixavo seemed to have no problem, swaying slightly from foot to foot to hold his own against the tilting deck. It was almost as if he was not standing on the deck but simply resting on it, sustained by some other equilibrium, merely simulating his response to gravity. "Steady the helm!" he called back to her. "I need everything to fill the sail. *Steady it.* Use the Lodestone." And: "What's the matter with you? You have the Gift. Use it *now!*"

She didn't react, didn't answer. Ahead of her on the foredeck the helm spun out of control. He rounded on her, crossing the space between in three long paces: the ship lurched but he didn't even stumble. "Do you want to ruin us?" His voice was a snarl that seemed to come from many throats. A lightning flash illumined her with glaring clarity: over her bodice, only the wet veil clung to her chest. For an instant she saw his face convulsed; his eyes appeared to be full of blood. "What have you done with it?" he shrieked, seizing her by the neck, shaking her as if to rattle the key from its hiding place among her bones.

"I lost it when I dived in the sea. I threw it away. I gave it away. You'll never have it!"

He thrust his face closer: the lightning showed his skin green with death, his eyes red without iris or pupil, blind with blood. "You're my creature—" the words were spoken through his voice, not with it, in a whisper deeper than the storm "—you *cannot* betray me. Ten thousand years in the future I put my thumb-mark in your mind. Your strength is too new: you could never erase it." His blind gaze was groping in her brain like a ray of dark, probing, stabbing—recoiling at last unrewarded. "*He* did this, didn't he? Caracandal the charlatan—Caracandal the dispossessed—he touched the key and the Stone paid him in power. But I'll take it yet and see him damned. Where is it? Tell me, or I'll split your mind open like a ripe fruit, I'll spill out your thoughts like seed. You *gave* it away—is that it? To the vagabond—the vagabond sailing that flimsy *carrarc* ahead. The vagabond!" He flung her aside and turned, crying to the ship in the many tongues of the sea, the scream of birds long extinct, the booming groan of the kraken stirring, the howl of tempests that raged in the ages before Man. A great wind bellied the sail, straining at the halyards: the waves gaped into a trough before them, the clouds arched into a tunnel above. Fern was sprawled half stunned against the boards but she pulled herself onto hands and knees and crawled to the ship's side. The deck no longer swayed: drawing on all his power, Ixavo held the ship suspended, every plank, every rope shuddering with the force that drove it onward. Closer and closer to the wave-tossed, storm-beleaguered shape of the *Norne*. But Fern had gone beyond all feelings now save one: the urge to win. Against fate, against Ixavo, against whatever demon inhabited him. The impetus that had carried her through the past few days—something often little more than a reflex, instinctive as programming—had hardened, knuckling itself into a resolve. Her head spun and her physical strength was almost gone but another strength rose in her that was more than physical, clearing her brain, tensing her sinews. A strength that was neither the Stone nor the Gift, but only *her*. She tugged Ipthor's knife from her waistband and hacked at one of the halyards anchoring the sail.

The knife was sharp, the rope taut: it snapped almost at once. The sail whipped free and was rent between stormwind and werewind, one useless shred flying like a banner while the other wrapped itself around the rigging. Ixavo's cry of fury was the raptor's screech, the clamor of primordial sea-beasts—but it did no good. Without the sail, the power had nothing to take hold of, no instrument to control. Will alone could not propel a vessel of that size through such a sea. The walls of the trough collapsed, re-assembling into rocking heights on which the ship bucked like a wild horse. Ixavo, his power flagging, clutched at the mast, trying to bind himself to it with his sash. Something must have struck his head: the wound had opened wider and a section of his scalp was hanging loose, like a piece of ripped cloth. Fern held on to severed rope and sodden timber, eyes narrowed against the splashback of

incessant waves, peering ahead through a blackness of spray, wondering in which direction ahead lay. And then they were lifted up,
and there was a second, less than a second, when the lightning
showed her the *Norne*, far away now, careening from wave-peak to
wave-peak, running with the true wind. They'll make it, she
thought, they'll ride out the storm, I've won—but the ship dived
down and the *Norne* was lost to view, and even the lightning was
blotted out. High above, the arching clouds had bowed into a
vault, the darkness had turned from black to a somber red. She
saw the spire of a tornado reaching down from the rim of the
cloud-vault, but its outline was oddly fixed, unwavering, and there
was another away to her left, like gigantic fangs scything toward
the sea, and the storm-tunnel had become a throat, half as big as
the sky, and they were being sucked into it in a vast mouthful of
ocean. Ixavo screamed, a human scream—*The Nenheedra! The
Nenheedra has woken!*—and his hands tore at the knots he had
made, but the flesh was slipping from his skull and his fingers
would no longer coordinate. Fern saw an enormous globe of moisture, darker than rain, dropping toward her: it struck the deck
inches from her foot, shearing through the planks, leaving a hole
whose charred edges seemed to smoke even in the wet. And
then—as in an occult room beyond the reach of memory—she
was soaring up and up, the sea was rising through the sky, the tempest fell away beneath. The great Snake reared its head above
cloud and lightning, slowly closing its yawning mouth, and the
ocean streamed in waterfalls from its jaw. The ship listed and Fern
half tumbled, half plunged over the side, and was swept away—
away and away—eluding the descending fangs, borne over the lipless jaw, falling endlessly through the turmoil of the sky. Her last
gleam of thought was a fleeting exultation, because she had
evaded both demon and serpent, and she would die in the Sea.

Epilogue
The Unicorn

There was something pressing against her cheek, a hard smooth surface, faintly textured. She thought about it for a while and realized she was lying on her side, and the hard smoothness was beneath her; when she opened her eyes she could see it stretching away, shining dimly silver in the darkness. She had the impression of more light above, and the shadows of unseen mountains, and low waves breaking over her, though she did not seem to be wet. And then she knew where she was. She sat up, and the endless beaches at the margin of being extended on either hand, curving into infinity, and every star in the universe crowded the midnight sky. She inhaled the glittering air, listening to the breathing of the sea and the hissing of the stars. Looking down, she saw she was dressed in rags; between them her bare legs shone like pearl. How she came to be there, or why, was not so much unknown as unimportant. She was there, and in being there she was herself, nameless and eternal. A cool peace filled her. When he came, she knew she had been waiting for him. He nuzzled her with his nose; his horn gleamed more brightly than her star-lustered limbs. Then suddenly he tossed his head, and his dark eyes were wild with hurt. Unicorns love jeal-

ously: they will not share. He would have run from her but she
sprang to her feet and wound her arms around his neck. "Stay for
me," she said, "once more, just once more. Then I will let you go."
She mounted: he bucked and reared, but her hands were meshed
in his mane, and she held on. Then he leaped away, streaking along
the sand, and the night streamed around them. "Take me home,"
she said. The stars frayed into long tassels of light, and the world
glimmered into nothingness, and when the nothingness had faded
the sun was shining, and the grass was green beneath his hooves.

She slid from his back and turned, but he was gone without
thanks, vanishing into a thinning mist: he would not come again.
The moor was under her feet, the heather and the wildflowers
and the butterflies, and the sunlight was warm on her face. She
was Fernani, Fernani and Fernanda, she was whole again, and all
that she had forgotten came flooding back, stirring her dormant
memory, knocking at her heart. And far below was the gray house
of her dream, but close by were three figures sitting on the slope,
a man, a boy, and a dog. "I am Fern Capel," she said aloud, and
began to cry, and so they found her, and she hugged Will, and
clasped the Watcher's coat, weeping as she had not wept since
she was a child, not since her mother died when she thought the
tears were frozen inside her forever. As the story poured out of her
so the two halves of her knowledge fitted together, and at last,
with a horror that stopped her tears, she understood. "You did
well," said Ragginbone, "better than my best hope—if hope it
could be called, since I dared not indulge it. The key is caught in
a time-trap: none will ever retrieve it again. And with the loss of
so powerful an ambulant, the Oldest Spirit may be crippled in
strength for many years."

"But what about the rest of the Lodestone—the other
pieces?" Will asked. "What became of them?"

"That is another story," the Watcher replied, "and still unfinished. Our story is over—for a while. Yes, you have done well.

Few have ventured so far, or ever returned. Do not regret the price. It all happened a long, long time ago. Atlantis crumbled into sand ere Rome was built or Troy burned. Its people are less than a memory."

"I *loved* them!" Fern cried, and Will saw her eyes were fierce and her face desperate, and he recognized with an odd pang that she would never be a child again. "Ezramé, and Uuinarde, and Ipthor who was my friend—and Raf. I wanted to save him, I gave my life for him—but I lived, and he died. I sent him to his death. How can I go on living—living here and now—when I was in Atlantis with him?" And as she spoke she clutched unseeing at the strip of gossamer still bound around the rags of her unfamiliar clothes.

"We all go on," said Ragginbone, and the lines were deep in his brow. "Don't despair. You are young, and despair comes easily to the young, but it is ultimately . . . unprofitable. Who knows? If you loved him—if he loved you—you and no other—he may come again. The Gate opens both ways, or so they say. Remember, where there is no hope, you can still have faith. You may meet again—someday. Eternity is a long time to say never." He got to his feet: Lougarry was at his side. "You should go home now. Your father is waiting."

"You've been gone five days," Will told her. "Dad's been frantic: he called the police and they were going to search the moor, but then they found out about Javier and they thought you'd run off with him. It's been awful."

She was staring after Ragginbone: he was moving with his ageless, tireless stride, receding swiftly into a haze of summer. She called out: "When is Someday?" but his answer, if there was one, blew away on the breeze, and man and dog—wizard and wolf—seemed to dwindle, fading into a memory.

"Come on," Will said, putting his arm around her, and together they walked down the hill toward their home.

The boat battled on through the towering seas. A curling cliff of water—had they but known it, the backwash of the Nenheedra's rising—bore them up and carried them onward, until they rode its fall and plunged again into a night-green chasm where the lightning could not come. Now he knew she was gone he was not surprised: he felt as if he had always expected to lose her, in the end. There was no mockery left in him, no anger: he must carry his grief ungrieved, like a stone in his heart. His friends had waited for him; the boat needed him. She was brave and sea-crafty, rolling with the waves, running with the gale; but already her sails were storm-shredded, her timbers leaking, her mast cracked. A shattering collision of wave on wave took her rudder: the wheel slid in his grasp. But still he held on, though there was nothing to hold on to, determined to ride his last tempest until the deck broke beneath him, to keep faith—if he had faith to keep—with his companions, his vessel, with her. She who would never know if he had kept faith at all. And so the hurricane screamed over him, and the Sea raged around him, and the dark poured down from above.

The mermaid rose out of deep water into the stormheart.

THE BEGINNING

Glossary

Names

Alimond   The name Alys Giddings took in honor of her Gift, probably from the Latin, *alius* other, *mundus* world, though it would also have been chosen for its similarity to her own name. Since the fall of Atlantis, most of the Gifted have taken a different name for magical purposes, one not used in their everyday lives; only the very arrogant or the very simple may not do so. Sometimes they choose their own name, more often it is given to them by a mentor. Its origins may come from any language but it usually has a meaning of significance to the named.

The reason for this may be partly to do with concealing their Gift from other people. Atlanteans wielded their power without pseudonyms, needing no other identity, but after the fall the Gifted were often called Accursed, and took many names to hide themselves.

Aliph   (Al-eef) The servant of Ezramé.

Atlantis   In Atlantean, the pronunciation is similar to the French, but the final consonant is almost always sounded. Thus, At-lon-teess. (The nasal *an*, as in the French, sounds almost like *on*).

Azmordis   One of the many names of the Old Spirit, pronounced
as written and probably a variant of Asmodeus, in Christian
legend one of the right-hand demons of Satan. Azimuth may
come from the same source, or it may be a version of
Ashtaroth, a Middle-Eastern goddess with sinister aspects.
Azmordis is generally considered a male spirit but will use female ambulants and identities when it suits him. Of the other
names he mentions, Jhavé (Zh-ah-vay) is obscure, but could
have an oblique connection with Jahweh, the ancient Jewish
god—masquerading as a god always appealed to him, it gave
him more scope than manifestation as a demon, though modern theology has made it far less practicable. Jezreel may be
related to Azrael, the Angel of Death, Xicatli to Xiuhtecuhtli,
the Aztec fire god, Ingré Manu to Angra Mainya, the principle
of evil in Persian mythology. The origin of Babbaloukis is unknown, but it could be the name of another demon derived
from Babel or Babylon, both seen by old-fashioned Chris-
tianity as symbols of chaos and wickedness.

Azmodel, the valley in the hinterland of reality where the
Old Spirit is still worshipped, obviously comes from the same
source as Azmordis.

Caracandal   The Gift-name of Ragginbone, Latin or Italian in
origin, derived from his true-name of Candido, meaning white
or pure—an unlikely meaning presumably intended to apply
to something in his spirit rather than his outward character.
The addition of *cara*, dear, suggests the name was chosen by
someone particularly close to him in affection.

Dévornine   (Day-vor-neen) One of the twelve Ruling Families
(ie. the most Gifted) in Atlantis.

Ezramé   (Ez-ra-may) The title of Cidame (See-dam) was given to
all the women of the Ruling Families after coming-of-age at
sixteen; Cidé is the masculine equivalent. It is possible that
the Spanish *el Cid* may be a latterday derivative.

Fernani   (Fur-nah-nee) This is northern, not Atlantean, in origin, but from what region or language it is impossible to tell. After the fall the empire disintegrated and many peoples—and their tongues—were lost.

Gogoth   (Goh-goth) Probably a mainlander name, since although Atlantean uses the sound *th* (sounded as in the English *sloth*), it rarely occurs at the end of a word.

Goulabey   (Goo-la-bay) The name of the Thirteenth House, the last of the Ruling Families to rise to prominence in Atlantis. Characterized by their ruthlessness and rapacity, they were considered upstarts by the rest of the aristocracy. The Thirteenth House is invariably mentioned separately from the other twelve. However, Pharouq (Fa-rook), the Wizard-King, was in many ways an efficient and practical ruler who did much to strengthen the empire and increase its prosperity. This wealth improved the lot of citizens, peasants, and slaves, so that Atlantis in its last days was more affluent than any other city of ancient times, even Athens or Rome.

Hexaté   (Heks-ah-tay) Also written Hex-Âté, in the days when she was first worshipped as a goddess. The name was probably the origin of the Greek Hecate, goddess of witches, and the German word *hex*.

Ipthor   (Eep-thor) A common forename in Atlantis.

Lougarry   This almost certainly derives, as Gus Dinsdale suggested, from the French *loup garou*, werewolf. Her true-name of Vashtari has an eastern flavor, which, since Ragginbone speaks of "northern forests" when relating her history, hints at a background in one of the Asian countries bordering on Russia.

Malmorth   Also Malmorff, meaning misshapen. Of mixed Latin and Greek origin, the name is a term of derision applied almost exclusively to goblins.

Mithraïs (Mith-rae-eess) The oldest of the twelve Ruling Houses.

The Nenheedra The origins of this word come from the Old Tongue, which pre-dated Atlantean and was said to be the first language ever spoken by man. The name, roughly translated, means Darkserpent, using Dark in the sense of the void, the abyss. The Old Tongue *næân* became the Atlantean *néan*, while *hyadr*, meaning giant snake, recurs as the Greek hydra.

Pegwillen This was presumably a nickname given to the house-goblin by his child-playmates. It comes from Pig William, a character in a folk tale. The youngest of three brothers, he was exceptionally ugly and apparently stupid, and his smarter and handsomer elders left him to take care of the pigs while they set off to win the hand of the local princess. Inevitably, they failed, while Pig William's down-to-earth common sense enabled him to outwit an invading giant, and his sincerity gained him the love of an unusually discerning royal.

Rafarl The pronunciation of this name demonstrates both Atlantean Rs. They use the R as in French, i.e. at the back of the throat, and also as in Italian, rolled off the tip of the tongue. The double R is normally French, the single Italian, except when it is preceded by a vowel. Thus in Rafarl the first R comes off the tip of the tongue while the second is in the back of the throat: Ra-farrrl.

Rahil (Ra-heel) Both Rahil and Rafarl may be sources for the later name Raphael.

Tamiszandre (Tam-eess-zondr) The wife of Pharouq and mother of Zohrâne.

Uuinarde (Oo-ee-narrrd) The French R occurs here, and the double U at the beginning is particularly common among the names of *nymphelins*, as in the case of her brother Uuinoor

(Oo-ee-noor). In Atlantean *uu* and *ou* are both generally pronounced oo, but a preceding H—*huu*—can change the sound
to hew. A single U is always pronounced ew.

Nymphelins (neem-feh-lin) were human mutations unique to
Atlantis—mutations occurred frequently in the vicinity of the
Lodestone—not magical creatures like mermaids. They were
natural swimmers who could hold their breath for long peri-
ods and seemed unaffected by water pressure even at depths
of several fathoms. None remain, although their genes may
have been passed on to certain races in the South Seas.

Zohrâne (Zoh-rahn) Literally Evertime, or eternity, this is a
name from the Old Tongue, where *zohr* meant time and
ân, ever. In Atlantean *zoor* meant time as in an age, or era,
also zone.

Language

ittle Atlantean survives nowadays: the descendants of the Exiles no longer use it and the Gifted learn it as a dead language, like Latin or Ancient Greek. Only the very skilled employ it for spells and incantations; lesser magic uses other tongues. Alone among Prospero's Children Fern traveled to the Forbidden Past, and thus the language became a part of her inborn knowledge, though her accent was always that of the north. We can surmise that it was the linguistic ancestor of many modern languages, specifically European ones. The pronunciation closely resembles French, with the epiglottal R and several nasal inflections like *an* and *on*, although in Atlantean the final consonant is generally sounded. However, there is also the German *ch*, the Russian *zh*, and the English *th*. Rules are erratic and, since the language is long dead, open to debate. For example, *th* is also pronounced as *t* in some proper names.

The Atlanteans claimed they created the first fully developed human speech; the Old Tongue, they said, contained many primitive sounds and even animal noises which pre-dated the subtleties of true communication. Certainly Atlantean holds a power which other tongues do not possess, as if an echo of the Lodestone's magnetism was transmuted into its sounds and rhythms. As a language of summoning it is irresistible: even the Old Spirits respond to it, though they were part of the world long before speech was invented. It is worth noting that they often use elemental noises rather than words to release their powers. Words are the skill of Men. Few among the Immortals learned from such transient beings, but those who did, whether in love or enmity, became fascinated and absorbed, and the words they had not made bound them irrevocably to the fate of humankind. Of these the strongest, and the closest to Man, is Azmordis.